Twenty-Twenty Hindsight

Tim Hind

Book Reality

Helping Writers Become Independent Authors

Copyright © Tim Hind, 2021
Published: 2021 by The Book Reality Experience
Western Australia

ISBN: 978-0-6487188-4-0 Paperback Edition
ISBN: 978-0-6451532-8-6 E-Book Edition
ISBN: 978-1-922670-11-3 Audio Book Edition

Typeset in 11.5pt Garamond

Cover Design by Luke Buxton | www.lukebuxton.com

For

Ian and Jacki

The Luke Frankland Novels

1

Macau – January 2007

Mac woke and stared into a dead girl's eyes.

It took a moment to comprehend what he was looking at. Then he propelled himself backwards off the bed and let out a guttural moan of despair. Her unseeing gaze remained fixed on him.

He pulled the covers back from her body. She was as naked as she had been when he'd climbed off her a few hours before. The exotic mix of Chinese and Portuguese looks, so prized by him in the girls he paid for, was succumbing quickly to death's decay.

The right hand side of her face was a deeply discoloured purple against the pristine white of the pillow. Her open eyes bored through him and he wanted to break contact with them, but couldn't. He felt himself retching, but still he took in the smallest details. Her lower eyelids had started to brown through dehydration. Her mouth had slackened, drooping like some melted plastic effigy. Her tongue slightly protruding, and her lips, those soft and firm young lips that had pleasured him only hours before, were taking on a leather-like appearance.

A subtle green spread across her lower abdomen and her previous flat stomach was already a little distended. The purple discolouration to her face spread down the whole of her right side. Her right arm, partially tucked under her body was a deep ruby.

'How the fuck?' Mac said, gazing around the room. She'd been twenty years old, only he knew that wasn't true. She'd been younger. He'd always wanted them as young as he could get but without ever admitting he was breaking any laws. The former Portuguese colony's hotels turned their blind eyes towards him and he to them. They catered for him. They always would. He made them as much money as he made himself.

'How the fuck?' he said again and once more looked around the room. Searching for some assassin that he could blame this disaster on. He stared back down at her body. Focussing in on the inner elbow of the left arm. There were no track marks, neither could he see any on the heavily discoloured right arm, but they could be there. Perhaps. He looked closer, and scanned across her torso, legs, down to her feet. There, in between her toes. Pin pricks so discreet as to never be noticed by him or any of her clients. Normally.

'For fuck's sake.' He moved away from the bed and turned unsteadily on his feet. Her bag sat on the dressing table. He grabbed the fake Stella McCartney clutch and emptied its contents onto the floor. A leather pouch dropped at his feet. A tied bundle that he didn't need to open to know the contents of.

'Fucker. Fuck. Fu—' His tirade was interrupted by a melodic 'ding-dong' on the hotel room's doorbell.

He glanced at the bedside table clock, 06:00. He'd booked an in-room breakfast. The French concierge, Julien, always made sure everything was on time and exactly how Mac wanted it. From breakfast to… he glanced back at the bed. To dead hookers. Most times the young Frenchman even made the in-room deliveries himself. Mac muttered a prayer to a God he didn't believe in that Julien was on the other side of the door now. He pulled the covers up the bed as high as they would go and grabbed the robe off the floor where he'd dropped it the night before. The room was more a suite so if it wasn't Julien he could shield the bed easily enough, but then what? This wasn't some uneaten food on a room service tray that he could dump in the corridor. He managed a last, under-breath, 'Fuck,' and opened the door.

'Bonjour, Monsieur MacLellan, greetings on this wond—'

'Get the fuck inside,' Mac said and pulled the trolley and the startled concierge into the room. He forced both past him and swung the door shut as hard as he could. The effect was dampened by the heavy automatic closing struts and rather than a stress relieving bang, Mac got a half-hearted swoosh.

'Monsieur?' Julien's voice quivered and the young man's face was caught halfway between surprise and fear.

'She's dead, Julien.'

'Monsieur?'

'Cut all the phoney French crap. I know you speak immaculate fucking English. She,' Mac punctuated his sentence with a jabbed finger towards the bed, 'is fucking dead. You sent me a fucking junkie you little prick.'

He may well have spoken immaculate English, but now Julien reverted to a stream of French expletives that even Mac, with his rudimentary French-Canadian language skills, translated easily enough.

'Exactly. I'm finished if I'm caught with a dead underage junkie in my room. Do you have any idea what the Chinese will do to me?'

Julien's face matched the white of his concierge jacket. His eyes were wide with alarm.

'DO YOU?' Mac bellowed and it served to knock the shock out of the young man's face. He became animated again.

'It is okay. Mac, it is okay. I will look after things. I will make all of this go away.' He took a notepad from his jacket pocket and scanned the first page. Then he unclipped the staff keycard from his belt and handed it to Mac.

'Leave now, in your robe, no one is about, go to Room 1093. It is empty. I will bring your clothes and belongings. I can change the hotel records. You were never in this room. Go, go now. I will sort it out.'

Mac took the offered card and the anger he had felt moments earlier dissipated, leaving him physically and mentally exhausted. He turned back as he got to the room door, 'Thank you, Julien. I won't forget this.'

2

Fort Benning, Georgia – October 2009

The drum beat was soft and low, but easily heard despite the squeals and shrieks of laughing from the children playing catch. Dan walked past them, leaving their noise behind and concentrated on stepping in time to the thud, thud, thud. A couple of people walked in front of him but their outlines were mere shimmers in the afternoon heat. One man walked behind him. He knew he was there, but couldn't turn round, couldn't twist his body to look. He felt stiff, like he was being constrained by some strange bindings. He heard the soft singing of another man up ahead and recognised the words of Green Day's song, *Nice Guys Finish Last*. He started to hum the tune. A breeze blew across the sand covered street and on it a fragrance that he knew but couldn't name. A strange mix of gun oil and candy. Leather polish and pancakes, toothpaste and sweat. He tried again to twist around, to look at the figure behind and as he turned, a man appeared beside him. Smiling, kind featured. They exchanged a friendly nod and walked along, in step to the soft thud, thud, thud. Dan tried once more to look behind. This time, straining with the effort, he managed it.

The figure following was hopping along on one leg. Thud, thud, thud. The other leg was missing. Half his torso was gone, the rest hung in bloody shreds. Half of his head was torn away. The remaining eye stared at Dan. The exposed teeth of half a jaw moved and screamed for him to take cover. Dan turned to the man who still walked alongside him. He saw the smiling eyes and heard the kind words of encouragement. 'Don't be sad, that's an old comrade coming along for the ride.'

Dan tried to speak, to tell this kind man that the body following was only half there. He opened his mouth but no words came. He gasped for air but couldn't breathe. He watched, in infinite slow motion, the sniper's bullet cross the floor of the valley and enter the kind man's head. The drum beat stopped, the world collapsed into silence and Dan was coated with grey and red. He finally caught a breath and woke to his own screams.

***

Shirlene sat at the breakfast bar and seethed anger. Dan could feel it coming from her every pore. Lilly-Anne, their 5-month old daughter, lay asleep in a bright red bouncer. Ryan, their 6-year old was in First Grade now and Dan had just returned from walking him over to his elementary school. As he came into the house he was still wondering how the years had passed so quickly. His baby boy was a First Grader. In the same instant he wondered how those same years had dragged on for so long in a miserable marriage. How many more could he take with Shirlene?

'Well?' she barked at him as he came into the kitchen. Lilly-Anne stirred with the volume of her mother's voice.

'Well what?'

'Well, did he say anything about your screaming the house down last night?'

Dan poured a coffee from the half-cold pot. 'No. He didn't. I told you he hadn't woken up when I checked on him last night.'

'Well I sure as shit woke up, soldier boy. You need to get it together. What sort of grown-ass man wakes up screaming every night with nightmares for God's sake?'

'It's not every night,' Dan said, and felt as pathetic for saying it as it had sounded coming out.

'You need to sort your shit out, Dan. I mean you were only intelligence for God's sake. It's not like you were a Marine storming the shores of Iwo fucking Jima. Get it sorted. And her.' Shirlene said and stood up, ignoring Lilly-Anne's cries. 'I'm going back to bed.'

Dan waited for his wife to leave then lifted the baby and soothed her back to sleep as he walked softly into the lounge room. The only two good things in his life were Ryan and Lilly-Anne and he knew he couldn't lose them, but any possibility of leaving Shirlene and keeping custody had been ripped away in a whirlwind of violence one night in London so many years ago.

He saw a tear fall onto the brow of his beautiful daughter as he sat on the chair facing the television. Its blank screen showed him and the baby clearly. Dan hadn't shaved for the previous few days and now, wearing old jeans with an older jumper, he looked less like an officer of the United States Army than he did some hobo waiting for the next freight train out of Georgia. A sigh escaped him as he realised if it weren't for the children, he'd swap places with any of those old train riders.

If he ran he would definitely lose the children. Shirlene would make it as hard as possible for him to even see them, let alone keep them. She would use the fact that he had attended conversion therapy, albeit at the insistence of her and his own parents, to cite him as unfit. She'd make damn sure the proceedings happened in their home state. Any hint that he had what the Nebraska Family Court would call, 'homosexual relationships', would scupper all hope of gaining custody, even if his active service in the US Military hadn't been a factor. If that came out in court he'd also be out of a job. *'Don't ask, don't tell'* did not include admitting to having an affair with a man. Even if you loved him. Perhaps especially if you loved him. With no job, he wouldn't be able to afford a house and that meant no visitation rights. It was all so final and bleak.

He knew Shirlene would arrive at any future court date looking like some apple-pie cooking, cheer-leading, all-Miss-America hometown girl done good and Dan's parents, with their warped religion and their misplaced sentiments, would side with their bat-shit-crazy daughter-in-law.

Reality was likely to be even harsher. Shirlene checked his email and phone records every month and monitored the bank accounts. If he made one move to reach out to Luke, she would know. She had a controlling streak as wide as her anger. Unlikely as it was, even if he could make contact and find Luke, if he could get away and if he could get custody of the kids, given the time that had passed, the chances were Luke wouldn't want to know him. That hurt more than all the rest. He knew he should have walked away from everything and got on a flight to London years ago, but he'd been too scared. Now, even if he did it, what would be waiting for him? A couple of years missed probably meant a lifetime of loss.

He absent-mindedly rubbed his shoulder, where the scar of a knife wound was still prominent and still occasionally ached. When he took his shirt off, Shirlene would sometimes look away. When she made him fuck her, she almost always kissed it. A couple of inches across and she would have stabbed him in the heart.

A couple of inches to the left and the sniper bullet that hit Staff Sergeant Morrie Lieberman as he patrolled alongside Dan would have missed. A couple of inches to the right and Dan would have been dead. A couple of years earlier or later and he could have been happy. Life was all about small fractions and missed opportunities. Hindsight was a wonderful thing.

Perhaps the darkness would have been better.

Captain Daniel Stückl held still and allowed more tears to fall onto his sleeping daughter.

3

Mid-Atlantic Ocean, 40,000 feet, Mach 0.8 – October 2009

The interior of the Bombardier Challenger 605 was a mix of soft beige leathers and high gloss walnut laminates. I'd thought Mac's 604 had been a luxury private jet, but this 605 was even more upmarket.

We'd taken off to the strains of John Denver's *Take Me Home, Country Roads*. It was just one of Mac's quirks. This cowboy-booted, Alberta born and bred Canadian who I had mistaken for a Texan on first meeting him four years ago, never allowed his private jets to take off or land without the song playing on full volume. Added to that was a never ending supply of Coors Light beer, a love bordering on obsession with the Dallas Cowboys American Football team and a loud, brash complete self-belief in his own abilities, real or imagined. It all made me wonder why I had accepted his offer to come on this unusual and extended job interview. Yet, as I settled back into the leather, I knew the answer.

Stuart Campbell MacLellan the Third, might be a narcissistic snakeskin remedy showman, but he couldn't be as stupid as my former boss at Bateleur Bank, Dickie Lessen, and he certainly wasn't as insipid as dreary dishcloth Dickie. Plus the fact was that I'd officially been made redundant from the bank only a day before and although the settlement cheque meant I had no short-term money worries, I also knew that me being bored and laying around in a London apartment was a recipe for a drinking disaster. I needed to keep busy and since first Mac had mentioned his new venture I had been intrigued. In fact more than intrigued. Excited.

That a private company could provide intelligence-led cyber security to mainstream commercial businesses and governments globally was potentially game-changing. I had pondered and explored the idea, allowing myself to consider the what-ifs and so-whats. Now I was enthused and inspired by what the possibilities could lead to. This was a brand new concept and as much as I'd been in on the ground floor of cyber threat intelligence in the UK military and almost in on the ground floor of it in the banking sector, it was another opportunity to really make my mark in a developing arena. Also, despite having more money in the bank than I'd ever had, Mac offering me even more straightaway couldn't be a bad thing. I liked my apartment in London, I liked my Saville Row suits and fine cigars. Having Mac finance my lifestyle without having to dip into my savings seemed a win-win. Not that I would let Mac in on all of my thoughts.

I'd picked up quite a few commercial lessons during my year with the bank and my financial safety-net meant I was in a good position to negotiate from strength. In the back of my mind I heard my inner voice give a non-committal grunt.

A good place? Money wise perhaps. The rest of you is still on a knife-edge. The rest of you is broken, Luke and you're hiding from it.

I felt my hand clinch. The last thing I needed was an internal dialogue that would end up with me despairing of myself as usual. If I had been at home I'd have taken the edge of my own disparaging monologue with a healthy shot of gin. Here on Mac's private jet the best I could hope for was a Coors Light. Like handing a drowning man a slowly deflating rubber ring. It would do for a while, but ultimately it would have to be replaced with something much stronger. Although I couldn't fault the speed of service within the private jet.

Mandy, the attractive young flight attendant, handed me the drink and retook her seat on the long couch that was sideways to the executive cabin. It allowed her to constantly keep an eye on Mac's and my refreshment requirements and, I suspected, allowed Mac to keep an eye on her long and shapely legs. She, much like the plane, was an upgrade to a younger version. In the same way that the Challenger 605 bore a resemblance to the 604, but was a newer model, so Mandy bore a remarkable re-semblance to the previous attendant, Betsy, I'd met on Mac's old jet. Both women looked like they'd been moulded from a "Mary-Lou" all-star Miss Southern Belle production line, and Mandy, like Betsy, spoke with an accent suffused with overtones of Georgia and a twang of Tupelo, Mississippi.

'You okay, kid?' Mac said, nodding toward my still clinched fist.

'Yeah, a bit of cramp, nothing really. Like I told you, I'd only touched down from Qatar when you'd phoned me, so I feel as if I've been flying for days. But yeah, I'm good,' I said giving him a smile at the same time as relaxing my hand.

'Good. Real glad you decided to join me for the flight back. Real glad you're deciding to join my company too,' he said with a self-assuredness that I figured was the start of his pitch.

'Well, I'm happy to fly in a private jet to Ottawa, Mac and you know me, always happy to join you for a trip to catch up on the latest news and games of the mighty Dallas Cowboys,' I said, raising my beer in a mock toast. 'But I haven't agreed to come work for you yet. You still haven't told me what the company is actually trying to do or what you want me for.'

He pushed a button to the side of his leather chair and it rotated from front facing to angle towards me. I found the same button on mine and reciprocated. We stopped short of facing off directly across the aisle.

'Kid, I told you. I've been pondering all that cyber stuff you were into back when I flew you out to Hong Kong. Made me think about it, off and on. But I was too busy with my usual business. No time to consider.'

I recalled Mac's usual business from my run-in with him four years ago. Flying high-roller gamblers in and out of Macau and Hong Kong whilst bypassing the usual Chinese travel restrictions. I had absolutely no doubt he also transported all manner of other merchandise that wouldn't have coped well with scrutiny. Not that I could judge. Had it not been for his connections then I couldn't have done what I had needed to do. The memory of those days seemed so long ago, yet the pain of losing Lily, more than that, the pain of me having caused her death hadn't diminished. *A good place?* I ignored the nagging voice again and refocussed on Mac. 'What's changed?'

Mac uncharacteristically hesitated, but only for a moment. 'Ah those little Communist bastards are changing the way Macau and Hong Kong work. Even down to the way you can travel between the two places. Can you believe they are actually going to build that crazy bridge idea? Thirty plus miles stretching from Hong Kong to Zhuhai to Macau. I saw the writing on the wall a couple of years ago. No need for flying in and out when you can drive it. Hell the taxying of the aircraft onto Macau's runway will take longer than driving from casino door to door in a limo.'

'But cyber?' I asked, still not too sure how he'd made the leap to my specialisation.

'Told you before kid. I'd not heard of it until I met you and then it kept cropping up. You know how it is. You don't know anything about something and then every time you lift a paper or a magazine, there it is. Maybes it always was there and maybes you never noticed it. So I read more about it and looked into it. Thing is, I know about investments, I made some good choices back when I was younger. Every investment I ever made was based on good information. Strength of the company, strength of the stock, the revenue, the net income, earnings per share, the price-earnings ratio and on and on. Yeah, knowledge of what went before didn't guarantee things, but having good intelligence on the sector and the competition meant you could make a well-worked out strategy rather than a Hail Mary pass.'

I had no idea what a Hail Mary pass was, but I guessed it likely had something to do with American Football. I could have asked him, but I didn't want to interrupt his flow, and quite honestly I was amazed. I knew he'd had to have made his money somewhere and somehow, but investments, stocks and shares had caught me on the hop. Much more surprising was that Mac had been clued-up and almost Warren Buffet-esque. It was a long way from the man I thought I'd known.

'...even the temperatures of the seasons got in on the act when I used to buy agricultural stocks. Yet, here I was reading all about scams and cons taking place all over the world, from those dang stupid emails from Nigerian Princes, to all that so-phisticated stuff attacking big business and nowhere could I find out information on the details.'

He paused to take a drink and nodded for the sleek Mandy to grab him a refill. I noticed his gaze traverse her legs as she slowly uncrossed them and stood. Even I could appreciate the sensual frisson she sent out allowing the top of her stockings to be visible for a moment. I also noticed the quick glance she gave me and the flash of a smile. Bless. I hadn't the heart, will or opportunity to tell her she was most definitely barking up the wrong tree trying to come on to me. The thought that her duties included servicing Mac's other needs made me feel very sorry for her career choices.

He took a long pull from the new beer and continued. 'There I was reading all about it and thinking I'd found a new niche to get into when there you were, boy. Your name, all over the articles. Giving speeches and conference papers and being heralded as the new kid on the block in banking cyber intelli-gence and the next thing you were calling me up. Destiny, Luke. That's what that is… destiny. So what do you say?'

It took a moment before I realised he was asking me if I'd come and work for him without any further explanation as to the job. I almost laughed, but managed to drown the noise by taking a drink. 'Eh. Yeah that's all great, but doing what exactly? What's the business plan?'

Mac leaned forward and tilted his head in a way that re-minded me of a Labrador somewhat confused by a word of command. 'The job? Didn't I explain it on that first call with you?'

'Eh, no. Not at all. You told me you had started a company called Twenty-Twenty Security Incorporated and you told me it would be a ground-breaker in terms of commercially available cyber intelligence, but that's it Mac. I'm still in the dark as to what the plan is or what my job would be. I assume you want me to set up an intelligence gathering division much like I did in the military and at the bank, but that's all I have, an assumption.'

He gave a short snort of a laugh, took another drink and relaxed back into his chair. 'Well hell kid, that's an awfully big leap of faith you darn took to come and get onto this plane. Heck, what if I wanted to offer you a janitor's job?'

'You said you'd pay off any notice periods I had to work and make good on any bonuses I would lose out on. Given that, I'm guessing the salary will be worth having, so Mac if you want me to sweep floors for you and still pay me top dollar, I'm willing to listen... but I don't think you want me as a janitor.' I took a drink, but kept my eyes on him and saw what I'd been waiting for. A subtle change to his demeanour. Very slight but enough to let me know the preliminaries were over. We were into negotiation now.

'No. That I don't. I want you as my London based, head of client relations. The business plan is simple. I am going to turn Twenty-Twenty into the world's leading provider of commercial cyber threat intelligence products. Our clients will be governments and the biggest companies on the planet and we will be their key enabler in avoiding cyber scams and cyber-attacks through predictive intelligence. We are going to get more major clients than any of the other fledging providers out there and we are going to be regarded as the best in the field. Once I've done that I intend to sell the company as a going concern. If I can't sell it privately, then I'll float it on the stock market, but private will be quicker and easier, more efficient. I intend to make myself a second fortune and if you come help me, I'll make you rich too, son.'

What value Mac gave to a second fortune was left unsaid, but the idea made me draw breath. This would be major money, but he still hadn't got to the crux. 'And specifically?' I asked.

'Specifically I want your name. Your reputation, kid. You're consistently mentioned as being in the top tier of what you do worldwide. I've spoken to likely investors in the financial sector and they say good cyber intelligence that would allow them to protect their networks would give a real competitive advantage. You get it?'

I nodded. It was obvious and at that moment I was surprised no one had thought of it before. Mac was still talking.

'...it's all about numbers and if they can show a return on investment for what they spend on cyber security then they'll make the initial outlay. The people I have been talking to know roughly what you did at the British Ministry of Defence and in detail what you did at Bateleur Bank so with your name attached to the company then those people will back us.'

I tried to say that there were others out in the world with the skills I had, but he cut me off.

'Hell yeah there are others, but I don't know them and I don't like them. I like you. Have done from that first trip we took and you started appreciating the Cowboys.'

'My name? You want me to recruit the best team—'

'No, son. I want you to make the client base wide and deep. I need your name to attract the clients. The best clients. You will be schmoozing them. Hosting them. Splashing cash on them. All the things I used to do with my high-rollers, but you'll be doing it with the heads of the departments at most risk from cyber-crime. I want you to wine and dine them and at the same time, show them how much money they could save their business by paying us to provide predictive intelligence on potential attacks.'

'But what about the actual job, the intelligence gathering?'

'I have that already. Working out of Paris with a full team of researchers and analysts headed up by a smart guy I trust. He's on top of things. No problem. But he ain't connected like you are. We have the product, we have the sources, we even have the undercover contacts and straightforward spies on the Dark Web. What I don't have is the known name that can get us into the boardrooms of the US, the UK, Europe, the Far East and the rest of the emerging markets. *That's* where you come in.'

I was surprised. Again. Seemed Mac was full of them today. My speciality was pulling a disparate team of technically savvy and intelligence-aware individuals together so they could provide top-notch cyber intelligence into the mix. I had, on occasion, got far more involved in the anti-cyber-crime operations than I would have preferred, but I had never been asked to be the known name in the room. In fact, since my days as a military intelligence officer, being the grey-man in any room was much more my thing. That said, I'd been fairly certain I was going to take whatever job he offered when I'd stepped on board the plane, so I was in. All I had to do now was remember the skills my mentor at the bank, Pat Harris had taught me about the subtle art of deal negotiations.

'Okay,' I said, eyeing Mac. 'How much?'

'The business is currently privately held with employee-owned share options. You'll come on board as an executive partner with the shareholdings appropriate to that level. I'll pay the rent on your London apartment, and provide you a base in Ottawa too. All travel will be minimum business class, or alternatively on this old bird,' he said, meaning the 605, but somehow pointing his beer-holding hand at Mandy, 'and I'll double your salary from the bank. When we sell you get your share value paid out in cash. Agreed?'

I forgot all Pat had ever told me. 'Agreed.'

***

We landed at Ottawa's Macdonald–Cartier International Airport and taxied to the private arrivals hangar. Unlike my previous trip with Mac, when he bribed a Chinese customs official to look anywhere but at us, this time we dutifully waited for the aircraft to park, the engines to idle down and for Mandy to open the door to allow two Canadian Customs Officers on board. They checked our passports whilst a colleague of theirs checked our luggage as it came out of the hold. It didn't take five minutes, by which time a black Range Rover had pulled up to the aircraft steps.

I was beginning to realise Mac was definitely a creature of habit. It wasn't only *Country Roads* or the beers or the football, but it obviously stretched to his cars too. He'd had black Range Rovers meet us in Macau. Perhaps it saved him from making mundane choices and freed his mind for more important things, or perhaps it was simply good old-fashioned OCD.

I said farewell to Mandy, a thing Mac neglected to do, followed him down the aircraft steps and climbed into the back seat of the Rover. Twenty minutes later, after a scenic drive along the banks of the Rideau Canal, we pulled into the side entrance of the stunning Fairmont Château Laurier Hotel on Mackenzie Avenue. I understood why it had château in its name. The hotel looked like it should have been sitting in a massive stretch of rolling estate somewhere in the Loire Valley. It was a majestic, gothic creation of turrets and towers, spires and black roofs that also reminded me of the Louvre in Paris. In the midst of Ottawa it should have looked like some strange cuckoo, yet it perfectly complimented the copper-roofed Parliament Buildings across the canal and also, in a juxtaposed way, the Tudor-

Gothic grandeur of a massive lump of a building that sat squat and rectangular across the road.

'That's the Connaught,' Mac said stepping up beside me.

'Someone wanted to build a castle?' I asked, nodding towards the central façade of the building opposite, rising as it did in two rampart style towers and with large wooden doors made to look like a set of faux portcullis.

'Yeah, you could say that. It's home to the Canadian Revenue Agency.'

'Ah, tax men. Nice digs.'

'And that monstrosity,' Mac said pointing further down the street towards a building surrounded with security fencing and anti-vehicle bollards.

'Is the American Embassy?' I offered, given it had the Stars and Stripes flying high above it.

'Yeah. It used to look a lot more subtle before 9/11 made them increase all their security requirements. No idea what for. Hell, this is Ottawa, not Beirut.'

'And that?' I asked pointing to the other side of the Connaught, where a modern cream and glass square of a building tried hard to hold its own in the street. Despite its attractive and sleek lines, it was always going to be overshadowed by the splendour of the Connaught and the Château. Like a much younger sibling being overawed by its older, cultured, and cleverer brother and sister.

'Ah,' Mac said, clapping me on my shoulder. 'That's your new home away from home. Or it will be once my lawyer gets the keys off the realtor.'

'Seriously?'

'Seriously, kid. Right in the heart of the city, within walking distance of what will be my Ottawa office, across the road from the Canadian Defence HQ, surrounded by the corporate head offices of banks and commercial enterprises and a stone's throw from the Byward Market.'

'A market?'

'Yeah, but not fish and vegetables. Think cappuccinos and wine bars. Good restaurants and high-end retail. Figured that as you liked that side of life in London, you'd want to be surrounded by it here too. That condominium block is where the elite of Ottawa live, Luke.'

'And you live there too?'

He thumbed over his shoulder and turned me around to face the hotel. 'I don't live in Ottawa. I live in Toronto. That's where the head office of Twenty-Twenty is. I stay here,' he said nodding at the hotel, 'when I'm in town. So you need to be close. Across the road is as close as I could get you. Although you're also in here for a few nights. Till we get the keys for the condo.'

I was confused and the fact that I'd been in Qatar only a day earlier and that my body clock was not so much out of synch as upside down, was making my head throb. 'So you want me to stay mainly in London, but I live here when I'm needed in Canada, in a luxury apartment owned by you?'

'Rented son, remember this is all temporary to get us to where we need to be.'

I should have known, but I let it pass. 'Sorry, rented. But you'll be in Toronto?'

'When I'm not down in the US or over in Paris, yeah. We need to be seen, Luke. It's all about impressions. We need to be seen as the people in the places meeting the people that frequent those places.'

I felt the tiniest of warning tremors up my spine. 'And my job here is the same as in London?'

'Sure is. We need to be talking to high-powered executives in the Canadian top tiers of commerce, industry and government. If I'm not around, then you'll be the man that fills in for me. I mean you'll have to come to Toronto too, but I have my home there so we can host anything we need to. Up here though,' he said making a gesture that was meant to take in the whole city, 'we need a good place and that condominium block comes with an executive style boardroom that can be reserved by residents. Also has an entertainment area next to a garden courtyard. Perfect for what I need you to do.'

'You did all of this without knowing I would say yes?'

Mac laughed and started to walk me towards the hotel's main doors. 'I knew you'd say yes, kid. What else are you going to do? You were made redundant from Bateleur yesterday and you only get to keep a reputation in an industry for so long.'

I almost missed the first step leading into the hotel's side foyer. Of course Mac's call to me, delayed by weeks yet coming as I made my way home from my final duties with the bank, hadn't been a coincidence. He'd been keeping tabs on me and I was only realising it now. The annoyance I felt with myself was overshadowed by a spike of greater annoyance at him. He'd played me.

'Take tonight to work out all that jetlag,' he said as a bell boy passed us with my bags. 'Follow him. You're in a top floor suite. Relax, unwind. It's got a bath you could hold a party in. There's a pool and a sauna in the hotel too. Even a spa. It's all expenses paid, order whatever you need or want. I'll see you bright, but not too early, for breakfast. Say ten in the restaurant?' He wheeled away to follow another bell boy.

The surge of annoyance left me and I managed a fairly weak, 'Fine.' I was really tired and frankly, Mac was right.

If I wanted to continue to cement my reputation in cyber intelligence, then sitting on the dole at home was not the way to do it. Let alone what I knew being idle would do for me. Keeping busy was my only option. Otherwise I'd dwell on lost opportunities and missed chances. The image of Dan, laying back in a crumpled bed and smiling up at me, the sun streaming through the windows on a lazy Sunday morning up in the English Lake District, made me falter. His face brought the same familiar feelings to me. A gripping tightness to my chest, like my heart was being squeezed. A lurch in the pit of my stomach. A nullifying sadness to my thoughts. I took a deep breath and forced myself to walk.

The bellboy delayed enough for me to catch up and led me through the opulent main foyer of the hotel. It was tastefully decorated in a mix of everything I liked. Edwardian luxury with modern amenities. I had to admit, if Mac was trying to ensure my commitment he definitely was going about things the right way. I realised that the surroundings alone had lifted my mood again.

The suite was equally grand although I had to shrug at the bell boy and apologise for having absolutely no Canadian cash on me.

'Can I offer you Qatar Riyals or catch you next time?'

'It's okay, Sir. Mr MacLellan will look after us,' he said with a tap of his forefinger on his forehead.

I had no doubt he was right. Just like Mac was about to look after me. The Coors Light rubber ring was about to get replaced with a proper life-preserver. I opened the suite's extensive mini-bar and withdrew five small bottles of gin and one of tonic.

Walking to the window I caught my breath at the panoramic view. Below, four locks of the Rideau Canal led down in steps to a wide expanse of water. Behind the canal and a break of trees stood the majestic Canadian Parliament Buildings. What had looked impressive at ground level now looked magnificent.

On an occasional table next to the window, in testimony to Canadian efficiency, lay a small card with a line-drawing outline of the view from the room's window. I peered to the left and right, checking the landmarks off one by one, whilst finishing my first gin.

Pouring the next and adding the smallest dash of tonic, I returned to the view. One building on Parliament Hill must have had a roof renovation recently as it was a copper colour instead of the rich green verdigris that topped off its neighbours. I considered that this rich copper tone was what the great domes of so many city halls and, of course, the Statue of Liberty in New York, would have looked like when 'new'.

Picking the card up again it told me the expanse of water to the front was the Ottawa River and off to the right was the Alexandra Bridge. It told me no more about this last feature, yet as usual when I looked at a bridge, words from my original intelligence training popped into my head unbidden. Truss bridge, five span, centre cantilever, road and pedestrian now but given its construction, probably rail traffic in the past. I gave a wry smile as I twisted the top of the next bottle of gin. Why my brain retained useless information like that was a mystery.

The memories of those days spent in a classroom learning about civilian infrastructure, including bridges and ports, power stations and factories, in case in some future scenario we would return to total war and have to flatten whole cities, made me sigh. Cyber could do most of the destruction and disruption with minimal physical damage.

I sipped my third gin in contrast to having knocked back the first two. My mind reflected on those early training courses. No one had even mentioned cyber back then and *back then* wasn't that long ago. How quickly things change.

'Don't they just,' I said to myself.

Eighteen months earlier I'd been on the dole. Signing in each fortnight for about fifty pounds of unemployment benefit. I gazed at the view outside and then back at the room. The trappings of wealth could be intoxicating, but almost on a daily basis I remembered my dad's words. 'Don't ever forget where you came from, Luke.'

4

Paris, Boulevard Haussmann – October 2009

Jules logged into a peer-to-peer network and navigated through a series of security protocols to enter the chatroom. He waited for his screen to refresh with a token that showed his connection was not only secure, but anonymous. He could only type with two fingers but if he kept his eyes on the keyboard he was relatively proficient. It was all he needed to be.

Reading from a secure fob, he typed the randomly generated number, adding his own pin to the end.

3873481093

He knew that the fob's twin, half a world away, would confirm his access to the chatroom and the pin, also known to his contact, proved it was actually Jules.

A few seconds later the screen split into two columns. The instructions were simple. The script was ready and the attack would start at 1am his time on Saturday. The screen went blank.

Jules logged out of the chatroom and pasted the link he'd been sent into another peer-to-peer relay. A single hyperlink nestled at the bottom of his screen and when he clicked on it a file named Aurora began to download to his laptop. A digital counter tracked the data transfer and when it finished, Jules dragged the file icon over to his USB memory stick. Then he ejected the stick, shut down his computer and left the office.

Stepping out on to Boulevard Haussmann he walked west towards Saint-Augustin Metro station. It was mid-week and almost eleven at night, but the wide tree-lined avenue was far from empty. He hesitated at the entrance to the station and purposefully checked his watch before glancing at a green-logoed Starbucks. Stepping forward he paused in front of the large windows, as if considering the scene inside the bland franchise. Then he turned away and crossed the road to a proper French café. To anyone with a passing interest in him, it appeared that Jules' patriotism had won out. On his late night stops for coffee, it always did. He valued his patronage of the Café Édith and not only for the coffee.

Given the lateness of the hour there were only a handful of customers and Jules was greeted with a friendly wave from Pascal and Monique, the engaged couple who worked the late shift most weekdays.

'Bonjour Jules, ton habituel?' Monique asked, dusting down a small space at the counter.

'S'il te plaît Monique. Tu me connais trop bien.'

The other customers in the café ignored the friendly greetings and if any had been looking up, they went back to their phones or books or simply staring into their brandy or cognac or coffee.

Jules slid a folded five Euro note across the counter. Monique picked it up and deftly allowed the USB stick to slip into her apron pocket before walking over to the cash register.

***

The phone rang on the bedside table and I fumbled in the dark for the receiver. It took me a few moments to orientate myself. I was still in Canada. It was six days since I'd arrived. In that time I'd been in a constant stream of meetings with Mac as he outlined his top targets within the Fortune100 companies and I'd managed to take preliminary meetings with executives from a couple of them. Nothing game-changing as yet, but to catch big fish sometimes you needed to hook a few smaller ones as bait. I had also managed to move into my new apartment, or condo as the locals called it.

Not that the move had entailed more than me walking myself and my suitcase across the road from the Château Hotel to the modern building I now knew was called, 7000 Sussex. The two-bedroom unit was big and as Mac had promised, designed for the elite of Ottawa. It came fully equipped and although a bit too modern for my tastes, I couldn't fault the quality of the fittings and furnishings. Everything about it was understated luxury. I had expected to have to buy some items, but when the Canadians said, 'Fully Furnished' they meant it. It came with almost everything I needed, down to cups, plates and cutlery, all brand new. The only things I had to provide were a couple of sets of bed linen, some food... and a few bottles of my preferred brands to help me sleep. Jetlag had been keeping me up and I simply needed a few shots to ease it off.

Mac had been right about the Byward Market area. It came with restaurants and bars, patisseries and crucially, two liquor stores. All in all I figured that I couldn't have asked for much better after Bateleur Bank. The evening before I had left Mac talking on the phone to his wife after we'd arranged to meet again for breakfast in the hotel. Now the condo phone was ringing and I didn't know anyone had the number.

'Hello?'

'Luke, it's Mac. Get up and get ready. We're needed in Paris.'

I struggled to find the light switch and when it eventually clicked on I checked my watch. 03:23. 'Now?'

'Yes now. We have a tip off about a possible cyber threat that might be on the horizon. I'll need you to talk to the analysts and then get out to the clients in London. The car will be outside yours in thirty minutes.' The phone clicked off.

I struggled out of bed and into the shower. Trading the time needed to shave for making a cup of tea, I topped off the cup with a nip of vodka. The first of the day always felt good to my throat. Like a warming scarf, comforting against the winds of the world. I only needed it because I had to be on top of my game with Mac regardless of the time of day. A small nip made me alert and switched on, so much more than anything else. I could have been as bright if he'd given me a few hours, but in the circumstances, a small nip was justified.

***

I'd been through Charles De Gaulle airport on many occasions. Round and confusing had been my main takeaway. That and the fact French customs officials were as full of Gallic indifference, arrogance and bloody-mindedness as they could squeeze into their uniforms.

I expected this time to be different, but I was mistaken. The protectors of French borders were at least still loyal to one of their nation's central tenets. I had no idea about *liberté* or *fraternité* but *égalité* was certainly alive and well. It mattered not that we had arrived on a private jet from the home of their Canadian half-cousins, the French Customs officials obviously prided themselves on treating rich and poor alike.

We had to wait on board the jet for almost half an hour and when they finally did deign to arrive, they were in every way as officious as any I'd encountered flying commercial. By the time the senior officer, a massive man who looked like he could have held his own in the French rugby union first XV, had asked his questions, stamped Mac's Canadian passport and barely looked at my UK European Union one, I thought Mac might have exploded in a show of petulant rich-privilege anger, but strangely he had been the epitome of calm. There had been no blustering or rants as I might have expected, instead he had stayed in his seat watching a re-run of the early season victory of his beloved Cowboys over the Carolina Panthers, 21-7. I had found it strangely comforting to hear the American twang of the commentators and pundits. One of them spoke just like Dan. I forced myself to concentrate on the game and pushed the image of him from my head.

Ninety minutes after landing we drove down the wide, tree-lined Boulevard Haussmann and pulled up in front of a typically Parisian triangular-shaped block of buildings, all modelled in the same style as the Fairmont Château Laurier Hotel back in Ottawa, replete with mansard roofs and cream-colored, Lutetian limestone frontage. To left and right of the building's double-height, double-width main door was a shoe shop, chemist, ladies boutique and various other small retail outlets. At either corner of the frontage was a brasserie, and nearest to me, a café-bistro. A light sandwich and a couple of white wines wouldn't have gone amiss, but as we stepped out onto the pavement the impressive door swung open and Mac bustled straight through.

'Good afternoon, Alicia, this is Luke,' he said, raising a hand in greeting to the tall, broad-shouldered black woman who had opened the door. 'Luke, stick with Alicia, she'll show you round.' He glanced at his watch. 'We'll meet in ten minutes, conference room,' he said, taking the stairs leading up from the main entrance hall two at a time. I hadn't even shaken hands with the woman before Mac had ascended the tight twist of the internal staircase and was out of sight.

The hallway and stairs seemed more in keeping with an actual apartment block and it disorientated me. Alicia sensed my discomfort. 'You were expecting a modern, refurbished, fit for purpose open plan office space nestling behind the Haussmann façade?' She asked in perfect English, with only the slightest hint of a French accent.

'Eh, well, yes, I suppose I was.'

'Yeah, so was I. Hi,' she said extending her hand. 'I'm Alicia Halder, head of the Production and Analysis team.' She waved me to follow and led me up to the second floor landing. To the side of a door, which looked like the entrance to a typical apartment, was a brushed aluminium plaque, laser engraved with Twenty-Twenty Security Incorporated and next to it a black glass panel. She held a plastic card against the glass, the door opened with a click and Alicia stepped aside to let me enter.

'Do we have the floors above and below,' I asked, still hesitating in the hallway and glancing up and down the twisting staircase.

'No. Just this floor.'

'And above and below?'

'Residential apartments,' she answered with a slight roll of her eyes. 'I know. I was weirded out by it too. I can imagine with where you've come from you definitely are.'

I didn't get a chance to ask her what she meant as the frown on my face had done it for me.

'We all knew Mac was trying to recruit you, Luke. And we all know your background in banking and the military. I imagine those workplaces were very isolated.'

'Yeah. You could say that,' I said, holding my hand out for her to go into the office first. She was right. The locations I'd been used to in the military or banking sectors were stand-alone secure units within bigger secure buildings belonging to very security-conscious organisations. Twenty-Twenty's configuration meant French families were living one floor up and down from a cyber-intelligence outfit. It was peculiar, but not something I could do anything about and so not worth the time to dwell on.

Entering the office I found it laid out much as I'd expected. Spaced desks with multiple screens for Alicia's P and A team and on the far side of the open plan area a triple-deep bank of computer servers. What I hadn't expected was a partition wall running the full width of the building and dividing off almost a third of the total floor space.

'Welcome to my humble abode, Luke.' she said, leading me across to a semi-circular configuration of desks topped with an array of monitors and a small wooden plinth that was exquisitely carved with *Dr. Alicia Halder* and underneath it, *Khedidja Oil*. She sat on a leather swivel chair and toe-poked another across to me. 'There's not much of a tour to take you on. This is it. My P and A crew are here. Tech folks live over with the servers and the intelligence collections guys are in there,' she said pointing to the partition wall.

'Really?' I found that most peculiar. My teams in the past had made the point of embedding the intelligence analysts in with the production teams so that there were no feelings of "them and us". Intelligence drove the efforts of production teams so they could provide real-world solutions to potential cyber threats. Having 'Int' tucked away in a secret world of their own seemed counter-productive to me. 'The intelligence collections team aren't in here with you?' I asked.

Alicia gave me another eye roll. 'Mmm, yeah. Not what I've been used to either. But, not my call.'

'This is Jules, yes?' I asked and couldn't miss the expression pass across Alicia's face. It was fleeting, but it had been there. I tried to work out what it had revealed, but the closest I could get was a strange mix of scepticism and pity.

'Yes,' Alicia replied. 'Jules… and his intelligence analysts. They like to keep themselves to themselves. All nerds, geeks and black-hats versus white-hats. Full of dark web intrigue and dark net hacking.'

'You don't sound convinced?'

Alicia hesitated and glanced over her shoulder to the secure door set into the middle of the partition wall. 'Umm, no, I mean we haven't been up and running that long and I can't fault their results to date, but… it's… well it's not…' she paused and corrected herself. 'He's not exactly what I was used to.'

'Where did Mac hire you from?' I asked, still curious at how he'd assembled a team of cyber professionals without making approaches to anyone I'd worked with or was familiar with.

'I was working for a multi-national oil exploration company called Khedidja Oil, out of Algiers. They had suffered multiple denial of service attacks and associated ransom demands. Also they hadn't realised all their geodetic data was vulnerable to being ripped off and one of their competitors was paying a bunch of Bulgarian and Czech hackers to syphon their ground surveys across to a Russian oil company.'

'Nice. All the fun of finding resources without having to go out and drill for them?'

'Pretty much. The execs knew they needed to shore up their computer security and so they brought in a few former US and Australian military guys to setup a cyber defence team.'

I was surprised. 'Oh, I thought you were French,' I said.

Alicia sat back with a laugh. 'I am. Well, dual. Algerian and French. They recruited me directly out of the National School of Computer Science in Algiers. I'd recently finished my doctorate and whilst the Americans and Aussies knew their way around code, they didn't know French or Algerian customs or languages. I was asked to pull together some local help from the Algerian computer industry. Worked there for five years until the company wrapped up their exploration operations. Took a year off to travel and was standing at Angkor Wat when I got a phone call from a French-Canadian recruitment agency to setup up for Mac here.' She swivelled in her chair and indicated the five or six people dotted about the office. 'I managed to reassemble some of my old team from Algiers. The intelligence team were pulled together separately.'

'Under this Jules guy?'

'Yeah.'

'And where's he from?'

'I'm sure you're parched. Would you like a coffee?' she asked standing up and walking off towards a small table setup as a coffee station. I followed, intrigued at her ignoring my enquiry. I knew better than to press it. I'd find out in good time so instead we talked about trivialities until it was time to join Mac.

'C'mon,' Alicia said, 'We better go through. I'm sure you know Mac doesn't like to be kept waiting.'

I nodded and followed her to the partition wall's only door which was protected by a digital keypad. '254817,' she said, keying in the numbers. 'If you need to get in.'

The door opened into a corridor with four doors on either side and one at the far end. It reminded me of walking into a low-budget hotel. That or a scene from *The Shining*.

'Oh, I was expecting the same as out here. Open plan space and a few terminals. This is very dark and foreboding.'

'Mmm,' Alicia managed but said nothing more.

As we walked to the far end of the corridor I could see each door was named. The labelling was crude, an A5 sheet of paper in a plastic sleeve stuck with tape, but the names were inventive, if you were into your Greek myths and legends. I could see the door at the far end of the corridor was tagged with Mount Olympus. 'I assume that's the conference room?' I asked.

'Yep.' Alicia said, giving me another of her idiosyncratic eye rolls whilst reaching for the handle and opening the door to reveal a large, bright and well-appointed room that would have been a main living salon when it had been an apartment. Mac sat at the head of a polished mahogany boardroom table. Next to him was a small, wiry man whom I guessed was in his mid-twenties. His hair was styled in an Elvis-like quiff and he wore black chinos with a crisp white shirt, the top three buttons of which were undone.

'Ah,' Mac said, getting to his feet. 'Luke, meet Jules. He's the head of my intelligence operations for the whole of Twenty-Twenty. We're very lucky to have him. He's our ace in the hole and will make your job in getting clients all the more easy.'

Jules stood slowly and extended his hand. 'Hello. Mac has told me much about you,' he said in heavily accented English. His limp-fish handshake was weak and incongruent for someone who looked relatively confident and assured.

I forced a smile to cover the distaste I felt at such an insipid grip and accompanied it with the usual response expected in such conversations. 'All good, I trust?'

Jules smiled as weakly as his handshake and sat back down.

Mac pressed a button and a projector whirred up, casting a square of light towards the screen at the end of the room. 'Alicia, honey, pull some of the window shutters closed. Okay, Jules. Take us through what your guys have found out.'

The first slide had a single word on it, NEMEAN.

'This is what we have called the threat,' Jules said and clicked for the next slide. An icon of Microsoft's Internet Explorer web browser came up on screen. The young Frenchman stayed seated and led us through a critical vulnerability in the browser that one of his team had been told about by a contact on the dark net. It seemed that the rooms I had passed in the corridor were each linked to separate dark net systems. From there Jules' team infiltrated the various illicit, and frankly disturbing, cha-trooms to 'listen in' to the real hackers and cyber-criminals. The analysts worked liked undercover agents taking on the persona of the room they were working in and that enabled round the clock intelligence gathering. Each room's 'persona' used the name of the Greek mythological character tacked to the door, so that multiple agents could work the same contacts and an-gles. So it was that *Hercules* had been monitoring chat from a couple of Far Eastern contacts and, eventually, had started to post into the chatrooms.

I knew the dangers. They weren't physical in nature, not usually, but some of the gangs and Nation States operating in the dark net space would, I was certain, reach out into the 'real world' or IRL, In Real Life, and take kinetic action if necessary, but thankfully that was far from normal. No, the dangers were more ethical. To gain the trust of hackers and criminals, the intelligence agents, source handlers and especially undercovers going into chatrooms had to be plausible. That meant more than knowing terminology or the history of previous cyber-attacks, sometimes it meant crossing over less than hard borders between passive monitoring and active engagement. My guys back in the military and in banking had walked fine lines sometimes. The step over from chatting and gaining trust to actively collaborating in the activities was easily made if the agent got carried away with the game.

It wasn't a new problem. Intelligence agents had always risked the potential of being drawn into collusion. It happened on more than one occasion during the Cold War, the dirty wars in Northern Ireland, and even within law enforcement when detectives, trying to catch paedophiles, had ended up having to trade images that were illegal and so nullified their cases through entrapment.

Jules' team needed to be trusted and as hackers were an ego-driven collective, so the proof of ability was in boasting about what you had done, were doing and would be doing. The 'Holy Grail' for a cyber-intelligence team was to become trusted so much as to be brought into an active cyber threat vector and so have insider knowledge of what was happening, what vulnerabilities it was targeting and therefore, how to stop it. The likelihood of gaining such access was extremely remote, yet in talking me through what was occurring, it seemed Jules himself had managed it.

'My main contact on the team goes by the name, Ushas. I have been cultivating him for a while. Even before I came to work for Mac,' Jules said, giving Mac what I figured was his idea of a smile but which came across to me as a half-smirk, half-scowl. I'd been in Jules' company for less than fifteen minutes and the drippy little man was getting under my skin. I couldn't put my finger on why, but I trusted my intuition. However, I couldn't deny the information he had gained was significant.

Ushas was part of a team planning a consolidated effort to gather background information on a number of key employees within a number of leading IT companies. The information would be used in emails directly targeting those people with topics that they would find of interest. I'd encountered this type of attack before. Rather than a simple phishing email sent out to millions in an effort to get a few unsuspecting souls to click on links, this was a much more sophisticated operation. Because of the individuals it was going after, it needed to be.

Serious high-end users within IT companies knew all about the dangers of unsolicited emails and therefore did not click on links or download random files. However, as I had seen during a cyber-attack on a British military exercise, if you could engage a senior leader with an email targeting their specific interests, the effect could be devastating. It was called spear-phishing and it needed a few things to work.

The list of targets had to be precise and that meant the hackers that Ushas belonged to had to have additional sources of intelligence on their targets. Did they like tennis, football, books about wildlife or conferences on psychology? In the case within the British military that I'd been involved with it had been an interest in mine-resistant, ambush protected vehicles. Niche, but effective.

Once you had the interest identified, then the phishing email had to be engineered to appear as if it originated from a trusted source. Even easier if you knew that your target had signed up to receive emails from a specific website. You could masquerade as an email from the real site, which in hacking terms was child's play, and send out a fake communique.

Lastly, the email you sent had to include a link to a website or a file that looked legitimate but in actual fact contained malware; malicious software that would run on the target's host computer and usually, though not always, would embed some form of backdoor into the system and allow the hackers access for future exploitation.

Spear-phishing wasn't new, but it was an incredibly involved, sophisticated attack vector and one that I had only ever known to be executed by a Nation State, namely China. When Jules paused in his self-congratulatory retelling of how he had groomed Ushas and thereby been 'recruited' into his inner circle, I interrupted. 'This is unusual for a set of lone hackers.'

'*Non*. Not really. I have encountered such things before. Ushas is a, how do you English say? Run at the mill criminal?'

'Near enough, Jules, near enough,' Mac interjected. 'So he's a good old boy trying to get what? Money?'

'I would say so. He is thinking to send specific emails to these people,' Jules added as the next slide came on screen.

It took me a moment to process what I was seeing. The CEOs of Yahoo, Symantec, Norton Security, Adobe and Google were only the top line of five lines of photos. 'That's the target list?' I asked, frankly amazed that any set of hackers would attempt to compromise these people.

Jules nodded. 'Oui. There are more, but these are the most notable.'

Mac was energised and almost bouncing up and down in his seat. 'Now you see, Luke. See what we can do if we have access to what's happening. See how valuable our ability to warn these guys is going to be?'

I nodded slowly. 'I can. So what is the actual attack system, Jules? What can we deploy to defeat it?' I asked the last question to Alicia who so far, had stayed quiet.

'That's quite an easy task,' she began. 'If we know what the source for the emails is then we can ensu—'

'Yeah, just hold on there a second,' Mac interrupted. 'We need to take this one step at a time. We need a few things to happen before we go shutting this all down.'

'Sorry?' I asked. 'We know who the actors are, we know who they intend to target and the methods they intend to use. If Jules has penetrated their operation to that level we know the specifics of the email. We need to get Alicia to deploy some defensive software and then brief the targets.'

'Yeah, well you might have done that in the old days from where you came from, Luke, but this is business. I want you to set up meetings in London with the representatives of that top row. Tell them we're getting undertones of a threat. Rumours, innuendos, nothing concrete. Make it out that we're working hard. Trying to get specifics, trying to develop a counter, but for now would they like to sign up for our intelligence products? Threat analysis, latest developments, up-to-date deployment of defensive software. If they pay they get it all. If they don't they don't.'

'But Mac, if Jules is righ—'

Mac stood up abruptly cutting me off in mid-sentence. 'Thank you Alicia. That's all for now. You too Jules.'

Mac walked to the windows and swung the wooden shutters back. The afternoon sun flooded the room. Jules clicked off the projector and he and Alicia left. As soon as the door shut Mac turned to face me and I noticed the rise of colour in his cheeks. 'I like you kid. Always have done, but don't ever fucking contradict me in front of anyone again. You hear me?'

I was stunned and lost for any type of response. He continued to glare at me. 'Well?'

'Sure. Fine,' I said and even to my ears it sounded petulant.

'Good. Now, what was it you were going to say?'

'Pardon?'

He sat back down, the flush in his cheeks dissipating. 'You wanted to contradict me,' he said, in a voice that had lost the sternness of moments before. 'What were you going to say?'

I hesitated. Was this meant to be some sort of test? Was I meant to say nothing?

'Speak up kid. I value your judgement.'

The roller-coaster of his emotional response had left me disorientated, but I figured I would have to take him at his word. Taking a breath, I said, 'I was going to suggest that this type of breach, targeted against the specific companies identified by Jules, has the potential to be catastrophic. If malware gets into their systems it could drop whole networks or lose untold amounts of data. These companies in a lot of ways protect the majority of other companies, or at least help facilitate their operations. If something gets in behind their defences it would be disastrous.'

'Good. That's exactly what we've been waiting for.'

'What?'

'Hear me out. You set up the meetings in London. Get them all on-board or not. Whatever way they handle it, you give our product and our prepared defensive software to the companies that were on the bottom two rows of Jules' slide. They'll be defended against the attack and the big boys that don't take our product, won't. When they finally realise that we're ahead of the game the ones that haven't already, will come crawling to us, begging for our help. That's how we'll consolidate our place in the market. Now do you understand?'

Despite my best efforts, I knew my face had conveyed my dismay, but it was more than that.

Mac continued, 'You once told me you'd never played poker, kid. I can see now it ain't a game for you to take up. You're as transparent as hell. What's the matter now?'

'I'm not convinced Jules is right about this, Ushas, being in a criminal gang. The level of social engineering needed to do this type of attack is really sophisticated. Also, how did Jules get into the inside circle of the hack?'

'Yeah, well that's not your concern. Jules is my intel guy. You're my customer facing business development guy. You do what I need you to do and Jules does what he needs to do. Okay, we're done here. Let's go get something to eat.'

He stood before I could say anything more and hustled me up out of my seat, through the door and along the corridor. As we entered the main production space he announced to the waiting Alicia and Jules that I was going to be heading to London, but first he was taking us out to dinner. I could do nothing else but tag along, bemused and confused.

***

As I'd discovered eating with him in Canada, Mac's dining rituals were strange and unusual. In Paris they were unchanged and as we entered the restaurant, he ordered for the whole table. Potato salad starter and steak main course. He stuck to his light beer, but insisted we order whatever alcohol we wanted. There are worse places to be given a free choice of a wine list than a Parisian restaurant. I made do with a bottle of Chablis. As we waited for the starter to arrive I figured I should really try to engage with Jules, despite my almost instant dislike of him. 'So, Jules, what's your background then?'

'I do not like to talk about it. Intelligence operators never like to discuss. I am sure you would know,' he said with that peculiar half-scowl, sneering smirk.

'Oh. An operator? Really? I thought you were like me, as in an intelligence officer?'

'*Non*, I was a special operator with the Dutch and French intelligence agencies. But even now I have said too much.'

'Wow. That's impressive. You must be one of those men who look younger than they are,' I said and took a long drink of my wine. *Patronising little prick.* 'The Dutch and the French?'

'*Oui*, but I cannot elaborate. I was trained from very young. I was recruited at school.'

'You mean university. They recruited you from there?'

Another sneer. Not often have I felt like throwing a good glass of Chablis over someone, but Jules was heading in the right direction.

'*Non!* At high school. I was the youngest ever recruited. I ran special operations for them when I was fifteen.'

Despite his apparent wish to shut up and say nothing, Jules seemed very keen to drop in details. I had no clue to his background, but I knew what mine was and I recognised bullshit when I heard it. 'Fifteen! You're kidding. Wow!'

He gave me the most stereotypical Gallic shrug I'd ever seen and then Mac leant in.

'Ah, stop interrogating him Luke. You know he can't tell you and if he did he'd have to kill ya!' Mac said with a loud laugh that made the rest of the restaurant patrons look round to our table. 'Anyway, I need to talk to Jules, but I need a piss, so two birds and all that. Come on,' he said standing and Jules dutifully followed him to the toilets.

I turned towards Alicia. 'I know he's got his quirks, but I can't imagine he invites you for a chat in the toilets?'

'No, thank goodness. Although that's a new one on me.'

'As opposed to all his other, umm…foibles?'

'Quite,' she said but with a hesitancy.

'It's okay Alicia, I'm not in his pocket that deep. I know he's a strange bird with some, let's call them peculiarities?' I nodded towards the glass of red wine that sat before her, untouched. 'No good?'

'Oh, no, it's fine.'

'Yeah, I'm sure it is, but I'm also going to guess, you don't actually drink.'

She smiled and gave a small shake of her head.

I continued, 'But you know as well as I do, because I have no doubt he announced it to you guys like he did to me,' I paused and in my best accent mimicked, *I don't trust no one that don't drink alcohol.*'

Alicia let out a laugh. 'First time he ever took us out. I figured, order a glass of something, drink water, hope he doesn't notice. So far so good… and it could be worse.'

'How?'

'Two of my team are vegetarians.'

'Ah. How'd they cope with Mac's never-changing menu choices?'

'They were okay initially. Eating the potato salad starter and pushing the steak around on their plate, but then Mac thumped his hand on the table and shouted—'

'Oh God. In a restaurant?' I interjected.

'This restaurant,' Alicia said checking over her shoulder to make sure Mac and Jules weren't coming back. 'He shouted that when the main arrived the *fucking potato salad was off-limits.*'

'Seriously?' I asked, knowing full-well it was something weird enough to be what I was now calling, a Mac-ism.

'Yeah. Poor guys. Then the next day, he gave them both a cash bonus for the month. I tell you, the money is great but I'm not sure how long I'll last riding his roller-coaster.'

I felt much the same, but decided not to share. I had a more pressing matter. 'Alicia, what's with Jules? Fifteen and recruited by two intelligence agencies. That's surely bullshit?' I expected another eye roll of disbelief and wasn't disappointed.

'I can't tell you if it's true or not, Luke, but it seemed pretty incredulous to me when I first heard it. I have a few friends in and around DGSE, on their Algiers desk and they've never heard of Jules, but they also said that if he was a special case like that, they'd never know about him anyway.'

That was true enough. Strange, off-the-books intelligence techniques, operations and personnel were exactly that for the most part, off-the-books. My instincts screamed at me about Jules, yet the fact was undeniable, he worked for Mac and Mac seemed to recruit top-level people. Well, I *would* think that. I pondered asking Alicia to put me in touch with her DGSE contacts, but Mac and Jules re-entered the restaurant and I resigned myself to giving the sneering little Frenchman the benefit of the doubt. As long as he provided good intelligence product.

The quality of it should have been the least of my concerns.

5

Surrey, England – October 2009

Charlie Buchanan checked his new Facebook page and tried desperately not to look towards his daughter and her friends.

It had all been so much easier being a dad a decade and more ago. Mandy and her four friends had idolised the Spice Girls, like so many little girls in the nineties. They'd taken the nicknames of their particular idol, except poor Denise, who'd been named Scary only because she was the tallest and roughest of the five. Still, the names had stuck and when they'd been little and come round to swim in 'Mandy's Pool', Charlie and his wife had kept an eye on them whilst they did underwater handstands and dive 'bombed', swum endlessly and played 'Marco Polo' until Charlie had been driven nearly insane by the endless call and response of a game he never saw the point of.

Mandy, his and Annie's only child had, because of the house and pool, naturally been tagged as 'Posh'. Lindsey was 'Ginger' due to her hair, Jess was 'Sporty' because she was the fastest swimmer and Christine was 'Baby' because she was, by about two months, the youngest. It seemed so long ago, and now all five girls were young women, attending universities dotted about the country but still the firmest of friends. Even now, in the early October break before Michaelmas term began, the five had met up and were, like all those years ago, swimming and splashing about in 'Mandy's Pool'. It helped it was indoor and heated. It also helped that they no longer played 'Marco Polo' at the top of their lungs, but it didn't help Charlie's embarrassment as he sat in his study with a clear view of the pool. No longer were Mandy's little friends, little. Now they were all in their early twenties and Charlie didn't have a clue where to look when they waltzed in, stripped off to their underwear like they had as kids and dived into the water. He wished Annie was here. She'd have laughed at his awkwardness and teased him about blushing.

Charlie stared at the silver framed photo of Annie on his desk and mouthed, 'I love you'. He stayed still for a while, concentrating on his breath until the wave of sadness passed.

He switched his focus back to his computer and the Facebook profile his daughter had set up for him. He'd had no interest in having any form of social profile, but Mandy had said it would be good for him. Allow him to reconnect to friends and colleagues that, by the nature of his career in IT, were scattered from Sydney to Silicon Valley. He'd spent a while in both places as a young man, before he'd met Annie, before the two of them had ridden the dot com bubble to a Surrey mansion, an indoor pool and a beautiful daughter. Before the breast cancer.

He checked the notifications and the pictures that had come up on his timeline. He had of course been aware of the platform before his daughter set up a profile. He'd actually met Zuckerberg briefly at a conference in Dublin when Facebook had established their international headquarters there twelve months ago, but it had been a hurried hello and handshake. Charlie hadn't been that interested in what was being called the Social Media revolution. He had, from a professional aspect, been interested in how secure the systems were and had been impressed at Zuckerberg's zeal for the whole thing. In a way he reminded Charlie of Charlie. The younger version. The driven IT security programmer who had become an industry forerunner in anti-virus software and, as an aside, a multi-millionaire. He figured Zuckerberg was well on the way to his own riches and if the Social Media bubble didn't burst too quickly, then there was scope for it to be a major influencer in the world of computer networks, but it was still early days. Charlie, like most in the industry, suspected Social Media could well be here one day and gone the next in as spectacular a manner as the whole dot com world had.

He shut down his browser and opened his email client. There were a few warning notices of new scam emails doing the rounds, a couple of requests from conference organisers for him to be a keynote speaker in the spring and a few from the small number of clients that he still acted for in a senior consultancy role. The duties were mostly background stuff, figurehead roles that allowed him to help out their internal teams or be seen as a guiding hand when they advertised their services. He rarely did hands-on programming or active network defence nowadays, but on occasion, if the threat was massively complex, he could login remotely and help out. The fees he was paid as a retained 'name' made him shake his head each and every time he checked his bank account. For a boy who'd been raised in a modest terraced house in the middle of Watford, Charlie always wondered what his dad would have made of it. He knew that the monthly payments he received from just one of the big anti-virus companies were more than his old man had made in a year. It was obscene, but it also allowed Charlie to indulge his altruistic passions and meant Mandy would never have to want for anything.

About to shut down his computer and go sit in the kitchen to avoid having to inadvertently look at 'Scary' as she sauntered about the edge of the pool like a barely-clad supermodel, Charlie saw an email from the Widower Support Group he'd joined after Annie's illness. He opened it, read the usual introductory paragraph and clicked on the link for the group's latest newsletter.

Computer programs take a finite time to run. Longer on slower machines. Charlie Buchanan's PC was as fast and as powerful as you could buy in non-Government environments. It meant the backdoor malware he had inadvertently activated ripped through it and every client system he had access to in the time it took him to walk to his kitchen.

6

London, England – April 2010

The headline read, 'Twenty-Twenty secure another FTSE100 client.'

It was six months since Jules' team had first penetrated the spear-phishing scam and, as Mac had wanted, we'd protected the lower-level companies. As soon as the power of the malware intrusions was evident and Alicia's team had deployed protection software based on the intelligence product from Jules, the top-end clients had been knocking at, and almost knocking down, our door. As we protected more and more, so the attacks petered out. Our reputation was riding high.

My role was simple and perfectly suited. I hosted events, chats, forums, and, most importantly, informal drinks receptions. The budget was unrestrained and I had carte blanche to hire industry experts to deliver a series of free-to-attend presentations on topics of interest. They might have been free, but were strictly by invite only.

The attendees came from industry, government and to make for a more rounded audience, Not-for-Profit organisations, although it took quite a lot of convincing Mac that they were a worthwhile addition. The presentations were enlightening but the receptions were the meal-ticket. Boxes of fine cigars, crates of champagne and more wines and spirits than even I could make a dent in.

It mattered not that the attendees knew we were on the prowl for their business and it mattered not that, surely, they could see through it, but high-end, quality schmoosing with high-end, quality food, drink and giveaways worked.

During the days after an event, I'd follow-up with individual clients, most often over a good meal at one of the preferred restaurants that I was becoming increasingly familiar with. The lifestyle suited me perfectly. I would arrange working dinners, or late lunches or, at a push, breakfast meetings. Lunch allowed me a few Tanqueray gins; breakfast always worked well for a few Veuve Clicquot mimosas, without the orange juice to spoil the champagne, and of course working dinners were accompanied by a bottle or two of Stellenbosch Chenin Blanc. It wasn't a big deal. I was always in control, never, ever drunk and my clients weren't aware I had turned up a good half hour before they arrived. I mean that was what a good host would do. I made sure I had time to ease my way into the meeting in advance. It wasn't like I needed to drink. It was simply sociable. A nice way to lubricate the mechanics of business. And there were a lot of mechanics.

Annoyingly, I also had to hand it to the little Frenchman, sneering and full of bull he may have been, but his intel product was proving to be unsurpassed. The queuing he was able to give Alicia allowed her team to develop software protection algorithms in almost real-time. The massively reduced levels of intrusive damage to clients' networks was putting Twenty-Twenty into a league of its own and there weren't too many in the commercial cyber game to begin with. Mac was delighted and had started the preliminary rounds of talks with potential future buyers. Twenty-Twenty opened a Washington DC office, a Singapore office, expanded the Paris operations centre and I was about to be joined by a new sales development force for Europe. All in all things were going well.

As the ideas for the private sale of the company developed and as I won high-level clients, Mac showered me with praise and with shares in the private company. I was now officially a senior partner and wondering how on earth I had fallen into this deep and luxurious bed of clover.

Until night-time drew in and I tried to sleep. Then I knew how I'd fallen into it. Everything has a balance and I got the job, and the lifestyle that went with it, by having a broken, thoroughly unhealed heart. Dan was somewhere in America. Living a lie of a life but unable to do anything about it, or that was the story I told myself. He'd never reached out to contact me so I had no real way of knowing what he was doing. My internal monologue, filled with angst at a reality that he simply didn't love me enough, was kept quiet by a nightcap. Or two. I needed to be able to sleep.

***

On the evening of April Fool's Day I received a LinkedIn request from a journalist. The Twenty-Twenty defensive software that we had been running since the spear-phishing scam didn't flag anything of note in regard to the contact information.

I didn't have a massive LinkedIn network, but I'd joined it back in January 2009 and mostly used it to identify high-level movers-and-shakers in potential client companies. Less often I used it to vet possible recruitment targets, but I always ran them through a sanity check with a London-based head-hunter called Emma Murray. She had recruited me to Bateleur Bank and I'd met up with her on the odd occasion at conferences and functions. I made a point of inviting her to all of my cocktail events, not just for her connections and industry knowledge, but she was intelligent, quick-witted and great company. She also knew a good gin from a bad one and over the preceding months I'd come to think of her as a friend. When I got a new connection on LinkedIn, first and foremost I checked if they were already connected to Emma as that was a shorthand for them being worth knowing in their own right.

This new connection request was from a Brian Hargreaves, who was listed as a freelance journalist and who had written contributions to most of the well-known computer magazines and periodicals. I'd never heard of him. Checking his LinkedIn network showed he wasn't connected to Emma, but was connected to some major players in a wide range of sectors from IT to oil and gas, military contractors, politics, finance and the media. He certainly looked interesting and being a journalist a diverse network like that wouldn't have been unexpected, but something niggled at me.

I stood up and stretched, feeling the kinks in my back working their way through a series of unsuccessful attempts to undo the knots in my muscles. Going via the kitchen to top up my white wine, I walked across to the lounge room windows and gazed out over the lights of the city. My own hazy and half-formed reflection stared back at me and for a moment I focussed on it.

I felt a mix of irritation with myself, regret and bloody-mindedness. My body's profile, once trim and fit was now looking markedly different to the man I had been even a year ago.

Somehow I had gained a belly. My neck and chin had lost some of their usual demarcation and my face was rounder and more ruddy. I turned sideways and placed my hand on my stomach. I breathed in and drew myself up to my full height, straightening my shoulders and raising my head like I was back on parade in the military. The roundness of my girth flattened a little and I breathed out, satisfied.

I lingered at the window and recalled another apartment overlooking the city. Another window where I had stood with a glass of wine in hand and Dan had come to stand next to me. Our first kiss. Our first night together. The torment inside me had diminished, I knew it had, yet it was far from gone. The continued physicality of my emotions in moments like this, when I remembered so vividly the life we had shared, was still enough to cause my breath to catch. Like a hand had reached inside my now fat stomach and twisted my innards. I swore softly at my own reflection again, drained my glass, turned on my heel and via a detour to the wine fridge, went back to the computer.

Brian Hargreaves' headshot stared back at me. I scanned his connections again and my misgivings became clear. There were no *nobodies*. Everyone he was connected to was significant; a person of standing within their chosen profession. I set my wine down and scrolled through the list more slowly. Where were the "also rans"? The not-so-high-flyers? The guy you went to school with who was now a middle-level administrator, or the woman who was on a career break and being a dedicated stay-at-home mum. I referenced my own list of connections. Yes, I had top-level executives and high-powered senior man-agers, but I also had others. Brian Hargreaves had no one similar to my own diverse bunch of flight attendants, nurses, chemists or GPs, journalists, construction project managers or plumbers. He definitely didn't have a bartender like the one I had in my LinkedIn network.

This lack of "others" wasn't an absolute red-flag, but I had seen enough within cyber to make me extremely cautious when presented with slight discrepancies. My LinkedIn profile, along with all my other social media profiles, was locked down tight. You needed to *know* me to see the rest, so allowing Brian to join my network meant Brian would get a lot more information about me and, given his profile, I figured he was worthy of a longer, more in-depth check. Easy enough when I had a whole cyber intelligence team sitting in Paris. I glanced at my watch, 11pm in London, midnight in France. This could wait for the morning. I drained my wine and turned in.

***

Waking early I made a cup of tea and found that I'd received three more invites to network connections on LinkedIn and two friend requests on Facebook. I knew none of the contacts.

Opening my emails there was the usual raft of unsolicited and unsophisticated spam and a few work-related missives that I could get to later. Halfway down the inbox was a very flattering enquiry about my availability to be a guest speaker at a cyber warfare conference. It was the type of email I received regularly enough and like most of them, this one specifically mentioned some of my background and experience.

It waxed on at considerable length about how great a fit I would be for the conference, how the currently secured speakers included major global influencers and captains of industry, how my skills would enhance the breadth of topics and how my joining the line-up would add rigour and legitimacy to the proceedings. By the time I had finished reading I was caught in a dichotomy between my ego, purring like a kitten at the flattery and my thoroughly British need to self-deprecate and feel awkward at any form of praise. I finished off my tea, with its usual morning kicker, and saw the link to the conference organisers' homepage. They wanted me to examine the conference agenda and suggest a topic that I might like to present on. A free choice. A handsomely well-paid free choice. Unlike the military or the bank where I had worked, Mac's policy was a lot more liberal. If I got offered money to take part in what he called, "an outside gig" then every cent of it was mine to keep.

'Hell kid, get them to pay you in cash. Then even the IRS don't need to know.'

I was a little more circumspect about that and I had no doubt that the US Inland Revenue Service and Her Majesty's Revenue and Customs were both capable of tracing cash payments and anyway, there was no way this conference organiser was going to pay me a four-figure speaking fee with a bundle of notes in a plastic bag.

I smiled to myself at how once, not so long ago, I had been on unemployment benefit and now, from a flat in London I could accept a couple of thousand pounds for speaking for forty minutes on a topic I knew inside out and upside down. I refocussed on the screen and positioned the mouse pointer over the link. And stopped.

The link address at the bottom of the browser looked correct, but I knew that was an easy thing to mask. The email was addressed to me, so not a generic "Dear Sir or Dear Customer" and I had heard of the company organising the conference. I was even vaguely aware the conference was running later in the year as I'd seen it mentioned in an online forum. Yet, lesson 101 in cyber-security was never, EVER click on a link within an unsolicited email. Despite the fact I had no need for technical programming skills, I was far from ignorant about the delivery methods of viruses.

I backed out of the email and scanned the rest of my inbox. There were another two similar offers for conferences and a couple inviting me to subscribe to well-respected cyber periodicals, all of which I already subscribed to. It didn't take a genius to work out that I was being targeted. I had to give it to whoever was behind it, they had balls, probably.

Given the protection we had offered after the 'Nemean' spear-phishing campaign that Jules' team had broken, to try a similar approach could be viewed as stupid in the extreme, but if the new vector could circumvent our existing defences, then it may be clever in the extreme. Companies and individuals, like me, would consider their systems protected against malware being delivered by social media links and so could be a little more laissez-faire. Even so, to go after random cyber-victims was one thing, to go after specific people another, but to go after someone in the industry, well that was either courageous in the extreme or very, very dumb. Instinctively I was veering towards the latter, but Paris would sort it out. Given how effective that snide little Frenchman's team was, I reckoned he'd crack this open in short-order and we could think about going after the perpetrators. I lifted my mobile and dialled Jules' cell-phone number.

'Yes?'

I waited a beat for a good morning, or a hello, or perhaps a what can I do for you. Nothing came. I stifled my annoyance. 'Good morning, Jules. I think the spear-phishing scam is back up and running. Obviously different links from a different source, as our protection software didn't quarantine it, but I'm sure it's a new threat vector. Can you track the false links and find out what their end-game is.'

'Are you sure it is phishing?'

Of course I am you patronising little shit… 'Yes, I'm fairly sure. I've received eleven separate potential hooks sent my way in the last,' I checked my watch, 'ten hours.' A pause. I waited. Then he made a sound which I took as the verbal equivalent of a Gallic shrug.

'Nughh. I am sure it is noth-zing to be concerned about. Delete them. It will stop.'

'Actually, Jules, that's not really your call to ma— Hello? Jules?' I took my phone from my ear and confirmed he'd hung up on me. 'You little prick!'

I called back and it went straight to voicemail.

It took me half an hour to get showered and dressed. By 7:30am I was ensconced in a First Class carriage of the Eurostar out of St Pancras. By 11:30am I was letting myself into Twenty-Twenty's second floor office on the Boulevard Haussmann. Alicia Halder rose out of her chair as soon as she saw me, her face reflecting concern which I guessed came from her observation of my expression. The journey had done little to assuage my annoyance.

'Hi Luke, are you okay?' She asked, leaning forward to greet me in typical Parisian fashion.

'Not really, Alicia. Hi to you too,' I said bobbing my head from side to side of hers whilst kissing the air. Handshakes were much swifter, but when in Rome. Or Paris. As she stepped back, I continued, 'Where's Jules?'

'Umm, he's taken a few days off. Back Monday.'

'For fu—' I stopped short of jumping up and down and stamping my feet. The annoyance and anger that should have erupted inside me fizzled out in a frank realisation that I'd been an idiot. I hadn't thought to call Alicia, or anyone else for that matter. I'd stormed out of my apartment straight to Paris in order to tear a strip off Jules and his grandiose, arrogant attitude and once and for all confront him about his bullshit resume. The flush of embarrassment was rising in my cheeks.

'Coffee?' Alicia offered.

'Eh, yes, please.'

'Where is he?' I asked, following her across the office space.

'Planning his wedding apparently. He's taken a trip down to his hotel.'

I figured she had simply misspoke. 'The hotel he's getting married at? Where's that?'

'Lisbon, Portugal. And yes, he is getting married there, but it is actually his hotel.'

'His?' I asked a little too forcefully. 'He has a hotel? I hardly pictured him as the hospitable type.'

'I know,' Alicia agreed. 'He's a bit too moody, antagonistic and frankly unhospitable for me, but yes he owns a hotel, or rather he and his fiancée own one. A three-storey, Spanish-villa style, or perhaps that's Portuguese-villa style, boutique hotel with verandas and one-off room designs and a swimming pool. He told us all about it, in great detail. In fact, he likes to tell us, *all the time,*' she said, stressing the last few words.

'Yeah, I can imagine. So this girlfriend, her family have money? Seems that Jules just can't help coming up smelling of roses.'

'Oh no,' Alicia said, filling the coffee machine hopper with beans. 'He bought it with her.'

'Really? How does he afford to buy a hotel? I know we're all doing okay, but a hotel?'

Alicia shrugged. 'Huh, that's not the half of it, Luke. Ask me how he is affording to hire a private jet to fly him up and down to Portugal for the weekend.'

'You're serious?' I asked, but it was a redundant question as the look on her face told me she was.

'Mm-mmm, completely. That and he has an apartment up near Montmartre. I agree with what you said, we make an okay salary but I'm like you, I rent an inner-city apartment, I certainly don't own one in Montmartre, and a hotel, *and* take private flights up and down to it.'

I took two mugs from a cupboard and positioned them under the twenty-thousand Euro coffee machine that Jules had expensed for the office. It didn't even taste that good.

'Anyway,' Alicia said, switching subject, 'enough of Jules. Why are you here?'

I took her through the spear-phishing and how I had called Jules to get him to set his intelligence team onto the matter and how he had hung up the phone on me.

'Charming little freak, isn't he,' she said. 'However, just because he isn't here doesn't mean we can't task the intel guys. C'mon,' she said and set off to the inner intelligence sanctum.

Once we'd briefed a couple of Jules' guys and I'd handed over a memory stick with the various emails I'd received and links to the connection requests, Alicia and I returned to the main office space.

'Well, if he's not here for me to argue with, I guess I'll head back to London,' I said.

'Yeah, but let me treat you to lunch first, downstairs, in the little bistro on the corner.'

I was about to make my apologies, but there was something about the way Alicia had made the offer, and the strange expression on her face, which made me agree.

The bistro was a minute's walk from the street door of the office. We were seated with menus, a carafe of white wine and one of water in less than five.

'Okay, so I guess it's my turn to ask what's wrong?' I said, pouring water into her glass.

'Thanks and nothing… maybe. But…'

'But?' I asked and waited for her to continue. She didn't. 'It's okay, Alicia, you can trust me. Is someone giving you a hard time?' I knew from my own experience that cyber was a male-dominated arena and I could imagine a woman, and a black woman at that, might have been on the receiving end of some subtle or maybe not so subtle put-downs.

'No, it's nothing like that. Believe me, I'd be able to handle that,' she said and smiled in a manner that made me think she would indeed be able to hold her own against any likely office bully.

'So what then?'

'The same thing that brought you here today.'

'Jules.' I said as a statement rather than a question.

'Yeah, Jules. I know we've scoffed at his claims of being an intelligence operator and we haven't turned up any information that he is what he says he is, but the results he and his team have been achieving are superb. We can scoff all we like, but results talk. Especially with…' again she hesitated.

'With Mac,' I finished for her.

'Yes. But the last couple of months, what with the apartment and the hotel and the flights, I can't figure out where the money is coming from.'

I took a drink from my wine and sat back, considering what could be happening. 'You think he's selling his information to others? Outsourcing his team? Getting paid on the side?'

'I did at first, but that makes no sense. If we build the business up the way we're going then, when Mac sells it, we all stand to make a heap. Selling info on the side is a very short term gain, and anyway, I don't think that one or two additional customers makes the money Jules is seemingly into.'

'It sounds like you have a theory?'

'Not so much a theory. Let's call it a loose hypothesis,' she said.

We paused while the waitress came over and took our order of soup and flatbreads. 'Go on then, what do you think is happening?' I asked when we were on our own again.

'I think, or rather I worry, that his guys on the intel team have gotten so far into bed with the hackers and extortionists that they might be turning a blind eye to some of the more targeted scams out there. I think they might be getting paid off to ignore them.'

For a working hypothesis it made sense. There was a lot of money to be had in cyber-crime, almost as much as in the illegal drugs industry. A micro percentage of it to have an intelligence team as effective as the one Jules was heading up look the other way was feasible and would result in major windfalls. 'Have you done any digging?'

Alicia shook her head. 'No. I don't have the skills needed to get into his accounts or to find another source of information on him.' She tilted her head and smiled.

'Hah! You want me to do it?'

'Well, not you necessarily, but I know you still know an awful lot of people out in the world and in the banking sector. I'm sure some of them might be able to help you?'

'I think you mean us, Alicia. Are we to be co-conspirators in the taking down of an arrogant little weasel?'

'Well, possibly?'

'Oh? Only possibly?'

'Thing is Luke, I'm getting to the end of my tether with the whole setup. Even if it turns out Jules is squeaky clean, he's still an annoying shit and despite the information he provides being gold, frankly it's disjointed and fractured.'

'How do you mean?'

'He should be working to a set of actual intelligence requirements but instead he's lurching between whatever takes his fancy, or if I'm right, what he's being paid off to ignore. It's not what I'm used to. Add to that Mac's emotional responses to everything and I might just jump ship the next time I get an offer.'

I understood her reservations. Jules' intelligence team and Alicia's operations were meant to work together. In my previous jobs that's what I'd made sure of. The operations were led by the intelligence and the intelligence work was directed by the potential risks that might be present. In the military that had been risks to the country, in the bank it had been risks to their financial stability and now, in Twenty-Twenty, it should be all about the potential risks to our clients. I hadn't much to offer her in consolation.

'However, whilst I'm still here,' she continued, 'Yes, I'd like to work with you on the Jules problem.' She lifted her glass of water, holding it toward the centre of the table. 'Are you game?'

I let her hand hover in mid-air for a moment more and saw a slight doubt creeping into her eyes, before I reached my wine glass forward and clinked it gently against hers. 'Of course I'm in. Let's hope we find something to get him exposed and fired, or better still, arrested.'

***

I was back in London by half past five and home before the six o'clock evening news. It was a Friday and I knew it would be more appropriate to wait until Monday before ringing up the people I needed, but then again, I figured they were probably all still in work mode.

'Steve?'

'Luke, is that you, La?' The scouse accent was as thick as ever and it brought an instant smile to my face. Steve Bryant had worked for me at Bateleur Bank and both he and his protégé, Paul Malone, had taken the voluntary redundancy packages at the same time as I had. In fact the whole cyber team of the bank had left when the prospect of working for a man called Dickie Lessen had been explained to them. Now Steve and Paul, a most unlikely looking duo, had formed their own cyber consultancy. Had I been running the intelligence gathering or operations side of Twenty-Twenty they'd have been some of the first people I would have tried to recruit, but that wasn't my job and so I was glad that they were making a success of their own business.

'Yeah it's me Steve. I was wondering if you and Paul would like to help me out.'

'Sure, what's up?'

'I need to know where someone is getting their money from.'

***

On the following Monday my phone rang at 6:30am. I'd expected it and I also expected Jules to be annoyed that I had tasked his team. What I hadn't expected was him to flatly refuse to allow his guys to work on the attack vector. My immediate response was to tell him exactly what I thought of him, but that wouldn't achieve anything and moreover his response certainly lent credence to Alicia's theory. I told him I thought he was being short-sighted, hung up the call and quietly fumed. Then I waited for the clock to tick down the hours.

At 8am their time, I called Canada. I needed to advise Mac what Jules was potentially up to and make him aware of the investigation I had launched.

'Good morning, Twenty-Twenty Security Incorporated, how may I direct your call?'

'Oh. Sorry, I was expecting this to go straight to Mac's phone. It's Luke Frankland… in London?'

'I'm sorry Mr Frankland, but Mr MacLellan's unavailable at the moment. Can I put you through to Mr Harris in the DC office?'

'Eh? Sure,' I said hesitantly, wondering with equal measure who Mr Harris was and what had happened to Mac that would cause him to be unavailable. The man was a machine, he was always at work. A few seconds of silence was followed by a laidback Arkansas voice I recognised.

'Pat Harris, how can I help you Luke?'

I was so stunned I only managed a stumbled reply, 'Pat? Pat Harris?'

I heard his familiar laugh 'Yes, the one and the same. I had intended to reach out and say hi a few days ago but things got a bit frantic.'

I was genuinely lost for words. Pat Harris was the man who had recruited me for Bateleur Bank. He had also engineered for me to get my redundancy and a relatively handsome payoff from the organisation. Pat himself had received a much more significant pay-out through the same redundancy scheme and as far as I knew had retired to live off his newly acquired wealth in a veranda-style house overlooking Lake Greeson in his native Arkansas. He was also a man I owed most of my commercial savviness to, if I had acquired any at all, and had been the key in me transitioning from a military mindset to a business one.

He was most certainly not meant to be answering the phone in Twenty-Twenty's DC office.

'Luke, you still there?' he asked.

'Eh, yes,' I said, unsure which one of the myriad questions to ask first. Pat, obviously sensing my confusion, allowed me time to orientate myself by stating the obvious.

'You're probably wondering why I'm answering the phone?'

'Yes, a little. Are you working for us now? Did Mac approach you?' It seemed a reasonable question. I knew Mac had been trying to recruit many of the leading figures from banks and financial institutions who had experience with cyber at the 'finger-to-keyboard' level, but Pat wasn't close to the 'frontline' of that. He was all about strategic thinking and business acumen. He had been born and bred in the American banking system and knew it inside-out, but he wasn't a coder or a white-hat hacker. He wasn't even an intelligence-team builder like me, so if he'd been approached by Mac that was a major deviation.

'Yeah, he approached me. Seems he wants a name to help with the due diligence.'

I took a breath. That made sense. I knew, in line with Mac's main goal, when we did finally come to sell the company, there would be a significant process of checks and balances to go through. It was usually referred to as due diligence and ensured the balance sheets were correct, the company could do what it said it could and ultimately was worth the selling price being asked. Having a name like Pat Harris involved would certainly help and he would no doubt do a sweeping series of pre-emptive audits to ensure all was well in advance of any future sale. On even a momentary reflection, it made good sense. But to scoop up Pat Harris was a coup and a half.

'I couldn't think of anyone better, but how did he pluck you from retirement?' I asked, still a little shocked by the coincidence.

'Simple really. He'd approached me at I'm guessing about the same time as he first approached you. Obviously neither one of us had heard back from him for months and so you took your redundancy and I took mine. I knew you'd been recruited in short order but I heard nothing and was quite happy walking the dogs and fishing, but a few weeks ago I was contacted by a recruiter and invited for a chat. The wife was getting a bit antsy with me being around the house all day, so I figured a part-time return might be just the thing.'

'That's brilliant, Pat,' I said and meant it. Pat was not only a great commercial brain to have on board, ethical and honest, but I liked him. 'So you've come on as what, the commercial manager?'

'No, not quite. Mac wondered if I'd also like to invest in Twenty-Twenty, so I've come on as a Senior Vice President.'

Now I knew why there had been no fanfare about the new arrival. Mac liked to play all his money cards extremely close to his chest. Twenty-Twenty was a privately owned company with nominal shares, the same ones that Mac gifted to me when I did things that pleased him. But to actually increase the number of shares meant more seed-funding, which both helped the company establish more capability, but also increased the over-all worth of it when it came to sell. It was common knowledge that there were some individuals in the background who had helped Mac with the initial financial resources and they, in turn, held large numbers of shares. While we knew of them, even the senior partners like me, knew nothing about them. They were, very much, silent partners. The only two initial seed-funders we did know about were the two men who had seeded the most investment into the company and had, in turn, been given the titles and real job roles of Senior Vice Presidents. Now, we had a third.

'Wow! Congratulations. So you're SVP of...?'

'Nominally, operations.'

He said it with no inflection in his voice, but I knew exactly what he meant. Mac was a control-freak at the best of times, even down at my level. I could barely imagine what the SVPs had to endure.

"But that's even better. You're my boss,' I said, and added, 'Again. What a thrill for you.'

Pat laughed. 'Yes, for sure. I do have to say though, without making you uncomfortable, you were a big reason I came on board.'

Once more I was rendered speechless. I didn't really *do* compliments and was always unsure how to react to them, especially if I felt they were particularly unworthy. It was I who owed Pat and he would have been a reason for me to follow along. For him to state the reciprocal was humbling. The silence could have become awkward, but I was saved by Pat's familiarity with me.

'Ah Luke, you haven't changed a bit. Now, you rang for a reason? What's up?'

'Oh, yes. Umm... Sorry Pat, before we start, where's Mac?'

'Hospital. With a football injury.'

'What?' I knew Mac MacLellan for a lot of things, but a football *player* would never have featured in my wildest dreams.

Pat laughed. 'Yeah, well, sort of. He was standing on a chair adjusting one of his wall-mounted flat-screens to better watch the Cowboys' game last night and over-balanced.'

'Shit! Is he okay?'

'Yes, and no. He managed to avoid landing on his head, but his knee took a battering. Alexis had to call an ambulance.'

'I can't imagine that went well,' I said, thinking of Mac's aversion to losing any form of control over anything, let alone having to be taken to a hospital.

'Yeah, he was a bit resistant, but he couldn't stand and his kneecap was pointing in the wrong direction, so there wasn't much choice. He's being operated on later today and will be out of action for a while.'

'Is Alexis okay?' I asked, knowing that Mac's wife was more than capable of being okay without Mac around. I didn't know exactly the age difference, but it was at least twenty years in her favour and on the occasions I had met her she had surprised me at not being what I had imagined. Rather than a mere beauty accessory for the multi-millionaire, although she was most certainly that, she also had humour, an innate witty sarcasm and a surfeit of brains behind the pretty façade. On the odd time I had met her at a function in Ottawa, I did wonder why she put up with his fairly demeaning attitude to her, but I suppose the multiple houses, indoor swimming pools, chauffer driven cars and private jet went a long way towards explaining it.

'Yeah, she's fine. She thinks he'll be in hospital for a couple of days, then recuperating at home for a few weeks, but she expects that as soon as he's out of hospital he'll be straight back working, even if he has to do it all from the home study.'

'Sounds about right,' I agreed.

'So, until he's back up and about, you have me. What can I do for you, Luke?'

Despite our longstanding relationship and his professionalism, I was unsure what his reaction might be to my news. Mac, officious, controlling and a complete pain in the backside on occasions, nevertheless liked and trusted me. I was fairly sure he'd back what I was doing about Jules. Pat also liked and trusted me, but he was new into his role and as he had said, it was a *nominal* one at best. As it turned out, I needn't have doubted my former, and I happily reminded myself, current, boss. 'It's complicated, Pat,' I began.

'Isn't everything? C'mon Luke, spit it out.'

I took a breath. 'I think we might have a problem with Jules and his team in Paris.'

'Really. Now that is interesting,' he said with sincerity and no trace of sarcasm.

'It is?' I asked, a little surprised at his tone.

'Yeah. You're the third person to say as much to me over the last few days.'

'Really?'

'Really.'

'What did Mac say? I assume you told him?'

'Oh yeah, I told him alright, but it was all a bit… weird if I'm honest. He told me not to worry about it. Just straight out denied there was an issue. Yet here you are telling me that might not be right.'

'What were the other two complaints?' I asked.

'Not really complaints, but a couple of the guys here in Washington were getting snippets of a new threat coming into manufacturing sites. Fancied it might be a good way into the big blue-collar industries up in the rust belt, but when they tried to get Jules and his team to investigate they got nothing back. Not even a reasonable report of attempts made within the cha-trooms that they've exploited so well in the past. Just stonewalled them. As soon as I was appointed they came to me hoping to get some movement on it.'

The scenarios fitted with Alicia's theory. My theory too now. I told Pat about my concerns and the broader issues of the disconnect between intelligence collections and operations. He listened without interruption. When I finished he stayed quiet. I waited. As I was wondering if I'd been cut-off, he finally gave a sigh. 'This isn't the way things are meant to work at their most optimal,' he finally said. 'Certainly isn't how we ran them at Bateleur.'

'No,' I agreed. It had been Pat who gave me my position as global head of cyber with Bateleur and he had been adamant that intelligence had to, in absolute terms, lead operations. I knew he'd be as confused as me at how Twenty-Twenty was doing things in Paris.

There was quiet on the line, but I waited. I knew the man on the other end. I knew he'd be measuring and weighing the circumstances and any likely response that he might be able to make to Mac. A potential course of action to be taken. In fact, I was wrong. Mac was not in Pat's thoughts. Instead, a former manager of both of us back at the bank was in Pat's thoughts.

'When is your next function event?' Pat asked.

'Two weeks.'

'Great, we can recruit a couple of sales and administration types to come and help you out with that. In the meantime, as I'm in charge of operations and at the minute, the acting head of Twenty-Twenty, I'm offering you a new position.'

'O-kay,' I said, stretching the sound out so that he knew I had reservations. 'What exactly?'

'Global Head of Cyber Intelligence and Operations. It'll be a Vice President position. I want the teams integrated. You'll be in charge of Paris and you'll have to recruit the equivalent for Singapore and Washington in due course. They'll all report to you. It makes sense that we have a round-the-clock capability and not just a European-centric one. And it also allows me to authorise you to pull the disparate bits of Paris together.'

'Eh, that's one hell of a job change. Are you sure? Will Mac buy it?'

'Yeah I'm sure and yeah, he'll buy it, because he wants what we all want. When we come to sell this company I intend to make back a lot more money than I put into it. Then I'm calling it quits, going back home and buying a bigger boat to spend my days fishing further out in the lake and thereby having a happy wife and a happy life. I don't plan for some potential scandal surrounding a Frenchman of all things to derail us, so go find out what's going on. Okay?'

'Eh, okay,' I said, hesitating a little as I'd just gone from a cushy job based in London back to being a global player in cyber. It hadn't been my plan for the phone call. Pat mistook the tone in my response.

'It's alright, Luke. Thank Dickie Lessen.'

'Seriously?' I said, thinking of a man I had considered an idiot. He systematically stymied our good decisions and made bad ones seemingly with ease and certainly with no thought as to potential consequences. 'Pat, are you sure you want to make decisions like him?' I asked.

Another laugh came down the line. 'No. Not like him, but I did promise myself that if I ever found myself in a position to make decisions I wasn't going to be frustrated by an idiot like Lessen again. You and I know this is the right decision. I'll sort out the specific titles and salary increase later, but trust me, you won't be disappointed. Meanwhile, get yourself across to Paris, launch a proper investigation of what the hell Jules is up to and get the intel team to work for the ops team. Alright?'

I remembered how the speed of Bateleur Bank reacting to events had surprised me when compared to the military. Now I had discovered how much faster decisions and appointments could be made in a private start-up where a Senior Vice

President had, as Pat himself would have said, skin in the game. There was no HR to go through, no public shareholders to convince. Pat, by my best quick reckoning, owned a third share of two thirds of the company and if he wanted to appoint me as Global Head of Cyber Intelligence and Operations, then he could. And he just had.

'Alright,' I answered, a lot more forcefully.

'Great. I'll fly over tomorrow. And Luke?' Pat added.

'Yes?'

'If it turns out Jules is screwing with us, I want him hung out to dry.'

It was unfortunate that Pat couldn't see the size of the smile I had on my face.

***

Mac was passionate about American Football but at heart he was proudly Canadian, so he insisted that Twenty-Twenty used the Canadian-owned Four Seasons Hotel Group. It worked out fairly well in most cities, but in Paris the result was exceptional. The George V was a sumptuous art-deco masterpiece and my room had a view across the city towards the Eiffel Tower. Pat had told me to put it all to the company card and he'd answer to Mac as and when it came up. I figured, looking at the minibar and the price tabs on the Champagne and spirits, that I might not take too much advantage. Perhaps I'd pay for my own drinks.

I met Pat for breakfast on Wednesday morning before we took a picturesque walk down the Avenue des Champs-Élysées, making a left at the Place de la Concorde and up the narrow tree lined Rue Tronchet. When we reached the Boulevard Haussmann and the heavy-set double doors of the street entrance for Twenty-Twenty he put a hand on my arm.

'Showtime. You all set?'

'Yes. I think so.'

'Remember, this is about finding out what's going on and making sure we're solid for when we come to sell the company. I can't simply storm in there and fire Jules; his results are too good and an action like that would itself cause questions with potential buyers. So we play it slow.'

'He'll be pissed off that I'm his new boss,' I said, figuring that was an understatement.

'Yeah, well that I can take care of. Best case scenario is that he gets so annoyed that he quits.'

'What's the worst case?' I asked.

'That he stays and you start getting his team to do what we want, meanwhile finding out what he's really up to. All good?'

'All good,' I repeated and followed Pat in.

***

It was worst case.

Not that there weren't moments when I wondered if Jules would storm out and one instance where I thought Pat might fire him for his language and attitude, but in the end Jules calmed down, shook my hand and followed me to a bigger meeting with his team, Alicia and all of her team.

I started by congratulating Jules' guys on their intelligence collection activities. There was no doubt how remarkably successful they had been. Jules looked as smug as usual but the rest seemed much more modest and almost embarrassed at being praised. I guessed Jules hadn't showered them with much in the way of thanks. I also told Alicia and her team that the software defences they had invented and deployed against the threats had put us at the forefront of the fledgling cyber intelligence industry. They seemed a lot more comfortable about my speech. I didn't doubt that Alicia had managed to put together a well-balanced team who knew their leader valued them.

Then I recapped the potential industrial threats that the guys in Washington had seen and the new spear-phishing I had been subjected to. I wanted all the current intelligence collection to continue, but I also tasked Jules with a new list of intelligence requirements. I wanted his guys to start reaching out through the layers of the dark web and the nefarious chatrooms they frequented. Find out who and what was behind the two specific threat vectors and feed that information as quickly as possible to Alicia's team.

I dragged a whiteboard forward and wrote RustBelt as the name for our operations against the industrial threat. 'Anyone got any suggestions for the new spear-phishing?' I asked.

One of Alicia's team tentatively raised his hand.

'It's Mo, isn't it?' I asked, suppressing a chuckle at his gesture. I was used to my teams in the Bank or the MOD freely speaking their minds and offering their opinions.

'They seem to be using social media as the cornerstone to their attempts at social engineering. So, Cornerstone?'

7

Fort Benning, Georgia – April 2010

Dan stood under the shower and let the heat of the water soak into his shoulders. He'd kicked-off the working day as he always did, with a ten klick run. It kept him fit and let him get out of the house as soon as he woke. By the time he was back, Shirlene usually had Ryan washed, dressed and sitting up at the breakfast bar eating a mixed bowl of Cheerios and Lucky Charms. Lilly-Anne would be twirling and undulating in her Jolly Jumper with a mauled rusk oozing out through her fingers and a smile that lit up Dan's world like nothing else could.

Coming in through the back door, he'd filled the coffee maker and then gone up for a shower. The water felt good against his skin. He realised he craved something touching him, for Shirlene hadn't so much as hugged him over the previous few months. Not that he wanted her to, but it was in stark contrast to how she had made him screw her every day for months after the first conversion therapy sessions and when he'd first come back from the Korengal. Not now though. Now she was wrapped up with the baby and whatever else she filled her days with on the Fort. She occasionally mentioned the Officers' Wives get-togethers and impromptu crèches, baby playdates, charity thrift drives and of course her work with the on-post Religious Support Office. Not that Dan thought she had the brains to interpret the scriptures. He was sure it was simply to make herself feel good and appear like a kind and true believer to others.

He lathered shampoo into his shorn hair and quietly cursed his wife. Everyone saw the hometown, high school beauty queen that she'd been. No one saw the manipulative bitch she'd become. The only part of her external persona and her internal beliefs that meshed was the Church and even then he had his doubts. God, Family, Country, Service was her mantra and she delivered it so forthrightly and so consistently she'd convinced everybody of her genuine belief in it. He remembered Luke had once shown him a stick of English candy, called 'rock'. It had the name of the town where they'd bought it twirled all the way through in contrasting candy strands. He figured if he cut Shirlene through the middle she'd have those four words twisted through her... perhaps. Rinsing the shampoo off, he wondered if it would only be one word; hypocrite.

Yet it was Shirlene's expressed belief, and his own father's backing of her, that had forced Dan to attend the conversion therapy with Pastor Harold's church. Back then the military's policy was still 'Don't ask, Don't Tell' but he knew they had very much approved of his time spent being 'cured'.

Now he wondered just what the fall out would be in the coming years. A lot of his fellow serving Officers had railed and sworn and called out President Obama's State of the Union Address where he declared he was going to *"finally repeal the law that denies gay Americans the right to serve the country they love because of who they are"*, but they'd been nothing when compared to what Shirlene had said. She hated the man in the Oval Office and when Dan reminded her that Jesus would have wanted her to love everyone, she told him it didn't apply to *that man*. When he taunted her again that only God could judge, she'd flung a half-full wine glass at his head and told him to fuck off.

He let the hot water cascade down his face and allowed his thoughts to meander. Was Shirlene the hypocrite? He knew he definitely was. He kept up the pretence so that he could stay with his kids. Was that hypocritical? He figured it was. Especially as he allowed his father and Shirlene to force him into actions he did not want to do.

Every three months travelling north to Pastor Harold's church. Applying for a long weekend duty pass, Friday through to Monday, so he could attend conversion refresher camps. Like his love for Luke was some recurring disease that could only be kept at bay by top-ups of a vaccine. The next one was in two days' time and he knew that he would go, as he had before and as he would again. Because apparently Shirlene's God was all about loving your fellow man, unless you took that literally.

Dan turned off the water, towelled himself dry and got dressed into his uniform. He'd go downstairs, kiss Lilly-Anne, walk Ryan to elementary school and then continue to the head-quarters of the 1st Battalion of the 96th Infantry Regiment. It was a post he should have left months ago, but the Army re-neging on a deal was not a surprise. He'd been assured that the Korengal was only a diversion and when he got back he'd be on track for the tour he'd been promised. Intelligence Officer for the 173rd Airborne Brigade in Vicenza, Italy.

'Yeah, right,' he said as he checked out his reflection in the bedroom mirror. 'All those who expect to be treated fairly, take one pace forward... Where do you think you're going Stückl?'

He laughed at the old joke and headed for the stairs. Before the day was out he knew what true unfairness was.

***

'But I only just got back?'

'Technically it's been over six months and it'll be another five before you actually deploy.'

Dan stared incredulously at his Colonel. He knew instinctively that when the Army had made its mind up there was little point in expending the energy to argue, but just because it was useless didn't mean he wouldn't try. 'But Sir, surely there has to be—'

The Colonel stood, cutting Dan off in mid-sentence. 'Look Captain Stückl.' The use of his rank was enough of a warning shot for Dan. Colonels didn't call their officers by their rank unless the conversation was effectively over.

'You're going to ask is there no one else. The truth is no, there isn't. We're over extended and so the tours are longer and the gaps are shorter. Occasionally we have to plug holes and your name is next up. It's not like we're sending you back to the Korengal. Hell, we aren't even sending you back to Afghanistan, so think yourself lucky. You leave in September. Clear?'

'Yes, Sir.' Dan stepped back and saluted.

On the walk home he decided that telling Shirlene straight away would mean his nine month deployment in Mosul, Iraq would come at the end of five months of an insurgent war at home. He'd stay quiet for now and he'd be careful not to mention anything to Pastor Harold during the coming weekend. The man was meant to be a confidant, but Dan knew everything he said to Harold made its way back to Shirlene via Dan's father.

He got home to be greeted by a beaming Lilly-Anne, a

napping Ryan and Shirlene, wearing tight-fitting jeans and a loose fitting top.

'I have to go out. Officers' Wives meeting. See you later,' she said, heading out the backdoor.

Dan gave thanks for small mercies. At least he'd have a quiet evening and maybe he'd be in bed by the time she came home. He reached for a beer from the fridge and for a fleeting moment recalled the flat in London. He'd have poured Luke a drink and they'd have settled down to talk. He breathed deeply, pushing away the thoughts of how life could have been. He imagined sealing the memories in a box and welding the lid shut. Except they always worked their way out.

***

I drained the last of the gin and reached to answer my phone. It was late and the lights of Paris shone through my hotel room window, casting a myriad of multi-coloured starbursts as they prismed in the raindrops from the earlier mid-summer shower. The phone display showed it was 11.42pm, later than I thought and much later than I'd have expected Steve Bryant to be calling, even allowing for the time difference. I hoped it boded well. I was wrong.

'Steve, what have you found?'

'Hi Luke, yeah, well that's just it. I thought I better call you so that you can be prepared for it.'

'It? That doesn't sound good. What's up?'

'Paul and I have been trying to track the money just like you asked, but we're not finding it. We started with those account details you lifted from his payroll record and ran all manner of combinations against potential other accounts. We can see his regular payments from Twenty-Twenty, but they're clean. There's no suspicious activity at all, so we ran a deep dive into any small amounts of money coming into his main transaction account in case he was being stupid and trying to clean small amounts of bad money through his own debit accounts.'

'He wouldn't be that stupid,' I said, but noted the pause at the end of the line. 'Was he?'

'Yeah. We think so. We got a repeating hit on a secondary account in a name not dissimilar to your man, but with a slightly different spelling to the first name. Something that would be easily managed in a relatively cheap forgery, like a street-made driving license, or of course the alternate might actually be his real name. Anyway, we thought we'd struck gold as there are big cash payments hitting into this one, but...'

'But?'

'We couldn't trace anything on where they were coming from.'

'Unlike you guys,' I said and meant it. Steve was an expert of tracing financial pathways.

'Yeah, I know. Anyway, we were about to call it quits when Paul decided to go off on one of his tangents.'

'And,' I said, sitting up straighter and feeling the buzz of the gin dissipate. Paul Malone was, by Steve's own admission, the brightest programmer working in the financial cyber sector. His tangents usually were flashes of genius. 'What did he find?'

'That's it, Luke. He didn't. He was blocked at every turn. He can't get through whatever is protecting the final identifiers.'

I stood up, instantly sober. 'Paul can't break it?'

'No.'

'Umm, has that happened before?'

'No.'

'How long's he been trying?'

'All last night and today. If we were going to get through we'd have done it by now. We're stuck.'

'Bugger. But you're telling me there is something there? Something that calls Jules' motivations or actions into question?'

'Oh yes, there's something, but it isn't a Mafiosi payment plan or a hacker-network reaching out to either compromise him, bribe him or just pay him off.'

'So if it isn't that, what's your best guess?'

'It's not a guess, Luke. Me and Paul are absolutely certain. This is government encryption. Military-grade.'

I was pacing back and forth with the phone held to my ear. Now I stopped and looked at the kaleidoscope nature of the colours on the window, diffusing the Parisian skyline. 'French? DGSE?'

'No idea. But you know some folks who might be able to help. We can pass everything over if you can convince them to take a look.'

I checked my watch again. 'Can you and Paul meet me there? Say, day after tomorrow?'

'Eh, yes, but are you that sure they'll be interested?'

'Yeah, I'm sure. And even if they're not, I'm owed a favour or two.'

***

I left Paris on the 06:43 Eurostar and, with the time difference of an hour recouped, was in London by 08:00. Even with the tube transfer from St Pancras International to Paddington, I was at the exit of Cheltenham's railway station at 10:30. Steve and Paul, who had driven down to the West Country spa town, were waiting for me. Our meeting with Rob Curzon was scheduled for 11:00 in the *Doughnut*.

I didn't know what the proper name of the building that housed the United Kingdom's Government Communications

Headquarters was. The torus-shaped structure, with a total floor area of 140,000 square metres, was only ever referred to as the Doughnut.

Surprisingly this nickname had gone quite a way towards fulfilling the aspirations of GCHQ senior management that their 'Top Secret' building would become as famous as the United States' Pentagon. I had always thought it a strange ambition, but back in 2000 when the plans for the new headquarters were being discussed publicly, the GCHQ director was keen to be more transparent. Well, more transparent where it suited. The work that went on inside its new 'open spaces' was still highly-classified and the budget to move from the old twin sites within the Gloucestershire town was also not as transparent as the Treasury might have liked. It ended up costing at least seven times the initial estimate, with the majority of the massive over-spend going towards moving the super-computers. Apparently maintaining operational capability whilst relocating super-computers was not as easy as switching them off, throwing them into a removals van and switching them back on again. Who knew?

I had my suspicions that GCHQ had known full well what the issues were, but had they announced them at the start the Government would have baulked. However, the huge amount of money was worth it to allow the whole of GCHQ to reside in a single location.

Such a shame that by the time they finally moved in, the Doughnut wasn't big enough and so now about a thousand or so people worked in an undisclosed location, 'Somewhere in Cheltenham'. You couldn't have made it up.

Despite their lack of ability with building projects or accommodation quotas, GCHQ, or simply 'Cheltenham' as most intelligence staff referred to it, was still extremely capable in cryptography, ciphers, signals intelligence and cyber-warfare. The man I was coming to see, Rob Curzon, had been attached to my old team in the Ministry of Defence. Back in the days when I had known little about cyber, Rob and his contacts had been invaluable. Through those same relationships, I had done a favour for Cheltenham during my tenure in Bateleur Bank, managing to provide them with an inside track into Chinese cyber warfare units. Enabling that opportunity had required quite a lot of risk on my part and now I was calling in the debt. Not that I expected Cheltenham to admit they owed me anything.

The signing-in process to the Doughnut took a good fifteen minutes, elongated by having to get special clearances for the memory stick Paul had brought with him, but once through the secure access area, Rob greeted me with a warm smile and a hearty handshake. I was a little surprised. Rob was a tall, thin man with over twenty five years' experience in GCHQ, and he was usually quite reserved. Not withdrawn, just quiet. This was the most affable I'd seen him. Perhaps the new building's openness had rubbed off on him.

'It's really good to see you, Luke. Really good.'

'Good to see you too, Rob.'

I introduced him to Steve and Paul as he led us towards a wide circular avenue that seemed to run the complete circumference of the building.

'We're in here,' he said, opening a door to a medium sized room, dominated by a central oval table on which rested a laptop and a secure telephone. 'There's tea and coffee on the side,' he said, pointing to trays that had been prepped for our arrival. Once sorted, we settled ourselves around the table and Rob looked expectantly at me.

My initial call to him, made on my usual mobile phone from

Paris, had simply said I had a problem that I needed his *company's* help with. Given that I didn't have access to a secure line and that Rob couldn't even acknowledge he worked at GCHQ on a standard telephone line, the conversation had, by necessity, been obscure. Now I let Paul and Steve talk Rob through what we were up against. They spent a good half hour taking him through the various methods and approaches they had used in tracing Jules' financial records and finally brought him up to the point where their investigations had stalled. They finished by sliding the memory stick across the table.

'We know it's military grade. I just don't have the skill sets to know who it is and by extension, what it is they are actually using,' Paul said.

Rob took the stick and plugged it into the laptop. I noted that the screen remained angled away from Paul, Steve and myself. Not that me seeing it would have made a blind bit of difference. My skills had never been in the technical weeds of cyber. The likes of Paul and Rob were coding experts and I never hoped to rival them in their chosen field. My skills were more strategic and always had been. The ability to see a bigger picture and to think through complex scenarios within its context was my speciality. Blessed or gifted with the skill, I was unsure how or why I had it, but I had it. Dyslexia probably. Yet even with the talent, I was struggling to see what on earth Jules was up to that needed military-grade encryption.

We waited patiently for what seemed like a considerable time, but from the clock on the wall was only a couple of minutes.

'Ah...' Rob said eventually. 'This is what you found whilst investigating one of your current team members?' he asked.

'Yes. Kind of,' I said. 'He's mine now, but I didn't recruit him. Sort of... inherited him. Is it that bad?'

'I'm going to need to hold on to this,' Rob said, indicating the memory stick and without directly answering my question. Paul and Steve both answered, 'Of course.'

'Thing is guys, I'm really sorry to do this, but I don't think I'm going to be able to talk you through what you have found. Or rather what I think you've found,' Rob said whilst looking between Paul and Steve. 'Luke, I might be able to take you through it, because of... well... because... Yes?'

I nodded. Paul and Steve had no knowledge of what I had been up to on the bank's time when I'd visited Shanghai the previous year.

'I'm really sorry guys,' Rob added and looked awkwardly embarrassed.

'That's okay, La. Me and Paul are well used to security firewalls and confidential information. No need to apologise. It's all good,' Steve said in his lyrical Scouse accent. 'Just happy that you might think it's worthwhile info.'

'Oh that I *can* tell you; yes, I think it's very worthwhile info, but I need to run it past some others. Can you bear with me?' Rob asked, while reaching for the secure phone. A few minutes after his call a younger man, introduced only as Danny, came into the room.

Rob stood up, shut his laptop and tucked it under his arm. 'I'm not too sure how long I'll be guys, but Danny will stay with you. It's almost lunch so he can escort you down to the canteen and look after you until I get back. Only problem is there's only one of him, so if you need to go to the loo, then you'll all have to go together,' he said with a laugh. 'Right! Back soon.'

***

Soon was almost three and a half hours, although Rob did call the meeting room's phone on a couple of occasions to ask Paul and Steve for clarification about how they had found the code on the memory stick. Eventually he reappeared without his laptop and said, 'Really sorry to have kept you all this time and I'm even sorrier to do this…' he hesitated again looking awkwardly at Steve and Paul. 'If it's alright with you, Luke, I need you to come with me, but umm…'

'You need us to exit the building?' Steve said with a laugh.

'Afraid so guys. Sorry. Especially after all the help you've been.'

'No need to be sorry,' Steve said. 'Luke, we'll probably head straight back to London if that's okay? I assume you were planning on taking the train home?'

I had been, so after exchanging handshakes, Danny escorted Steve and Paul out and I followed Rob around the main avenue thoroughfare. 'Is it bad?' I asked as we ascended the first of two flights of stairs.

'Not bad, per se. Just different from what I thought I might be looking at. Thing is, I'm not the expert in this particular data set, so I needed to speak to some people who are and that gets complicated,' he said as we alighted onto a similar central avenue but now on the third floor.

I looked to my right and the open vista of the Doughnut stopped me in my tracks. I wasn't sure who the architect was, and I doubted any award committee would have been allowed in to view their work, but they should have won something for it. The space was magnificent. 'Quite a change from lots of tightly secured little offices with solid walls, isn't it?' I said, gazing across the light-filled amphitheatre.

'Yes it is.'

I turned to look at the speaker. 'Eugene!'

'Hi Luke, good to see you again. Seems you've been keeping busy?'

'Yes. It seems so,' I replied to the man who I had last seen in the British Consulate within the Shanghai Centre.

'I'll be taking you from here. Thanks Rob,' Eugene said.

Rob shook hands with me and I thanked him for his help. We promised, as all old colleagues do, to keep in touch. We wouldn't, but that didn't lessen our former bonds, nor did it mean that if and when we did run into one another again, our friendship would be diminished.

'This way Luke,' Eugene said and led me into a spoke corridor running off the main avenue. It narrowed slightly, then turned left, ending a few metres further on at a double set of plain-wood doors with an electronic scanner mounted on the wall to the right. Eugene paused. 'Okay. A quick heads-up, Luke. The Doughnut is a bit different from the old guard, as you've already seen. Believe it or not, our Director doesn't even have her own office. No executive suite or salubrious sprawl of leather and chrome. Her usual desk is out on the floor space with everyone else. It's all about being seamless and flattening the hierarchy. However, sometimes even she needs a space to hold more confidential meetings.'

'Eh, are you saying you're taking me to meet the Director?'

'Yes.'

'What the hell was on that memory stick?' I asked.

'All in good time, mate. I'll take you through it, but given what it is, and given that you were in the building, she figured now was the opportune moment to finally meet you.'

I considered that even when I had carried out the tasking in Shanghai, the Director had never thought to reach out to meet me. 'Eugene?' I asked, not yet ready to step forward to the doors.

'Yes?'

'You used to be a specialist on Chinese matters.'

'Yes, that's right.'

'Are you telling me that the memory stick has Ch—'

'All in good time,' he said, cutting me off as he raised his ID pass to the electronic scanner. A single chirp was accompanied by a green LED illuminating and the click of the door lock releasing. 'Oh, I'm sure you know, but a little reminder, the Director's name is Kelly Martin. You can call her Ma'am, Ms Martin or Kelly. She doesn't mind which.'

I stepped forward but Eugene put out his arm and stopped me. 'One more thing Luke.'

'Yes?'

'Try not to swear.'

I frowned at him. During the previous year I had spent a considerable amount of time with Eugene, planning and practising for the job I was to do in a Shanghai data centre, but during all that time I couldn't remember, or indeed imagine, any time when I'd sworn at him. I swore infrequently in general and even more rarely within my working life. The idea that I would start swearing in the presence of the Director of GCHQ was simply ludicrous.

Eugene swung the door open and I walked into the room.

A woman I recognised from news bulletins as Kelly Martin sat at the head of a small meeting table. A man I knew, Andy Gibson, an operative of MI6, sat on her left hand side, facing me. A woman sitting to Kelly Martin's right had her back to me. She stood and turned as Eugene shut the door behind us and I managed to forget his warning.

'Fucking hell! Lily.'

8

Cheltenham – April 2010

The young Asian woman stepped forward and hugged me so tightly I thought, despite my extra pounds, she'd break my ribs. I hugged her back and along with the avalanche of questions came a tsunami of emotions. Happiness, heart-filling joy, sorrow, relief, pity, anguish and above all a deep undercurrent of intense anger.

I waited for her hug to soften, before holding her back at arm's length. My anger wasn't with her. She looked up with tears in her eyes that I knew mirrored my own.

'Hello, Luke.'

'Lily. I... I don't underst—' I stopped myself because in that instant, I did understand. I understood it all. It had been four and a half years, almost to the day, since I had huddled on the north bank of the Thames and watched her body being lifted from the dark, cold water. Only, I had never seen her body. Andy Gibson, a serving member of MI6, more properly called the Secret Intelligence Service, whose headquarters in Vauxhall

Cross had shone like a green and cream beacon on the other bank from where our tragic tableau was occurring, was the only one to have breached the police cordon.

It was he, with his official ID, who had talked to the on-scene supervisor. He, with sorrow in his voice, who had reported back to the rest of us that the description fitted with Lily. He, no doubt under orders from Sir Colin Hope, the SIS Director, who I now realised had been the key to faking Lily's death. Yet it was me, because of the circumstances that had led the police to my door on that terrible night, who had suffered the real guilt for Lily's death. It was me who had carried it and reflected on it every day for the previous four and a half years. That guilt was now ebbing rapidly; forced out by an increasing tide of frustration with myself. How or why would anyone have allowed me to carry the crushing guilt for Lily all this time? How or why would they have let me fume at the ineptitude and complete lack of concern shown by the then Foreign Secretary, Mary South? She who had sent Lily's mother and brother back to China to face incarceration if not death.

A Foreign Secretary who had subsequently been exposed as having an affair with one of her ministerial colleagues. Both disgraced, she eventually had to resign from Parliament following a messy and expensive divorce. I had read the headlines and been grateful for her fall, seeing it as appropriate karma for her actions. Now, I looked to Lily and Andy and I wondered if it had indeed been karma.

'Your family, Lily? Your mother? Your brother?'

Lily glanced over her shoulder to Andy Gibson. He nodded.

'They are safe and well and living close-by, Luke. We are all safe and well.'

'That's really, really good news to hear, Lily,' I said, my anger being tempered with waves of relief. I had helped Veronica,

Lily's mother and Ethan, her younger brother, out of Chinese Hong Kong. Their lives had also weighed on my conscience. I had lain awake many a night with their faces in my mind. My relief was short-lived; overcome again with frustration. 'Why the hell didn't you tell me, Andy?'

He sat placidly at the table and gave the smallest of shrugs. 'You know why, Luke. We had gone against the direct wishes of a Cabinet Minister, we'd faked deaths and misappropriated corpses. We'd blind-sided the Chinese government and gained one of the most significant cyber intelligence assets ever to come into our sphere of influence. The need-to-know bubble was extremely small. It still is. There are no more than a dozen privy to what was done and to who Lily really is. Or was,' he added as an afterthought. 'That's why you'll need to sign this,' he said, sliding forward a sheet of paper.

I picked up the document and noted the bold heading:

TOP SECRET//JASMINE TREE//UK EYES ALPHA

I'd seen similar during my time in the Ministry of Defence. A compartmentalised Codeword clearance strictly limited to UK personnel only. Not even our closest allies would see it.

The Americans had a similar caveat, NOFORN. It belonged to what they called Sensitive Compartmented Information or SCI. The Brits just referred to it as Codeword. It all meant the same. When Top Secret, the highest level of security classification, wasn't controlled enough, you restricted it further by limiting the number of people allowed to be in an 'inner sanctum'. The document laid out the standard threats of prosecution and the requirement to say nothing to anyone about anything, or face untold years in prison. I always figured the old penalties for treason, being hung or shot, carried a little more in the way of deterrence. I imagined Julian Assange might have thought twice about his recent leaks if faced with a noose.

Or perhaps not.

The document ended with two signature lines. One for me and one for the reading-on officer. I signed and handed it back to Andy who counter-signed before saying, 'Excellent. Luke, meet Paula Young.'

Lily's new name. I assumed Paula in memory of her twin brother Paul, whose death had been one of the catalysts for her defection in the first place.

'I never got a chance to thank you, Luke. Neither did my mother or Ethan. We always wanted to, but... well, circumstances... you know,' she said in flawless English that now carried a tiny trace of a Gloucestershire twang.

I recalled how she had not only been a leading cyber-warfare exponent for the Chinese People's Liberation Army, but that she'd once told me how each cyber unit had linguistic advisors to help others who might not be as fluent in the language of their particular target-sets. Lily— Paula, I corrected myself, had been one of the advisors for English because her father and mother were both privately educated within the British schools in Hong Kong.

I stared at her for a long time before turning to Andy again. 'And I wasn't worthy of notifying? Seriously? You left me regretting this for years.'

'You quit, Luke. You do recall resigning right in front of the Foreign Secretary? You remember walking out of the military? Surrendering your clearances? Yes?'

I didn't acknowledge his questions, but continued staring at him.

'Then you were working for a bank that was developing close ties to China. We wanted to bring you into the fold at that point, but the job Eugene had you help out on had risks involved.'

'You think I'd have ever compromised Lily?' I said, trying hard not to shout across the table at him.

'No. Of course not, but if you'd been caught in Shanghai…' he paused and Lily said softly, 'Trust me, Luke. Everyone talks. Everyone.'

Another moment of clarity swept through me. If anyone knew what the regime was capable of, it was Lily. As a teenager she'd been subjected to sufferings I could only imagine. I let a small piece of my anger go and took a deep breath. 'How did you manage it?' I asked Andy.

He shook his head.

Obviously the *hows* of the operation were still need-to-know and I didn't. 'Fair enough. Just one question then. Mary South. Was that you too?'

Andy shook his head again. 'That was just a lucky break,' he said. 'Which happily worked out to be in the best interests of everybody.'

I considered his words. Andy Gibson was a consummate professional in the world of Human Intelligence. He carefully considered his every response for in his world, words mattered. I neither smiled nor nodded, but once more, I understood.

'Why now?' I asked.

Andy looked sideways to Kelly Martin.

The GCHQ Director spoke for the first time since I had entered the room. 'Take a seat next to Paula, Luke. Eugene will bring you up to speed.'

I did as I was asked.

Eugene opened the laptop that sat on the table and turned on a projector. The laptop display showed on the large screen. 'This is the code wall that stopped your efforts in tracing your current employee's financial transactions,' he said, highlighting a dense block of what looked like meaningless characters to me.

'Okay, I'll take your word for it, but you know the technical aspects of this aren't my forte,' I answered.

'The thing is,' Kelly Martin pitched in. 'Rob Curzon said you thought this Jules fellow was scamming commercial customers and was perhaps being paid off by organised crime, yes?'

'Yes, Ma'am,' I said, unable to square away calling her Kelly. It seemed a little too informal for me.

'Rob thought this code looked familiar somehow, but he couldn't be sure. He, like the chaps you'd called on, recognised it as military-grade but as you know, Rob's more of a generalist, so he had to reach out to a few teams,' she continued, before nodding towards Eugene.

'It landed on my desk,' Eugene said, 'and I was fairly sure where I'd seen it before, but it raised all sorts of complications. They took a bit of time to sort out and not least was a phone call to Vauxhall Cross and a quick trip up the M40 for Andy.'

'That's why I had to wait?' I asked, looking around the table.

'Yes. Sorry,' Kelly said, 'but I needed SIS to countersign the authorisation for the disclosure and Sir Colin thought it would be good for you in particular if Andy was also present when that happened.'

'What disclosure? You mean Lily being alive?' I asked turning to look at the young woman sitting next to me. I saw in my peripheral vision Andy and Kelly nodding towards her.

'Not quite, Luke,' Lily said. 'The disclosure is that the code wall your employee is being protected by is very familiar to me.'

'It is? Why?' I asked, wondering what Jules had gotten himself into.

'Because I wrote it for Battalion 60288 of the PLA's cyber units.'

I forgot Eugene's warning again. 'For fuck's sake.'

9

Toronto – April 2010

I was met at Pearson International by Pat and we drove to Mac's home together. Mac, as I suspected he would, had signed himself out of hospital early, despite doctor's advice. An hour after setting up in his den-cum-home-office, Pat had briefed him on my new job role. It was a wonder I hadn't heard the explosion of rage in Paris. As it was, I was ordered to attend, *immediately*.

Given simple logistics, immediately was eleven hours later, eight of which were spent in the air. The time difference between Paris and Canada meant I took off at 11am and landed 'two hours' later at 1pm. Had it not been for multiple champagnes to aid a fitful few hours of sleep on board, I would have been wiped out by the jetlag. It would catch-up with me later, but for now, I felt relatively robust. I figured I would need to.

Twenty minutes after leaving the airport we drove into the district of Kleinburg, north of Toronto. My first impression was that it was green. Lusciously green, with open stretches of paddocks interrupted by copses of trees. Older, taller trees lined the banks of the meandering Humber River and the houses, or rather the gated driveways to large houses, were spaced far enough apart to allow for wealthy isolation, yet close enough to allow for a feeling of belonging in an exclusive area.

Pat took his telephone from his inside pocket and handed it to me. 'Speed dial one. Call it and tell him we're almost there.'

I did as asked and Mac barely grunted in response. I hung up as Pat swung the black Range Rover off Highway 27. As we made the turn I realised Pat had driven here without satnav.

'Have you been here before?'

'Three times. A couple of discussions about coming in to the company and then to sign up on the dotted line.'

Intriguing I thought. I was making my first visit but I'd been summoned, not invited.

A minute later we pulled up to a double width entrance where the ornate metal fretwork gates were swinging open automatically. As well as the intricate swirl designs within the gates, I noticed the 'Private Property – No Trespassers' signs mounted on both. Combinations of cleverly positioned fir trees and low, well-maintained shrubs and hedges blocked all but a glimpse of the house.

Pat eased the car forward, onto the driveway proper and headed for the semi-circular sweep in front of the now, fully-visible house. Except it wasn't a house. A mansion would have been a better description. Slate grey and dark hues should have given it an 'Addams Family' feel, but the manicured lawns and shaped trees, the large windows and the treble-gabled frontage complemented the whole, lending the building a welcoming feel. An expensive and luxurious type of welcome. As we swung around to approach the front, I glimpsed a large expanse of water in the rear grounds.

'That's a massive pool.'

Pat laughed. 'Yeah, because Mac swims a lot. No… that's a private boating and fishing lake. Even has a little island in the middle with a barbeque area and a cabin all wired for cable TV. You know he has to be able to watch his sports.'

'How the other half…' I trailed off, realising that Pat too was rich enough to be considered in that other half. Thankfully, his laconic southern style couldn't be battered down by money.

'Yeah, very true. Him and the rest of the capitalist money-grabbers will be first against the wall when the peasants revolt. Except me of course. I'm much too altruistic for that.' He laughed again and stopped the car at the steps leading to the front door just as it was being opened by Mac's Brazilian wife, Alexis. She looked immaculate, as usual. Greeting us with a wave she waited for us to join her at the top of the steps. 'Go right on in. You know the way, Pat. He's waiting for you in his office. I'll have Randy fetch you some drinks.'

I followed Pat into a sumptuous entrance hall with wooden floors and cream walls. To the left was a majestic staircase that led up through a circular balustrade gallery to the second floor. To the right was an opening leading through to a massive formal lounge. Pat walked past both and into the main body of the house. Behind the staircase a few steps led down into another lounge whilst on the right the floorplan opened into a stunningly appointed kitchen, breakfast bar, dining room and I guessed a butler's pantry that was itself three times the size of my actual kitchen in London. To our front was a final room with leather settees and chairs set in front of a very wide, brick-built chimney and fireplace. The back wall of the room was floor to ceiling glass looking out over the grounds towards the boating lake. Every room I had glimpsed was decorated with a calm, subdued freshness. The artwork on the walls and the sculptures in cabinets and on plinths were subtle, refined and I assumed, beyond expensive. Pat led me through this final room to a recess beyond the fireplace and there, through a small arched passage way, was Mac's den-cum-office. It was furnished in walnuts and dark brown leathers and I estimated the floor space was almost as big as the full size of my London apartment. The wall to the left was dominated by the largest flat screen television I had seen outside of a commercial sports bar. The wall to the right was as the previous room, floor to ceiling glass looking out over the grounds. Mac's semi-circular desk, that held centre stage in the room and must have been at least ten feet along its curved frontage, sat in front of what I would have called an honour-wall. Various framed certificates competed for space with multiple photos of Mac shaking hands with, or standing next to, people who I had to assume were famous for something or other. A quick mental inventory registered Mac and a few footballers in the colours of the Dallas Cowboys, Mac and quite a lot of middle-aged white men in suits and Mac with a few women who were potentially models, actresses, beauty pageant winners or potentially all three. As I was about to look away I saw a set of four photos of Mac with people I did recognise. President George H. W. Bush, President George W. Bush, Dick Cheney and Colin Powell.

On the expansive desktop was an array of football memorabilia that included a plinth-mounted full-sized ball, flags, pennants, miniature helmets and a Perspex trophy lazer engraved with various signatures and the words, 'Mac – One in a million - Thanks for your Support'. In the desk's relatively clear central section was a pad of A4 legal paper, a pencil and a can of Coors Light beer. A second can was in Mac's hand. He motioned with it for us both to sit. I took the leather and wood luxury of the Eames lounge chair. I'd seen replicas of them sell for a couple of thousand dollars, but I suspected this was the real thing. Pat perched himself on the end of a wide leather couch.

A good-looking man, maybe in his mid-twenties and dressed in deck shoes, board shorts and a casual linen shirt entered through the archway, retrieved two Coors Light from the built-in fridge in the corner of the office and handed one each to Pat and me. I guessed this was Randy. He didn't speak and left as quietly as he'd come in.

Once he was gone, Mac said, 'Well, Luke. Seems Pat and you think something's wrong with the people *I* put in charge of our intel collections team?' He emphasised the I.

The likelihood of a difficult conversation had been on my mind since I'd left Paris. I'd flip-flopped in my approach between conciliation and confrontation. In the end I'd decided on the truth. Albeit not the whole truth. That was going to have to be limited to between me and Cheltenham and what Mac didn't know wouldn't hurt him. Or me, I hoped.

'Look Mac. I don't want to get into a contest here. The simple facts are that I was targeted by a new threat vector and when I tried to get Jules to investigate I was blanked. I called you to talk about it, but you were in hospital and I got Pat instead. He told me he also had reservations and so I took the job being offered. Only to try to find out what is going on and to better coordinate the teams.'

'Better? Better than I had set up?' Mac interjected, sounding like a petulant toddler.

'Frankly? Yes,' I said and expected him to explode, to fire me on the spot and to potentially throw his beer can at me. Instead, he sat back a little and eyed me like I was a complete stranger deposited into his office by some mysterious force. I waited.

'Why better?' he asked in a neutral tone that surprised me.

'Eh, well, you brought me in to Twenty-Twenty for my name, but remember Mac, I spent a long time putting cyber teams together.'

'So what?'

'Well, the intelligence should be directed by the requirement and in turn, it feeds the operational response. If the ops and intel don't work closely together then things are disjointed. We still get the job done, most times, but not as quickly or as smoothly as we should. So what Pat and I did was take a good setup and streamline it a bit,' I offered in a spirit of conciliation.

'Yeah. Blow smoke all you want. What've you found on Jules?'

Pat had briefed me on the drive over that he'd told Mac about our concerns about Jules. Now we seemed to be cutting straight to the crux of things. I'd been practising for this question since I'd left the meeting room at GCHQ.

'Nothing,' I lied smoothly. 'So far. However, my investigators are running into some issues with his cash flow.'

Mac drained his beer and reached for the other can on his desk. 'What issues?' He asked as he flipped the ring pull open.

'Succinctly, he has too much of it, Mac. He has a hotel, he uses private jets, his younger, foreign wife drives a top-of-the-range Mercedes, he—'

'Do you think I'm dirty too?' Mac asked cutting me off.

I realised, too late, that despite rehearsing my answer I had failed to notice that by describing Jules I was also describing Mac. If you swapped his mansion for a hotel. 'I...no...I didn't mean how you're taking this.'

'Really?' he almost sneered the word. 'You sure this isn't you being petty-minded because my pick for head of intelligence is doing things better than you could? You're jealous, of him, his results, his lifestyle and probably his wife too. I don't notice you with a beautiful woman on your arm. Is that what this is about?'

As I'd practised for his question about the investigation into Jules, I'd also contemplated how this meeting with Mac might ultimately play out. Of the various scenarios I'd imagined, the one I least wanted was, given his last remarks, the one I was left with. I made my decision instantly.

Standing up, I took my Twenty-Twenty ID from my inside pocket and walked over to Mac's desk. 'Here,' I said, setting the edge of the plastic card on the leather desktop. 'Personally, I don't give a shit what you think Mac. Your head of intel is dirty. I haven't found out what or why yet,' I lied again, 'but he's dirty. You want to sell this company and make a lot of money, good luck. The first due diligence check will fail inside a day. However, it won't be my concern, because I resign. I expect you'll want me to sign a non-disclosure agreement and I will, as soon as you come up with a reasonably sized severance amount. I suggest a year's salary.' I punctuated the last word by allowing the rest of my ID card to flick down onto his desk with a satisfying 'thwick'. Then I turned on my heel and walked towards the office's exit. 'Can I get a lift back to the airport, please, Pat?' I asked as I passed him. My departure was going to be a lot less dramatic if he said no and I ended up standing in Mac's hallway waiting for a cab. Thankfully Pat started to get up from the couch, which I took as an encouraging sign.

Two steps from the archway I heard Mac say, 'Okay, okay, whoa up you sonofabitch. Stop where you are. I don't want your damned resignation.'

I stopped walking and turned around. Both Mac and Pat were standing.

'Are you sure he's dirty?' Mac asked. 'Like really sure?'

'As sure as the three of us are in this room, Mac. I think he's being paid to look the other way. I think he's directing his intel team to investigate certain issues, and ignore other ones and for that he's being rewarded in cash and by snippets of information that actually does make his team and by extension, the company, look good. We get the jump on certain threats, but not the ones that are actually out there doing the real harm.'

Mac slumped back into his chair and waved towards me. 'Come back in, Luke. Sit down and tell me what you mean.'

I hesitated momentarily.

'Don't make me beg you,' he said. 'That I won't do. If you wanna go that badly, then go. But I'd rather you stayed, kid. I've always said, I liked you from the first time I met you. Pat and I both know the company will benefit from you being with us, and if Jules is screwing us over, I wanna know what he's doing.' He finished by holding his hand out towards the Eames chair.

I retook my seat and explained to Mac how Pat and I were initially concerned about Jules deflecting his intelligence team away from certain known threat vectors. 'That could be because he's being paid off by organised crime,' I said. That wasn't technically a lie. It was what I had suspected until Lily's code wall had dissuaded me, but Mac didn't need to know that. In fact, Mac couldn't be told that.

'More so,' I continued, 'the fidelity of the intelligence he is managing to get on certain threats is so good that I'm sure it's being fed to him by the people actually writing the code. It makes us look good, but it's hardly ethical. We get choice scraps to feed on if we look the other way on the big stuff.'

Mac looked crestfallen.

Pat added, 'If Jules' team is being seeded information from organised crime and we've been charging clients for defences, then we are in a bad position.'

'Well, hell Pat, that's a major understatement. If the little French bastard's been doing that, then we're truly screwed,' Mac said and the can in his right hand buckled a little.

I waited.

Eventually Mac said, 'Okay, Luke. I'm confirming you as Global Head of Cyber Intelligence and Operations. Find out exactly what's going on.'

'Thank you,' I said.

'Oh and one last thing. You answer to Pat now. I don't want you calling me direct anymore. You want to be a VP and play power games, then you learn how to play them properly. Clear?'

'Clear,' I said wondering how the hell a petulant idiot like this got to have the millions he had. I felt like shouting back, I hadn't wanted to be a bloody VP and what the hell did he mean power games? But I knew that would only make me look more petty than him. Instead I said nothing more, although I also knew he would never leave the last word to me.

'Glad to hear it.'

***

He watched the Range Rover drive away and went back into the house. Alexis was stretched out on a recliner in the lounge and Randy was fussing in the kitchen. Mac figured he'd be making something or other too goddam fancy for Alexis's evening meal. At least the boy did a reasonable burger, onion rings and fries.

Sliding the door to his office shut, Mac retrieved a burner phone from the safe hidden behind the A3-sized photograph of the Cowboy's AT&T Stadium.

'It's me. Shut up and listen. You better be sure we're clean.'

'I don't understand Mac, why have you not fired him?'

'Because it doesn't work like that. I can't just get rid of him. There are wider concerns and we have to be seen to be clean by the outside world. I can't do anything that screws that up and firing Luke Frankland would most definitely screw things. You don't think people would ask questions? Do you want to be left selling the company for chicken feed?'

The line stayed silent.

'Well? Do you?' Mac half yelled the question. He knew the veins in his neck and on his temple were standing out. Why the good God had he hired Luke Frankland? The question had hammered around inside his head ever since Pat had decided to promote the kid. It wasn't meant to be like this. It was meant to be simple. It was meant to be easy money for a couple of years' worth of effort.

Jules had assured him it was simple. Why the hell had he trusted the little French bast— He stopped his thoughts. He hadn't trusted him. Not really. Not in the way he would had he been free of the threat that hung over him. His own damned Sword of Damocles.

Mac had been a mediocre student. Average, save for his ambition, but he had liked history more so than most other subjects. He'd had to study Canada's hesitant reaction to the Cuban Missile Crisis and the interactions between then Prime Minister Diefenbaker, President Kennedy and the Soviet Premier Khrushchev. In the year prior to the crisis, referring to nuclear weapons, Kennedy said they hung over the world like the Sword of Damocles. Later, Khrushchev boasted that he wanted the USSR's H-bomb, *Tsar Bomba*, to threaten the imperialists in the same manner. Mac had been intrigued; what was this sword that two rivals would call upon separately?

For one of the very few times in his school career, Mac had voluntarily visited the library to read about King Dionysius and the sword that he had hung over his throne by a single horse hair. Done to show his servant, Damocles, how having a fortune and power was always offset by the fear and anxiety of potential dangers that threatened to overtake a ruler; Mac had been scornful.

He had always imagined Dionysius had been weak at heart. That young version of Mac, not quite sixteen, had considered if one was truly powerful, and to him that meant wealthy, then you could always look after any threats that came your way. Not for the first time in the last few years he rued his dismissal of Dionysius' concerns.

The sword that hung above Mac was not suspended by a hair, but by a debt owed and, more significantly, the information Jules held on him. Mac had seriously considered hiring a hitman to look after the little bastard, but that wasn't as simple as it sounded in the movies. How, or where do you find a hitman in upmarket Ontario? His thoughts quietened and he returned his focus to the call.

'I asked you a question.' He forced the words through gritted teeth.

'No. I do not want to lose the money, Mac.'

'So are we clean? Are you sure?'

The hesitation before the reply confirmed Mac's worst fears.

'You can never be completely sure, Mac. Yes, we are safe and secure from the majority of people, but there is always risk. I know this is not what you want to hear, but it is the truth. You have let it get to this. This is your fault.'

The truth of Jules' words bit into him. It *was* his fault. He had recruited the kid to make the customers flock to the fledgling company. Now it threatened to undo it all. A fleeting thought of how difficult it was to hire a hitman flashed through his head again. 'We might be lucky. He's fixated on the money.'

'So nothing about the code?' Jules asked.

'No. Well, a little. He thinks it's coming from the same place.'

'You see,' Jules laughed. 'Maybe he is not such a golden child after all. You are sure, he said nothing else?'

'No, he hasn't mentioned anything else. Only the money. You couldn't have kept it a little low-key? A fucking private plane to fly up and down to your hotel?'

'Yes. I hire a private plane, Mac. You of course, *own* one.'

Mac wanted to shout and rage, instead he sighed and said, 'At least he hasn't found anything yet. Maybe you're right. Maybe he isn't as good as I thought.' Mac's words sounded lame even to his own ears.

'Yes. That is true. That is good. No?' Jules agreed.

'I want you to throw him something. Make it enough that he gets diverted.'

'What would you suggest?' Jules asked with typical cynicism.

Mac's anger flared back to life. 'I don't Goddam know, boy. You're the one at that end. Sort it out.'

Jules remained placid. 'I can give him the US manufacturing plants. We have not developed them so much as to make the defence worth what it should be. You will lose maybe 100 or 200 million in value. It is difficult to sell high priced defensive software if no one knows there is a problem, yes?'

'Will it distract him? Will it give you time to make damn sure we are untraceable?'

'It will distract him and yes, it will give me time, but like I said before, Mac. Even if he is bad at his job, he was once well connected back at the bank, and maybe in the military. He may have friends he can reach out to and they might be able to trace, regardless of what I do. However...' Jules hesitated.

'However what?'

'If you cannot fire him, maybe you would like me to make some contingency calls? Perhaps arrange a more, how shall I say… permanent solution?'

Mac reached for his beer. The full implications of the question were not lost on him. The men Jules dealt with to make the cyber threats appear didn't just work in a digital world of ones and noughts. They had real world operations running real world businesses which needed to have real world minders to protect them. Ontario might not have hitmen, but the people Jules knew lived a long, long way from the exclusive northern suburbs of Toronto.

'I asked *you* a question, Mac.'

Mac took a long swig of his beer, emptying the can before crushing it. 'Yes.'

10

London – April 2010

My eyes opened and dragged the rest of me unwillingly into consciousness. Sunlight glared and for a moment I wasn't sure if I was in Toronto, Ottawa, Paris or London. Focussing on the skyline visible through my bedroom window, the Millennium Dome and the tall towers of Canary Wharf gave me the answer. I reached for the half empty wine glass on the bedside table and finished off the room-temperature Chardonnay.

By the time I'd had a shower, wrapped myself in a robe and made a couple of cups of my version of morning tea, I was feeling a lot more focussed.

With no plans for the day I contemplated giving an old friend, Liam, a call. He and I had never been a proper couple, but he served to scratch an itch every so often.

I pulled on my jeans and tightened my belt, but to a hole I'd not had to use before. Moving to stand in front of the mirrored door on my wardrobe I looked at myself, as I had done in Paris. The annoyance at what I saw threatened to overwhelm me. My gut was bulbous, my cheeks ruddy. I quickly pulled on a loose fitting collarless polo shirt and stalked through to the kitchen. Another 'tea' served to mellow me a little.

As I was placing the cup in the dishwasher, my mobile phone rang. Steve Bryant's name scrolled across the screen.

'Hi Steve, it's Saturday morning, this can't be good news?'

'Depends on your definition really. The present we were loaned by your friends in the west has done the trick.'

I knew he meant the code that the director of GCHQ had allowed me to pass on to him. Kelly Martin couldn't authorise an unsanctioned track and trace against a French national or a Canadian owned company, but she'd been happy to allow Lily's decryption software to be passed on by me. Given the right tools, I knew Paul and Steve would have a reasonably good chance of success. The only surprise was how quickly they had managed it. Although I tempered my enthusiasm; I didn't know what 'it' was yet.

'When can we meet?' he asked.

'Anytime. Now if you want. Where?'

***

All Bar One hadn't changed since it was the regular haunt of my team at Bateleur. So regular that we'd eventually christened it "Meeting Room AB1". Even the bar manager, a Spaniard called Sebastian, was still there and happily, and if I was honest quite surprisingly, he recalled my preference for a good South African Chenin Blanc at lunchtime.

Steve and Paul found me sitting at an outside table with my second glass half consumed. They fetched their own pints and a waitress delivered a grazing board with a selection of Chorizo and halloumi skewers, salt & pepper calamari, nachos, fish goujons and mustard glazed cocktail sausages.

Once she'd departed, Paul slid a thin flat device across.

'Is that what I think it is?' I asked.

Paul nodded like some proud father proffering his first born. 'Yep. One of the first ones into the country.'

I picked up the iPad. Apple had made much of its release earlier in the spring, but I'd yet to see an actual one. It had looked impressive in the news reports, on-line videos and marketing campaigns, but was even more impressive in the flesh.

'Nice,' I said, turning the tablet over in my hands.

'And this is the wi-fi and 3G version, so it's got its own sim card. Means it's online constantly,' Paul said, as if telling me that his new progeny could walk and talk.

I nodded and looked again at the screen. Paul leant across and touched an icon. The display turned into a facsimile of a yellow legal pad, complete with margin.

'A truly mobile computer, but designed for leisure and fun,' Steve said. 'With all the connectivity of a laptop or regular PC and absolutely none of the requirements for its users to be aware of any form of security,' he added, taking a bite of a cocktail sausage.

'You sound worried,' I said.

'I am. You've seen how quickly Facebook is spreading. They reckon there's over five hundred million users now. Once you add this,' he said pointing to the iPad, 'into the mix, it'll all go nuts. I tell you Luke, this is what Steve Jobs says it is. It's a game changer, but I'm not sure anyone outside of paranoid folks like us has considered what sort of changes it's gonna bring.'

'What are you most worried about?' I asked.

Steve considered the question while chewing on a piece of Chorizo. 'That the average Joe public walks into their workplace with one of these in their bag bringing God alone knows what sort of software piggy-backing onto their networks.'

'Look on the bright side,' I offered. 'More ignorance of cyber security out there means more work for the likes of us. How bad can it be? Aren't Apple devices much more resilient against viruses and the like.'

Paul nodded. 'Yeah, but this thing has a really decent camera, a good quality microphone and a live internet connection. If I can get into it from anywhere on the planet then I have access to you and your work. Or your home. It's a high definition portable spy-cam.'

I laughed. 'Yeah, you really want to see me getting ready to take a shower.'

'But what if it was your niece?' Steve said.

'True, that would be different, but parents aren't going to hand one of these to their kids without supervision. It's not going to end up being in a child's bedroom. Anyway, I like the concept of it and let's be fair, it is very sci-fi.' I said, handing the tablet back to Paul. 'But let's press on, what have you found?'

Paul turned the tablet in his hand so I could see the screen. The legal pad was still displayed, but he scrolled down a page and revealed a tight paragraph of text that I read quickly and then reread more slowly. I took note of the bank name and the city location.

'And you're sure about this?' I asked, not looking away from the screen.

'Yes. Positive. The code you got us broke through the various defences that had been keeping us out like a hot knife through butter. I don't know how your west country friends developed a code like that, but it's quite a leveller. I like to think I'm quite talented, but I'm nothing compared to what they can bring to the table,' Paul said with a slight catch to his voice.

I wasn't sure if it was regret or envy. Perhaps it was a little of both.

'Yeah but chin up, La,' Steve said. 'If I gifted you a couple of Cray supercomputers, you'd have cracked it too.'

Or if you had written the original code in the first place, I thought, but didn't add. Lily and her circumstances were not up for discussion, despite my complete trust in Steve and Paul. Need to know was always the bottom line.

'Is this as far as we can go electronically?' I asked.

Both men nodded. Paul spoke again, 'We know the bank and the account number, but the name and any other details of the person behind it will be false. I already ran a trace on the name and it came up blank. It's what we've seen before and no software, good, bad or ugly is gonna get that level of information.'

'On the plus side, you definitely know your French boy is as dirty as sin,' Steve added. 'But unless you happen to know a couple of Romanian Godfather types, then I'm afraid this is the end of the trail. However, you don't really care who's doing the paying, do you? You just needed to know that he's being paid by others outside of your company. Yeah?' Steve asked.

He was right on one point. Sort of. Mac had made it very clear that he needed a smoking gun. The fact Jules was being sent substantial sums of money from an account in Bucharest was enough to prove to me that he was dirty, but I had an inkling Mac would want more. He'd recruited Jules and he'd seem to want to argue in his favour often enough. I worried he'd want absolute proof. However, although Steve had been sort of right on one point, he'd been quite wrong on another. It just so happened I might well know a few Romanian Godfathers, or at least I knew a man who might. Yet again though, need to know was the reason Paul and Steve were in the dark about that.

I raised my glass and toasted them. 'Thanks guys. Seriously, thank you. What can I offer to show my appreciation?'

Steve picked up the last of the cocktail sausages. 'Another of these grazing boards and a few more of these,' he said raising his Stella Artois glass in response. 'And if you throw in the taxi fare to pour me home at the end of the day I think we'll be quits. What do you say, Paul?'

'Yep, suits me,' the younger man said, clicking his glass into mine.

An afternoon's drinking session with former colleagues seemed quite the most pleasant thing I could think of for an early summer Saturday in London. Calling the waitress over I ordered food and drink and was once more surprised to find that Sebastian the bar manager also remembered exactly how I liked my G&Ts. The Tanqueray No. Ten arrived with the merest hint of tonic added.

As I raised my glass again to Steve and Paul, I thought of how I would go about getting in touch with Tom Solomon.

11

Nebraska – April 2010

Dan rose, dressed and went for a run. He kept it shorter than usual as he found it quite depressing doing loops around the inner compound of the Church of the Risen Son.

The perimeter fence, high and finished in a battleship grey colour, reminded him of a prison camp instead of a spiritual retreat. He figured his impression was closer to the truth. This was meant to be his spirit's sanctuary. The place he came to have his faith topped up and his sins atoned for, like the rest of the... the what? Inmates, sinners... or was it pilgrims, or disciples? He wasn't quite sure what he thought of the others who made the trek to Nebraska for the weekend conversion retreats. Pastor Harold called them his flock; his chosen. Those who had seen the error of their ways and repented. 'Praise the Lord.'

Except Dan hadn't repented. He'd merely repressed. The feelings he had for Luke were still there, buried under his need to stay with his children. He couldn't lose them to Shirlene, which was a certainty had he been dishonourably discharged from the military. So he had given in to going along with the so called, conversion therapy. Yet the strangest thing he found about the pseudoscientific nonsense, with its widely discredited capabilities and its likelihood of doing more harm than any good, was that even if, in some alternate reality, it had worked, he didn't need it.

He wasn't gay. He'd never been gay. He loved Luke, that was all. They used to joke about it. He was Luke-sexual. A hetero-sexual man who had simply fallen for another man. He'd never seen any other male that he'd in anyway been attracted to. He felt no desire to continue any other gay relationship. Of course, when he had said that at the first conversion therapy camp he'd been forced to attend, Pastor Harold had declared him, 'cured'. Like it was a disease. Dan had barely managed to keep control of his temper. Luke was a gay man and there was nothing 'wrong' with him, yet Dan had said nothing. He'd gone along with the charade, for his career and to keep his family. Every time he denied his true feelings and played along with Shirlene and his own father's need for him to come close to these aber-rations in Nebraska, he felt a little more of his soul wither. He wondered how much more he could endure. One thing he was sure of; religion poisoned everything.

Turning away from the fence he jogged towards the accom-modation blocks and realised he might only ever have to attend this weekend and one more, three months from now. After that he'd be in Mosul for nearly a year. Maybe the insurgents would take care of everything. Like they had for Morrie.

He pulled up and doubled over, feeling a wave of nausea envelop him. He gagged and vomited. It was an involuntary spasm that caused only a small amount of bile to fill his mouth. He spat it out and spat again. It wasn't a shock, he was used to it now. It happened when the suddenness of the memory and the intensity of the relived scene caused his body to react. Thankfully it happened mostly when he was on his own. It was also helpful if it happened when he was exercising. At least that gave an excuse for the whole-body sheen of sweat that accompanied the episodes. Straightening up he quickly looked around to see if he'd been observed. There was no one out in the grounds at this time of the morning other than him. The thick, darkly coloured bile was already soaking into the sand of the compound, but he kicked at the dirt a few times to make sure it was completely covered. The last thing he needed was for this aspect of his personality to be examined by Pastor Harold and the rest of the group as he sat in the midst of the conversion circle.

Dan set off again for the accommodation blocks. Picking up his pace for the final one hundred metres, he wiped his tears on the sweatbands he wore on each wrist.

***

The weekend was all it ever was. Prayers, followed by group discussions, followed by each individual moving into the middle of the circle to give their 'Testimony'. All of it led by the good Pastor. A Pastor who had always been relatively circumspect about his own past, but who allowed enough to infer he had undergone quite a conversion. He was a big man, almost three hundred pounds, and spoke in a sing-song lilt, yet the words always carried an edge. This was the delivery of a man who had, by his own admission, run with the wrong type of people as he had grown up in Anacostia. The Washington DC neighbourhood was only two miles south east of Capitol Hill, but it might as well have been on a different planet.

During the crack cocaine epidemic of the late 1980s and early '90s, DC had more than one murder a day, every day, for seven straight years. It only missed nine in a row by a whisker.

Harold had seen the inside of prison cells and as he testified at the end of every session, he was only here in the Church of the Risen Son by the glory of Psalm 34:4; for *'I sought the Lord, and he answered me and delivered me from all my fears.'*

Dan had always been equally impressed and annoyed by how some people could recite passages from the Bible at will. His own father could do it, as could quite a number of Shirlene's family, yet their hypocrisy in being able to spout the words but not live the spirit of their meaning rankled Dan. Pastor Harold's repertoire was more extensive than most and he at least did seem to believe in the words, although the heavy reliance on reminding all of the 'flock' that they were weak and of sin was difficult to bear. In one of the first camps he'd attended, Dan had counted ninety quotes that all centred around the same theme of the flesh being sinful and the spirit weak. He had no ability to recall Bible passages at will, but one or two of Harold's almost mantras had stuck. The most favoured of the big Pastors go-to phrases was from Romans: *Let not sin therefore reign in your mortal body, to make you obey its passions.* Now though, the time for quotes was over.

The weekend camp had finally drawn to a close and Dan hurriedly packed his holdall, threw it onto the passenger seat of his hire car and was eager to be on the road. It was only a half hour drive to Eppley Airfield where he'd get a direct flight to Atlanta. From there, after a short wait, he'd take another hop to Columbus and then hail a cab to take him the fifteen minutes home. He'd get in at about 10pm and hopefully Shirlene would already be asleep. He waved goodbye to Pastor Harold and one of the attendees, a kid called Cody, who was waiting to be picked up later by his sister. He'd been a new face this weekend. Only fifteen, his father had caught him with another boy from school and beat the living crap out of them both.

Cody's old man ran a car repair shop and had been the first pick center offensive lineman for the town's high school football team back in the day. He was charged with a misdemeanour by a cop who'd been the quarterback he'd snapped to for their junior and senior years. Later, he was sentenced by a county court judge who had used his repair shop for more than a decade, to three months' probation and walked from the courtroom. Cody agreed to attend conversion therapy. Dan suspected it was that or get further beatings. As soon as the other kid made it out of the hospital he'd dropped out of school and had last been heard of making his way to New York.

Cody had spent a lot of the weekend in tears, but the rules of the camp said no one was allowed to even give him a hug. Dan wondered just what was Christian about allowing someone so young to suffer in isolation.

Halfway to Eppley Dan's phone began to ring and then immediately died due to lack of battery. The hire car came with a USB charging port, but no built in lead. Figuring he could use the one from his normal iPhone plug, he reached for the zipper on his bag. With one hand on the wheel and one eye on the road, he tried to feel and glance his way to retrieving the cord, stopping a couple of times to correct his steering. When the insistent horn of a truck alerted him to the fact he had drifted across the yellow median line, he decided to pull over at the next layby.

After a fruitless search he eventually realised he had left his charging cord plugged into the wall socket beside his bed. He checked his watch. There was plenty of time to go back to the camp and retrieve the plug and lead. He had nearly two hours before check-in would close. The alternative was to keep going and buy a new plug and lead at the airport, but a strange mix of frugalness and not wanting to leave anything of his at the camp for a second longer than necessary decided it. He swung the car around and drove back the way he had come.

***

Parking up in the bays to the front of the church, next to Pastor Harold's 2010 Chevy Silverado, Dan went up the steps and through the heavy oak doors. The accommodation blocks, a motel style strip of self-contained ensuite rooms were on the other side of the grounds, but the keys for each room hung in a cabinet in Harold's office. The Pastor himself lived in a single storey, small but neat house set side on to the rear of the church.

Walking down the central aisle, Dan looked up to the cross mounted above the altar. Plain and unadorned. No statue of Christ hanging from it as he had seen in the Catholic cathedrals in Europe. This was stripped back Christianity.

He pushed through the doors leading to the office, but it was empty. Coming back outside he walked around the church and headed towards the Pastor's house. Traversing the small patch of tended lawn he smiled to himself as his army conditioning berated himself for walking on the grass. A definite breach of etiquette on any military base, but the pathway to the front of the house was on the other side of the building and although he had time, he decided to take the short cut. It wasn't like a Gunnery Sergeant was going to yell at him like they had in Officer Candidate School. Still smiling he looked up, his gaze falling on the nearest side window of the house. The open slated drapes afforded a clear view into a kitchen-dining room. Dan stopped dead.

Pastor Harold was hugging Cody. The teenager was enveloped in the big man's arms. At first glance Dan was immediately moved by what he was seeing. The boy had needed someone to reach out and give him the comfort of a simple hug. Perhaps the bare, stripped back Christianity that passed itself off inside the camp's weekend retreats had finally been too much for even the good Pastor to bear. Or maybe it wasn't Christianity, but Humanity that had finally won through. A feeling of warmth and kindness swept through Dan as he continued to watch and then, as he went to step forward again, the empathy and kindness were replaced with the burning rage of anger.

Cody was not being hugged. He was struggling against the Pastor's grip. As the youth twisted and turned, Dan could see the boy's trousers were undone at the front. The left hand of Harold, previously masked until Cody pivoted his hips, was down the front of the boy's underpants.

The Pastor's right hand was not, as Dan had first thought, comforting the boys head, but instead was pressing it hard into Harold's own shoulder, presumably to prevent the boy from shouting.

Cody kicked out and struck Harold's ankle. The Pastor merely leant his bulk backwards and lifted the boy off the floor. He moved in a lurch, turning Cody around and pressing him face first into the kitchen bench; holding him securely with one hand, whilst his other tugged the boy's trousers down.

The teenager turned his head and looked out through the window. Dan knew it was unlikely the boy could see anything through the slated drapes and yet it seemed like he was staring directly into Dan's eyes. The surge of adrenaline finally flooded Dan's body.

He ran like a starter had fired a gun. Bolting for the front door of the house he was about to hit it with his shoulder when another of the lessons from his extensive army training asserted itself; *'try the easy before attempting the hard'*; he reached out and turned the door's handle. It was unlocked. He pushed it open and ran into the kitchen.

Pastor Harold's trousers and underwear were now around his ankles. He had one hand on Cody's head, holding him firm to the bench, whilst his other hand was pulling the boys waist backwards. Dan took in the scene at a glance and ran forward.

The squeak of his shoes on the tiled floor alerted Harold, whose head started to turn. Dan reached for the man's right shoulder and dragged him round whilst throwing a punch that contained the fury of every day he had ever spent in conversion therapy, every day that he had denied his love for Luke, every day he had relived the visions of a sniper's bullet blowing apart the head of Staff Sergeant Morrie Lieberman.

Captain Daniel Stückl had been in the US Army for almost thirteen years. He was an Afghan veteran. He'd fought in the hellhole that was the Korengal Valley, yet in all of his service, in fact in all of his life, he'd never actually punched anyone. He registered the fact that he had probably broken two or more of his fingers as his fist connected with hard jaw bone, but it only served to ensure he put the rest of his body's momentum behind the punch. The Pastor, all three hundred pounds of him, lifted off his feet. The resulting crump as the unconscious body hit the kitchen floor made every cup, plate and bowl in the racks above the benches bounce out onto the tiles. Crockery exploded into pieces and showered Harold's unmoving form.

Cody was hurriedly trying to cover himself up, his breaths coming in sobbed gasps, a strangled cry sounding between his teeth as blood ran down the backs and sides of his legs. The boy could barely stand. Dan shushed him and held his hands out, arms spread, palms upwards to show he was no threat.

'It's okay. You're okay,' Dan said, reaching over to grab a few clean drying cloths from a pile next to the sink. He handed them to the boy and motioned for him to wipe the blood from his legs. 'Has this been happening all weekend?' Dan asked, wondering out loud if this was the reason the kid had been in such an emotional state over the previous few days.

Cody focussed on Dan's face and shook his head. 'No.'

The single word, but more so in the expression on the boy's face convinced Dan he was telling the truth. It would have been a hard task for the Pastor to have managed something like this when the rest of his 'flock' had been about, but in the same instance, Dan recalled every camp he had attended. The other young men who had stayed later, waiting for lifts from family or friends. Remaining behind after all the rest had departed. He had no idea if anything like this had occurred, but as his mind swam through the images, a number of those late departures had never come back for more sessions. His anger, subsiding, threatened to flare again. He looked to the body still on the floor, covered in slivers of ceramics. He could see the chest rise and fall. 'Mores the pity,' he thought and then considered that going to prison for the hypocritical sonofabitch was not what he wanted to do. Instead he asked the now fully dressed, but still sobbing Cody, 'When are your family coming?'

Between stifled breaths he managed to reply, 'Meant to be in two hours... My sister's...driving here...after her shift.'

'Where's home?'

'Waverly, near Lincoln.'

Dan went to reach for his phone but remembered it lay uncharged in his car. He called to mind his own internal map of Nebraska. 'That's about an hour from here?'

Cody nodded. 'Three quarters, but yeah.'

Dan knew he wouldn't make it back in time for his flight, but he'd catch the next one. It meant getting home a few hours later. No big deal. He could hardly leave the boy sitting here, waiting for his sister to turn up and, given what he'd learnt about his story during the weekend, ringing his father for a lift might not be a great idea. As Dan pondered on that he realised there would be no chance of Cody ever making any form of complaint against Pastor Harold. The boy's father would never allow anything like that to become public about his son. Neither would any of the rest of the families of others this might have happened to. They were shamed even by the hint of their sons being gay and there'd be no chance any of them would ever have made a complaint. Dan looked again to the man lying on the floor. He'd targeted the weak and the innocent and knew he could rely completely on their silence. 'Well you won't get away with it this time, you prick,' Dan said under his breath.

Cody looked up from a half squatting position on the floor. 'What did you say?'

'Nothing, Cody, nothing. It's okay. I'll take you home now if you're alright to come with me?'

The boy merely nodded.

'Where's your bag?'

Cody pointed towards the front room, visible through an archway opening.

Crunching across shards of crockery, Dan retrieved a back-pack from the lounge room. Turning to leave he saw an iPhone charging plug and lead in a socket next to the large flat-screen television. He took the plug out of the wall and coiled the lead around a hand that was beginning to colour purple and black.

Walking back through to the kitchen he looked at the Pastor who was showing signs of coming round. He thought about kicking him in the head, a number of times, leaving him in a state where he'd never recover, but once more the idea of doing hard time for such a worthless piece of shit stopped him.

Instead, in the instant he passed the stricken Pastor, from some deep subconscious layer of knowledge that Dan had long forgotten, a phrase came to his mind. *This day will the Lord deliver thee into mine hand; and I will smite thee,'* he said to the supine body at his feet. Then he dangled the charging cord from his hand and added, 'And I'm taking this you bastard. Call it spoils of war.'

Heaving the backpack onto his shoulder he asked, 'You ready?'

Cody staggered to his feet and stumbled after Dan.

12

I decided to give easy a go before embarking on hard. Coming out of Russell Square Tube Station, it took me about ten minutes, wandering along in the bright May sunshine, to get to Thomas Elijah Solomon's house.

I'd been here a few times. On the first occasion in the company of a Metropolitan Police Specialist Firearms Unit. On the second, I'd forced my way in with the help of a companion. Subsequently, I'd been invited in on much more cordial terms, however, I had no clue if Tom still lived here. The old man was meant to have retired to the sun. I smiled to myself remembering how, being born on a Leap Year 'day', Tom always rendered his age in the number of real birthdays he'd celebrated. Born in 1928, he was proudly 20-years-old, in an 82-year-old's body. Even then, the last time I'd seen him, ten months ago, he was as sprightly as someone a decade or two younger. I looked down at my own bulbous frame and realised Tom was more sprightly than me, and I wasn't even half his age. The thought took the shine off my mood.

I lifted the lion's head knocker on the door of 115 Guilford Street and rapped it twice. After a minute, I went to rap again, but as I reached up the door opened inwards. Tom, dressed in loose chinos and a short sleeve shirt looked as dapper as usual, although the tartan slippers rather detracted from the ensemble. He greeted me with real warmth and my mood brightened again.

'Luke. What a pleasure. An absolute delight,' he said in a re-fined voice, which like his physical condition was still firm and strong despite his years. Extending his hand to shake mine, he popped his head out the door and made an overly theatrical check of up and down the street. 'Unless you've brought the cops again and then it'll be, Luke, ya prick, what ya want?' He delivered the last half of the sentence in his best 'Pearly King' cockney accent that I knew he'd cultivated to make him fit in when he'd first arrived in England after the war. It was just a part of him, that he could slip on and off, like his tartan foot-wear.

He guided me through to the kitchen.

'I thought you were going to be in Cuba, or some other far flung island,' I asked.

'Yeah, I was, I was. I did go. Beautiful. Loved it, but couldn't live there. Not for any extended time. Decided to keep my gaff and spend maybe the late spring, summer in good old London and the winter away wherever I fancy. Do you take sugar?' he said opening a cutlery drawer.

'No, thanks. Just milk,' I answered, remembering the last time I'd opened that same cutlery drawer I'd found a Browning 9mm high-power handgun nestling inside it. Tom was far from the standard octogenarian.

We continued to swap small talk until he'd taken a seat opposite me, two cups of tea and a plate of biscuits between us.

'So what can I do for you, Luke. I'm assuming you didn't just call round on a passing whim to get an update on my holiday plans.'

He reached out to take a ginger nut off the plate and I saw again the faint line of numbers tattooed on his inner arm. Though I'd seen it before, each time never really lessened the impact of it on me. That the Nazi regime had, in the lifetime of the man sitting opposite, thought it appropriate to number humans like livestock and plan for their mass murder never ceased to amaze me. That some, also in that time, chose to stand against the regime, in spite of all terror and if necessary alone, was part of the reason I had a gilt framed portrait of Winston Churchill hanging in my apartment. I knew a lot of my acquaintances thought me a little strange. Personally, I thought every home should have one.

'No Tom, not quite.' I spent the next fifteen minutes bringing him up to speed on what I knew was happening within Twenty-Twenty, what I was hypothesising about Jules and what I was guessing about the source of the money.

'So you want me to put the word out through my former business associates to see who's financing the Frenchman?'

'Yeah. If possible?'

'Everything's possible, Luke. It just might take a bit of time. You remember I said my old mate had died and a couple of his sons had picked up the reins?'

I nodded.

'Well they started trying to take the business legit, but they needed a few cleanskins to help and—'

'Sorry, Tom,' I interrupted. 'Cleanskins? I thought that was unlabelled wine sold off cheap?'

'Yeah, it is, but it's also anyone with no criminal record. Clean. They needed a couple of them and ideally they also needed some previously unlinked businesses to put the money through. Turns out after the last little show you and me ran, my niece Monika decided she wanted to play a bigger part. She was perfect for it.'

'Monika? But I thought she was going to be Lufthansa cabin crew.'

'Yeah, she was. I mean, she is. But you saw her. She's that great combination of clever and beautiful. Good head on her shoulders in both regards and street smart with it. And her folks run a hotel up in the Alps. It seemed a perfect fit. Add to that her ability to fly round the world with no one asking any questions and my only surprise was why I hadn't thought of it.'

'Wow, so she's you now?' I asked, recalling the girl who had helped Tom and I put right a wrong the previous year. She was everything Tom said.

'Sort of. She's not doing anything illegal…well, not directly,' he said with a wink. 'She's just looking after some interests of mine and garnering some of her own. Think of her like a Board Director of a company that is, mmm, transitioning.'

'Okay, so how does she factor in this?'

'Well, I said I was packing it all in and I did. I don't have any contact with my old mate's sons. Nor with any of the rest of the organisation in Romania. It works better that way. A complete break you see. No loose threads. So if I'm gonna find out anything for you, I need to go through Monika. That takes a bit of time.'

'But you reckon they might be able to get me a name?'

'You got the account details?'

I handed over a slip of paper.

'Then yeah, I reckon we'll get you something to go on.'

***

I got back to Paris at 11pm, dumped my bags and collapsed on top of my bed in the George V hotel.

The following day was already scheduled down to each half hour, from 7am through to at least 6pm and it was likely Pat, who was due to fly in from DC in the early evening, would want to catch up on his arrival.

My body felt exhausted but my mind was buzzing. Added to meeting Pat, I actually had to run a cyber-intelligence team again, ensure Alicia Halder's operational team were being guided to provide the correct responses for Twenty-Twenty's increasingly impressive client list and try to meet Pat's brief of recruiting whole new intelligence teams for Singapore and Washington DC. All whilst trying to keep tabs on where Jules was getting his money and bringing every single aspect of the operation into good order for any future sale. I was beginning to feel a little overwhelmed. I needed some sleep, but my mind wouldn't quieten.

I got up and walked through to the other half of the room-cum-suite. Taking a bottle of Chardonnay from the fridge I opened it and poured a large glass. By the time I'd finished three quarters of the bottle, I felt a little more relaxed.

***

I rose at 6am and went for a shower. As I went to have a shave, I noticed my hand was shaking. Not just a small tremor but severe enough that were I to try to shave with it, I'd have sliced myself open. With a towel wrapped around me, I fetched the in-room kettle and with two hands steadying it, managed to fill it under the tap. Whilst I waited for it to boil I examined the tremors. I wasn't scared, rather I was a little fascinated by it. I wondered what it could be.

My impatience for the kettle to boil so I could make my usual morning tea got the better of me. I stalked over to the fridge and retrieved the quarter-full bottle of Chardonnay. Again, with both hands steadying it, I tipped the neck of the bottle to my lips and let the ice-cold liquid burn into me. As I finished it, my hands returned to normal. I went back to the bathroom and prepared for my day.

***

Alicia Halder met me as I came through the front door of Twenty-Twenty.

'Got a minute?'

'Sure,' I answered, not really certain if I did. 'What's up?'

She turned about and beckoned for me to follow her into the small briefing room her ops team used. Mo, the guy who had raised his hand at my previous meeting and suggested the name of 'Cornerstone' was sitting in front of a laptop, whose display was projected onto the wall.

'Hi, what's up?' I asked taking a seat and looking at the display. It seemed to show a view of another office that I didn't recognise. A handful of people could be seen working at various terminals in the background. From a side window it also appeared to be dark wherever it was. 'What am I looking at?'

'This is the administration office of a US manufacturing firm in Youngtown, Ohio. The camera and microphone from a currently unused computer terminal are being routed through to us and they have no knowledge the system is even on,' Alicia said, taking the seat next to me.

'What?' I sat forward looking intensely at the screen. 'This is real-time? You're hacking into a US company's systems?'

Mo turned to face me. 'Technically, yes, but not for malicious purpose or gain, so it isn't strictly a hack.'

I was caught off-guard by his defence. He might have a point but I was also sure that was not what Twenty-Twenty were in business for. 'You're arguing semantics. Shut it down. Now!'

Mo reached across and tapped a series of keys on the laptop. The display on the wall reverted to his standard desktop.

'Alicia?' I asked, turning towards her.

She sat with her hands held up. 'Okay, okay, I know it was a bit of a cheap stunt, but I needed you to see it.'

'Why?'

'Because despite being clearly tasked to find out about the attack vectors you wanted to know about on the Cornerstone side of things, we've had nothing, yet yesterday Jules meandered in and handed us this piece of code. He said it had come from his team's investigations into the RustBelt attacks. Said it was malware that they'd got from a dark web contact they'd been cultivating for months.'

'And?' I asked, knowing there was more to come.

'And it's quite brilliant. Mo?' Alicia said, handing things to her senior programmer.

'We have an amazingly intrusive software stub that exploits a Trojan Horse to install a Remote Administration Tool giving full control over the target terminal.'

'That sounds very impressive,' I said, 'Could you explain it in simpler terms?'

'Oh, sorry. Eh, when I install the malware, which I can do by having access to the machine, or getting the user to open an infected attachment, I can immediately take over the target computer's resources and use them to run any type of process I want in the background. I could literally use the whole of a manufacturing plant's PCs as a massive spamming network, or I could use it to run any other type of intrusive code.'

'And no one would know?'

'Not if I didn't want them to. I mean if I ran too many processes they would notice their own operations slowing, but if I was cautious, then no. But that's not the best bit.'

I knew he meant worst, but I let it go. 'Carry on,' I said.

'It also allows me to sit in the background capturing every keystroke and screen display, thereby handing me access to real-time control mechanisms.'

'Mmm, but that's not new. There's been malware like that for quite a while,' I said, reflecting on multiple threat vectors of that type which we had encountered in my time at the bank.

'True, but not like this,' Mo said. 'This is developed in a completely different way. Not only will it do it to live terminals, it will also allow me to take over sleeping terminals on the same network and activate their cameras and microphones. If they aren't physically switched off at the wall, I can turn them on with no indication that would give away their status. I can also jump security protocols that were specifically designed to stop that type of malware and that yes, as you say, have been around for a while. But this is new. This is literally genius.' Mo sounded the way I'd heard so many, even Dan, speak with high praise about their adversaries' skill sets.

Immediately a few other uses for this type of software came to my mind and I felt both sickened by some possibilities and enthused by the potential of others. 'How widespread is it?' I asked.

'Don't know yet,' Alicia answered. 'We've only just got it working and then we needed to test it.' She pointed up to the now blank display on the wall. 'I figured a manufacturing plant right in the heart of the real rust belt was as good an example of what the original hackers were planning to go after. I isolated all of the other systems and then asked Mo to run it. We made sure there was no way it could come back to bite us. Seems it works.'

'Can we run a trace?' I asked, knowing that would be the next step to find out if we could track down tell-tale signs of infection across wider networks.

'We can,' Alicia said, 'But that's not the thing, Luke. The thing is that after refusing to do any investigations into this we've now been handed the exact code that would go to the heart of an ability to construct a surveillance ghost network on any target's intranet. Don't you think that's remarkable?'

I frowned and looked towards Mo. Alicia waved her hand. 'Don't fret about Mo. One, he knows what I think about Jules already. Two, he needs to be up to speed on this as he's the lead defensive programmer I have and three, I trust him.'

I figured I trusted her and she was trusting me, so a bit of mutual trust in Mo would have to be an acceptable price. 'Okay. Well isn't this just more weight to our theory? Jules was being paid to ignore it and now he has to do something or be subject to scrutiny?' I asked, not too sure what Alicia was meaning.

'Yes, this is true,' Mo added. 'But surely the first step would be to find out a little about the potential threat vectors. To begin to gather more information, slowly, and to drip feed it to us in operations. We could begin to develop possible strategies and all the time, if he is being paid off, it gives his paymasters the chance to distance themselves. Instead, what we have here is the whole attack vector code in one neat package. It is, how you say in English, tied up with a bow?'

'But he said his team had a contact on the dark web they'd been cultivating. Couldn't he or she have given it to him,' I countered.

'Yeah, he said he got it from an Access Broker. Pah!'

Mo accompanied his verbal dismissal with an eye roll worthy of Alicia. I knew the type of broker he was referring to was a hacker who specialised in gathering logon details. They didn't use them to breach systems themselves, but rather sold them to others. It seemed the code was ideal for that.

'Wouldn't this be exactly the code an Access Broker could use?' I asked.

'Yes, but no,' Mo said.

'Go on,' I prompted.

He gave a quick look across to Alicia, who gave a subtle nod.

'I know how hacking teams work, and I know how the dark web informants work. I should, I used to be on the other side,' Mo said, without making it sound either boastful or something he was ashamed of. I reflected that most white-hat hackers had once been on the dark side. Again an image of Dan came to my mind. He'd been destined for a jail cell before the US Army had scooped him up.

Mo was still talking. 'The programmers would never give the heart of their code away and the informants are never on the inside of the coding teams. They're peripheral players. They know about strategies, or they'll know about the vulnerabilities being exploited or perhaps they'll know the individuals behind the code, but they aren't the coders.' He shook his head as if to reinforce his thoughts.

'Like in Project Nemean, the contact Jules' intel team had, that Ushas person, wasn't the coder. He informed on the vulnerability that was being exploited and on how the social engineering was working, but he didn't just give up the code. No coder would give up their efforts via a dark web contact when, presumably, they are in it for money or fame.

'If it's the former they go to the target systems and blackmail their way to riches, or in the case of an Access Broker, sell the logon data. If the latter, they simply go public and declare what they did and how clever they were.'

I tried to process what I was being told. 'So you *don't* think Jules is being paid off now?' I asked.

'Oh, I still do,' Alicia said. 'But I also think there's another side to it. I think Jules has been panicked into needing to be seen to do something.'

The pieces fell into place in my mind like a jigsaw forming in quick order.

'Oh! You think he overreacted and gave us too much?'

Alicia and Mo both nodded.

'But surely he would know how suspicious it would look?'

This time Alicia shook her head. 'I don't think so. Honestly Luke, Jules' ego is unbelievable. He seriously believes he is always the smartest person in the room. I reckon he thinks we're incapable of seeing through this.'

Mo was nodding rapidly in agreement.

'And I don't actually think he understands anything about how real hackers work. He really is dumb as fu—' she stopped herself. 'Sorry. Let's just say he's a naïve child trying to play with the grownups,' she added.

I hesitated, confused and a little stunned by her last statement. 'If that's true, how did he manage to…' I stalled, my mind trying to extrapolate a conclusion. Even if nothing else was true, I couldn't believe Jules was some genius code writer. Alicia saw my confusion.

'Oh, I don't think he wrote it, Luke. I think he paid someone to write it.'

The picture came into sharp focus. I saw the whole solution and once again thanked my brain for being a bit quirky in how it solved puzzles.

'Oh my good God,' I said and cradled my chin in my hands. 'If that's correct then we are royally screwed.'

This time Alicia and Mo frowned.

'If that phrase is an English way of saying we are in big trouble, then yes. Yes we are,' Mo offered.

Alicia pushed her chair back a little. 'Although, you have to give him some credit. If we're right, then he's being paid by organised criminals to ignore threats whilst using some of that money to pay coders to write malicious software that he releases into the world.' She stood, picked up a board marker and drew a rough flow diagram on a white board as she spoke.

'Then he points his intel team to places on the dark web that he's already arranged and they talk to informants he has already paid.

'They provide superb insights into the threats that they wrote in the first place and that intelligence product comes to my team.

'We write the defences which Twenty-Twenty sell to our ever-increasing client list, and that list gets bigger and bigger, because our insight into the threats and our ability to provide protection is better than anyone else out there.'

She ended by drawing a very large dollar sign and underlining it. 'I mean, it's pretty smart.'

Alicia was right, but she was missing a piece of the jigsaw that I had. Jules was also being protected by Chinese PLA provided code walls and that meant direct involvement with the Chinese Government, so those threats he was being paid to ignore were not necessarily criminal, but much more likely to be significant strategic threats to the international community in general and Western Powers specifically.

It should have been simple. I go to Mac and tell him what I know, then we go to the Canadian authorities, who ultimately had control over Twenty-Twenty's commercial setup. Then all of us would go to the US Government who would have a say in any future sale of the company to one of the big American IT giants. When everyone was assembled, I would reveal the proof I already had, or rather that GCHQ had, about the PLA code. Simple, but impossible.

Director Kelly Martin and the classification of JASMINE TREE had made it very clear that I couldn't expose the fact we knew Jules' operation was being protected by Chinese cyber units. It was a significant problem with heavily compartmented intelligence sources. You couldn't act on everything they could tell you as that would risk exposing the source and that in turn risked compromising the very thing that made them valuable. It had always been the same.

When the Allies broke the Enigma code in World War II they couldn't act directly on every intercepted signal that was decoded. If they did, then even the stupidest Nazi would have figured out something was amiss.

If each U-Boat 'Wolfpack' had been found and destroyed shortly after signalling Kriegsmarine Headquarters to confirm its patrol position, then the reasonable assumption by enemy commanders would have been that their communication codes had been broken. The immediate reaction would have been to change encryption methods and the intelligence advantage would have been lost to the Allies.

So they had to be smarter. An excuse of bad weather could be used to reroute a convoy away from the threat. The Germans could put that down to bad luck. Likewise, if a lone RAF aircraft occasionally and "fortuitously" stumbled upon a target, that would be believable, but not if it occurred each and every time. In that manner the Allies kept their Enigma secret.

In fact, they kept the secret of having broken Enigma until 1974. That alone gave a good indication of how important GCHQ, and their forerunners in the Government Code and Cipher School took source protection.

In the same manner, if only one person in the world could possibly be the source for a piece of information, then it was imperative that information was never disclosed in a raw state. It was paramount that Lily's role in the UK's knowledge of the PLA code could never be divulged. If I was going to be able to prove to Mac, and any others outside of the UK Government, that Twenty-Twenty's operations were being compromised by Jules, I needed to find alternative sources of evidence that would come to the same conclusion.

I looked between Alicia and Mo. 'It is smart. You're right. Now all we have to do is prove it.'

13

Fort Benning, Georgia – May 2010

His hand was almost fully healed. Two broken knuckles and two severely bruised ones, that he'd passed off as an airport sliding door closing onto his hand whilst he'd been holding his kit bag. Shirlene, not really giving a damn, bought it, or didn't care enough to query it. The Fort Benning medic gave him a wry look and asked, 'You gonna sue the airport?'

'Nah, it was just an accident, no one at fault,' Dan answered.

The corpsman nodded slowly, 'Um-hmm. Must have been a badass door.'

'How's that?'

'Hit your hand like a punch. Only ever see injuries like this after a good old fashioned bar brawl.'

'Interesting,' Dan said and winced as the splint was shifted into place.

'It is that, Sir. But a door's a door and as long as it isn't likely to come to Fort Benning to sue *you*, then I think you're good to go. Come back in three weeks and we'll take a follow-up x-ray.'

Now, three weeks later, he had the firm splint replaced with a looser bandage slip-on glove and the prognosis was that in another three he'd be back to full fitness.

'Any word on the door?' the corpsman asked as he finished off checking the circulation in Dan's fingers to make sure the glove wasn't too tight.

'Nope. Like I suspected, it just took the hit and moved on.'

'Good to hear.'

As Dan walked back to his office in the headquarters building of the 96th Infantry Regiment's 1st Battalion, he mulled over what he'd said about the door taking the hit and moving on. In the previous three weeks he'd spent a lot of time, usually when he was out for his morning run, trying to figure out what he could do to stop Pastor Harold and the Church of the Risen Son. Each fanciful idea of dragging him in front of a courtroom met the same fate. No witnesses, no case. It would be his word against a man of God and a reformed sinner no less. That whole part of Nebraska loved a man of God, but a sinner who'd repented and was now working to 'convert homosexual devils' was akin to the second coming.

The example of Cody and how his father had gotten away with a misdemeanour for what had actually been the Class II felony of first degree assault was not encouraging. Less likely was any of the families allowing the assaulted to testify. Even if some of them were now adults, the individuals had been forced into conversion therapy so they, like Dan himself, had controlling circumstances that had made them submissive. Be that parents in the case of Cody, or in Dan's own case, threats to lose access to kids or career.

In wilder moments of free-wheeling thoughts he considered flying back up to Nebraska, hiring a car and firebombing the church. Or sneaking in at the dead of night and slitting the good Pastor's throat. The idea made his spirits light for a moment or two, but he knew it was ridiculous. Had he had a weapon with him when he found the Pastor with Cody, he may well have killed the man, but that was a surge of anger that he'd had little control of. His fingers were testament to how little he had thought through his actions. Yet to go back there and in cold blood murder someone was as far from Dan's capabilities as sprouting wings and flying to Nebraska.

What he needed was to shame the man himself into quitting, but that was also unlikely. The two things Dan knew about the conversion therapy camps were that they didn't work and they were a lucrative source of income. Proof of the latter was the new model Chevy the Pastor drove and, even though he'd only been in the house for a few minutes, Dan had noticed the fixtures, fittings, furniture and accessories it was equipped with, including the impressive scale of the flat-screen TV. Giving that up, as well as the rest of the income derived from the Church of the Risen Son was a longshot. Even more so as it was a church and therefore, under US law, paid no taxes whatsoever. Not only hypocrites, but rich hypocrites. Dan wondered if Jesus ever decided to come back, who he'd be most angry with, the atheists or the Christians?

A couple of enlisted men ran past him, saluting as they went. Dan returned the gesture and as he brought his hand back down he looked again at the glove supporting his knuckles. The surge of anger he had experienced confronting Pastor Harold was like nothing he had ever known. The intensity of it had allowed him to hit out with such a satisfying force, but it also scared Dan a little. What if Harold had been a smaller man? Hitting someone Cody's size with a punch like that, could very well have killed them. The worry of that and the stress levels he felt even thinking about Harold and his God-forsaken church weren't helping Dan come to any rational decisions about what actions he could take.

And then there was Cody. He had driven the boy home but dropped him off, at the kid's insistence, a street back from his house. Throughout the journey, Dan had tried to gently infer he'd be happy to go to the cops with him, but the kid refused point blank.

Finally Dan had asked, 'What are you going to do?'

Cody shrugged.

Nearing the boy's hometown, Dan tried to form a sentence in his head, but each time it sounded wrong. Like another older man, who after all had also been an attendee at the camp, was trying to push himself forward. What he wanted to do was offer the kid his phone number, so he could reach out if things got bad, or worse, as Dan suspected they were already bad and that today's events had just heaped more misery on young shoulders. In the end he managed, 'Look, Cody. Do you want to take my phone number? Save it as US Army Recruitment or something that won't attract attention. Don't give me your number, so you don't have to worry about me calling you, but take mine. If you ever need to talk. Yeah?'

Cody had stared at him for a long time, but eventually he nodded. It had been three weeks and the boy hadn't called. Dan didn't expect he ever would.

The tightness in his chest threatened to overwhelm him again. He couldn't let that happen walking through the middle of the administration buildings on Fort Benning. Forcing deep breaths into his lungs he strode forward and on entering the 1st Battalion's headquarters went straight to the men's room. Thankfully it was empty. He closed the stall door and spat out the bile he'd regurgitated. The frustration he felt at his inability to do anything, remained deep inside.

His plan had been to delay telling Shirlene about his deployment for as long as possible. He couldn't delay it indefinitely as a month before he was due to have his boots on the ground in Mosul he'd be sent for pre-deployment refresher training and orientation. Mosul was an urban environment; as far removed from the Afghan countryside as could be imagined, and that meant new types of training had to be undertaken. Four weeks of it, six weeks prior to his embarkation date. That meant he had about twelve weeks before he needed to confess he'd be leaving her alone again.

Not that she would be concerned about the lack of him as a companion, but the lack of him as a second pair of hands, a babysitter, a children's cook and entertainer when she was out at her 'committees and functions' was a different matter. He could already foresee the argument, although it wouldn't really be an argument. He would remain quiet while she ranted at him, possibly threw things at him and called him all the cuss words she could think of, and she could think of a few. Then she'd threaten to storm off to her parents, take the kids, stop him from ever seeing them again, except not even the family courts up there would allow that if he was still a serving officer in the US Army with a distinguished record. She would probably head back to Nebraska for a while, maybe spend some time with her folks. He considered the pleasures of that trip and figured a few months in Mosul might have some bonuses.

However, all of his plans were about to fall apart. As he settled himself behind his desk and turned on his PC, the first email he saw was a warning order for movement to a training course at Fort Hood, Texas. Dan scanned the email and his heart sunk. His pre-deployment training was being extended. About to read more, his phone rang.

The Regiment's adjutant asked him to attend a briefing, Colonel's office, five minutes.

Thirty five minutes later, Dan and the rest of the Regiment's command team had been brought up to speed with the latest in the United States' bright ideas about extricating itself out of the Middle East. Apparently it was to be centred around something called, Advise and Assist Brigades. No one had a clue what that meant, but it seemed to be tied in with plans by the Obama administration to end combat operations completely. All combat troops were, according to the rumour mill, going to be pulling out of Iraq. Dan, like every other officer in the briefing, thought that meant no more Iraq, no more deployments at all, no more war…

He and every other officer was wrong. It simply meant a bit of strategic rebranding. Troops would still go to Iraq, but to help the Iraqis try to stabilise and secure the country that the Americans and the British had completely unsecured and destabilised back in 2003. It didn't mean that the troops wouldn't still get shot at, bombed, ambushed, blown up and generally screwed over. It just meant they'd be getting all of that done to them in a new spirit of cooperation.

The immediate impact was that the Advise and Assist role was different and the Army didn't like different. When it came across 'different' it determined to train the hell out of it and make it 'normal'. The first training course, for thirty officers, was going to run in only three weeks' time at Fort Hood in Texas, and Dan was on the list.

He'd have to tell Shirlene and though she was many things, stupid about army procedures was not one of them. She'd ask what was going on and he'd have to tell her that between now and September, he'd be away for a total of eight weeks' training separated by a few weeks at home. Then she'd ask what happens in September and he'd tell her about the nine months in Mosul. Then the shit would hit the fan.

As Dan returned to his desk he felt the tightness in his chest return with a vengeance.

14

London – May 2010

Monika and Tom sat at one of the outdoor wooden tables on the small rear decking of the Mayflower Pub, overlooking the Thames. Tom raised a hand in greeting and Monika raced over to give me a hug.

'What can I get you to drink?' I asked.

'Oh no, no need. We have ordered already. I got you a bottle of Chenin Blanc, like you had when we went out to the meal, last time. Is that okay?' she said with a smile that lightened the overcast grey of a London trying to remember it was meant to be in the height of spring.

'Perfect,' I answered and followed her across to the table.

'How's it going Luke?' Tom asked.

'Good, thanks. This is some place,' I said, pointing towards the river and the view northwards to Wapping, the City and the Canary Wharf skyline. To the left, the square central core of what was to be London's tallest building, the Shard, was visible with a construction crane perched atop it.

'Oldest pub on the Thames me old mate,' Tom said, reverting to his wide boy cockney.

'Is it?'

'Yeah. Like all the rest of the oldest pubs on the Thames,' he said and laughed.

I turned back around and pointed into the main bar behind me. 'I've never been here before, but it certainly looks the part.'

'Yeah, to be fair it definitely does,' Tom agreed. 'Monika here loves it, don't you sweetheart.'

'Yes. It is all I think any tourist wants when they come to London,' she enthused. 'The history and the feel of it is very special.'

'So what's the connection with the Mayflower?' I asked.

Tom pointed down to the river. 'Apparently down there's the final London mooring from where the Mayflower left for its voyage to America with the Pilgrims.'

'And the pub was here then?'

'Yeah. It's 16th century.'

I turned again to look into the main bar. The narrow pub, replete with leadlight windows, candle sconces, a bar that looked like it had been cleaved from a ship's hull, pitched black wood panelling and enough accessories to dress every nook and cranny, including blunderbusses and various antique books, all looked, in some strange way that it had been put together by a set designer in order to make the perfect Ye Olde English Pub. It was, I realised, the other way round. Set designers would likely use it for inspiration, as being 16th century this was the genuine article.

'Wellll, I say that,' Tom said, with a fair amount of air being sucked between his teeth.

I turned back around to face the smiling old man. 'Go on. I feel there a fairly big, but coming.'

'I mean, there's been a pub here for all that time, that's true enough, but it's a bit like Trigger's Broom.'

Monika and I shared the same look of confusion.

'Trigger's what?' she asked beating me to the same question.

'In Only Fools and 'Orses. You wouldn't know it sweetheart, it's a British TV comedy show, but you know it Luke.'

I nodded. It was an iconic comedy show, but I was still lost as to what Trigger's Broom was.

'Well, Trigger gets a medal for saving the council money by having had the same broom for twenty years, but when he's asked about it he says it's had 17 new heads and 14 new handles.' Tom gave a laugh. 'Same with this place. Yeah, there's been a pub here in Rotherhithe for 400 years, but it was called the Shippe Inn and that burned down in the 1700s. They replaced it with the Spread Eagle and Crown and my former countrymen blew that one up in the Blitz, and now here we sit in the Mayflower. All of that stuff you see in there, well I doubt most of it's any older than me. Anyway, let's order something 'cos I'm starving and then Monika can tell you about your money.'

'Oh yes. That sounds good.' Monika said, lifting the plastic covered menu.

'Do we have good news on that front?' I asked, already knowing I was going to have the beer battered fish and chips.

'Yes, but it is more complicated than you might have hoped for,' she said, 'May I have the steak, please, medium?'

I went to get up, but Tom waved me back into my seat. 'No, you sit there. I'll get this and then you two can talk and I don't have to know,' he said.

I told him my order and he ambled into the pub. Monika stood and walked across to the rear fence of the pub's decking. I lifted my glass and joined her, looking out over the Thames.

'The Bucharest account that you provided the information

for checks out with all the details you gave me, but of course the name it is opened under is completely false. Also the setup is more complex than usual. I had hoped that some of my new colleagues,' she paused and turned to me, her eyes twinkling, 'Who would have thought I would be taking on Tom's work, ha!' she laughed and I couldn't help but be beguiled. Monika and the Mayflower Pub. New faces that had replaced older ones; new name, same purpose.

'Yes. And there's me thinking you'd be flying high and happy with the airlines,' I said.

'Oh but I am, Luke. It is just the rest of it also gives me a buzz that being aircrew cannot. Anyway, my new colleagues; I had hoped that perhaps one of them was paying your person off. We are still running many... mmm... let's just call them projects. I thought maybe if they recognised the account then the answer would be easy. Alas not. It isn't us.'

'Oh. So there's no way of finding it out?'

'No, I didn't mean it like that. We found out who is paying the money in. That was relatively easy. We paid one of the bank, eh,' she paused. 'Is the word... cashier?'

Her English was so good I often forgot that Monika's first language was, like Tom's too, German. 'If you mean a person behind a bank counter then yes, cashier.'

'Good. Well we paid one of the cash—'

I held my hand up to stop her. 'I think probably best you don't tell me exactly what you did to get the information?'

Another twinkle in her eye. 'Okay. We found out the man who is making the deposits into the account. Very clever that he is doing it.'

'Clever?' I asked, wondering how paying your own money into an account was clever. 'Who is he?'

'He is no one. He is only an air gap between the source of

the money and the account that your person is being paid from. All the account details are worthless. The name on the account is not where the money comes from.'

I frowned.

'The man paying the money in is only a courier. He is not the source of the money. It comes from an completely different place,' she clarified.

'Ah, I see. Ah well, thanks anyw—'

It was her turn to interrupt me. 'But Luke, we didn't stop there. My friends visited the man at the house they followed him back to.'

I felt my heart sink. I figured that a friendly chat wouldn't have been in the repertoire of Monika's 'new friends'.

She was continuing, 'Apparently it didn't take long for him to tell them everything he knew.'

I imagined it would have taken no time at all.

'The account that he withdraws from is not only used by him. That is clever too. It means that even if you had those account details, you would not necessarily know which deposit to follow. If there were multiple accounts feeding into it, the law enforcement authorities would have a very hard time getting warrants to follow the proper money trail. Very smart.'

'So he goes to this account and draws money out to a pre-arranged schedule?' I asked, trying to understand the mechanics of how it worked.

'No. He gets notified when a deposit is made and the amount he is to withdraw. He takes the money in cash from that account and pays it into the account you traced. Very simple and very effective in providing a gap in electronic surveillance.'

I didn't want to ask, but felt I'd better know. 'Did your new friends leave this man alive?'

'It seems that the notifications and the account details were all anonymously arranged. The man never met the people who had originally reached out to him. He gets a text message, he withdraws cash. He takes his very lucrative cut and pays in the deposit. I would imagine if your person didn't receive his money, then the originators would know the Bucharest man had not done his part. But it is all faceless.'

I hadn't missed that Monika hadn't answered my question. I had to press it. 'Monika?'

'Yes,' she said chirpily. 'He is alive. Given what he had told my friends, they explained that they could do what he was doing and no one would be wiser. Or he could keep doing it, keep his mouth shut and stay alive and healthy.'

'And he chose to be smart and stay quiet and alive?'

'Yes,' she said with a smile. 'I mean, that is a sensible choice, given the alternative. Wouldn't you agree?'

'Most definitely. It's also good that my person as you refer to him, will still be getting his money, so won't be worried that anything is wrong.' I paused and took a sip of wine. 'Ah well. Like I said, thanks for trying Monika. I really do appreciate it.'

She turned to face me, frowning. 'Ah well?'

'Yeah, you know, the air gap and the multiple deposits pretty much puts an end to my trace.'

She reached into her jacket pocket and took out a piece of paper. 'No, silly. My friends let him live, but only if he gave us all the information he knew. These are the account details for where the deposits go into.' From her other pocket she took a small non-smart mobile phone. 'And this is a cloned burner that will receive the text notifications at the same time as the man does, so you can run an instant trace against the amount and the source. Cheers,' she said raising her glass and clinking it against mine.

15

London – June 2010

The first time I had asked Steve and Paul for help, they'd done the work as a favour. I couldn't go back to them for another freebie, but as the new Global Head of Cyber Intelligence and Operations, I had a budget that could easily look after a short-term contract for some freelance consultants, and they would work out of their usual London offices so wouldn't cause any suspicions within Paris. I handed them the new account details, and the phone, over a long and relaxed lunch in AB1.

Returning to my apartment in the late afternoon, I poured myself a good quantity of gin and picked up my phone. Steve and Paul were excellent at what they did. When I'd first been introduced to them, by Pat Harris on my first day at Bateleur Bank, he'd told me they were the best operational programmers and system engineers in the business. Coincidently that was also the day Lehman Brothers went bust in a move that signalled the Global Financial Crisis. On reflection, it had been a mixed start to my banking career. However, what Paul and Steve weren't, were systematic investigators. They could run the traces on accounts and dismantle protective firewalls to get 'in behind' the complex web of financial transactions, especially with the tools GCHQ had gifted them, but to figure out if Jules was indeed paying others to write specific threat code within the dark web, needed a whole different skillset. One that not only had technical ability, but a detective's methodical approach to investigations. Thankfully, I knew just the chap.

'Mark, it's Luke. How's life?'

A former RAF Flight Sergeant policeman, Mark Donoghue had been widely acknowledged as the UK military's top cyber counter-intelligence and computer security expert. During my time at the MOD, he'd been my de facto second-in-command. On leaving the Air Force he'd tried his hand at early retirement and been bored senseless. When I'd offered for him to come work with me at Bateleur Bank, he'd said yes before I'd finished the question. On leaving the bank, another to take the redundancy and get far away from Dickie Lessen, he had not tried to wrestle with retirement again and instead had, like Steve and Paul, set himself up as a consultant. Now I was hoping he'd have some spare capacity to help me out.

'Luke! Life is terrific. Couldn't be better. You catch me sitting in a café in Paphos harbour!'

'Paphos? As in Cyprus Paphos?'

'The very same.'

'Oh, I'm sorry Mark, I didn't mean to disturb you on holiday. I can ring when yo—'

'Nope, not on holiday, Luke, you're okay, what do you need?'

'Not on holiday? Are you there for work?'

'I'm living out here. Well, for some of the time. Me and the missus decided we'd take the opportunity with the bank's money and buy a place. Plan to spend at least half the year over here. We always liked it, from back when we were posted to Ackers on one of my first tours of duty.'

I knew he meant RAF Akrotiri, but I hadn't known he'd been posted out there during his career. Then again, he'd done almost twenty-seven years in uniform, so there was probably a lot of his early career I knew nothing about. 'Oh, nice. How's Paphos then?'

'Beautiful. We're just about to have an early evening meze, a few more drinks and watch the sun go down over the old castle in the company of a few meandering pelicans who call the sea front home. All in all, quite idyllic.'

'Sounds wonderful. Well, listen I won't disturb you.'

'No, it's okay. Not disturbing me. What do you need? Is it work?'

'Well, it was, but if you've packed all that in then—'

'Nope. Not at all. I'm still a consultant. Still working. The speed of networks just means I can work from out here as well as I can from an office in Yorkshire. So what's up?'

I felt a great wave of relief pass over me. Mark was realistically the only one with his skills that I actually knew and it also helped I trusted him. Completely. 'I think I might need to come talk to you, face to face about it. Would that be okay?'

'Certainly. Though BA canned their direct flights for the rest of the year, so you'll have to use a low-budget airline. You okay with slumming it?' he asked with a laugh, knowing that my idea of slumming it on airlines was business class.

'Ha, very funny! But you're not even joking are you?'

'Nope. Or you can come into Larnaca on a posher flight, but then you'll have an almost two hour drive ahead of you.'

'Guess I'll slum it. So if you're okay with it could I and a new colleague of mine meet you on Thursday?'

'Yeah. I'll text you my details.'

***

I met Mo at the arrivals hall in Paphos Airport. His flight from Paris, strangely also on a UK low-budget carrier, had arrived a half hour ahead of mine and meant he had already arranged the hire car. I'd told him in advance that I didn't need to be added as a driver. I rationalised that if we were to go out for a meal or two, then at least one of us could have a drink.

The drive to the 5-star luxury of the Elysium Hotel, that I had booked as a counter to the definite non-luxury of a low-budget flight, took only twenty-five minutes, but by the time we'd arrived I could understand why Mark had decided to live out here for part of the year. Cyprus in June was extremely pleasant.

Dropping my bag into my suite and grabbing a small gin out of the mini-bar to give myself a little boost after the flight, I met Mo back at reception. Mark's place was another ten minutes north and the route took us past the Tombs of the Kings. I smiled to myself, hoping it was a good omen. I really wanted to bury Jules.

I wasn't sure what I had expected, but a three bedroom, three bathroom, wrap around verandah, with glistening white walls and terracotta roof-tiles bungalow was not it. Stepping out of the car and turning to look at the view across a wide plateau towards the Mediterranean Sea, I wondered if Mark managed to get any work done at all.

Ushered in and through the house, we made our way out to the rear garden, neatly landscaped and incorporating a small but perfectly functional swimming pool. A round table with snacks and drinks waited for us, courtesy of Mark's wife who made a fuss of me, as she always had done. Once she had gone back inside, Mark got down to business.

A half hour later we had briefed him as fully as we could on what we thought Jules was up to.

'And you want to go catfishing?' he asked.

Mo nodded vigorously. I asked, 'Do I?'

Mark laughed and stood up to stretch. 'Yes, you do. It's the online act of pretending to be someone you're not.'

'Ah, then yes, that's exactly what I want,' I said. 'Although it will need to be a little more than just pretending to be a hacker.'

'Yeah and therein lies your problem,' Mark said. 'From what Mo's just told me of his misspent youth, I have no doubt that he could represent as a black-hat easily enough and we could make some code that would be fit for purpose. I also know that if Jules takes the bait, then I can follow him through whatever nefarious pathways he takes and provide enough forensics to tie him to it completely.'

'But how do we get Jules to commission Mo in the first place?' I asked, knowing that was the crux of the problem.

'Exactly. The dark web is full of ne'er-do-wells looking to make a buck and we don't know if Jules has a single go-to guy for all of his coding needs. If he does, then setting Mo up to be a new provider probably doesn't work.'

I couldn't tell Mo, or even Mark, about my main concern. It had plagued me since Alicia mooted the possibility Jules wasn't only being paid to ignore certain threats, but might be paying people to come up with new ones. What if the Chinese weren't simply protecting the payoffs to Jules, which I had initially thought were for him to look the other way? What if the PLA were actually providing the new threats that were making Twenty-Twenty the stand out company in the sector?

'What you really need,' Mark said, interrupting my thoughts, 'Is the ability to clandestinely monitor every single device that Jules has access to. Then you could see where he goes on line and who he talks to. Once you knew that, it'd be easy to not so much catfish, but masquerade.'

I frowned. 'What's the difference?'

'Catfishing is Mo pretending to be a black-hat hacker called Bob. Some made up, fictitious identity who doesn't exist in real life. Masquerading is Mo pretending to be me.'

'Right, I see. But how do we clandes—' I was stopped by the sight of Mo raising his hand. I could see Mark hiding a smile. 'It's okay, Mo, just shout it out, you don't need permission to speak.'

'We can do that,' he said, lowering his hand and looking extremely happy about something.

'Do what?' I asked.

'We can monitor every single device he goes onto, without him ever knowing. We can certainly do it to the computers in work and if we are a little clever, then I am sure we would be able to do the same on any personal systems he has.'

Mark interjected, 'I like the sound of that, but if he's using peer-to-peer networks with the usual security protocols of the dark web, then the usual track and trace software won't work. It would be pinged as a notification to the user and either shutdown automatically or the user would know he was being monitored. Sorry, Mo.'

'No need to be sorry. Until Monday, I would have certainly agreed with you.'

Mark beat me to the question. 'What happened on Monday?'

Mo took a USB drive from his pocket. 'We got handed this,' he said and slid the drive across the table.

I started to laugh. 'Are you telling me the RustBelt software stub Jules gave us can do that?'

Mo nodded.

'You were right, Mo. It's genius.'

Mark looked a little perplexed. 'Surely if you got this from the man we're going to use it against he would be savvy to its capabilities?'

Mo gave a beaming smile. 'No. Absolutely not. Whilst he has told all sorts of stories about his past and none of us really know if they are true or not, the one thing I know for sure is that Jules is no coder. He can use a computer, and he might have a rudimentary knowledge of what this code can do, but there is not a chance he has the first idea of how it does it.'

***

I left Cyprus and flew to Singapore to begin the process of re-cruiting a new team of analysts. Four days there, then back to London for two days, during which I hosted a reception for clients, of which although Pat had hired the two sales helpers he had promised, Mac still expected me to be the 'face'. In the afternoon of the second day I had a meeting in a coffee shop near Vauxhall Bridge with Andy Gibson.

Now intricately linked with Lily, Andy had also, for quite a long time by his own admission, worked with the French. He'd told me that in passing small talk at a reception we had once attended back in my MOD days. Knowing what SIS operators were like, I had no idea if that meant he had worked alongside them, or spied on them. I wasn't bothered either way. I simply needed him to have some of his current SIS colleagues in Paris do me a small favour. I figured given how he had kept Lily's survival from me it was the least he could do. Also, I had a gift for him.

Once I'd told him the details he shrugged and said, 'That's a piece of cake. If you're going to call in a favour on the debt of Lily, you need to make it a much bigger request. Consider this one gratis.' He checked his watch. 'I can have the assets briefed and in place in let's say... three hours? Is that fast enough?'

'More than fast enough.'

'Great. Then you text me when the place is clear and we'll get it done. Should be in and out in about five minutes assuming no major issues. However, given what we know about that code wall, we might just take some extra counter-surveillance precautions.'

'Will that complicate the matter?' I asked, not having any real idea what measures would be needed.

'No, not really. Might take us ten minutes to be in and out instead,' he said with a grin. 'We really are very good at this type of thing. Oh the stories I could tell you.' He reached for his coffee still chuckling.

I figured the cliché of 'But then I'd have to kill you,' had never been more apt.

'Now, you mentioned a gift?'

***

The following morning I flew to Ottawa. Two days of client meetings would follow a full day spent with Mac bringing him up to speed on new business opportunities, a full update on how the newly coordinated intelligence and production teams were panning out and of course, a full brief on anything I had managed to find out about Jules. At present, that amounted to nothing. Although for reasons I couldn't quite understand, I didn't tell him about Steve, Paul or Mark. I definitely didn't mention Andy.

In return for all my news he informed me that he had opened negotiations with a potential buyer for the firm, but couldn't tell me who. Then added, 'So I'll be flying across to San Francisco as soon as we're finished here.'

I asked nothing further, which I figured would annoy him quite a lot, because I knew he was itching to tell me. I also thought he wouldn't have coped well in Andy Gibson's world.

By the time I got back into London, ten days after I had left for Cyprus, I'd flown 20,485 miles, crossed and re-crossed twenty four time zones, renewed my British Airways Executive Club, Gold tier membership a few times over, and been living on an almost constant diet of airline food. And drink. At least, I could never complain about having a good selection of wine, port and gins in BA Business, and more often than not nowadays, First Class. Still, I never took the luxury for granted and was always grateful that my work allowed me such comfort.

I did enjoy being back in my own apartment though. A few civilised Chardonnays helped me wind down to sleep, which was important as I'd be up early in the morning for the Eurostar back to Paris and a meeting with Jules. Knowing that, I also left a good measure in the bottle. I found the shake in my hand was better if I gave myself a small boost in the morning. It didn't bother me, but I'd determined the next time I was going to see my parents I'd make an appointment with my home town GP.

***

The briefing ended with an image of the newly opened, yet strangely still under construction, Marina Bay Sands hotel. The futuristic three tower hotel appeared to have an oil tanker perched on top of it. Although I hadn't visited it, I knew from my recent trip to Singapore that the top deck was actually a SkyPark, linking all three towers and playing host to an infinity-edged swimming pool nearly 200 metres above the city. I thought the whole thing was ostentatious and like the other Sands resort I had once stayed at in Macau, a lot of window dressing for the real money earner, a casino.

What I hadn't fully appreciated, until I read a report in the Straits Times on the morning I was flying home, was just how big an earner the casino would be. According to latest estimates, the Marina Bay Sands' tables and slot machines would generate $1B per year. The figure was staggering. It would be almost 0.3% of Singapore's Gross Domestic Product. From a single casino. I knew casinos were a cash rich environment, in fact they could be a perfect front for money laundering, not that there was any hint of that being the case in Singapore, but in the modern world, they would also rely heavily on electronic monitoring of customers. The data collected on the hotel guest, their room preferences, their gambling habits, the amount they used loyalty cards, where they went, what they ate and how they paid for it all would, at some point, become baseline data for a potential cyber-attack. I was convinced of it and more than that, as I looked up at the Singapore skyline, I realised I knew how to task Jules.

As I finished the brief to Jules, Alicia and their attendant deputies, of which Mo was Alicia's and Louis was Jules', I could see the nods coming from around the table.

'It makes good sense and is not something we have even considered before,' Louis said in heavily accented French. He came from a relatively wealthy background, his family owned properties down near Toulouse and he was a Masters graduate of the Sorbonne. Unlike many of the cyber intelligence analysts I had either worked with, or was now in the process of recruiting, Louis had joined straight from university and not via law enforcement, the military or the financial sector. By Alicia and Mo's opinion, he was an all-round 'good guy'. None of which detracted from the fact that he was a heavy-set, short, mean-looking bearded man who I first thought of as a cross between a Viking and a hobbit, until I realised he was more accurately a Tolkien dwarf.

Nonetheless, his opinion, something I hadn't known going into the briefing, backed with Alicia's and Mo's, which I had, worked to ensure Jules could only give one reply.

'I think it is an intriguing new market that we have not looked at before,' he said, surprising me with his enthusiasm.

'Great,' I said. 'If we can find out any potential threats within an amazingly lucrative market and begin to develop some defences that could be of use to not just the Singaporeans, but perhaps even the American casino markets, then it can only strengthen Mac's negotiating position. I assume you all know we've started preliminary discussions on an acquisition and merger deal?'

All four gave nods and smiles. All four, like me, held shares in the start-up. I imagined that all four, like me, were desperate for Mac not to screw up the discussions. What all four did not know was my concern at the company being valued at nothing, if we didn't manage to divest ourselves of Jules. That rested largely with him picking up my suggestion and, once again, coming up with a marvellous opportunity for the company.

The only difference was this time, rather than showing me how brilliant an intel operator he was, I hoped he'd prove to me he was as corrupt as I suspected.

I didn't expect immediate results, even Jules's likely criminal contacts would take time to produce a product and anyway, in the meantime I had more jet setting to do.

16

Fort Benning, Georgia – July 2010

The house was quiet, save for the light tinkle of the broken glass as he placed it into the kitchen bin. Neither of the kids had woken up and thankfully, Shirlene had managed to keep her expletives down to a level that meant the neighbours might not have heard. Hopefully. Although if she stuck to her usual form, they would probably hear her come back in at some hour of the night and slam the front door with enough force to waken the dead.

He looked up at the cupboard mounted on the kitchen wall. Its glass fronted door showed two cut crystal highballs. Dan quietly chuckled as he imagined the glasses were shying away, trying to back themselves into an unseen corner. He didn't blame them. The other nine of their original companions had met a similar fate to the one he was now laying to rest in the bin. They were the two survivors from a wedding gift, seven years earlier. Although that any of them survived meant they had fared better over the years than the numerous beer glasses, shot glasses, a whiskey decanter, countless plates and once, a full one gallon milk bottle, though thankfully that last one had been plastic. It had still split and disgorged its contents in a most spectacular way. He sighed and reached for a slice of bread. The trick to picking up the tiniest shards of glass had been taught to him by some long forgotten TV show that he'd watched as a kid. A life hack is apparently what YouTube called it now. He was fairly sure it had just been a domestic cleaning tip when he'd first seen it. He was also absolutely sure that the young Dan would never have guessed he'd have had to use it so often in his adult life.

Placing the bread slice in the bin, he wiped for a final time with a dampened piece of kitchen paper towel and straightened up. The sudden wave of despair that hit him was physical. He felt his heart racing and slumped against the kitchen counter, before sinking down onto the floor.

Images of Shirlene, Ryan and Lilly-Anne mixed with the fading face of Luke, standing on the approach to a bridge looking at a sculpture. A small Chinese woman, being carried out of the Thames. Morrie Lieberman smiling and throwing candy to a group of kids in the middle of a village being raked by gunfire and explosions. A young boy being held down and abused while a faceless crowd looked on and all of it sinking to black as Luke stretched his hand down and down and down, but Dan, his breath shallow and his heart hammering in his chest, slipped further and further and further away.

***

He came to and checked the wall clock. Only a couple of minutes had passed. Pushing himself up into a sitting position he felt like he'd taken a bath with his clothes on. His brow was damp with sweat and his t-shirt clung to his torso. The anger he could feel coursing through his body was being met and overtaken by shame. The lingering memory he had was of Luke's face, staring down at him. Tears began to add to the wetness of his t-shirt. It was another five minutes before the feelings passed and he could get to his feet. He stared at the half full bottle of Jack Daniels that Shirlene had left on the kitchen table. Perhaps it would take the edge off?

Drink had never been an issue for him. Luke liked to drink and Dan had joined him on almost every occasion, but he could never hold his liquor in the same way. For every one glass he could handle, Luke could muster two or maybe three, yet he never seemed to get drunk or hungover. Shirlene on the other hand could drink a bottle at a time, but it only served her as an amplifier. If she was happy, she got happier. Back in days past if she'd been horny, she got hornier. Now, she was mostly angry and it served to make her like a hornets nest of fury.

Maybe it would be different for him. Maybe it would simply wash away his memories and stop the flashbacks that were getting steadily worse. Maybe it would let him sleep. Taking a step towards the table he heard the kitchen door open. Ryan stood in his Buzz Lightyear pyjamas, teddy in hand.

'Can I have a drink of water, Daddy?'

'Sure, Son. Of course. Then do you want me to read to you until you fall back asleep?'

The boys whole face lit up.

Dan lifted the bottle of Jack's and as he ran the faucet for Ryan's water, he emptied the liquor down the sink.

***

Landing at Ronald Reagan International, I was met by Pat and whisked away to the Four Seasons in Georgetown. It seemed like my life was becoming, another day another country. I'd been on a round robin for the previous fifteen-days, leaving Paris for Singapore, then Jakarta, back to Singapore, Oman, Kenya, South Africa, London and now the States. My body clock had given up trying to cope.

At least this time I'd be in the US for a full week, but only in DC for three days. Then Pat, me and the rest of the DC team, bar a skeleton crew left to hold the fort, would fly out to Las Vegas. There we were to be met by nearly 90 percent of the Twenty-Twenty employees as we were to attend, en masse, *Black Hat*, the biggest international exhibition and conference dealing with digital defence in the world. And being Vegas, it was going to be glitzy.

Mac had been insistent that all bar a handful of the staff would attend. He wanted the profile of the company raised as high as possible and, as Pat said, with more than a hint of cynicism, apparently if we can bring a hundred, then it looks like we have a real force of experience and talent.

I'd countered that it would leave about ten people keeping the whole company running for the two days of the event.

'It'll be nearer five days when you factor in the travelling, but it'll look good,' Pat said. Before adding, 'As long as you don't peek behind the curtain.'

I had to laugh in agreement. Many years before, I'd been advised that Mac was a showman. Vegas and he were meant for each other and Twenty-Twenty would be putting on a show. Mac had arranged for logoed t-shirts, polo shirts and windbreaker jackets to be designed and provided for all of us. Then, because apparently he liked it, he booked over one hundred King Suites within the Venetian Resort's Palazzo Tower for us all to stay at. He and Alexis would, according to Pat, be in the Penthouse Suite, but only because the Presidential and the

Chairman suites were already booked and no amount of jumping up and down could change that. We would also have the exclusive use of the Palazzo's largest hospitality suite and would be hosting a continuous stream of the biggest and best in the industry.

As Pat finished telling me all about the arrangements that he and his guys had been putting the final touches to, I could see he was nonplussed about the whole thing.

'You don't agree we should be at the event?' I asked, as we followed the George Washington Memorial Parkway and crossed the Potomac. I knew DC well and I'd have probably headed for one of the more northerly bridges, the Arlington Memorial, or Teddy Roosevelt or more likely the Key, but I figured Pat was taking me this way so he could bisect the National Mall, before turning left onto Constitution Avenue. It was the best route to see the Capitol, the Washington Monument, the White House and the Lincoln Memorial. If you ever wanted to impress a Brit with DC's architecture, you took them this way. I knew Pat was well aware I had been in the city many times before, but still, I saw nothing wrong with a bit of national pride. His answer drew me back to Mac, a Canadian who seemed more interested in being a modern day PT Barnum.

'No, I think we should be at the event and it makes good sense to be seen there in the run up to any likely sale or flotation, but I'm not sure a small army of Twenty-Twenty employees walking into the buffet for breakfast will send the right message. Especially as Mac has made it very clear to me that he wants everyone there at exactly the same time.'

'You think just a select few would have been better?'

'Yeah, Luke, I do. I think maybe two dozen would have been perfectly sufficient. A hundred of us is going to make it look like a cult's descended.'

'Yeah, but I bet Mac will be as happy as a sand-boy.'

It was Pat's turn to laugh. 'I guess he will, but while you're over here, that would be happy as a clam.'

'Really?'

'Yeah really.'

'Just a shame Mac's mouth wouldn't be as shut as one,' I thought, but didn't say.

***

The Four Seasons in Georgetown was as pleasant as all the rest of the chain, although I did find myself thinking that, 'Oh, I only got a deluxe room,' and 'it's a bit small.' Putting my bag down on the exquisite Egyptian cotton covered quilt on top of the king sized bed in a room that was next to a good-sized ensuite, my next thought was, 'Don't be so full of yourself.' I recalled some of the accommodation I'd stayed in during my time in the Air Force.

I gazed about the room again and reframed my thoughts. 'Wow, I got a deluxe ensuite and I'm in DC and it's not costing me a cent.' Although I couldn't fully reframe my disappointment that the deluxe room's mini-bar offered a relatively limited inventory. To compensate, on the ground-floor was a very well-appointed lounge bar. However, I was dog-tired and couldn't face the prospect of having to be socially engaging. Instead, I ordered room service and included a few bottles of wine and a single bottle of tonic. I had used my duty free allowance to bring in a bottle of Tanqueray. That was my usual routine now wherever I was flying to. It helped me wind down from the journey, get a reasonable night's sleep and be sharp for work as soon as possible. I couldn't spend days being constantly jet lagged. Especially on trips like this.

Before I left for Vegas with the rest of the 'cult', I had to finish off the recruiting for the Washington based intelligence and production team that Pat had tasked me with on my promotion.

The Singapore team was up to full strength and once DC was the same we would have round the clock capability. Added to those teams, I had also had to recruit various outliers. People who reported to the teams but were based in remote offices. It was essential if we were going to try to get information on threats from the more obscure hacking groups. I'd spent quite a lot of the previous week recruiting a couple of personnel in Jakarta.

The so called, 'Indonesian Security Down Team' had boasted online of their growing capabilities and allegedly been behind some incursions into Australian networks. If I wanted my team to provide information on, and subsequently defences against, them and other threats coming out of Indonesia, then we needed fluent Indonesian speakers who could engage and exploit the relevant dark web sources. That meant I had to recruit within Indonesia. The same was true of South American countries, for which I needed Spanish and Portuguese speakers and of course, I needed Chinese and Russian speakers. Singapore had helped massively with the first of those. I worried that I didn't have enough of the latter and that was another reason I was in DC.

The candidates I looked for all shared similar resumes, for the most part. That was good, as it made narrowing down the field easier, and bad, as it could be excessively restrictive. I had worried about finding any suitable people when Pat had first tasked me, but it turned out that in the six years since I had first encountered cyber, the number of cyber security orientated analysts had increased exponentially.

Still, I usually needed someone with hands-on experience, although for the DC, Paris and Singapore teams I would take new graduates as they had people to instruct and mentor them. But for the remotes, preferably they would have government and commercial experience, usually within the law, military or financial sectors and above all be 'self-starters' as I was told the modern HR phrase was. I preferred my take on it; they had to have a bit of get up and go, coupled with common-sense.

I had four interviews lined up for the following day. Two were for junior intelligence analyst roles and the candidates came from Patrick Henry College and Mercyhurst University. I was a bit concerned at the very intense religious overtones of each academic facility. I had little truck with organised religion, felt they were a bunch of hypocrites and had shared many an evening discussing the subject with Dan, who had been equally mistrusting of them.

As ever, when I thought of him, my heart lurched and the weight in my stomach threatened to bring me to my knees. It was even worse knowing I was in the US and he was too. Well, probably. He could have been anywhere, but he could also have been in DC. I could pass him in the street, or look sideways at a traffic light and there he'd be.

In the afternoon, I'd be meeting with a woman whose CV suggested she was a technical malware reverse engineer and the last of the day was with a US Marine Corp Military Police Officer, recent retiree who was, at least according to his CV, a potential 'Mark Donoghue'.

***

The Blue Duck Tavern was Pat's choice for dinner.

I wasn't inclined to disagree, although a more inappropriate name I could not think of. Far from some rustic tavern, this was fine dining at its best and the honour wall of awards testified to an establishment that had, since its opening four years before, been consistently listed as one of the top restaurants in the country, let alone DC. It was also highly regarded for its wine list, which pleased me greatly.

Like a conversational plate of breads and dips, we swapped news of homes and families and old colleagues before our starters arrived. Once my charcuterie board of locally sourced Virginia hams turned up, Pat asked, 'How'd today go?'

'Okay. Two from four. The Mercyhurst guy was a no, the Patrick Henry guy looks to have a lot of potential and the woman, Hannah Clarke is a real find.'

Pat's eyebrows raised. 'What's her background?'

'Former Department of Defence Contractor, worked in the National Computer Security Center and then hopped over into a different part of NSA, as she put it.'

'I'm assuming she wasn't forthcoming on what?'

'No,' I said, laughing. It was good to be able to talk this through with Pat. He understood the limitations some of the people we would want to recruit suffered when it came to being open about their full careers. Hannah Clarke was not going to be able to tell anyone about what she had actually done in NSA until she was likely a little old lady, and maybe not even then, but for now, she said she could reverse engineer malware and her previous employment lent her all the credence I needed. I took some more of my starter and then continued.

'We got her to do the reverse coding test that Mo and Alicia put together for potential candidates. Thankfully the software shell that Alicia built spits out the results. Ms Clarke aced it. We'll hire her on a three-month probation period and give her a couple of preliminary cases to work on. If she continues to do what she says she can, and I have no reason to doubt her, then we'll sign her on permanently.'

Pat nodded. 'Good work. And the fourth? I had hopes of him being our new Mark.'

The trust that Pat put into his people, and more specifically me, since the first day I had worked for him in Bateleur was heart-warming. There was no second guessing or trying to over-see my every decision. He trusted the people who worked for him and continued to do so until they disappointed him. My first experience of that trust had been when he allowed me to recruit Mark and another former colleague into the bank, on my first day. He had known Mark's work and knew how good a coup it would be to find 'another one' of him. Alas, I was going to have to disappoint him. 'Eh no. Not by a country mile.'

'Oh, that's a shame. What was wrong with him?'

'His name was Joe Merwaki, former USMC police officer. Kept telling me about all the amazing things he had done and all the amazing things he could do and all the amazing things he had been trained in. If he said amazing things once he said it fifty times in the first half hour.'

'Uh-oh.'

'Yeah, uh-oh's right. I gave him the usual brief, took him through what we would expect of him, listened to him some more and then gave him the scenario examples that we've been using for potential new security staff.'

'And?'

'Let's say it was a day of extremes. Hannah had scored the highest results in her set of tests that I've seen since you tasked me with recruiting the teams.'

'And Marine Joe crashed and burned?'

'Yep. Not just a little either. Worst results I've seen. Seriously, I know they're who you want when you have to kick in doors and fight your way through hostile territory, but I doubt he had one transferrable skill that I could use. I also think he really believed all the Corps bullshit he must have been told, because he was incredulous that he hadn't passed. Looked bemused that he wasn't God's gift to cyber.'

'So we are yet to find another Mark,' Pat said with a comedic overtone of sadness. 'Maybe you should try again to make him an offer he can't refuse?'

'Yeah, and maybe if you could see his place in Cyprus and the view from his front door, you'd understand why he's not going to come.'

'Ah well. So two from four isn't a bad hit rate for recruitment. How many are we short for the DC team then?'

'Well, technically, three, but I have another series of interviews tomorrow and that should hopefully see it done and dusted.'

'Great. Good Job, Luke. I am, as usual, impressed. You holding up with all the travel?'

'Yeah.'

'And the Jules thing?'

'As expected. I figure I might have something to report to you and Mac in a week or so.'

'Good. The sooner we get him nailed and out, the better.'

We paused and ate and Pat poured a couple of glasses of a top of the range Chenin Blanc. By the time the mains arrived I had briefed him on all that was occurring with Jules and some of those things I hadn't shared with Mac. Andy Gibson's help and of course Lily's, remained with me only. They were not for sharing with anyone.

Cutting into my prime New York strip steak, that had been cooked to perfection, I moved the conversation onto my other concerns. 'Pat, the teams have come together well and currently, we've got all three up and running and 12 other remotes in various places.'

He nodded as he lifted another one of his braised ribs up. US restaurants were a bit of a congruence to me. Fine dining in superb surrounds with great wine lists, yet when they had brought Pat's ribs out they had also adorned him with quite a cheap and tacky bib. And a plastic side bowl of water to wash his fingers in. No one else in the place turned an eye. So I went with my 'when in Rome' mantra.

His hand turned a circle, indicating I should continue.

'I think we're pretty well covered albeit we're light in one or two places. I could probably do with a few back-ups, especially in and around the Middle East, but my main concern is Russia. We are very light on ability to penetrate any Russian threats and it'll be a gap potential buyers look at.'

Pat put his rib down and cleaned his face with one of the raft of napkins that had accompanied his bib. 'You want to start a team in Russia?' he asked incredulously.

'Yes, Pat. At Number One, Red Square, just down from Saint Basil's.'

He choked back a laugh and reached for his glass of wine. 'Okay, very funny. So what's the plan?'

'I think we should consider somewhere close to it. Belarus is a bit too in bed with Moscow and probably not Georgia given the Russians walked in there a couple of years ago and it could happen again.'

'The Baltic States?' Pat offered, reaching for another rib.

'Yes, potentially, but their level of criminal hacking teams isn't that high. I was thinking the Ukraine.'

He signalled again with his hand for me to continue.

'They aren't particularly close to their former Russian masters. That will make any potential conflict of interests less likely.

More so, given the level of criminal activity within the country and the links it has to organised crime throughout the former Warsaw Pact countries, especially Romania, it would give us a potential base for gathering a lot of useable intelligence. Finally, whilst most Ukrainians speak Ukrainian, most of them can also understand and converse in Russian, so exploiting potential contacts within Russian hacker networks should be doable.'

I cut another strip of my steak and waited. A thought, similar to ones I'd had before, floated through my mind. During my time in the Royal Air Force, I'd had ideas and my bosses were usually amazingly good at backing me, but the concept that I would suggest setting up a new RAF intelligence unit on foreign soil would have been ludicrous. Working at the bank, I'd found it paid to be cautious with suggestions, as Pat might just decide to move ahead with them, but as I'd considered before, there was a fixed structure, born of a century or more of banking activity, that meant decisions had to go through a controlled procedure. Now, as Pat chewed the last meat of his penultimate rib, I knew that the Ukraine go/no-go decision would be made here and now.

I poured another glass of the very good indeed Chenin Blanc. Pat shook his head when I offered to fill his glass.

After a few minutes, he put down the almost completely stripped bone, dipped his fingers and wiped both them and his mouth. 'Have you worked out the costs?'

'Yes. Annually, it would be half the price of the Singapore team. The wages would be the same but the real estate and fixed costs for Kyiv are mercifully less. The initial setup costs would also be less, by about 60 percent, as we have the contracts in place for infrastructure fixtures and fittings that we didn't have out in Asia.'

'How many people?'

'Six to begin with. Half and half split. Intel and P and A.'

Pat looked at the last rib on his plate. 'I think I'll leave that so I can fit in some of the Crémeux they do here. You?'

'Always happy to fit in a dessert.'

'Good. Coffee and port as well?'

'Certainly,' I said and relaxed. I didn't press him on the Ukraine. He knew what he needed to know and he'd tell me soon enough.

Soon enough was as the fine 20-year Taylor Fladgate Tawny was being poured for us. Once the waitress had departed, Pat reached out and raised his glass. 'To Kyiv,' he offered.

'To Kyiv,' I responded.

17

With the last of my interviews finished and having filled the final slots in the DC team, I took a taxi to Dulles Airport. American Airlines, as was becoming usual for me now given the amount I was flying with them and their partner airline, British Airways, had bumped me up to First Class.

I left the Four Seasons early and spent an extra couple of hours in the airline's Admiral's Club Lounge sampling a few very good quality labels that were on offer. Given the cost of a Business Class ticket, I felt it reasonable to recoup some of the expense in liquid form.

Weather scuppered an on-time take off and I knew Mac would be seriously pissed if I turned up late for the first of what he was calling his 'Senior Leadership' meetings. However, after sitting on the runway for forty minutes we eventually rolled forward.

Flying westwards meant I arrived into McCarran Airport 'two hours' after leaving DC. Clearing through arrivals was done with the usual US efficiency and a taxi deposited me in front of the Venetian Resort's high towers twenty minutes after I'd landed. Another ten and I walked into one of the biggest hotel suites I'd ever stayed in. The split level bedroom led down into a lounge that not only had a sofa, but chairs, a working table, a dining table, a coffee table, a sideboard-cum-bureau and a nest of occasional tables. The bed was huge and the head-board was leather, wood and chrome. As for the bathroom, with its marble topped double sink, marble tiled floor, large bath tub and shower, it was bigger on its own than the room I'd stayed in when I visited Jakarta.

Yet, as I made my way around the room, I could see that the leather headboard was faux and the marble tops were really a composite, which to the touch felt like plastic. The furniture looked solid mahogany or oak or darkened ash, but again, running my hand over it brought the reality into focus. The show far outweighed the substance. In an instant I understood a little about Vegas, although I had a feeling I may have subconsciously expected it. In the same moment I knew why Mac liked the place so much. It was a reflection of the man.

Unpacking, I unrolled my XXL polo shirt with the Twenty-Twenty logo and retrieved the couple of bottles of Tanqueray that I'd bought before leaving DC. Despite tipping out the rest of the contents of my bags, there was no tonic. Closing my eyes I remembered seeing it sitting on my bedside table back in the Four Seasons.

Pulling open the sideboard drawers to reveal what in all fair-ness could not be called a mini-bar, for it was more like a refreshment centre, I was a bit annoyed that it had every mixer I could think of, except tonic. A quick check of the time and I knew, because of the delayed departure, I'd be cutting it fine to make it to one of the liquor stores either in the hotel or out on the Strip.

Room service might also be a bit slower than I needed. Showman or not, Mac did not like to be kept waiting and there was a meeting in the hospitality suite in just over half an hour. It was fine. I'd sort it later. For now I opened one of the bottles of gin and took a few neat slugs.

***

The hospitality suite was what I'd expected. A series of drink and food stations for every conceivable type of finger food and every flavour of liquor I could imagine, and a few I'd never heard off. Thankfully, I noted, they had stocked up with tonic. The gin was Hendricks, but I'd cope.

The round black bottle caused a memory to flash into my mind, but it was gone before I could properly focus. It had something to do with Mac. I tried to recapture it, but with no luck. Instead, I looked around the room.

Beautiful wood-lined strips adorned the walls, partnered with divided ceiling sections, some of wood, some of plain plaster and some that stopped me in my tracks. A swathe of Renaissance frescoes that looked in every way authentic held me quite enthralled. Finally allowing my eyes to traverse down, I realised that the marble columns, baroque-inspired murals and trompe l'oeil ornamental features were, unlike in the guest suites, 100 percent authentic. Even the green stone of the floor extending out to a private pool area adjoining the function room, seemed to me to be authentic in its look.

'Quite the place,' Alicia said coming up behind me. 'That's Botticino marble if I am not mistaken,' she continued, inclining her head towards the columns. 'And that floor you were admiring is, I'm sure, Verde St. Denis hewn from the Italian alps.'

'It's all very impressive,' I agreed. 'How much do you think this is setting us back for the two days of Black Hat?'

'Ah,' she laughed. 'Probably a bit more than the polo shirts and blouses. Although I did a quick calculation on the accommodation costs for all of us.'

'And what did you come up with?' I asked turning to pour myself a drink. 'Are you okay?' I asked.

'Oh yes. Cranberry juice with a splash of blackcurrant. He'll think I'm on the red wine.'

I couldn't imagine facing two days of schmoozing clients with nothing to take the edge off. 'Anyway, sorry, you were saying?'

'Oh, yeah. Seventy thousand US at a pinch. But that doesn't include whatever suite Mac is in, as I imagine he isn't in the same as us, nor the cost of this little setup for the duration.'

'Apparently, he's in the Penthouse,' I said, reporting what Pat had told me.

'Nice.'

'Nope, he'll probably be annoyed. There are more exclusive rooms, but they'd already been booked.'

'By Gates or Jobs presumably,' she said and laughed again. 'I saw the exclusive suites on the hotel website, but there were no prices listed for them.'

'Have to ask, can't afford?' I offered.

'Probably. So if I was being conservative and adding in the same again, plus all our flights and our wages for being here and not working...' she hesitated for a second, 'Maybe half a million?'

'Sounds feasible,' I said. 'Where's Mo?' I asked, looking around.

'Oh he's not in this.'

'He's not? I thought we were all here en masse?'

'We are, but we shall also divide and conquer.'

'We shall?' I was confused.

'It's the same way he wanted it done last year, but there were obviously so many less of us then. Me and the other senior partners, you and your co-VPs and the SVPs will be in here round the clock. I worked 12-hour days last time. Mac expects us to wine and dine every executive we can. In here, out there by the pool and down on the tables if necessary.'

'But aren't we here to attend the seminars, workshops and technical presentations?'

'No. The technical staff, like Mo and his ilk, they will do all of that. Your newbies from Singapore and DC, they'll all be in there. We looked quite effective last year, this year we'll look like there's an army of us.'

I shook my head, about to be disparaging about the whole setup, but Alicia cut me off. 'Weirdly, Luke, it worked. We doubled our market share in two days. Partly, Black Hat '09 is the reason you and all the new people are here now. It gave us a massive push forward. Built the company faster than we would have, or could have, imagined.' She ended it with a small Gallic shrug.

Perhaps it made sense. After all, the London events I hosted definitely brought us clients. I was about to say that to Alicia when she put her hand on my arm and inclined her head towards the hospitality suite's entrance.

A man in a dark suit and sunglasses had opened the suite's wide door. Another, similarly attired, walked in ahead of Mac, who strode into the room wearing what I at first thought must have been the result of losing a bet.

We had all been given explicit and detailed instructions to wear black shoes, dark trousers and the black Twenty-Twenty polo shirts. Alternatively, if the temperature rose to the seasonal norms of Vegas in July, we could wear dark sandals, dark shorts and the Twenty-Twenty crew neck t-shirt. Women were to wear the same, or a black skirt in lieu of trousers. No one had mentioned we could wear bright orange shorts, a God-awful Hawaiian shirt opened a few buttons too low and all of it topped off with the Canadian version of a Stetson.

The three SVPs, all wearing the same dark corporate uniform as me, looked embarrassed to be trailing in Mac's wake. Pat especially looked uncomfortable. A third sunglasses wearing man brought up the rear and closed the double doors.

I whispered to Alicia, 'What's with the sunglasses?'

'Bodyguards. Mac brought them last year too.'

'What the f—,' I stopped myself and managed, 'Why?'

'I think he thinks it makes him look like Caesar,' she said quietly.

'We're in the wrong casino for that. Shouldn't we be in the Palace down the road?'

'True and anyway, if it was me, I don't think Caesar is a great role model,' she said looking up at me and smiling.

'Et tu,' I said, but further banter was stopped in its tracks.

'WELCOME TO VEGAS,' Mac yelled. 'We are gonna rock this place and by the time we leave, we're gonna have this little company of mine valued at a billion dollars. If we can do that and push the sale through to some of the folks I've already been talking to, then everyone of you in this room is gonna be smelling of roses. For now, grab some food, get a drink and relax. The hard work starts tomorrow.'

As if to punctuate his little speech, one of his 'bodyguards' tore the tab on a can of light beer and handed it over.

A few thoughts occurred to me. Not a real bodyguard was the first. What does Mac think he looks like was the second. And the third I voiced. 'Where's Jules?'

'Back in Paris. Said he had vital work to do.' Alicia smiled up at me again. 'Here's hoping he's successful.'

***

Fort Hood was the home of the Army's Operational Test Command and as well as proving new equipment, the Mission Directorate part of the Command were trying to rapidly get their act together on what Advise and Assist would look and feel like. Dan got the impression it was the blind leading the blind, but how that differed from most things in his career he couldn't work out.

The fort itself had a strange feel. He'd never been to Hood before, but there was little doubt it was still in the throes of recovering from the mass shooting that had occurred less than a year earlier. A serving Army Major had opened fire on fellow soldiers, killing thirteen and wounding thirty two others. Compared to most bases he'd visited or been stationed at in the Continental USA, Hood had a lot of security teams assigned, including the Army's own Military Police, but also a large number of contracted law enforcement. Although it could have been seen as too little too late, Dan understood the need to give the service personnel and their families a sense of well-being and safety.

The first three weeks of the training would be classroom based and centre a lot on the cultural norms of the forces that the deployed units would be working with.

That meant an in-depth understanding of the ancient schism between Sunni and Shia, how that affected pretty much everything within Iraq society and what would be acceptable for US troops to do or say when in the company of personnel of either sect. It would go on to examine the Kurds, the Assyrians and the Turkmen. Guest lecturers and US-based members of those communities would be invited to talk to the officers and discuss their own particular viewpoint on the history of the land they all, in one way or another, called home.

Next, the course would explore the structure and roles of the various security forces within Iraq, or at least those ones that had either survived the war or had been newly formed after it. A lot of effort was concentrated on the Iraqi Special Operations Forces and Dan was particularly interested in them, as their 2nd Special Operations Brigade had a whole battalion's worth of men based in Mosul.

Last on the theory syllabus was an in-depth examination of the brand new defence force units that were going to be established through the advice and assistance supplied by the men in the room and the rest of the US forces on the ground.

Dan was looking forward to it. He enjoyed study and always enjoyed the collegiate feel of a study team around him. He hated not being with his kids but at least he would talk to them daily. Well, until week four, but he would cross that when he came to it.

18

Las Vegas – July 2010

My phone was ringing. It was dark and my mouth felt fuzzy. Sitting up I fumbled for the light switch. The bedside clock read 02:22. 'Hello?'

'Luke, sorry, I know it's some ungodly hour with you. But he's active. Do you want the good news or the bad?''

I sat up, instantly alert. 'When, Mark? Where?'

'He initiated a contact an hour and a half ago. Just completed it in the last few minutes. As you thought he would, the initial approach was on his laptop in his flat at Montmartre. You still haven't told me how the heck you got that software of Mo's onto Jules' private laptop inside his house.'

'No. You're right… Moving on,' I said.

Mark Donoghue was a consummate security professional and knew, by my simple phrase, he wouldn't be finding out how I'd managed that seemingly impossible task. Of course, I hadn't. Not personally.

SIS clandestine operators belonging to what the media still incorrectly called MI6, possessed a wide range of skills, very few of them to do with Aston Martins or Martinis. One skillset was the rapid incursion into a property for the placement of a wide range of surveillance equipment. I'd briefed Andy Gibson that I wanted to know if Jules had computer equipment in his Montmartre flat and if he had, I'd like the RustBelt code stub to be installed on it. Just in case.

Getting it done was easy. The day after I had briefed Andy, Alicia texted me when Jules came into work. I texted Andy. His friends were as good as his word. In and out in seven minutes.

Andy had also thrown in a free piece of information as well. According to all his French and Dutch contacts, no one had ever heard of Jules Guérin within their operations. He was no more a fifteen-year-old boy wonder spy than I was a ballerina.

That had occurred a few weeks earlier, but Jules had played the long game, like I suspected he would. He couldn't simply hand me exactly what I had asked for a day or two after I had made the request. It had to look like he was doing the hard yards in source cultivation and pursuit of intelligence leads. However, I also knew he wouldn't wait too long. His ego wouldn't allow it. Now he'd made his first move and Mark Donoghue, armed with a suite of software tripwires and notification triggers was on the trail.

'Fair enough,' Mark said in response to me not telling him how I'd planted the software. 'Now Jules has established what he wants from the threat vector and the contact protocols, I imagine once he gets the malware he'll revert to the systems you have in your Paris office. He'll use those for the false leads and false dark web contacts. That way it'll look to you or anyone else, like he's getting the information legitimately. There will be logs and records and evidence of how smart he is. Have to say it is clever. If I didn't know he'd just spent ninety minutes sorting things out like times, dark web chatroom locations, cover names and exactly the code the supposed informer is going to give him information on, then it would look like he's an incredibly gifted operator.

'As it is, he's as clever as an actor playing a cop in a movie. He has his lines and his moves are blocked. He's going to follow all the clues and look like he's a clever boy at the end of it all when he comes up with the solution.'

I had reached for the half empty bottle of wine next to my bed and taken a quick hit while Mark had been talking. It was only to focus me. 'You said good news and bad?' I prompted.

'Yes. I have all the information and the key to proving he's corrupt will be to intercept him when he goes back to get the malware. That's when we cut him off from the real software he thinks he's getting, but Luke, Mo isn't going to be able to be the masquerading coder that we substitute in to the chatroom. Not unless he has skills I don't know about.'

'What do you mean?'

'You said you were sketchy on Jules' background. That you knew little about his history?'

'Yes. The story he told me sounded like bullshit and it was. Why Mark, what's up?'

'The reason I didn't ring you straight away when he tripped the software was because it took me a while to figure out what I was looking at. I had to put the text in the chat boxes through a translation program.'

'I thought you said you read passable French?'

'I do, mate. But my Pinyin Chinese is not at all up to scratch.'

I sat forward so quickly some wine in the bottle splashed on to the bed cover. 'What?'

'The contact script was all in Chinese. Assuming Mo doesn't speak Chinese, we're going to need someone who does. Can you bring in one of your team from Singapore to help?'

My mind wasn't quite ignoring Mark's question, but I couldn't get past what he was telling me. 'Is there any way he was using a translation tool?'

'No. His responses were much too fluid and too quick.'

'How the hell does Jules' speak fluent Chinese?'

'Good question, Luke. But gladly, not one I have to answer.'

***

The rest of Black Hat was a blur. My head was in London and Paris, trying to figure out what I would do as soon as I got home. Meanwhile I had to make small talk with a seemingly never-ending line of potential buyers from within medium sized, large and gigantic IT companies. That hadn't surprised me, but the number of men in suits from Venture Capital firms did. Also surprising were the men from the other cyber security companies, who were the same size as, or marginally bigger than, Twenty-Twenty.

Mac appeared from time to time when the likes of Norton, or Microsoft, Amazon or Apple showed up, whisking the men away to the side of the pool where young, beautiful women, most definitely not wearing logoed shirts, or indeed much of anything, kept their glasses refilled and their plates replenished.

He especially showered the party from Ailinka Software with a lot of time and attention. They were a major powerhouse based out of San Francisco with a wide portfolio encompassing everything from niche operating systems through to artificial intelligence projects. Their customer base was also diverse, from the governments of the 5-eyes community, through many of the major financial institutions I'd been familiar with at the bank to small businesses in the agricultural sector. I recalled Mac mentioning San Francisco when I'd last been in Canada. To have Ailinka Software buy us out would be a real coup; if he could pull it off.

Every now and again I would fall in next to Alicia. I hadn't told her yet what I'd discovered about Jules. There was no point at present. She and Mo were as stuck in Vegas as I was and Mark had made it clear to me that Jules' apparent 'discovery' of information was scheduled to go down when we were all back from Black Hat. The man's ego was going to be his downfall. Well, partly, I corrected myself.

I had dropped what I hoped she took as an innocent enquiry about language skills, framed around my concern at our lack of Russian. She confirmed that she spoke English, French and two separate dialects of her native Arabic. Mo, and the half of her team that had followed her from Algeria had similar abilities. The rest spoke French, English and some German.

The intelligence team she was less sure about but they had most of the Western European languages covered off.

'What about Jules?'

She pondered for a moment. 'French and English. Maybe a few other words in some of the other European languages.'

I nodded, and wondered if I could test that theory. I hadn't thought to before.

'Oh and of course, Portuguese,' she added.

'Because of his hotel?'

'Yes. I assume he will have to have some grasp of it to talk to his staff.'

'Quite,' I said. 'No others?'

'No. Not that I know of. Definitely not Russian. You know what he's like. He'd have boasted about that for certain.'

She was right. So why, I wondered, hadn't Jules boasted about what was a particularly unusual language skill for most Europeans?

I had to let the thoughts go as another round of smiling faces came into the Twenty-Twenty schmooze mill. Picking up another glass of gin, one of the better perks to the whole affair, I made my way to shake hands and be charming.

***

As the end of the final day drew to a close and I was looking forward to getting a few hours of my usual fitful sleep before flying back to London, Mac waltzed in looking for me.

'Luke, you're with me tomorrow. I'm flying up to New York to have a preliminary discussion with the board of VecThreat. As you're pulling together our new teams I want you there to outline our latest capabilities. Senior VPs are coming too, as well as VP of HR. Questions?'

'My flight's booked with American Airlines out of McCarron back to DC and then onto London.'

'Cancel it. Or don't turn up for it. We're taking the 605. Wheels up at 5am. You can arrange for a JFK to Heathrow flight in the evening or first thing Saturday, whichever suits you best. Book a hotel for overnight if you have to. I don't expect the VecThreat board to talk to anyone other than me, but it's always good to go in armed.'

I was frowning, but frankly too tired to ask. Sadly Mac saw my expression.

'Spit it out,' he said, reaching for the can of Coors Light his alleged bodyguard was holding out.

'I thought we were in negotiations to be bought out. Aren't VecThreat smaller than us?'

'Bigger by personnel but yeah, a lot less valuable. I figure if we were to buy them it might make us an even better, more lucrative catch. So I'm thinking we make an acquisition of our own in quick time.'

The arguments for why that was a massively bad idea tumbled into my head and I could imagine poor Pat Harris, with a hundredfold more business acumen than me, tearing his hair out. I merely nodded, smiled, toasted his can with my gin and willed the day to be done.

***

A day later and my trip to New York had been a waste of time. VecThreat's board had been bludgeoned by Mac while the rest of us sat along for the ride. I began to wonder if Mac's knee hadn't been the only thing he'd landed on when he'd fallen off that chair.

He hadn't so much laid out our capabilities as told them the many bonuses of us acquiring them. He'd share the use of his private jet with them. He'd host them at Black Hat next year. He'd double their salaries and grant them shares in the newly merged company that, when he sold it, would make them all rich. When they looked as bewildered as I felt, Mac motioned for me to tell them all about our global teams.

I did.

Then Pat had told them of our future operational expansion plans. The Senior VP for infrastructure, Chuck HJ Foale, who everyone called HJ, told them of our new campus plans, which was news to me. Apparently we were going to form our own teaching college for cyber. I shared a sideways glance with Pat. It was apparently news to him too.

Finally, Marvin Bridges, Senior VP in charge of all things administration, handed over almost immediately to Kimberly Fredricks our head of HR, who laid out our staffing levels.

Once that was done, we had lunch and then Mac, advising us we were no longer needed and that, 'It's getting down to the money shot boys and girls. I'll take it from here,' practically shooed us out of the building. Once more I shared a glance with Pat.

'Now what?' I asked as we stood on the corner of 6th and West 28th.

'Home I guess,' HJ said looking more than a little bemused.

Marvin chipped in, 'I'll get flights. Are we all going back to DC now?'

Pat looked over at me. I checked my watch. 'No. I'm staying overnight. I had no idea when this was going to finish so I've a flight booked from JFK for tomorrow.'

'I'll call,' Kimberley said taking out her phone. Mac had told us to ring the flight crew of the 605 and they'd arrange for everyone's luggage to be dropped wherever they wanted it.

We wandered across to the MacDonald's restaurant on the corner looking like a bunch of lost executives contemplating their fate.

I was nonetheless impressed. In the time it took for four drinks to be ordered from and handed over by the young kid behind the counter, who looked more stressed than us, Marvin had flights booked for himself, HJ and Pat.

Kimberley had arranged for their bags to meet them in JFK. Mine were on their way to the Four Seasons on East 57th and her own bags were being taken to her aunt's in Brooklyn who she said she was going to spend the weekend with.

'Might as well make the most of the opportunity. Lord alone knows what will be waiting for us on Monday.'

The rest of the faces around the table reflected her concern. I desperately wanted to tell them all that our main concern wasn't actually any hair-brained scheme of Mac's to buy up a company, but the fact that the whole value of ours might hinge on me being able to disentangle ourselves from whatever the hell Jules was up to.

I hadn't even been able to brief Pat on any of it as I knew he would ask what my plans were and I couldn't possibly share that with him. Not yet.

***

Friday night, New York City. Had someone told the teenage me that I'd be in the city that never sleeps, have enough money and a completely free pass to do whatever I wanted, I wasn't sure what the younger me would have said. This older version, gazed out across the New York skyline and was overcome by a deep sense of melancholy. Dan and I had often talked about travelling. He'd spoken of New York and wished to take me on walks through Central Park. Now, here I was and he was… somewhere. Maybe in the same country, but I had no clue.

Perhaps it was tiredness. Perhaps the stress of trying to do my multi-faceted job of building and running international teams, travelling so much, still having to host the London events and all the while trying to find a way to prove to Mac and the rest what Jules was up to, without compromising British national security. Perhaps it was the thoughts of Dan and how, when I flew out tomorrow, we would no longer have even the remotest chance of being in the same country.

Whatever the reason, I pulled the drapes of my room shut and blocked out the possibilities of New York. Going into the bathroom, I turned on the oversized faucet that hung over the edge of the overly deep tub and was mildly surprised at the volume of water that gushed out. The bath was nearly over-flowing in about two minutes. Staring down into the hot water,

I wondered what was the point of constantly feeling this heartache for a man I would never have. A man who hadn't once even tried to get in touch. I knew all the reasons he couldn't and still understood none of them. I dipped my hand in the water. Reaching lower I felt the soothing warmth caress my wrist. A tear drop fell into the bath. Clenching my fist, I watched the veins rise up on my reddening wrist and casually wondered what it would feel like.

Then I went back into the main room.

The whole suite was of course much smaller than the Vegas one had been, but this was midtown New York. This was 'old money' and every fixture and fitting was solid and real. The Italian marble in the bathroom, was. The large executive desk was oak, the other furniture I thought was perhaps ash and even I could recognise proper English sycamore wood panelling in the room and lining the closets. It was exquisite, expensive... and empty.

I recalled a small holiday home my parents kept in the Lake District. It was humble, homely and when Dan and I had shared days there, heavenly.

Opening my case, I took two large bottles of Tanqueray No. Ten out and placed them on the small table in front of the sofa. Then I called room service and ordered a burger and fries. It would come with all manner of flourishes, accoutrements and special garnishes, but it was at heart a good old fashioned New York burger. I also ordered two bottles of Chardonnay and a half dozen small mixer bottles of tonic. The promised twenty minutes delivery time allowed me to have a quick bath and be wrapped in an exceedingly heavy and fluffy bathrobe by the time the suite's bell rang.

The white liveried staff member pushed a dining trolley in and proceeded to layout the meal, the glasses, the cutlery, the bottles of wine and tonic and finally, with a flick of her wrist to unfurl it, she placed a maroon coloured linen napkin.

I had one of those strange fleeting memories again. Of white against maroon. Again it was too quick. Again I knew it had something to do with Mac, but I couldn't pin it down and then it was gone.

'Would you like me to open and pour the wine, Sir?'

'No. That's okay,' I said and passed her a twenty dollar note. She pocketed the folded bill without so much as a glance at it. I knew when she got back downstairs, or perhaps as soon as she got into the elevator, the portrait of President Andrew Jackson looking up at her wouldn't bring wonder to her eyes. There were people in this hotel who would drop a fistful of Benjamin Franklins as tips, still, Jackson was better than Washington.

Unscrewing the top of the first wine bottle I poured almost half the bottle into the large glass and took a long drink. It didn't erase the feelings of sadness or frustration, nor did it eradicate my stress. But it helped.

***

I woke late, finished the last quarter of the second bottle of Chardonnay, showered, shaved and repacked. Dumping the empty bottle of Tanqueray into the trash, I rerolled the other one and packed it securely in the middle of my bag. I bypassed breakfast and once cleared of check-out the concierge hailed me a cab. Thirty minutes later, thanks to light Saturday late-morning traffic, I was walking into JFK's Terminal-7.

The economy lines to the BA check-in desks were packed and slowly snaking their way around the multiple twists and turns of the corded avenues, that since I'd seen the cartoon movie Shrek had always made me smile. The straight approach to the Business Class desks were also busy. I reached into my wallet, withdrew my Gold card and walked straight up to the First Class desk.

'Good morning, Mr Frankland. Thank you for choosing to fly with us again. Oh!'

'Oh?' I asked.

He raised his head from his computer screen and with a broad grin said, 'I have something for you, Sir.'

I took the proffered envelope and opened it. Inside was a letter and a cardboard folder that held a credit-card sized white plastic card. The card was plain save for the gold lettering of my name, a validity date a year from now and the words at the top, 'The Concorde Room'.

'I'll be happy to check you in, Sir. We have upgraded you to First Class and as you have passed the required tier points, we are delighted to reward you with access to the Concorde Room in Heathrow and here at JFK.'

I knew about the Concorde Room and had also known that given the miles I was flying, I'd reach it at some point, but I hadn't realised I'd already done it. It was one of those elite but discrete things British Airways tried to do to keep frequent fly-ers like me loyal. The perks it carried were listed, in a long list, on the folder in the envelope but one of the most convenient was that, even if I was on an economy ticket, I could not only enter any first class lounge globally that BA or her partner air-lines operated like I currently could on my gold card, but I could also now use the very secluded and quiet Concorde Rooms.

The check-in staff member, Jonah according to his badge, was still smiling and still talking. 'As you will know Mr Frank-land, the Concorde Room card is only issued to a select few of our most frequent flyers and is a higher tier than your current Gold Card. Did you pack your bag yourself, Sir?'

Once checked-in I meandered off in search of the elusive Concorde Room.

I was greeted by 'Stephanie' who didn't do the usual thing of tapping on a computer or have me scan or swipe my card against any type of reader. Rather she opened a thin paper file in front of her, scanned the list of names and said in a subtle New York twang, 'Ah yes. Mr Frankland. A pleasure. Come right in, Sir.'

I thought it was a nice touch. I also appreciated Stephanie's colleague, 'Jessica' immediately offering me a glass of champagne. I didn't usually drink champagne, but I knew about it, like I knew about wines, and I recognised the label of Laurent-Perrier Grand Siècle. I also inherently knew the approximate value of wines. This one, I was certain, retailed at well over £100 in the UK. I took the glass with a smile and moved on.

The rest of the lounge, apart from being a lot less crowded than any First Class ones I'd been in, was furnished with a strange mix of brightly upholstered wingback chairs that mixed, or clashed, with modern glass, chrome and a couple of what I thought quite tacky Union Flag sofas. I sipped my champagne and forgave the designers.

Realising I was starving, I wandered through to the dining area and about thirty seconds after I had sat down, 'Melissa' appeared. The menu was almost as good as the one at The Blue Duck Tavern and the beverage list that Melissa handed over was better.

If this was what I could expect every time I flew out of Heathrow as well, then I reckoned I'd be checking in about four hours ahead of my flights. My previous efforts to recoup some of my ticket expenses in complimentary booze were going to be surpassed. Sipping on another glass of the Laurent-Perrier, while Melissa was fetching me a Tanqueray and a side of tonic so I could mix it myself, I wondered how BA and their partners managed to make a profit. As if to answer my unspoken question, I overheard the couple in the dining booth next to me order two orange juices. It seemed a wasted opportunity.

I took the Concorde Card out and set it on the pristine, white linen tablecloth. Opening my wallet, I retrieved a small plastic sleeve. It had once held my Bank ID, but prior to that it had been home to my Job Centre signing-on card. Now it would hold this elite membership token and every time I was asked to show it, I'd be reminded. Raising my glass I gave an imaginary toast to my dad for his lifelong lessons to me in staying humble.

A few hours later I departed for London. Thoughts of Dan, somewhere in the country I was leaving behind, crowded me again. The sadness threatened to overwhelm me and not for the first time I was glad of the isolation of a First Class suite to hide myself in.

19

London – July 2010

The call to Andy Gibson had taken five minutes. The pick and confirmation of a suitable location two days. The rest of the logistics another one. I got a call on Wednesday morning. I called Pat in Washington to tell him I was taking a couple of days leave. He didn't question it.

I left the Lord Moon of the Mall pub in Whitehall after a lone lunch, during which I'd recalled meeting in the same place, less than six years earlier, an American called Steve Jäeger. That day, like a very few other pivotal moments, had changed my life. It had quickly led to me meeting Dan. Given what occurred later, I supposed it had changed his life too. For certain it had radically changed the life of the person I was about to meet up with.

Coming level with the statue of the Duke of Cambridge, mounted high on his horse and with his Field Marshall's baton perched on his hip, I crossed Whitehall and walked up the few steps leading into the Old War Office Building. Ironically the

Duke, the last Royal to be the Commander-in-Chief of the Forces, would hardly have approved of the building he sat so resolutely outside of.

I'd been given an impromptu tour of OWOB as it was known, by a former boss of mine, John Leofric, about three months before that meeting with Jäeger. John, a former cavalry officer, had always been keen to share his love and passion for history. He felt it important his junior officers, be they the Guards of the Household Cavalry as in his past, or an RAF version like me, should have a proper sense of the people who had gone before and the buildings in which they had served.

So it was I knew that the old Duke had been very much against any reforms of the British Army and that the notion the commander-in-chief would answer to a politician in the form of the Secretary of War was abhorrent to him. He further re-sisted the formation of an Army Council or a General Staff, yet the building his statue was erected outside of in 1907, had been opened a year earlier to provide office space for those very things. As John had said, showing me how the old Duke's head was gazing up at the Portland and York stone façade of the Edwardian Baroque building, 'He must have been spinning in his grave. Silly old bugger.'

I also had John to thank for knowing far more about OWOB than I otherwise would have. He informed me the four domed towers on each corner had only been added to mask the fact it was a strange trapezium shape. He insisted on taking me round all four sides to show me the statues on the roof, which he was able to name but which I almost instantly forgot. He also, being as he held the civil service equivalent of a 1-star, wandered into various rooms without seeking permission and so was able to show me the Haldane Suite, saying as we walked into the grand room, 'This was Kitchener's Office. And Lloyd-George's. And Churchill's. And of course that rogue, Halifax.'

I had been quietly in awe and was swept up with John's imaginings of the meetings that had been held in the surrounds of the wood-panelling and stone fireplaces. Then he led me out onto the second floor's principal landing and cast his arm around at the symmetrical, double staircases leading down to the main foyer. He rued how the splendour of the entrance hall had been compromised for the inclusion of the modern day security desks and cylindrical entrance tubes, but also acknowledging they were by necessity, required.

'Ah well,' he had said, casting his eyes up to the light pouring through the glass dome above our heads, 'It's been here for a hundred years and it's good to know it'll be here for a hundred more. We, young man, are mere custodians of heritage, put here to defend it from those who would bring us to our knees.'

Pushing open the heavy oak door and entering into that secured entrance hall now, I figured John Leofric would be quite pleased by what I was about to do, considering it was he that had been instrumental in helping Lily to defect. In fact, despite political interference, setbacks and the obstacles placed in our way it was entirely down to him the rescue missions had been able to proceed. It was a shame I could never tell him and that he, like me so recently, believed Lily and her family dead.

Andy was waiting on the inside of the security pods. Before I could go through them, I was issued with a temporary visitor's pass and asked to sign into an old fashioned visitor's register.

In the years since I'd been earning good money, I'd treated myself to carrying a Mont Blanc fountain pen. It was my indulgence to myself. I didn't have a flash watch and I didn't even keep a car in London, so it felt okay. It had been born out of having been gifted one once, but infuriatingly I'd lost that original a long time ago. As I signed my name in the OWOB register and screwed the cap back on the pen, my mind had another one of those fleeting memories snap through it. I desperately tried to cling on to this one, but like the others in the last few days, it was gone. I stayed looking down at the book for a fraction too long.

The uniformed security guard asked, 'Sir, are you alright?'

Straightening up I said, 'Yes, sorry. Just a case of déjà vu.'

He smiled in a half-understanding, half-'who's the weirdo' way and ushered me through the security access pod.

Andy greeted me and didn't guide me up the grand staircase to the Haldane Suite, but instead led me down a non-descript staircase to the basement levels. After a mazy journey through labyrinthine corridors we came to a set of double oak doors which sported a card scanner set into the adjoining wall.

He scanned his ID and there was a high-tone beep followed by a low-toned 'thunk' as the heavy bolts withdrew. I was struck with the thought that, on various occasions, I'd met Andy in the SIS building at Vauxhall Cross. Also at the Permanent Joint Headquarters out at Northwood. Again at GCHQ and now here. He always had access and never registered as a visitor as I always had to. Even in my days as a serving military officer.

'How many security passes do you have?' I asked.

He gave me a quick grin. 'A few.'

I was almost rugby tackled by Lily before I'd taken more than a few steps into the room.

'Luke! I am so glad to see you again so soon. Thank you for allowing me to help on this.'

I let her hug me and the intensity of the happiness I felt almost threatened to make me cry. I swallowed hard and managed to stumble an answer, although I heard the crack in my voice. I hoped Andy would be kind enough not to notice. 'No Lily, it's me that has to thank you. There's no one I could have wished for more to help me. After all this time, we finally get a chance to do what I always imagined we would.'

She let go and stood back. 'Yes. Although I have worked quite a lot since Andy and his friends spirited me away, I always wished it could have been beside you and Dan. I am sorry for what happened.'

'It wasn't your fault. I should never have left the flat.'

She gave me another hug and Andy, who had remained quiet for our reunion spoke up. 'Okay. You'll have lots of time to chat as we do this. For now, this room is exclusively ours. There's an access pass for you Luke,' he said, handing me a blank yellow card. 'It'll get you in and out of here and the main security pods at the front and I'll need it back when we're done. That door,' he continued, pointing to the far end of the room, 'goes through to a corridor with toilets. There's a fridge and a kettle in the corner and we've setup the computers as you specified.' He ended his orientation by sweeping his arm over the three workstations set in a single line abreast in the middle of the room.

'Ha. Thanks, but you know Mark Donoghue specified it, I'm just the messenger.'

'Yeah, but I was big'ing you up,' Andy said and laughed.

'Well it is appreciated. I did think we'd be doing this in GCHQ or SIS.'

'Not a hope,' Andy said. 'Both of those are owned by the Foreign and Commonwealth and we like our new minister.'

'We do?' I asked knowing the new guy, a former Leader of the Opposition, had only been in a few months.

'We do. I mean it's early days so things could change, but yeah. He seems okay. More importantly, what we're doing here is much more likely to be preventing a clear and present danger to critical infrastructure within the United Kingdom,' Andy said, using a turn of phrase that sounded very well practised.

'It is?'

'It is. That means it's defence and that puts it squarely in here, or some other defence establishment, but this is the most secure and least visible, strangely being right in the heart of London. A lot less comings and goings than PJHQ or an active military base.'

I knew that thanks to OWOB being home to the Defence Intelligence Staff the level of computer security was good and the communications lines excellent. And it wasn't that far a commute for me. All in all I was very happy Andy had chosen it. 'Fair enough, and here's to the DIS,' I said.

'Only DI now,' Andy corrected.

'Oh, of course, I forgot.' I wondered if my sarcastic eye roll would have impressed Alicia had she been able to see it. The change of name to Defence Intelligence had occurred the previous year and no doubt resulted in a ludicrously hefty bill to the taxpayer for an unnecessary and completely superfluous renaming exercise.

Lily giggled. 'I think Luke would not be impressed at the waste of money those terrible Labour politicians would have spent on such a thing,' she said with a beaming smile.

'And you'd be right,' I said sharing the joke and remembering that when she had led a PLA cyber unit this woman had known almost as much about me, my motivations and my thoughts as any close friend or family member. I was beyond grateful that she was on our side now, although truth be told, she'd never really been on theirs.

'Shall we begin?' Lily asked, taking her seat at the middle set of twin screens.

***

Andy sat to her right, me to her left. I wore a single earpiece and thin boom mike that was connected to a secure telephone line. At the other end of the call was Alicia, still in Paris but talking quietly on a specially modified mobile phone that Andy had provided for the duration of our needs.

She knew nothing of where I was or who I was with, but I had travelled across to Paris two days beforehand to brief her and Mo on what was going to happen.

'I knew it,' she had exclaimed a little louder than I'd expected in the bistro on Haussmann Boulevard. The look of surprise on mine and Mo's face caused her voice to drop in volume to the extent I had to lean in to hear her. 'Oops, sorry. But I did. I knew that weasely little shit was selling us out. So when can we put Mo into the back end?'

'Yeah. About that,' I said and had then gone on to explain about the Chinese language Jules had used in his setting up of the false intelligence collection. They were both as shocked as I'd been. Mo raised his hand. I suppressed the urge to laugh. 'Yes Mo?'

'I can't speak Chinese.'

This time I couldn't help myself. He looked a little distraught. 'No Mo, I'm not laughing at you. I'm sorry, but that's funny. And I know you can't.'

'Oh, you asked me about this in Vegas. You knew back then?' Alicia asked.

'Yes, but there was no point burdening you with it out there. You had enough to do keeping that old Texan's hands off you.'

'Ha! You saw that did you?'

'Hard to miss. Especially when you nearly put him on the floor with that arm twist. I didn't know you did Kung Fu.'

'Aikido, actually,' she said and gave me the sign of the horns.

I mirrored her gesture and looked quizzically at it. 'I thought this was something to do with rock music?'

'Yeah, but I couldn't actually say, I rock. Could I? Anyway, that old man won't be using his right hand as freely for a while.'

This time Mo laughed.

The rest of the lunch had been spent outlining how I planned to ensnare Jules. I told them I had found a Chinese speaking hacker, but didn't expand on any details and they were shrewd enough not to ask, assuming I was hiring a black-hat hacker 'off-the-books'. Then we discussed what each of us would need to do to make this work. The tasks were simple enough, but the timing was crucial.

Now, according to the schedule Mark had intercepted on his initial trace of Jules' activity, we were set to go.

I adjusted the boom mic to sit properly and said, 'Alicia, are you ready?'

'Oui,' she answered. My French was very rudimentary, but we figured given she was in the Twenty-Twenty office it would be a better misdirection if she spoke it rather than English. Although if things got complex, Andy, who also had an earpiece connected to the call, would translate for me.

'Tell Mo to start it up, please.'

'Oui.'

I heard her speak into another phone. 'Allez maintenant.'

The screen to my left showed one of the chatrooms within the intelligence corridor in Paris. This one was called *Hermes*. Jules had once explained to me, in his usual patronising way, that Hermes was the God of communication. A herald. The messenger of the Gods. All true. However, that wasn't why I thought it was most appropriate that 'the Gods' or 'the Fates' or whatever other reason had made Mo choose to use this room today. Back in my days as a boarder at Sedbergh School, I'd done enough of the Greek Classics to know Hermes was also the God of cunning and thieves.

I could see the contents of the Hermes screen itself, courtesy of the RustBelt code stub. This one hadn't needed Andy Gibson's help to install. Mo had been able to plant the software on every system within Twenty-Twenty, although before he did that and before he had handed the version over to Mark, that I had also passed on to Andy, he'd ensured any backdoors the original coders had engineered in were firmly shut.

I knew Mo was currently sitting in front of the Hermes keyboard and that none of the intelligence analysts would query him being in there. Jules, who most certainly would have, wasn't in the office.

My right hand screen was split in two. The upper half showed a dark web chat screen from a forum that had been identified by Jules as the 'place' he would meet his contact. It was a repeat of the actual feed on Lily's workstation.

The bottom showed what appeared to be the same, but which was a dark web chat forum that Mo had manufactured and, from within Hermes, just launched. This display was direct from Jules' laptop in Montmartre, again courtesy of RustBelt.

The false chat room's location in the dark web, like everything within the multi-layered and hidden version of the Internet was accessed via an 'Onion' address. Like an IP address but mostly unsearchable. This was the TOR darknet and the easiest way to navigate to a site was to have a link to it. Jules had been provided that link by his Chinese contact during the chats that Mark had intercepted. Mark had also told me how that could be used to our advantage and that he reckoned Mo could easily do what was required.

During our lunch in the bistro, Mo confirmed that it would take an extremely simple two line piece of code to ensure that when Jules clicked on the link he'd been given, he would actually go to a false room that Mo could create. There were a couple of problems. One, the real room would be non-persistent, in as much as it would be created for the chat and then removed. That meant Mo had to create his version of the room in the minutes before the contact time and kill it off immediately afterwards. Otherwise the risk was Jules would check the link to ensure it was valid and if it showed up differently from what he expected, he'd be suspicious.

'That is not insurmountable,' Mo had said. 'But I would also have to install the two lines of code into Jules' laptop and I have to presume it is inside his apartment in Montmartre.'

I'd told him I had a friend who could help with that.

Everything was in place. I checked my watch. It was 1pm in London, 2pm in Paris and 8pm in China. An auspicious time.

As if reading my thoughts, Andy said, 'Showtime!'

The cursor in the upper chatroom, the real room, moved rapidly, leaving a series of Romanised Pinyin characters in its wake. Below it, a similar series were appearing in the false room.

Then a series of numbers appeared in the bottom screen.

'Well, that's that then,' I said. My biggest fear confirmed.

'Yep,' Andy agreed.

We recognised the numbers as a randomised, fob generated sequence with a pin number appended.

Prior to their appearance it was still possible that Jules had been in contact with Chinese criminals. The Triads were known to have cyber activities in their repertoire. The random numbers put paid to that theory.

Lily had, many years before, given a thorough debrief on

PLA cyber methods. I had, of course, not been privy to much of that information, retrieved as it was after her supposed 'death', but now she had been able to brief me fully. If Jules was working for the Chinese government through their PLA cyber units, then, she explained, there would be a security check.

'They use an electronic fob. Like in online banking. It generates a number which they can see on their end and they match it. That grants the person entry into the chat room, but they also need to identify the person. They know the pin number of their contact. If it matches too, then they are free to chat.'

What she had explained was exactly what I had now seen. Jules was PLA, or at least working for the PLA. Now all we had to do was convince him he was still talking to who he thought he was and that relied on Lily. I glanced to my right and watched open-mouthed at the speed she was typing.

On her twin screens were multiple windows. She was, in real time, taking what was being typed by the Chinese contact, and typing it into the chatroom Jules was in. With modifications to ensure he was doing what we wanted.

Jules would type his response and Lily would take that and, again with potential modifications, reply into the real room.

'Is that the number sequence you expected, Lily?' Andy asked.

'Yes. He's definitely PLA. Thankfully, I can see everything he is typing, so I only have to match it for now,' she replied without looking away from the screen. 'See, done,' she added and I watched more Pinyin appear in the top screen.

'They believe they are talking direct to him. We can begin.'

With a flurry of fingers she was running two conversations, making sure both were accurate but with enough subtle differences to make them play the game we wanted instead of their own. I also noticed she was modifying how she typed. Slowing her entries when she was 'Jules' and typing rapidly when she was whatever PLA member was behind the keyboard in what I now assumed to be Shanghai.

After a few minutes I heard a quiet, 'Umm,' from her.

'Umm?' I echoed.

'They have completed their instructions and he knows what he has to do, but they have sent a link to another location. He is to download the script they have prepared from there. I need a false download site. I need it now. Ask Mo please. I can stall for sixty seconds,' she said and I was struck by her calmness. There was no panic to her voice.

Unlike mine. 'Alicia, I need a false download site. In the next minute please.'

'Mais oui.'

Lily began to type something into the room Jules was in, but there had been no corresponding message in the real room.

I muted my microphone. 'What are you asking him?'

'I am telling him to wait. The script download link is not working. We are placing it elsewhere,' she glanced round at me with a grin. 'It is okay, Luke. This happens sometimes. When I did this for real in the PLA we always had contingencies. I admit we usually sent the file through the same chat window, which is what I thought they would do, but this makes sense. It is more secure. Of course back then I would have a team surrounding me who could launch four or five new TOR locations for me. Now I have you.' She gave a giggle and her eyes sparkled.

I was amazed at how calm she was.

'Fifteen seconds please,' she said returning her attention to the screens and copying the actual Chinese link. She pasted it into a new window and clicked on it. A series of scripts scrolled up inside the mini-window display.

Unmuting myself I repeated the time call to Alicia. A few seconds later she responded, saying in French that Mo said it was on his Hermes screen now.

I relayed the news and Lily looked across to her repeating display. Her fingers flashed again and the link appeared in the false chat room.

Jules closed his chat window down, Lily closed both of hers and the real PLA one disappeared a second later. On my screens I could see Mo rapidly typing on one screen whilst Jules was opening a new TOR browser on his laptop.

'What's going on?' I asked.

Lily indicated for me to mute my microphone again. Once I had, she said, 'Mo is loading the file we prepared onto the false download site he just created.' Her voice was still the modicum of calm. 'When Jules pastes in the link I sent him he will see a file for download and on clicking it he will receive the code script that he believes is from his PLA friends.'

I watched both screens. The commands on the Hermes screen were coming faster than I could read them and a small progress bar was filling excruciatingly slowly. It currently read 65% and seemed to have stalled.

On the other screen, Jules' laptop feed, I could see the link address appear in the TOR window.

The file progress bar was at 75%. 'Lily?' I said and heard the tension in my voice. 'He's going to go for a download that isn't there. Then what happens?'

'Then it would be a disaster, Luke,' she answered with the same lightness to her tone.

I glanced away from the progress bar and across at her. In my mind's eye I saw an image of Dan in front of a keyboard during our days in the MOD together. I'd been amazed at how fast he could type code. He was a quantum leap faster than my original team members had been, yet he'd always insisted he was average. I'd discounted his statement as false modesty, said only due to his humility. Now, watching Lily do what she had been trained to do by an army that had whole battalions dedicated to their cyber cause, I could see that Dan had been correct.

Glancing back to my screens I saw the progress of the uploaded file hit 82%. I looked to Jules' screen but it hadn't changed. It was still showing the 'Welcome to TOR Browser' screen with the iconic little onion graphic.

'Lily?' I asked and glanced at her again.

'All done,' she said. 'His browser has stalled.'

'Really?'

'Really,' she said. 'I do like this code by the way. It is very clever. You can see the screens, capture the keystrokes, but also take control of all the resources. I have his CPU doing somersaults for a moment,' she added with that delightful giggle again.

I breathed out and looked to the progress bar, which now, as my stress dissipated, seemed to be leaping forward.

Lily was continuing in her praise of the RustBelt stub. 'All those actions are very normal, but this new ability to monitor sleeping terminals and hop across peer-to-peer connections is very good. I wouldn't have expected less.'

I was intrigued by her last remark. 'How do you mean?'

'Now we know he is working with the PLA it makes sense that the stub was provided by them too. I am surprised they are not angry at him for having surrendered it.'

'Perhaps they don't know,' I offered and saw Andy straighten up in his chair.

'Might they *not* know, Lily?' he asked.

She pondered his question. 'I would think not. There was no sense or hint of animosity in the chat and it is a very clever piece of code. Worthy I would think of Shanghai's work. Maybe even from within my old unit. Maybe even some of my former *comrades*.' She delivered the last word with a comical sneer. 'Oh; the file's been uploaded,' she said, drawing my attention back to the progress bar which now sat at 100%.

I heard the keys of her keyboard clack like machine gun fire and Jules' TOR browser completed loading the link address.

'At most he will think his internet connection stalled for a moment. All is good,' she said. 'Can you thank Mo for me?'

Unmuting myself, I added her anonymous thanks to my own, passed both on to Alicia and told her that Mo could shut down and get out of Hermes. As I ended the call, I watched Jules' screen.

He was downloading a file that he thought was from his PLA masters. What he was actually getting was a dud, with added tracking capabilities.

The brief I had delivered about the Marina Bay Sands casino had been in an effort to get Jules to realise a data harvesting threat vector would be potentially profitable. If he was getting bad actors to write threat code then he would reach out to them.

They would write it and he would release it into the world. After a few weeks, or perhaps sooner, he'd begin to 'pick-up' snippets about it, learn more and more about it and finally deliver the intelligence to the operational teams that would allow Mo and his colleagues the ability to defend against the threat.

All the while Twenty-Twenty would continue to provide daily briefings and updates to our existing clients. They would feel we were looking out for them and that they were getting exceptional value for money. In tandem we'd also approach new clients, especially within the legal gambling sectors and advise them of this new threat looming on the horizon and how, if they came on board, we could provide exceptional intelligence that no one else in the market place had and of course, we could potentially protect them.

The brief about casinos was no more than me betting on Alicia, Mo and me being right. If we were, then Jules would reach out to his contacts and they would, after a short time, write an initial piece of malware that might be crude, but still be partially effective. Jules would develop intelligence on it and as we combatted its capabilities so it would develop over months. That's the way real threats went and he had to be seen to be real. My problem was that regardless of how ineffective the first iteration might be, in all good conscience, I couldn't allow real malware to propagate. I had to replace it with something suitable, but completely benign.

Our version would first and foremost leave a trail of breadcrumbs wherever it went so that we could use it in evidence.

Next, if introduced into a hotel's corporate Intranet by the usual delivery methods, file attachment, USB plug in, login credential brute-force attack or any other myriad of ways, it would trawl the customer databases for names, addresses, telephone numbers, emails and critically, loyalty card numbers. Then it would spread through looking for the data sources that came from the card scanners on the gaming tables themselves. It didn't do anything with the data, but in the real world, data like that could provide some amazing insights for future attacks or good old fashioned blackmail.

As I suspected, when I briefed Mo initially, he told me that a piece of code like that could take months to develop. When I pointed out that ours didn't actually have to do any of that, except for the breadcrumbs, he revised his development down to a couple of days. Maybe even a day if it only had to look enough of the part to fool Jules.

He hadn't gotten that far on it before Mark's revelation

about the Chinese connection. Once I knew Lily was on board, I was able to task her, but not wanting to annoy Mo I asked him to be an evaluator of the code I was going to get from my 'newly acquired' Chinese speaking hacker. It was true. I did want to keep Mo happy and part of the team. I liked him and his hand raising quirks.

His subsequent evaluation of the code script was delivered with a single word; outstanding.

I checked my watch. Not even twenty minutes since we had started and Lily's file, which Jules believed to be PLA malware, began to download on to the private laptop of Twenty-Twenty's Head of Intelligence Analysis (Europe).

I had him.

Lily swivelled around in her chair. 'Would you like me to see what their code does now?'

'Yes please,' I said and knew she was itching to get into it.

Andy got up and headed over to the fridge. His call of, 'Tea, coffee?' was accompanied by a tilt of his head for me to come and join him.

'What's up?' I asked setting out three mugs on top of a bench.

'If Lily is right, and the Chinese don't know we've been gifted RustBelt, how long do you think we can keep that quiet for?'

'Eh, not that long. Once we bust Jules his contacts… actually strike that, his PLA handlers as we know now, will presume everything he's been given is tarnished or compromised. It's what we would do,' I said, dropping a teabag into each mug, before looking directly at him. 'But you more than most know that, Andy. What's the real question?'

He grinned. 'When did you get so perceptive?'

'Always have been mate, just hide it so as not to dazzle you.'

'Ha. And yes, you're right. Okay then... I assume that to prosecute Jules you'll have to put that Chinese stub forward as evidence?'

I considered his question as I fetched the milk from the fridge. 'Probably. But it's no major drama. The Chinese will know we have their original so they won't try to deploy it because they know we can defend against it.'

'Yes, but if it was kept quiet, completely invisible, then no one other than the Chinese and us would know we have it?'

'Oh!' I said. 'I see. Do you want the SIS to able to take control of US manufacturing plants?'

'That's not really our bag. But the modified version you gave to me, the one Mo made sure wasn't reporting back to the original authors?'

'Yessss,' I said, drawing it out as I wasn't quite sure where Andy was headed with this.

'Imagine if that version could find its way into an embassy's Intranet,' he said softly as the kettle began to boil noisily.

'A camera and a microphone in every nook and cranny there was a PC and no requirement for clandestine entry or tell-tale bugs?' I asked, equally softly.

'Something like that.'

'Of course, if it was the Chinese deploying it, we'd be up in arms. Dastardly underhand spying,' I said with a smile.

'True. But it isn't. It would be us.'

I laughed as the kettle clicked off. 'Fine upstanding chaps, all round good eggs, keeping an eye on Johnny Foreigner?'

Andy began to pour the water into the mugs. 'Precisely. What do you think?'

'I think, in all seriousness, it would be difficult to prosecute Jules without it. We've got him linked to downloading software, but the file he has from us is completely benign. The case will rest on being able to say, yes m'lord, but here's one he down-loaded earlier and it's vicious and pervasive.'

'Mmm, so that's a no.'

'It is if you want Jules hung out to dry.'

Andy didn't answer that one. Instead he stirred each teabag, lifted them out and waited for me to add the milk.

'I hear, as I do, your company is going to be sold?'

'Why am I not surprised that you would know that, Andy,' I said, pouring the milk into the teas.

'How much less would it be worth if the news of what Jules has been up to gets known during a trial?'

I finished with the milk and put it back into the fridge. 'I had assumed I'd show the evidence to MacLellan, the owner, he'd fire Jules and then later, after the sale, we'd contact the French authorities and they'd make the arrest.'

'Yeah, I think you might need to rethink that.'

'Really?'

'I know the French and they'd be more inclined to turn an asset like Jules than throw him in to the modern equivalent of the Bastille.'

'What about the Brits?' I asked.

'Not our jurisdiction. No crime committed in our patch and even more difficult to actually prosecute him if the crime is cyber across national boundaries.'

I was about to try a counterargument, but Andy added, 'Also, what if, when he's fired, he blows the whistle on himself. Just to wreck the financial worth of the company?'

Returning to the workstations I had a peculiar feeling that my delight in bringing Jules down might be short lived. I'd let the likely consequences pass me by as I concentrated my efforts on exposing him. For now though, I had exposed him.

I revelled in it and my day was only going to get better.

20

London – August 2010

The summer sky was slowly turning orange, but there was still an hour or so until sunset as I turned back towards Vauxhall Tube Station.

Andy, Lily and I had shared a beautiful meal in the Pico Bar and Grill, under the railway arches opposite Vauxhall Cross, the SIS headquarters. I'd suggested it as it was convenient for Andy and Lily, who afterwards would be travelling by SIS car to a safe house located somewhere that I had no need to know about. I'd also picked the restaurant as it was a short stroll from the apartment I had shared with Dan and the little eatery had been a favourite of ours.

Waving goodbye to Lily as she ducked into the backseat of a black Jaguar, I contemplated not taking the tube and instead crossing the Vauxhall Bridge and strolling up to Westminster. It was a beautiful evening and the exercise would do me good.

I was rescued from myself by my phone ringing. The screen showed SB.

'Steve, I thought you were dead,' I said.

'Yeah, sorry, La. It's taken us a while. Been a bit more convoluted than we thought. Can we come see you?'

'I'm not in. But I can meet you somewhere?'

'We haven't eaten yet, could we do that little Italian place in Soho?'

'Yeah, but don't order for me, I *have* just eaten. See you there in fifteen?'

I hung up and hailed a black cab.

***

The little Italian place was inspirationally called, Little Italy and was almost full. Soft jazz, of a type I would usually have passed on but which in here sounded superb, mellowed the hum of conversation and added to the overall ambience. When we'd wanted a change from AB1 and a more 'sophisticated' evening out, we'd used this place, amongst others.

They also had an exceptional wine list and that had helped me make it a preferred stop for my Bateleur colleagues. I wasn't quite sure how often we'd spent late nights in here, but it must have been enough as I was delighted to still be recognised by the concierge.

'Ah, Mister Frankland, it has been a while,' he said in his Italian lilt, which may have been fake but added to the overall impression of the place. 'Of course I can squeeze you and your friends in.'

Waiting for Steve and Paul, I settled myself with a glass of Italian Chardonnay which sounded wrong the first time I'd seen it on a wine list yet turned out to be reasonable enough.

The dynamic duo turned up ten minutes later and by the time they'd ordered drinks, perused a menu and ordered food, I'd become peckish enough to indulge in some Calamari Frittis.

I also decided a bottle of the Ca del Bosco Chardonnay from the Lombardia region made more sense as it was only £140 and the quality of it over the house chardonnay was well worth it.

When all was settled and we were waiting the arrival of the food, I prompted them to start. 'Well, what have you managed to dig up?'

'Where to begin,' Paul said reaching out for some bread.

The back of his left hand looked like he had suffered from a terrible burn. I knew it for what it actually was, a ragged scar from falling sideways and impaling his hand on an ornamental railing in Cairo's City of the Dead. He'd had to tear his hand free with little concern for the damage done. I felt a deep pang of regret tinged with a shame that I struggled to shake. I alone knew why Paul had fallen sideways.

Reaching for a drink, I steadied myself. 'The beginning?'

'Okay. We waited to track the second starting account you gave us in Bucharest, but didn't receive a ping on the cloned mobile for ages. Then we got one last Wednesday at about 8am. The amount was for 460k in Romanian leu. That's a touch north of 100K in Euros at current rates.'

I thought back. Last Wednesday, am UK time would tie in with when Mark had seen the contact between Jules and China.

'Okay and so you started the trace?'

'Yeah, but it got a lot more complicated than following the bounces,' Steve said cramming in an olive oil soaked piece of focaccia.

'First hop went to Mexico, a bank in,' Paul paused and bent to his soft sided briefcase, taking out his iPad. Straightening up I could see the familiar yellow of the notepad he'd shown me in AB1. 'Mérida, it's in the Yucatán Peninsula, which is here,' he said turning the tablet so I could see a map.

I'd always thought of Mexico as being the shape of a fishing hook, with its point lying to the right and projecting up towards Cuba. In my mind, Mérida was almost exactly halfway between the point and the barb. 'And what's in Mérida?' I asked.

'Nothing, except it's in territory controlled by the Los Zetas cartel. It skipped out of there and went to Cali in Columbia.'

'As in the Cali Cartel?' I asked.

'Yeah,' said Steve, 'but that cartel's mostly been busted apart. However, the Los Zetas might be handling the production and supply routes from there up to Mexico now. So that might be a link.' He sat back into his chair and let Paul continue.

"From there it went to Brazil, where it bounced fourteen times in banks from Brasilia down to a bunch of smaller towns, then through more cities before landing in Natal—'

'Natal? As in KwaZulu-Natal, South Africa?' I asked.

'Eh, no,' Paul stopped. 'As in Natal, Brasil. It's eh,' he hesitated and called up another window on his iPad. 'Eh, north west Brasil, right on the Atlantic Coast. Its.. eh… the closest point in South America to Europe. Also founded by the Portuguese, so made the next jump a bit logical, I suppose.'

'Except,' Steve interjected, 'that's where we lost it.'

I paused from reaching for my glass again. 'Sorry?'

'Yeah,' Paul agreed. 'We lost complete sight of it. I had to go back in and start again, but we got to the same place and nothing. It all stopped.'

'Another air gap?' I said.

'That's what we reckoned too,' Steve said, 'so that's why we got delayed.'

'But Paul, you just said the next jump. Did you find it again?'

Paul nodded and then closed his iPad and sat back whilst the waiter brought our meals.

When we were on our own again, Paul continued. 'I figured there couldn't be that many ATMs in Natal.'

I put down my fork. 'Pardon?'

'I figured it would work like Bucharest. If I could find the ATM the withdrawal was made from then it would probably narrow down the area that the deposit would be made into. Working on the fact you probably don't want to be walking around town with a bag full of someone else's cash. Especially if it gets stolen and very bad people turn up to see you about it.'

'Okay,' I said slowly. 'And how many ATMs were there?'

'One hundred and ninety six.'

'And you're telling me you targeted each one to interrogate their withdrawal records?'

Steve started smiling. 'Yeah, he did. Crazy sod.'

'Seriously, Paul?' I asked incredulous at the amount of effort that would have taken.

'Well it wasn't so bad. I dropped out all the small ones in shopping malls and garages as I didn't think they'd be feasible. That brought the numbers down a bit.'

'How many did you have to do?'

'Not that many.'

'How many?'

'One shy of seventy,' he said, to the accompaniment of Steve laughing.

'When he told me he found it I had to congratulate him for his cunning—'

'Yeah, I get it,' I said, cutting Steve's punchline off. 'Well I congratulate your perseverance and your avoidance of juvenile toilet humour,' I continued, sharing a wink with Steve. 'Unlike your much more senior colleague.'

Steve reached out to pat Paul on the back. 'All due respect though, it was a hell of an endeavour. To find the locations, target the IPs, brute force into the records and identify the withdrawal. It was amazing. The script was probably one of the best I've ever seen, Luke.'

Since my first day in Bateleur when Pat Harris had told me that Steve considered Paul one of the brightest IT security minds in the business and had taken him under his wing, I don't think I'd ever seen the older man look prouder.

'Thing is, he struck gold. Turned out the air gap didn't go far. Next bank down the street. Tell him,' Steve said, obviously not wanting to steal Paul's thunder.

'We found the amount paid in, minus a reasonable cut and then the rest was fairly simple. No more air gaps.'

It hadn't passed me by that for him to have found the amount paid in, as he put it, he would have had to hack into yet another bank-standard security encryption. I marvelled at how matter-of-factly he had passed over a procedure so difficult as to be nigh on impossible. More than that, he'd done it and left absolutely no trace within any of the systems he had 'peeked' into. Before I had a chance to ask, he finished the trail.

'From Natal then it went to Lagos in Portugal, then Faro, Lisbon, Lisbon to Macau.'

I had my glass to my mouth, taking another drink of the Chardonnay. I expected him to finish with a final jump, but Paul too had reached for his drink.

'And from Macau to?' I asked.

'To nowhere,' Steve said. 'It ends in Macau.'

'Although,' Paul said, 'It could have been washed a hundred times over before then. Even that's a step too far for me.'

'So just to recap, it gets to Macau in cash, then Macau to Portugal, Portugal to Brazil with an air gap, Brazil to Columbia, then Mexico, on to Romania and a last air gap and then into the Paris account and then, because he's stupid, a small trickle feed to his actual account that we can definitely tie him to.'

'Yes,' Paul said having checked my path against the diagram on his iPad.

Steve nodded. 'They're all easy bounces to make as well. Old alliances and old trading partners. The Macau to Portugal jump is clever.'

'I agree. However, none of it counts for anything, does it?' I said cutting to the core of the matter.

'No. Not a jot,' Steve agreed. 'We don't have a clean trail. We can't prove it. The air gaps default on any potential evidence trail. There is no proof that the money going from one is the same going into the other. It is very clever.' He took a drink of his beer before continuing. 'I mean, if we were law enforcement we could break the chain easily enough and intercept it at any point we chose to, but that's not what this is about. This is about you being able to put a smoking gun into the hand of your man.'

'And that we can't do,' Paul said.

'Also, given that we thought it was Military Grade software that was initially blocking us and that our friends in the west country so kindly broke through that barrier, I'm gonna guess you wanted to pin this on the Chinese?' Steve said.

It wasn't a massive intuitive leap to have made. I nodded.

'Well we can't even trace it backwards that way either. The amount of money coming through Macau's casinos on a daily basis makes it a launderers' paradise. Like Paul said, it could be washed a hundred times over between a Chinese Government source and the initial Macau deposit.'

He was right. I'd seen the amount of money that was being flashed around Macau a lot of years ago. Reaching for another piece of calamari I suddenly felt the world lurch. A blackness, like toppling dominoes, crowded my peripheral vision and I put my hands on the table to stop myself from falling.

'Luke? Luke are you alright?' Steve's voice.

I panted and tried to take a longer breath. I coughed and coughed again and finally took a deeper breath in.

'Luke?' Steve repeated, now standing up.

'What? Eh, I'm okay,' I finally managed to say.

Steve and Paul were looking at me with genuine concern on their faces. I sat back in my chair. 'Eh yeah. I am. I just choked a little.'

'Are you sure you're okay? You've gone grey,' Steve said, stepping forward and offering me a glass of water.

I felt a wave of indigestion and severe heartburn course through me. The pain was intense and I rubbed my hand up and down my sternum to try to get some relief.

'Here, take a drink mate,' Steve said, holding the glass of water so I could take a mouthful.

I did as he told and breathed deeply. After a few minutes the worst had passed. I had no clue what had happened, but I tried to brush it off. 'Thanks Steve. Sorry, I think, well you know I'd said I'd already had dinner. I think it was just one calamari too many. Sorry. Didn't mean to startle you.'

'Just like you to be squids in,' he said.

Paul and I groaned and the incident was forgotten. I clenched my fist to stop the tremor I felt.

***

Pat Harris answered his phone on the third ring.

'It's Luke. We have him, but I wouldn't be able to prove any of it in a court of law.'

'The money?'

'I can show you the trail we've found.'

'The code buying?'

'Yes. But that's far worse than we expected.'

'Worse?'

'Much. Think China.'

'Oh boy… But we have him?'

'Yes. I'm scheduled for a week in Ottawa starting Monday, but I'll fly out tomorrow.'

'Excellent work, Luke. Let me check with Mac. I'll tell him you've found what we were looking for. I'll call you back.'

***

Mac answered on the first ring.

***

Jules answered on the fifth.

'Set it up. Kyiv.'

'Are you sure, Mac?'

'Yes I'm Goddamn sure and as for you, I don't know what the hell you have gotten me into, but once this is done, so are we. It was meant to be simple you sonofabitch. I've been paying real well for you to get those threats made by nobodies that we can't be traced back to. Now Pat Harris is yelling China down the phone at me. China. CHINA? Are you totally stupid, boy?'

There was no response.

Mac continued his rant. 'Well it's over. I'm gonna sell this damn company in a few weeks' time, you'll get your pay out and then that's us done. Quits. You hear me?'

'I hear you Mac. It's been a pleasure, but I agree. Time to part company now.'

***

I answered my phone on the third ring. It was force of habit. 'Luke Frankland.'

'Luke, it's Pat. Slight road bump. I called Mac, told him you have what we need and he was genuinely relieved. Said it couldn't come quick enough. When I started to tell him about the Chinese angle he cut me off. Said he wasn't happy to discuss any of it on the phone.'

'Why?'

'I have no idea, but he said it wasn't secure and stressed the word like he thought he was being bugged.'

'Oh for God's sake. He's getting worse.'

'Yeah, but if he's that paranoid maybe it explains the body-guards in Vegas.'

'Mmm, no comment,' I said.

Pat laughed. 'So he wants you and me to come see him on Saturday in Toronto.'

'But I can be there tomorrow.'

'Yes, as can I, but Mac's meeting with the executives from Ailinka Software tomorrow and Friday in San Francisco. If it goes well then all us SVPs and VPs will be invited to a prelimi-nary negotiation seminar in a week or so. The word is between 750 million and one billion.'

I couldn't begin to calculate how much that would mean for the principal shareholders and I hadn't a clue how much it would mean for me, but the words, 'A lot' sprung to mind. However, if I couldn't get us extricated from Jules and the fact we had been distributing PLA written threats into the market-place before commercially selling solutions to those same threats then we'd be lucky to get $7.50. I was still trying to phrase a suitable response other than, wow, when Pat contin-ued.

'He's also very keen that when he goes into these meetings he can truthfully say we're doing something about the Russian gap.'

'Okay. Well you know I've started running preliminary headhunting profiles on suitable candidates in Kyiv. The list is up to about fifteen potentials at present.'

'Yeah, I told him that.'

'And the premises are down to just the last two possibilities. HJ, you and I are scheduled to go look at them at the start of next month. It's all on track to meet the schedule you set me.'

'It was and we were,' Pat said.

I sighed. 'Let me guess, he wants everything accelerated so we look good to Ailinka Software?'

'Yeah, but I've argued most of it away. However, he said that as soon as we've briefed him in Toronto, he wants you to tidy up whatever you're doing in Ottawa and head directly to Ukraine. You're to interview the best potentials and make the offers for the local head of intelligence and head of production. Then you and them are to put a team together as quickly as possible.'

'He's nuts Pat.'

'I know, and it's become clearer to me every day since we arrived in Vegas, but if he pulls off a sale for a billion dollars are you gonna care?'

I paused.

'Honestly, Luke?'

'No.'

'Okay, call your head hunter, you're still using Emma, right?'

'Yes.'

'Excellent. Get her to setup the interviews and you make whatever other arrangements you need to for Kyiv. I'll meet you in Toronto on Saturday. Text me your arrival time but try to be there as early as possible.'

'That's fine,' I said, rejigging my schedules in my head. 'I'll still fly out to Ottawa first thing tomorrow. Spend Friday there trying to rearrange things, so I can be in Toronto really early.'

'Great, you can fill me in on the full story on the drive up. Then we'll tell Mac and hopefully he authorises us to fire Jules, we clean up any residual mess and Mac sells the company for an obscene amount of money. How does that sound?'

I had to agree it sounded reasonably okay when Pat put it like that. 'Fair enough. I'll get it done.'

'I know you will Luke, you've never let me down.'

I ended the call and put my phone down on the sideboard. I still had a burning sensation in my chest and the hand tremor was still there. That usually only happened in the morning. Clenching my fist I walked to my cabinet bar and then, with both hands steadying the bottle, poured myself a gin. Adding my normal dash of tonic was a bit hit and miss, but after swallowing the second long draught, everything relaxed. The tremor stopped and I felt at peace.

Before I turned in I called the British Airways Gold Guest List Card holders' line. Five minutes later I was booked into my preferred seat in Business Class, but expected to be bumped up to First when I arrived at the airport. A thing I intended to do way in advance of my departure time so I could sample the delights of the Concorde Room again.

I'd also call Emma Murray, my go-to recruiter as soon as it turned a reasonable hour in the morning. I'd need her on the ground in Kyiv to help me with the candidates she'd identified.

Draining my gin and tonic, I went to bed.

21

I liked the apartment in Ottawa, even if I got to stay in it a lot less than I had first thought. As soon as I finished my hurriedly rescheduled meetings on the Friday I strolled into the Byward Market area and paused to select one of a myriad of restaurants that competed for customers on a glorious summer's evening.

A softness to the atmosphere seemed to sum up Canada for me. There were plenty of people out and about on the streets, but those streets were clean, filled with vibrant looking shops and amazing architecture, street art and culture. Even the buskers seemed to be standardly, 'good'. My logical mind knew there must be parts of Canada, parts of Ottawa even, that were not as idyllic. There were no doubt homeless people and all manner of crimes, what else did they have the Mounties for, but overall it was... I searched for an appropriate word as I let my thoughts meander in company with my continued walk through the markets. The best I could manage was, 'Nice'.

My brother lived in Australia. Near Sydney. It was 'nice' too, but different. Sydney to me always seemed like London, with sunshine. The harbour was of course beautiful and the Opera House an amazing icon of culture, but the streets were busier and the city detritus more on view. I knew the population was about five times that of Ottawa and that went a long way to explaining the different feel, yet there was something more. Perhaps it was the history of how the nations were founded. Perhaps it was the climate. Perhaps it was a lot of things that I couldn't imagine, I just knew the feel of the places and I was certain I preferred Canada. Although Canada was birthplace and home to Mac, so there were always downsides.

As if to bring my thoughts to a neat conclusion and though not one to find meaning in symbols, I looked up to find myself outside the Oz Kafe, which might have called itself a café, but was most definitely a very cool looking restaurant. Of the many places I'd chosen to eat in the Byward, I'd never tried this one before.

Ten minutes later I had ordered the Nordic shrimp salad on toast, followed by grilled Enright beef. I'd start off with a few glasses of Aperol Spritz and to accompany the beef, I'd ordered a bottle of Marchesi di Barolo Riserva. Settling into the drink and the complimentary starter of olives and flat breads, I tried to calculate what my small share of a very, very big number would be if Mac managed to push the sale through. I still couldn't work it out as I didn't know how many total shares there were or what percentages would actually be left over for the VPs and 'also rans'. Still, it was a 'nice' daydream.

Reaching to tear off a strip of bread, I noticed a discolouration on the inside of my right elbow. Unusually for me, but because of the glorious weather, I was wearing sandals, shorts and a short sleeve shirt. Most normally, when not in a suit for work, I would wear casual shirts, but normally I preferred a long sleeve which I would roll up to mid forearm. Tonight was different. I checked my other arm. The same staining was visible on it too. I ran my hands over both but it didn't come off. Picking my napkin up I casually looked around to ensure no one was paying me any attention and dipped the point of the napkin into the glass of water the waiter had poured for me. The discolouration still didn't come off. It seemed likely that a dye from either a business shirt or perhaps a towel in the apartment, that did after all get infrequently used, had left a mark. Turning my arms over to check the backs of my elbows I was relieved to see it was only in the crook of my arms. Most people wouldn't even notice, which was a good thing, as it was a rather unsightly pale yellow colour.

***

I met Pat outside Pearson International Airport, which also served for domestic flights and we were pulling in through Mac's gated driveway by 07:30. Alexis, golden-tanned and immaculately made-up, opened the door in a pair of shorts that were extremely short and a top which barely met them. She smelt of vanilla and coconut as she gave me a beaming smile and leaned in to kiss me on the cheek. After greeting Pat in the same way and ushering us through to the office, she waved over her shoulder and wandered out onto the large rear patio overlooking the boating lake.

Mac looked neither golden nor beaming. Sitting behind his large desk he looked, as my father would have said, like a bulldog chewing a wasp. There were no preliminaries, and for the first time that I could remember, he didn't have a beer in his hand.

'Well, let's hear it,' he barked.

It took me twenty minutes to layout the same information I'd presented to Pat on the drive up from the airport. Mac never interrupted once, but nor did he make the ohs and ahs that Pat had made. It was truth, but not all of the truth. It was also not the neat ending I had hoped for. Andy Gibson's conversation as we had made the teas in OWOB had seen to that. Yet it was an ending.

As I'd eaten my meal in the Oz Kafe, I'd determined finally what I could and couldn't reveal and having practised it a couple of times and delivered the story to Pat already, I was fluent and consistent in the retelling to Mac.

He got to hear all of it apart from anything to do with GCHQ, the code that Lily had provided to trace the money, the fact that we had used her and the Old War Office Building to monitor the download or that I had tasked the British Secret Intelligence Service to plant code on Jules' laptop. Most were easy to omit, but the last one had required me to be creative with a scenario of Mo planting it on there at my order when Jules had brought his own laptop into work 'one day'.

I also didn't mention that the same RustBelt code stub had been modified by Mo or given to Andy Gibson by me.

Mac did get to think I had hired a freelance Chinese-speaking programmer in Singapore and he got a full rundown on what the code we had intercepted from the PLA chatroom was capable of. I explained that given the speed with which they had responded to Jules' initial contacts the code wasn't refined, but it provided an initial threat vector against hotel and casino data banks. The exact thing I had asked Jules to investigate. I ended with what I thought was a fairly succinct conclusion.

'Given Jules is receiving money from external sources and the PLA are providing him malware to order, I think we have no option but to get rid of him, but in a way that is done quietly and without fanfare. Otherwise we risk impacting our financial standing and credibility in the marketplace.'

There was silence in the office. Pat gave a supporting smile and a few nods of his head. Mac sat still. I waited.

'Is that it?' Mac finally asked.

'Eh, yes,' I said.

Standing, Mac came around to the front of his desk and perched on the edge. No more the shorts and shirts and hats of Vegas, he was back in his usual cowboy boots, jeans and plain white shirt. His belly hung over his belt and the large oval black and silver buckle with its intertwined monogram motif.

'So let me get this straight,' he said, sucking in a breath of air. 'You have some money coming into Jules' bank account from an external account?' he paused and looked at me, then raised his eyebrows. 'Am I right so far?'

'Yes.'

'And that other account, it may or may not be having deposits made from yet another account that might have been given up to us by some low-level courier who was being half scared to death by a bunch of Romanian criminals who might have been threatening to cut his balls off, for all we know.'

'That—'

'Whoa up son, I haven't finished yet,' he said cutting off my protests that Monika and her business contacts were convinced the information they had was correct.

'Then that money trail keeps going but it does a couple of jinks here and there when other gaps appear, but that's okay because some clever banking guys who you happen to know think they have filled in the missing pieces but can't prove it.' Again he paused and tilted his head quizzically. 'How am I going so far?'

Before I got a chance to speak, he pressed on.

'Then the money ends up in who knows where and can't possibly be traced back to some mythical bad guys in China, be that the head of some triad gang or the General Secretary of the Chinese Communist Party himself. Is that what I heard from you?'

Another pause.

'Well, is it?'

'That's not what I said, Mac and you know it.'

'But Luke, that is what you said and here's the kicker son. I pay money into a separate account for Jules to pay his dark web informants. How the hell do you think we get such good intelligence? We don't blackmail people or use some spy-shit honey traps. We pay for our information, and that isn't strictly illegal but it isn't strictly ethical either, so I hide the money we are using. I pay it into an account and Jules uses it. Did you find that account?'

I was stunned. 'Eh... I don—'

'I use a centrally funded account. A number of us pay into it. That little company in New York we visited? VecThreat? They do the same. We all need a way to pay informants that doesn't come straight off the company books. It isn't a big deal and I have no idea who else is paying into that account. That's the whole point. It's anonymous. Maybe there are some real bad folks. Maybe not. But your wild goose chase to follow the money seems to me to have followed the wrong trail. All you have told me so far is that Jules is taking some payments out of that account into his own. Well fuck me son, we all skim a little.'

I went to protest, but again he talked over me.

'Hell, I've seen your expenses. How many people do you entertain at company dinners that need four bottles of wine? Jules as far as I know doesn't go out to dinner on the company's dime. My dime. So he takes a little,' he shrugged. 'I'll have a word. But that isn't a firing offence.'

I looked across to Pat. He was staring fixedly at the floor. I could see his jaw clenched tightly. Without looking up he said, 'And what about the PLA code, Mac?'

'Yeah, let's move onto that. Has Jules deployed it against any companies as yet?'

'What?' I asked.

'Simple question, son. Has Jules released what he downloaded. The code you say you stepped in and replaced. You told me you put a trace on it, so you'd know when it got deployed?'

'Yes we did,' I answered.

'Well, you'd be able to track it. Has he deployed it?'

'Eh, no, not yet,' I answered.

'No. Not yet. And just on that topic. The RustBelt code, did he deploy that out to the world?'

'No,' I said flatly and knew where Mac was taking this.

'No. But you took it upon yourself to plant software on Jules' laptop and you're telling me he made contact with some PLA cyber unit.'

'Yes,' I said through almost gritted teeth.

'Okay, let me run another scenario by you. And mine isn't as sophisticated as yours. Jules is a great intelligence practitioner and knows he has to cultivate contacts. We pay quite a lot of money to our informers and most times we get snippets, but sometimes, just sometimes, we get real pearls, like the RustBelt code. We have gaps in our market information and until Pat here decided to make you Global Head of Intelligence, Jules was my only hope. Thinking about it, given where we sit now and our likely valuation, he hasn't done too bad. Has he?'

A pause, but I wasn't going to give him the satisfaction. He ploughed on.

'Well I think he's done okay and I run the company so I guess that counts for something. Anyhow... Jules reached out to a contact and got a file, which he hasn't used anywhere and maybe he is doing what he had planned all along, which is to evaluate what he was given and then hand it over to Alicia and her team. We don't know yet, because no one has asked Jules, but we do know he hasn't deployed it into the big wide world, because you would have been able to track it.'

'But it came from the PLA, Mac. Are you not listening?' I said, allowing my frustration to get the better of me.

'Did it? You're telling me it was a PLA contact because Jules used an identifier code?'

'Yes.'

'I use an identifier code to login to my bank account. Is the Royal Bank of Canada run by the Communist Party of China?'

'No, of course not, but what he used is a known method of PLA cyber units.'

'And how the hell do you know the PLA cyber units use identifier codes?'

I stopped myself before I even opened my mouth. I could feel the pain in my chest again, Like heartburn. Taking a deep breath, I said, weakly, 'I can't say. It was from my time in the military.'

Mac straightened up and walked back around his desk. Taking his seat he looked directly at me. 'You can't say. That's handy. Here's what I think. You don't like him because he's young and rich and French. Hell, I don't like the French either but I don't hate them like you seem to hate Jules.' He held up his hand to prevent me interrupting. 'You have nothing of material evidence to prove any of what you are suggesting and not even enough to give me reasonable cause to fire him. We may be a private company and not subject to all the problems of bigger, more public ones, but unfair dismissal is still a thing we can be sued for and I do NOT want to jeopardise the negotiations I am currently in the middle of. So, unless you have something else?

I straightened up in the Eames chair. 'It was a PLA unit, Mac.'

'If it's not too classified,' he said with a cynical edge, 'how good are the PLA cyber units, Luke?'

'They're very good. Probably the best at offensive cyber in the world.'

'Yet the code you apparently intercepted was, in your own words, not refined? Would that be the same as what I'd call, rough and ready?'

'Yes.'

'Hardly what I would expect from the world's best.' He leant back in his chair. 'I like you, Luke. Always have done and you certainly are a talent. The whole of the cyber community knows that. The clients you've gained for us in Ottawa and London and elsewhere are all great and I don't think we would have them if not for you. Also turns out, Pat was right to promote you, because your new teams and the remotes have certainly boosted our profile and added to our portfolio, but…you need to give this Jules nonsense up.'

I felt completely defeated. I had nothing else to give and as Mac's words poured over me, I realised that in the cold light of day, to an unbiased mind, it could well look like I was wrong. Yet, I knew I wasn't.

'So, you concentrate on getting our Kyiv office opened as soon as possible, and I'll concentrate on making us all rich, how does that sound?' Mac said, standing.

Pat stood and I stood too. Walking to the office door, I paused and turned back. 'Okay, Mac. Can I say one last thing?'

'Sure.'

'I'm convinced Jules is connected to the Chinese. If he isn't then how the hell does he speak fluent Chinese?'

'Hell Luke,' Mac said, his voice raising and a flush of anger coming to his face, 'because he lived in Macau for nine years. That's where he met his Portuguese wife. Did you ever think to ask him, son? Seriously, Luke, you need to build your own friendship bridge with the man.'

The final brick in the wall I had built to incarcerate Jules fell away. My mind and body felt numb. This man who I considered egotistical, with no skills for the job he was doing and whose background was obviously bogus, might actually turn out to be a multi-lingual intelligence specialist with a skillset outstripping my own. My plunge into depressive thoughts was halted by a series of micro-memories flashing through my brain.

Mac and me landing into Macau in the teeth of a gathering storm. A three mile long, 'stretched-W' of a bridge reaching into the black of the night. As before, these new micro-images were fleeting, but unlike before the rest came tumbling back too. A reception area, a Mont Blanc pen, a staff member dressed in white and maroon. A bottle of Hendricks gin.

Then a new image. This one steady, not fleeting. Sharply in focus. A door opening. A concierge entering the room. His heavy French accent adding to the cosmopolitan mix of Macau. 'Hello, Monsieur MacLellan, it is good to see you again.'

'Luke! Luke?'

I heard Pat's voice like he was a long way away.

My arms were being supported, my body being steered to the couch. Mac shouting for Randy to fetch water.

The smell of vanilla and coconut and something cool on my forehead.

I refocused to see four faces looking down at me. Alexis, Pat and Randy were concerned. Mac looked mildly annoyed.

'Eh... Oh... sorry,' I said struggling to sit up straight. Alexis helped me.

'Take it easy Luke. Are you sure you're okay to sit up?' she said, fussing over me.

'You might want to take five minutes,' Pat offered. 'Make sure you're okay. Probably the jetlag catching up with you.'

'Yeah, it'll do that if you ain't used to it,' Mac added.

Even now, coming out of a partial faint, I found myself thinking, 'Prick.' Not used to it? All I did was fly around the world for him. I let it pass and sat up. Assuring all and sundry that I was fine.

I saw the nudge in Mac's ribs from Alexis. 'You sure, Luke?' Mac asked. 'Maybe take a day in Ottawa before you head to Kyiv.'

I saw the scowl Alexis gave him. He didn't.

'Yeah, you're right, Mac. About it all,' I said and gave him my best conciliatory smile.

'Well that is good to know,' he said and clapped me on my shoulder.

Ten minutes later Pat and I made our goodbyes. As Mac shook my hand at the entrance to his house, he said, 'I know you only acted out of concern, Luke. But I need you to concentrate on your job. Get Kyiv set up, get more clients, let Jules do his job. Then we can move on to bigger and better things.'

'I agree, Mac. I agree. And I apologise.'

'No problem, it's already forgotten,' he said with a smile.

I hadn't told him what I was apologising for and I was sure of one thing; now that I had finally remembered, I wouldn't be forgetting about that concierge in Macau.

22

Fort Hood, Texas – August 2010

Moving into week four, the officers of the army's inaugural A&A Orientation Course were about to deploy into the west of Fort Hood's massive training area and put the lessons they'd learnt into a series of practical exercises that would increase in difficulty and duration. All of the course personnel would be taking part and the 'extras' were being supplied by additional units and a few actual Iraqi commandos.

Dan and the rest of the officers knew the rules of the game. It wasn't ideal, but it was what it was and it was only a week. He called Shirlene, ostensibly to talk to the kids and tell them he'd call them again, as soon as he was 'back'.

***

Dan was next to a translator and an Iraqi captain, who was, within the scenario, visiting a training exercise to watch US troops liaising with and overseeing the training of a squad of 'newly recruited' potential commandos. All eight recruits were currently 'leopard crawling' flat on their bellies, assault rifles balanced on their forearms towards an imaginary enemy bunker, represented by sandbags and half height oil drums.

The squad's 'commander', a sergeant of Kurdish heritage was berating all of his new troops in the manner a good training sergeant should, but seemed, to Dan, to be concentrating on one man in particular.

The Texan heat in the Fort Hood training area wasn't far off what Dan imagined the Iraqi desert would be like at the height of summer. The sand also seemed to be relevantly accurate and the small area of Iraqi townsite the US Army's engineers had built meant that had you been dropped here unknowingly you could realistically have convinced yourself you were, in fact, in Iraq.

Added to that, the shouting in Arabic of the sergeant while the translator tried to keep up with the Iraqi captain's questions to Dan about methods and techniques, whilst also trying to answer Dan directly as he queried what the sergeant was saying to recruit number four, all contributed to the overall effect.

Dan stopped the Iraqi captain with a gently raised hand and directed the translator to tell him why the sergeant was giving the number four man such a hard time when it seemed to Dan the man was doing as well, or as badly, as his colleagues.

Not having even a passable knowledge of the 'local' language meant Dan was reliant on his translator, just as he had been back in Afghanistan, but that experience also allowed him to pick up hesitations, inferences and tonal pitches that were a good indicator that the translator was not actually translating, but interpreting and potentially putting his own narrative on things. Sometimes this was done to satisfy what the translator might have thought the US officer would have wanted to hear and sometimes it was done simply to obfuscate the truth. Either way, it wasn't what a translator was paid for.

In answer to Dan's question the translator most definitely hesitated and looked away as he reported that the recruit had said something out of turn to the Sergeant. Dan was about to ask again, but was stopped as four things happened at once.

The recruit stopped crawling along the ground towards the objective his squad were meant to reach, and began to stand up.

The Iraqi captain to Dan's right started shouting loudly and gesticulating towards the training sergeant, in a manner that in any language meant he was far from happy.

The sergeant stopped shouting and began to run towards the rising recruit and Dan, in a reflex action that he was only partially aware of, sank to one knee whilst swinging his shoulder-slung M4 assault rifle from behind his back and into the aim. Then time seemed to slow.

The recruit, now standing, brought his assault rifle into his shoulder and fired a short three round burst into the on-rushing sergeant who dropped to the ground. The captain, struggling to get his own sidearm out of its holster continued to shout. The remaining recruits had all stopped crawling and were in various semi-prone positions as they twisted and turned to see what was happening. Dan saw the standing recruit turn and bring his weapon to bear on the captain, who was still struggling and still shouting.

Dan fired twice. Both aimed at centre mass. Both without hesitation. Then he adjusted aim and fired another two rounds at the recruit's head.

Everything stopped.

'Excellent, excellent. Well done. Superb reaction, Captain Stückl,' the Mission Directorate Major said, stepping up from his vantage point. 'Very good indeed. We only lost one friendly which is a great job, considering you can't legitimately open fire until the hostile does. Very good. Best result possible. Okay guys, dust yourselves off, take five and grab a drink. Then back here for a full debrief. Corporal Thomas?'

An enlisted soldier stepped forward and deactivated the flashing indicator light and high-pitched beep of the Multiple Integrated Laser Engagement System fitted to the 'training sergeant' and 'recruit'. As he did so he reported, 'Four hits. Two chest, stopped by Kevlar body plate, but likely impact wounds. Two head. Both fatal. Time from first to last, 1.28 seconds.'

'Outstanding, Captain,' the Major said, holding his hand out to help Dan up off his knee.

***

For the rest of the week long 'in-the-field' exercise Dan and his fellow students were put through an increasingly challenging set of scenarios. Some featured suicide bombers, some ambushes, some meetings with village committees, or Iraqi Government representatives. All kept the threat threshold high, all kept Dan in a constant state of anxiety and heightened awareness. He didn't sleep much, ate meagrely and, when away from prying eyes, coughed up bile. Yet in every scenario that required immediate action backed with an almost instant aggression, he excelled. His 'body count' at the end of those scenarios he was in charge of was 15-6.

The Major in charge of the Directing Staff consistently praised him for making superb decisions in real-time resulting in the rapid elimination of hostile threats with the minimum of coalition casualties. All Dan could reflect on each night were the 'friendlies' who had died before he'd reacted. He wondered what that would feel like on the ground in Mosul when the bodies didn't get back up and dust themselves off as they had in Texas.

23

Kyiv – August 2010

I waited patiently at the barrier lined walkway for the familiar face of Emma Murray and almost completely missed her until she was within a foot of me.

'You're not very good at all this target surveillance stuff then?' she said, laughing and reaching over the barrier to kiss me hello.

I returned the peck on her cheek and stood back to look at her. 'Well obviously not if all it takes is a bottle of dye,' I said and flicked her hair with a finger. 'What's with the blonde?'

'Fancied a change. Seemed like the easiest way to get one. You know, that or a full face tattoo and I thought that might be a little excessive.'

'And hard to get rid of if you change your mind,' I agreed.

'Yeah,' she said laughing and walked off to meet me at the end of the barrier.

'Where are we staying, somewhere suitably nice?' she asked as we made our way out of the airport.

'Middle of town, the InterContinental. I was trying to book a Four Seasons as per usual but couldn't find one. It looks okay, newish and has a couple of smaller function rooms. I've booked one for the three days so we should be all set.'

'Great, let's go,' she said striding off.

'Have you ever been here before?'

'No.'

'Okay, just to warn you, it's about an hour and a quarter to get from the airport to the city, depending on traffic.'

'Oh!' she said, slipping her arm into mine and righting her suitcase onto its wheels. 'You can tell me all about your love life on the way in.'

'And what do you want to talk about for the other hour and ten minutes?'

***

We were met at the hotel by Kimberly Fredricks, the head of Twenty-Twenty HR. Emma and I would do the interviewing, but Kimberley would do the hiring and, given the time differences between DC and Ukraine, added to the speed Mac wanted things to happen here, it was a better solution for her to be here too.

Also already at the hotel was HJ Foale, the Senior VP for infrastructure. He and I were going to select an office space that he would sign off on and begin to have his team fit out. Pat was originally going to weigh in on that but had told me just to make the decision I thought was best. Once more I was grateful for his confidence in me.

I also wondered if he wanted to make sure at least two of the Senior VPs were on the right side of the world to stop Mac doing something strange and unusual in the negotiations with

Ailinka Software. It made sense, even if he couldn't say it out loud.

Monday was spent organising ourselves. Tuesday was a field trip to the two potential office locations. The first, located on Moskovska Street, close to the Svyato-Vvedenskyi Monastery, was a solid looking, four storey, squat building of pale yellow stone, that reminded me of the discolouration on my arms, which instead of having lessened, seemed I'd noted that morning, to be spreading.

The second location was in Borychiv Tik Street, further to the north of the city, out past St Sophia's Cathedral. The route took us past the Security Service of Ukraine's main headquarters.

In front of the impressive looking building, which reminded me of a cross between OWOB and Buckingham Palace there appeared to be a mini-riot happening on the wide, cordoned-off footpath. HJ, in his broad North Dakotan accent, asked what was happening. The taxi driver, in broken English, told us that the women who take their clothes off were protesting again. As I looked to my right, sure enough a small crowd of young women were holding placards, banners and what looked like hammers and long sticks. The police were struggling with a couple while the rest were yelling and generally doing what I'd seen protestors do in London, or elsewhere on television. The only difference was these young women were mostly topless. Some wore jeans and shoes, some wore hats. Some, not topless, wore either underwear or bikinis, it was difficult to tell as we drove past, waved on by police officers who didn't seem to be seeing anything amusing about the event.

The taxi driver was continuing, 'They protest about the women right. And corrupt government. They want the free press and not like our current President. Also not the Russians. They, eh, special not like Putin.'

'Crazy,' HJ said.

'No!' the taxi driver said loudly. 'No. Not crazy. They are right. They do the no cloth for the, eh… for the famous news?'

'Publicity,' I offered.

'Yes. The public. They do for that. They are not crazy. Brave. Braver than some men. I want my girls to be equal.'

I'd been in Ukraine once before and recalled another driver, Maksym, a security contractor to Bateleur, telling me about an Elton John concert. I had thought he was going to voice all sorts of anti-gay sentiments, but had been pleasantly surprised to learn he had held the opposite opinion. I recalled he too, a father of twin girls who would be six or seven now, was most adamant they would be brought up to have good ethical values and see the equality of all. I also recalled something else that he had said about Kyiv and felt a twinge of vague uneasiness that I couldn't pin down.

The sight of the Byzantine St Sophia's Cathedral, with its green and golden cupolas banished any feelings other than awe.

A large banner hung across a part of the Cathedral grounds but the Cyrillic lettering was a mystery to me. The Arabic numbers however suggested the Cathedral would celebrate its millennium the following year. I asked the driver.

'Yes. A thousand years. Big cellar.. cellar… big festival and concerts and party. Go on long time.'

I reckoned my pronunciation of celebrations in his native tongue would be equally difficult.

The second office location was modern, functional and strangely lacking in any of the solidity or permanence that the first one had. It was, according to HJ, two thirds of the lease costs, being further from the city centre and closer to the docks.

I figured, as and when I had to visit my new team, the drive past St Sophia's magnificence would compensate well for any fragility the office suffered.

By Thursday night I had my head of Intelligence, a woman called Zhenya Boiko and my choice for head of production, a man called Dima Sharapov, who could have passed for a male model.

I met Emma and Kimberley in the hotel bar prior to going to dinner.

'Where's HJ?' Kimberley asked.

'Flew back to the US this afternoon,' I answered, relaying what I'd been told in a phone call from Pat.

Kimberley looked a little taken aback. 'What on earth would make him leave a day early. I thought he was going to be signing the legal papers for the lease tomorrow?'

'He went to the lawyers on the way to the airport apparently. When we were in with Zhenya.' I took a drink of my gin. 'And as for what takes him back, Pat said Mac had insisted he, HJ and Marvin be in a meeting with him and *them* tomorrow.'

I gave Emma a quick wink. 'Secrets, what can I say?'

She gave me a knowing smile. 'Yeah, like I don't know what Mac's trying to do with Ailinka.'

'Oh, you do?' I asked, genuinely surprised. 'I thought, and I think Mac thinks, the whole deal's on the QT.'

'Well it might be, but you know me, I have contacts. And besides the rest of the industry knows something's going on.'

'They do?' I asked, concerned about how much information was out in the world regarding any deal.

'Yeah. He shouldn't have tried to raise the profile so much at Black Hat,' Emma answered.

'Were you there?' Kimberley asked, and took a sip of her espresso martini that almost drained the glass. I knew there was a reason I had warmed to her from our first meeting.

'Oh gosh no,' Emma said, 'far too expensive a trip for my company to pay for, but I heard about it from at least six, maybe seven executive level acquaintances who were and all of them are convinced that Mac is trying to get a buyout happening in weeks rather than months.'

'That doesn't explain why you just mentioned Ailinka,' I said. 'Whose your source?' I added with my best attempt at a threatening scowl. I got the reaction I expected.

'Yeah, right Inspector Clueless… Ha. But as it's you. I know a guy, who I might have hired into his first senior management role a while back. He's now at executive level with Ailinka. He was in the room for Mac's negotiations. Last time I was in the States he told me his thoughts.'

'Mmm, and what were his thoughts?' Kimberley asked while I ordered us some more drinks and the bar snack menu, as I had a feeling we weren't going to be going very far for a while.

'That depends,' Emma answered.

I turned back to the conversation. 'On what?'

I got a strange look from Emma. I'd known her for a while and had hit it off with her surprisingly quickly. She was smart, not merely intelligent, good fun and, rare in my opinion of her role and chosen career path, kind. That latter fact usually reflected in her eyes, but now those eyes had narrowed somewhat. I had a good read of expressions normally, but this one lost me.

'What?' I asked and received a sigh and an eye roll Alicia would have been proud of in return.

Through gritted teeth she said in a voice that obviously Kimberley, sitting next to her, could hear, 'How close are people to Mac?'

Kimberley burst out laughing. 'Oh God no hun, you fire away, I think he's bat-shit crazy. Or as you Brits say, crazy as a box of... mice?'

'Frogs,' Emma said laughing. 'But close enough. Okay then, well, the word is that he's severely overvalued the business but more importantly, much more importantly, the riders he keeps attaching to the negotiations are proving hard to take.'

Both Kimberley and I gave the same quizzical look. She beat me to asking the question.

'What riders?'

'Well you know I can't speak first hand, but one of my main clients got this from a guy who was in the room during one of the meetings in advance of Vegas.'

'And,' I asked, passing her a newly arrived glass of wine.

'And Mac wants to have a continued role after the buyout. A very specific role.'

'Oh God,' Kimberley sighed, taking her second espresso martini. 'What role?'

'The official spokesperson on cyber at any and all of the big conferences. He also insisted that as an employee he would not have to wear corporate suits, and would be allowed to stay in his boots and jeans.'

'Serious—'

She cut me off with, 'Yes, seriously. And to top it off, that private jet of his, isn't. Well, it is but it's licensed through the company for tax purposes so would form part of the assets. He was asking that he still be allowed to use it for all his personal trips.'

Kimberley put her drink down and brought her hands up to her face, sighing as she did.

I simply shook my head and took a long drink of my gin and tonic.

'Anyhow,' Emma said in an overly upbeat way, 'look on the bright side.'

'Which is?' I asked.

'He's picking up our bar bill for tonight!'

'And I get a long lie-in. My flight isn't leaving until 2pm,' Kimberley said, raising her glass in a toast and inadvertently, or perhaps not, leaning her hand on my thigh. 'Hope you aren't too superstitious, we'll all be flying on Friday the thirteenth,' she said giving a long squeeze with her hand.

'What time's ours?' Emma asked.

'Midday,' I said and could see Emma's eyes twinkling. One of the two of us was going to have to explain to Kimberley that she was most definitely barking up the wrong tree.

***

This time Jules answered on the first ring.

'You ready?'

'Yes, Mac. All is ready.'

'When?'

'In the morning. By the time you wake it will be done. Okay?' The line clicked off.

***

My phone buzzed in my pocket and I got up from my bar stool a little unsteadily. 'Hello,' I said, walking away from the main hubbub of the room.

'Is that Mr Frankland?' A heavily accented Ukrainian voice.

'Eh, yes,' I answered, looking back to where Kimberley and Emma were leaning in close to one another in a conspiratorial way. I was hoping upon hope that Emma was telling Twenty-Twenty's head of HR, who was most definitely leaning in to me and sitting closer to me at every opportunity, that I was a very bad bet for an 'in-Kyiv' fling.

'I am the duty solicitor for Zalnik and Sons,' the voice in my ear said, bring me back to the call. 'We are handling the property terms for your new office in Kyiv.'

I thought I vaguely recognised the name from the conversations I'd had with HJ. 'Yes?'

'I am sorry to call so late but I was told you were leaving tomorrow and did not want to miss you. Yes?'

'Yes, what's the matter?'

'Your colleague signed the lease on the documents?'

'That's right,' I said, finding a seat on the far side of the hotel lobby. 'Is there a problem?'

'Sadly, yes. One of the pages to be signed and witnessed was missed by your colleague. I have tried to call him, but I am getting no answer. You are listed as an alternative contact. Do you think I could send a car for you in the morning?'

HJ would still be in the air, no surprise he hadn't answered. 'Can you not bring me the papers,' I asked.

'Part of the witness process requires the papers to be stamped with our office seal. So, no.'

I put his forthright abruptness down to English not being his first language, but I was fairly sure we were paying him. I also didn't appreciate him saying HJ had missed the page to be signed. What were the lawyers in the room doing, looking on uninterested? Sighing and annoyed that civil society and my upbringing prevented me from ranting at someone who was likely to be a junior solicitor dumped into the night shift to file away documents, I instead said, 'Fine, but I have to be at the airport by ten at the latest. Can you manage that?'

'We are on the way. Fifteen minutes from you. Five minutes to sign. Then an hour more to the airport. If you bring your bags, we will have our car take you straight there. To be safe, can you meet our car in front of your hotel at 8.00am?'

'Yes. I'll be outside. Don't be late,' I said and ended the call. Walking back to take my stool at the bar, I hesitated and slowed to a stop. Turning back I retook the seat on the far side of the room.

The last time I'd visited Kyiv was in the middle of winter, a year and a half ago. It had been freezing. The city completely different from how it was now, in the height of summer. But... I wondered... had other things changed as much?

I scrolled through my contacts and pressed the call button.

When I returned to the bar, Emma swivelled around to catch the barman's eye and order more drinks. Kimberley leaned in to me, gave me a peck on the cheek and said, 'Typical. Ah well.' Then she straightened and drained her latest espresso martini. I figured she'd need the lie-in anyway.

***

My alarm woke me at 06:00. It was still dark due to the heavy curtains of the room. Laying still for a moment I was aware of a deeply unsatisfying taste in my mouth. Taking a deep breath I sat up straight and swung my legs out of bed, planting them on the floor. For the first time in as long as I could remember, my head hurt.

The longer I sat there, the more my temples were pounding. I pressed the heels of my shaking hands into the side of my head and squeezed. I didn't feel very well at all. This was one less thing I needed to be dealing with. A little unsteadily, I walked to the room's fridge. There was no wine left, my usual habit of leaving some for the morning had passed me by last night, so I took two of the small bottles of vodka from the mini bar. There was no gin either but I simply needed a drink to steady my hand and take the damned headache away. I never got a hangover. If I felt like this I wondered how Kimberley was feeling. Emma and I had literally had to carry her to bed.

In the shower I scrubbed at the yellow colour that now extended from my armpit to my wrist. I had no clue what it was, but it wasn't shifting. Next time I was back in the UK I'd go and see my folks. Get my father to make an appointment with our family GP. For now I stopped the water, wrapped myself in a towel and reached for the in-room phone.

By the time room service arrived with a pot of tea and four headache tablets, I'd had a shave, was dressed in my suit, my bags were packed and I was feeling slightly fresher if not on top of the world.

***

The car was a black Mercedes with tinted rear and side windows. The driver wore a black suit. The man who stepped out of the passenger seat was similarly attired.

'Mr Frankland?'

I gave a nod of my still fragile head. He pointed to the open boot and I placed my bags in. Then he opened the rear door for me. Climbing in, a man on the opposite side of the rear seat held his hand out. 'Mr Frankland, I spoke to you last night.'

The rear door shut and the car pulled away as soon as the front passenger had retaken his seat.

'I didn't catch your name,' I said to my new acquaintance.

'No.'

I stared sideways at him. 'What?'

He leaned forward. I felt the hard pressure in my ribs. Looking down my thoughts came in a rush. I put them down to mild shock. Why would a lawyer carry a handgun? I don't recognise what type of gun that is. Does that really matter? My headache's gone. I might die. I wish I could see home one more time.

I looked around hurriedly. The rear window was narrow. I couldn't see much out of it other than the fast receding Inter-Continental Hotel. I felt the gun poke deeper into me. In a voice much calmer than I felt, I said, 'What on earth do you think you're doing?'

'Sit still, do not make a fuss and I shall not hurt you.'

I was contemplating an answer when the passenger twisted around, leaned back through the gap in the seats and placed a hood over my head. I felt my arms being pulled forward and a plastic tie secured around my wrists.

I tried to suck in air and regulate my breathing. Despite the things I knew, or as the voice in my head corrected me, hoped I knew, my mind was tumbling. Those things could be wrong. All of it could be wrong. Concentrating, I told myself to shut up and willed my focus on likely certainties. This was a kidnap. It happened fairly regularly in the Ukraine. Mac would pay up and I'd be released. Panic threatened to swamp me. The burning sensation in my chest returned. I felt my hands begin to tremble. Breathing as deeply as I could, I tried to tell my body to relax. That small corrective voice in my head chipped in again. Pat would pay up. I'd be released. In the meantime, be calm. From some long-ago military training I'd been exposed to, I recalled suggestions to guestimate the time and concentrate on the things you can hear and feel.

***

With a guess of twenty minutes, so perhaps still in the city, and no massive change to road conditions, so not in some muddy field, the car came to a stop.

Doors opened and the weight in the car changed as the men got out. Sensing my own door opening and hearing a single word, 'Out!' I twisted myself around. Arms reached for mine and pulled me forward. A hand went on my head to stop me from hitting it. More surreal thoughts of how kind a thing that was, shame about the gun, came to me.

'Stand still.'

I did. With a hood still over my head there wasn't much choice.

That problem was removed.

I blinked in the early morning, but bright, sun. Two men stood in front of me. One was my 'lawyer'. The other held the hood. Both had guns. I turned my head and saw the shadow of another man on the ground behind me. The driver. My mind conjured out of some more long-ago training that given the time of day, I was facing approximately south west. That probably didn't help me, but I was becoming intrigued at how my mind was dealing with this.

Directly in front was an old, likely Soviet-era, three storey building. Its façade was faded and decaying across the whole of its frontage, which was easily fifty metres wide. The entrance doors, atop four cracked concrete steps, looked to be solid metal. I noticed the windows, at least twenty five to either side on every floor. All were barred. I wondered at it being an old prison. Looking to my left and right it obviously sat in grounds, but I could see high-rise buildings not too far away on the skyline. It could still be a prison. London had prisons inside its boundaries.

My lawyer led off and pushed open the right hand metal entrance door. With my eyes adjusted and only my hands bound it merely took the flick of the other man's gun to have me moving forward. For encouragement the driver pushed the muzzle of his gun into the small of my back.

On entering, a rectangular hall led into a narrow, forbidding corridor that disappeared into darkness both right and left. The building smelt of damp, decay and urine. In the weak light from the still open door behind me, I could see the floor was littered with broken glass, syringes and other drug detritus.

Still encouraged by the muzzle of a gun, I walked forward, crossing the corridor and entering a mirror hallway leading to another set of doors like the ones we had just come through. The lawyer opened the left hand one of this pair and walked down another four concrete steps that led into a massive inner courtyard. As I stepped down I realised the whole building was built as a hollow square. Fifty metres to each side. All the inner walls, as the outer, were lined with barred windows. This inner yard, a single, huge space had been laid in concrete, but the grey was almost completely overtaken by the vibrant green of weeds breaking through its wrecked surface.

I was pushed forward. My lawyer had stopped about fifteen metres further into the open space and was turning around, as if admiring his newly acquired kingdom. I assumed they wanted me to walk to him. So I did, stopping a few paces short as he completed his impromptu survey.

'How much have you asked for?' I asked.

He faced me. 'Asked for?'

'Yes. How much do you want? As a ransom?' I was quite impressed at how assured I sounded.

He laughed. Not an affected laugh, but a real, strong laugh. It surprised me. I hadn't expected that.

'You think this a… eh?' He called out to his colleagues in Ukrainian. The nearest, the passenger who had opened my door for me, said, 'Kidnap.'

'Yes. That is it,' my make-believe lawyer continued. He stepped forward, close enough for me to smell the stench of cigarettes on his breath. 'You think this is kidnap?' he asked.

About to answer I gave an involuntary cry as the two men behind me kicked the backs of my knees. I collapsed onto the concrete, pain shot through my kneecaps and up my thighs. My back went into spasm. One of the men held me upright by my collar. I felt tears in my eyes from the pain in my legs and the burning in my chest. The spasm in my back twisted the muscles from my waist to my shoulders. Gulping for breath I raised my still secured hands to wipe my eyes. The last thing I wanted was for any of them to see my tears.

'This is not a kidnap, Mr Frankland.' he reached inside my jacket pockets, removing my phone, my wallet and my Mont Blanc pen. Twirling it in his fingers he said, 'Pretty. Thank you. I shall use it well.'

'If this isn't a kidnap,' I said looking up and willing my back to relax. Willing my mind to relax. 'What is it you want?'

'Nothing. We have all we need. You have been…' he paused again and once more called to his colleagues in Ukrainian. This time the answer was, 'Upsetting.'

'Yes. This is it. You have been upsetting some people. Now you will not. It is that simple.' He gave a flick of his head. The man holding my collar let go and stepped away.

About to look around, my attention was instantly drawn back to my front. The lawyer cocked the pistol in his hand and my mind cleared of everything.

All that I had been doing, all that I had been wallowing about in. All that I had been wasting. All of it, was for nothing.

My heart hammered in my chest. I watched with fascination as he aimed the pistol at my head. My last strange thought was, 'Ah yes, that's a Glock-17.'

Then I decided, on my knees or not, to hold myself as straight as possible and look my killer in the eye.

Yet all I saw in my mind was an image of my parents and my brother.

Unlike all the stories I'd read, I heard the shot.

24

Kyiv – August 2010

A small, neat hole appeared in the middle of the lawyer's face. A bloom of red and brown and black burst from the back of his head, his gun hand, that had been so solid in its aim, fell to his side and his body crumpled in a heap.

The shouts of men, jumbled and panicked, mixed with other shouts, calm and assured.

I stayed perfectly still. Other than falling forward onto concrete there was not a lot else I could do and one thing I did remember clearly from training was that in a situation where armed men are running about, movement attracts attention.

Amidst the shouting, there were no more shots, yet I wondered if I would even hear them over the thundering of my heart and the pounding of the blood in my ears. Thoughts crowded in on me. Life didn't flash before me, nor had it at the vital, last moment, yet in a strange way, it sauntered through. Not in images or a movie reel, but with a feeling.

Hands reached under my armpits and pulled me to my feet while a short stocky man dressed in jeans and a black jumper came to stand in front of me and cut the plastic ties on my wrists with a knife. Once done, he nodded to the man still holding me up.

I was turned, like I was weightless and half carried-shuffled-run back up the steps, through the open door, across the corridor, out the other open door and into where the Mercedes had been parked. Two other dark sedans were fast approaching into the space. One skidded to a halt and four men, also in jeans and jumpers piled out and ran for the building. The other car looked to be heading straight for me but the driver executed an impressive handbrake turn and slid to a halt side on. The short stocky man ran forward and opened the nearest rear door.

I was bundled in and the man who had been carrying me slid in after me. I knew no Ukrainian but I imagined he shouted, Go! as we did. Rapidly. He reached across and pulled the seatbelt down over me before clipping it in. He did the same for his own. Only then did he turn his massive frame and look down on me. I stared back up at a fierce looking, bald, heavy browed, crooked nosed, barrel chested man who easily dwarfed my six foot two. He was dressed all in black, from his boots, to his jeans, to his jumper. Even his shoulder holster and handgun were the same.

'I told you I should have ridden in a car with you,' he said, in English much more practised than the first time we had met.

'Yes, Maksym, you were right.'

And he had been. Even after I'd tried to confirm the page signing, by ringing the lawyer's office this morning and there had been no answer. I'd put it down to being too early. They weren't open yet. My rational brain said, it was fine. My sense of fair play determined they'd be offended if I rocked up with my own massive version of a bodyguard. yet, I knew that hadn't been the main reason. The reason I'd eschewed Maksym's perfectly reasonable demands, given all the history of business executives being kidnapped in Ukraine, had been a much more stupid one.

Mac had looked like a complete idiot with his bodyguards in Vegas. A paranoid, hyper-egotistical idiot and I hadn't wanted to look the same, yet in denying it I had in fact pandered to my own ego. I was too good to look like Mac. I was not like him. I was not, as Kimberley had said, bat-shit-crazy.

Yet to make Maksym and his men be in a trail vehicle, just in case, had actually been the most bat-shit-crazy thing I could have done.

'We were lucky,' he said. 'That was not a kidnap.'

'No, I know. How did you know?'

'That old building, it is former Soviet hospital for the mind. Eh… Assembly?'

I frowned and tried to figure out what he meant. 'Asylum. An insane asylum?'

He twirled the fingers of one of his massive hands around his temple. 'Yes. Crazy people. Mental hospital. Insane asylum,' he said, sounding out the last words and no doubt committing them to his stock of English. 'Also now dumping ground for bodies. As soon as car started going east out of city I feared it might be going there. Most kidnap go north, direct for Belarus border. Sit over there so out of reach of police.'

'But how did you get there on foot?' I asked and he looked at me like I was insane.

'No, I have second car stay with you. In case I was wrong. My car and guys came here. Much faster than you. Your car careful not to be noticed. Drive safe. We were not. I got there two, three minutes before you. I tell Yevhen here,' he said pointing to the driver, 'to park car out of sight. Also he tell other car to come too and wait. Me and Stepan, the one who cut your ties, and Dmytro all went into building. It is not secure, always used by drug gangs, police lock it up with chains but they were stolen, so now it is open. Nothing left to steal. We went into corridor. You saw. It is very dark. My plan was to come behind them, make them talk, make them let you go, but it look like their leader not talk too long.'

'No. Seemed he had nothing much to say.'

'That is okay. I once told you I owed you and that I would be in your debt. Now I feel good. You want to come home and say hello to my Anastasia and Ksenia?'

I was struck by the strange normalness of the request. An invite to visit Maksym and his twin daughters. I'd seen a man die less than five minutes earlier. It was almost me dying five minutes earlier. Maksym was seemingly not bothered. Weirdly, neither was I. For now. Part of me wondered when the numb shock wore off, what the shellshock would be like.

'Eh, I'd love to, but I need to get to the air—Oh fuck.'

'What is wrong?' he said, his hand reaching for his pistol.

'My bags, all my stuff, my wallet, phone, pen, it is all back there.'

'Oh, okay,' he said moving his hand from his gun and taking out a phone.

A minute of conversation in Ukrainian and he ended the call. 'They will meet us at airport with all your things. Lucky you said, they were about to set fire to car. Ha!'

Knowing that I didn't want to know, but that I would ask anyway, I swallowed hard. 'Maksym, what happens, with the men back there?'

'The dead one is no concern. His body won't be found. Other two will agree to be quiet. Car will be burnt out. Easy.

Nothing to worry about.'

The clearness to my thoughts remained. The numbness to my feelings meant I couldn't grieve for the 'lawyer', but I did worry about the other two talking, or trying to do harm to Maksym. 'How can you be sure they will agree to be quiet? How can you be sure they won't seek revenge?'

He looked down and gave me a cheerful grin. 'You see things with British eyes. Here in Ukraine, since fall of Soviet, there are people who are hired for money. These three men probably do not know each other well. Even if they do, there is no money in revenge. As a contract kill, they have been paid already for the job. So no reason to die. That is why they put their guns down and put hands up. They go back and wait for next person to hire them.'

His words caused me to relive a moment from when I was on my knees. The sensation I felt was a thousand times more than a shiver and stilled to a calmness in seconds. 'Maksym, if your men haven't killed them yet, can you ask them to answer a question?'

The big man laughed. 'I told you, no more killing. When I talk to Dmytro about your bags, he say that the biggest concern for the other two was getting back into city. They asked for a lift. Ha! Funny, yes?'

My British eyes, nor my British head could understand. Thankfully they didn't have to.

'But you say you want a question answered?'

'Yes. Can you ask who hired them?'

'I would not expect them to have a name, but let us see,' he said, pulling out his phone again. The call lasted a little longer, but not so long that I began to worry I had put in motion some horrendous torture. He ended the call. 'No name. This is usual.'

I shrugged. 'Never mind.'

'But apparently he was French.'

***

The five days of field exercises had drawn to a close on the Friday with a live-firing session at Fort Hood's extended range. As Dan lay on the slightly raised firing point, he was shocked to realise he couldn't recall a single detail of any of the scenarios he'd been involved in, yet when he sighted along his M4's scope towards the stylised 'body' of the US Army's High Percentage Shot paper targets 100 yards away, he *could* see, in high-definition, each face belonging to the men he had 'killed' during the exercise. Rationally he knew it had been make-believe. The 'casualties' weren't dead. At the same time, he knew, without a shadow of doubt, he had not hesitated to pull the trigger and on each occasion he also knew that he had felt... nothing.

Now, lying prone with his eye to the scope of his assault rifle, his vision became blurred with tears. He fired and fired and fired again. When the 30-round magazine was empty, he swapped it out for another and engaged the next target set.

When the tally was completed for the day, Staff Sergeant Chappell, senior enlisted man in charge of range operations, gave a low whistle as he handed over a range score report.

'That's seriously good shooting, Sir. You are 149 on centre mass or head, for 150 rounds and the stray was in an arm.

Dan gave a shrug and said something about, 'being lucky, I guess.'

'No Sir, that is skill and practise,' the Staff Sergeant said with a knowing look. 'You are one fine example, Sir.'

Instead of satisfaction, all Dan could feel was numb, except for the intense weight pressing in on his head and crushing his chest.

25

London – August 2010

I had an hour between getting into my apartment and leaving to catch a train up to my parents' house near Newcastle.

Throughout the flight home from Kyiv, Emma and I had chatted amenably. My morning had been dismissed with a 'Yes, all done,' and I had functioned quite normally. The numb feelings when I tried to recall what had actually happened were still insulating me from myself, but I had noticed it had taken a few gins before, during and now, after to keep my hands steady.

Pouring another generous glass, I made the first of the three calls I planned to make. 'Andy, do you still owe me a favour?'

'Yep.'

'I'll send you a text soon. It's my preferred hotel in Macau. An American owned one. I stayed in it once, remember?'

Andy had been part of the operation that had seen me transit through Macau to reach Hong Kong.

'Yes. I remember when that was.'

'There was a concierge at that hotel. Excellent service. I am thinking of hiring some people but I can't recall his name. Could you get a staff list?'

'Only for that particular month?'

'Yeah and only the concierges. Is that possible?'

'Everything's possible, Luke.'

I laughed.

'What's funny?'

'Ah, just I heard that from an old friend not long ago. And yeah, it seems it is. Thanks.'

'Where shall I send it?'

'I'll text you two emails. Mine and a friend's. Can you send to both?'

'Sure. Talk soon.'

The call ended and I scrolled to another number. 'Steve?'

'Hello, Luke. You feeling better?'

I glanced down at my free hand. The tremor was easing with my latest gin, the colour of my arm was now a brownish-yellow. My mind was beginning to fill with glimpses of what had only been this morning and sweat was making my shirt cling to me in my air-conditioned apartment.

'Yeah, never been better. Listen, I wondered if you could do a couple of things for me?'

'Fire away. We like doing things for you. Your company pays well.'

His choice of phrase and the idea that others had been paid well for this morning crashed into me, threatening to knock me over. 'Good, glad to hear it. I need you to email me the name that you found attached to the secondary account.'

'The one that is close to the original?'

'Yeah, but I think you might be right, Steve. I think it's the original. Can you also copy it to an email I'll text you? '

269

'Sure, okay. What else?'

'That's a bit more sensitive. Can you meet me at King's Cross, entrance to Platform 6, in about forty-five minutes?'

'Yep. Paul too?'

'No, just you. Then if you say no, he hasn't had to be involved.'

'Okay,' Steve answered without hesitation. 'See you then.'

He rung off.

I called Washington DC.

'Luke. How are you feeling?'

Repeating the same lie I'd told Steve minutes earlier, I told Pat that I was going to send him an encrypted file. The contents of which I had written on the plane coming back from Kyiv. I also told him that he would hear it all first hand from Kimberley when she arrived into DC, but that it was confirmed by a source who worked for Ailinka and had been in the room during negotiations with Mac.

'How bad is it?' he asked.

'We'll be lucky if we can find a buyer if he keeps going the way he's going. But Pat,'

'Uh oh, that sounds worse, go on.'

'I'm sorry to do this, Pat, but I have to ask you something.'

'Go on.'

'Regarding my last trip to Toronto and our visit to Mac's. You've had time to process what Mac said. Time to consider it for a while. Do you still trust my take on the whole Jules thing?'

'I can see why you apologised before you asked me. If you think I didn't trust you, that is a bit disappointing, but I can understand it and I can assure you, yes, I still trust your instincts. I think the guy is as dirty as you think. My only issue is how the hell we get rid of him without derailing the whole company or Mac firing us both.'

'Thanks, Pat. I appreciate it and in return, I think I might have a way. If I'm right, our head of intelligence in Europe doesn't have the background he should have.'

'And what background does he have?'

'When I end this call, I'm going to text two separate sources to your email. They'll copy you into some information, one probably right away and one, well I don't know how long it will take him to get it. Anyway, the first will be a single name, the second will be a list of concierges that worked in a hotel in Macau that Mac used to use back in his days of running high-rollers through the casinos.'

'Okay, and?' Pat asked.

'And if the names get a match, then that is where Mac met Jules. He isn't an intel specialist, he's a concierge and for whatever reason, and this is what I don't know, Mac made him the head of his start-up's intel program.'

'Shit. Our credibility will go through the floor.'

'And our sales price,' I added.

'Why would he do that?'

'All I can tell you is Mac used to have some, let's call them creative methods of getting in and out of Chinese territories. Maybe he was rumbled by the Chinese authorities, maybe he got caught up in something he shouldn't have. I don't know, maybe Jules is his secret love child from a fling in Quebec. Whatever the reason, if those names match, we need to get rid of him, but if I go to Mac with it, he'll shut me down again and probably fire me on the spot.'

'He might not believe me either, but even if he does, you know Jules will get a severance pay-off. He won't be walking away a broken and destitute man,' Pat said in his usual reasonable manner.

'I know. And trust me, for all sorts of reasons I won't share, I really want him to be broken. Maybe even worse. But for the things that are driving me to hate him, I have no proof and even if I did, to bring them into the light of day would be dropping a very good friend of mine into a world of hurt.'

I thought of Maksym and his colleagues. There was no way I could mention what had happened even if it meant I could point the finger at Jules. I had to take what I could get.

'Okay then. I'll wait for the files and the names.'

'One last thing, Pat.'

'Yes?'

'When we do come to sell and the deal goes through, I'd recommend we make absolutely sure that our options are in cash or we can liquidate any residual shares immediately.'

***

The meeting with Steve at Kings Cross took less than ten minutes, most of it him checking if I was okay.

I told him part of what had happened to me in Kyiv, but obscured it as an attempted kidnap that had been thwarted at the outset. He told me to go to the cops and I explained there was no proof, but I knew who was responsible and what I had to do.

'And that is?' he asked.

'You kept all the bank account details in the trail you did from Macau to France?'

'Of course.'

'Are you familiar with a reverse?'

Steve looked blank. 'You mean a reverse engineered hack?'

'No, a reverse is when a pickpocket takes a mark's wallet or watch or whatever and plants it on someone else.'

Steve's face broke into a broad grin. 'How the hell do you know about pickpocketing? You never do cease to amaze me, matey.'

'A very old version of the Artful Dodger once told me,' I laughed. 'Although he might be young depending on how you count it.'

This time Steve looked properly confused.

'Never mind that. Can you and Paul lift money from Macau, with no air gaps and put it through a few accounts, leaving it ready for a final transfer, but with enough of a fingerprint to be traced?'

'It's easy to do. Is the final account owned by the person you know arranged your kidnap?'

I hadn't liked lying to Steve although he didn't need to know I'd nearly been shot, still the less lies the better. 'No, but it is owned by the man I am convinced asked for it to be done. Is that okay?'

'Yeah. It's fine by me and it'll be fine by Paul too. When do we make the transfer?'

'When I text you a go. Not before.'

'Sure. For me it'd be tough. For Paul, it'll be child's play.'

I stood, shook his hand and boarded the First Class carriage to take me north to Newcastle. The benefit of a larger seat and complimentary food and drink were never wasted on me. The speed of the complimentary service though, was not as quick as it needed to be and their gin and tonic was shocking, although the rose wine was of a good standard. Hence I'd brought my own supplies. I glanced at my watch. It was 4pm. The date indicator showed, as Kimberley had mentioned the night before, Friday the thirteenth. So far, despite Jules' best efforts, I'd been lucky. All I had to do now was make it through to mid-night, I said to myself and took another hit on the hipflask I had packed. I needed to keep the numbness from wearing off.

The taxi dropped me off at my parents' spacious house in its picturesque village at 7.35pm. The wonders of a north east summer and a sunset that wouldn't reach here until nearly 9pm, meant the sound of children playing and the smell of bar-b-ques was in the air. I walked into the hall, dropped my bag and continued through to the back garden. My father was relaxing in a deckchair and my mother was balanced on a small set of steps with a pair of shears in her hand.

'Good to see we have our priorities sorted,' I said.

They both came and hugged me. My mum, holding me out at arm's length. 'Are you okay, son? You look a little…'

'Peaky,' my dad finished for her. 'Your eyes are a bit… off colour?' he added. 'You sure you're feeling okay?'

'Yes, I'm fine. I'm just going to nip to the toilet, then I'll come back out.'

'Hungry?' my virtual chef of a mother asked. Just in case I had faded away having been at home for five minutes.

'No, it's okay, but thank you. I ate on the train,' I lied.

Ducking back inside I retrieved a bottle of Tanqueray from my bag and took a long drink before tucking it back under my shirts. Climbing the stairs I went to my childhood bedroom, dropped my bag on my bed, plugged my phone in to charge and went to the toilet.

The shock of seeing my urine a deep reddish black colour, almost caused me to fall. I felt tremors running through my body. Gasping for breath, I barely managed to finish and zip my trousers. The room was spinning and I could smell the damp and dank of the Soviet asylum crushing me from all sides.

I twisted the tap and ran cold water, bending my head to splash myself.

Slowly I felt more in control. I splashed more water and stood straighter. Running my hands through my hair I focussed on anything other than the pictures beginning to fill my mind of a man next to me with a gun in my ribs and that same man looking at me with a hole in his face.

Turning to the bathroom mirror I looked hard into my own eyes and saw that my mum had been right. The whites of my eyes were yellow. The same shade as the skin on my arms. My thoughts about Kyiv dissolved away. My breathing returned to normal, but the anxiety about my urine, my arms and now my eyes clawed at my insides.

I heard my mum's voice calling from the foot of the stairs. 'Luke, are you alright? Could you come and give me a hand? I'm too short to reach the top of the hedge and your father's no better,' she ended with a laugh that brought a smile to my face and allowed a weight to lift from me. I checked my appearance a last time in the mirror and headed downstairs.

Coming into the garden my mum was pointing to a single wayward shoot growing from the garden hedge, so tall, that even perched on the top of her admittedly small steps, she hadn't been able to reach. Handing me the shears she returned to her deckchair, next to my dad's.

I stood on the steps and with my height looked right over the hedge across the adjoining fields to the horizon. A beachball was floating there. A colourful, blow-up beachball, hovering on the horizon. I was mesmerised as it solidified into a marble of translucent glass which began to move slowly towards me.

My peripheral vision went to black. The marble shifted in the light, then accelerated violently, hurtling towards me down a black cylindrical tunnel. I could see nothing else. The ball and the blackness forming and coalescing, shifting and merging until my brain realised what it was seeing.

The muzzle of a pistol.

My body convulsed and my skin exploded in jagged prickles. The sound of my mother's screams accompanied my world turning to black as I toppled backwards.

26

The specialist in charge of the intensive care unit walked into the family seating area.

'Mr and Mrs Frankland?'

My parents stood and followed her into a separate room. Closing the door she waited for them to sit on the sofa, then took the chair next to them.

'Your son has alcoholic hepatitis. I'm afraid it's advanced. Very advanced.'

Neither of my parents spoke. The look on their faces, probably one the doctor had seen more times than she cared to recall, prompted her on.

'He is also suffering from severe tremors and there is a lot of electrical activity within his brain that is akin to, but different from epilepsy. I have put him into a temporary induced coma to allow us to run some more tests and scans, but I have to tell you that given his current physical condition, there is no way out of it. Not with current medicines and treatment plans.'

'What do you mean, there's no way out of it?' my dad asked, finally finding his voice.

'I mean that given the levels of toxicity in his body, it is an amazement to me how he has been functioning for the last, two or three weeks. Perhaps even the last month. He shouldn't have been able to keep going, but he did and I am afraid that leaves us where we are now.'

'Which is where? Just come out and say it,' said my dad, gripping my mother's hand.

'At best case, I would say forty days.'

'Oh my God,' my mum said as the tears began to stream down her face.

'And at worst?' my dad asked, trying to keep himself strong for his wife.

'Twenty? Twenty, maybe.'

***

It was almost 6pm on Friday evening by the time the students got back to their on-base accommodation in Fort Hood. Given their exertions, they were on free-time until midday of the following day, when they would spend the rest of the weekend sorting out 'admin' as the Army called it. Laundry, preparing uniform, cleaning up their personal space, plus a bit of down-time, maybe a trip to the PX. But it wasn't all a free pass as they'd also be expected to prepare for their end of course presentations. A half hour on a topic that had been assigned to them, relevant to what they had learnt, to be delivered to the Directing Staff and the rest of the course attendees. The students, or at least the twenty-two who had made it this far, would deliver the briefings over the Tuesday, Wednesday and Thursday of the following week, and, assuming all met the grade, they'd graduate at a small, non-formal event on Friday before dispersing back to their home units.

Dan closed the door to his room, threw his kit bag into the corner and stripped off to take his first proper shower in a week.

He picked his phone off the nightstand where it had lain for the duration of the field exercise. You didn't carry a personal cell phone on live operations, so it hadn't been a shock that they'd been 'banned' for the week. He'd told Ryan he'd call as soon as he got back. Not expecting to see anything on the screen, Shirlene wouldn't have been calling to wish him 'a nice day'. His heart gave a lurch when he saw seven missed calls. Three from Wednesday, two from Thursday and two from today. He opened the call log, but all were from a number that had no correlation to any of his phone's contacts. There was another notification, two voice messages. One from this morning and the first from Wednesday afternoon. He clicked on the earlier call and heard silence, then a cough, then a young man's voice.

'Dan? Dan? Are you there? It's Cody. Dan?'

A longer pause. A stifled sob.

'He's sending me back, Dan… My dad. He's making me go back to another weekend. The Pastor rang. Said I'd benefit from attending again, earlier than planned. I know the real reason Dan. You won't be there. He wants to get me on my own. Dan?'

A silence, like the kid had been hoping Dan might pick up.

'You said you'd help me. I'm frightened. I don't know what to do.'

Another silence, then the message ended.

Dan felt sick, but clicked on the next voice message. It was timed at 10.35am this morning.

'It's Cody, Dan. My dad's driving me to the Church tonight. You said you'd help. Can you come and get me? Please? Dan?'

A long drawn out silence ended with a sob and the message stopped.

The last missed call was timed at 1pm. Dan checked his watch. Nearly seven hours earlier. He scrolled to the call log and clicked on the number. The phone rang. Dan waited impatiently, pacing about his small room, feeling his anger rise, feeling his frustrations peak. Even if he had been here, even if he could have taken the calls, he couldn't get to Nebraska. You didn't simply go AWOL from Fort Hood and get a flight to Nebraska in short order, but maybe he could have listened, maybe he could have been an ear. Maybe, he decided he could have rung Pastor Harold and threatened all sorts of retribution on him if he laid even a finger on Cody. Maybe he could do…his thoughts trailed off as the phone rang out and clicked onto messenger.

'Cody, it's Dan. Call me back. I've been out on exercise for the last days. No phone. But I'm here now. Call me.'

He clicked off the call and stalked about the room like a caged tiger.

After five minutes of frantically jumbled thoughts, which only heightened his frustrations, he decided to call the Pastor's direct number. He had no clue whether it would work but he intended to threaten the man with everything he could think of. Opening his phone's browser he searched for the code needed to block an outgoing number. The last thing he needed was the Pastor recognising his cell phone number and not answering.

'Pastor Harold Williams, Church of the Rise—'

'Shut the fuck up you piece of shit and listen to me. It's Dan Stückl here. I swear to the God you hold high and mighty, that if you lay one hand on Cody I will rip you limb from fucking limb. Do you hear me. That punch from last time will be nothing. I'll tear your heart out and make you eat it. Are you hearing me?' Dan drew a breath and noticed his right hand was balled tight. He wished the Pastor was standing in front of him.

'Did you hear what I said?' He shouted into the phone.

A pause. Silence. Then Harold's voice, but much less assured than its usual sing-song lilt. A tremble to it. Dan registered it as fear. Good. He should be scared for once. After all the fear he'd no doubt instilled in those he'd abused. He wanted the big man to be terrified.

'I didn't. I promise. I didn't touch him.'

'You better not, I mean it Harold, I'll kill you if you do. Put him on the phone, go get him now and put him on the phone.'

Another pause. But Dan could still hear the man's breathing on the line. 'Harold, are you going to get him?'

'I...I can't, Dan.'

'Oh you can Harold. Go get Cody and put him on the damned phone.'

'I can't... You haven't heard... He isn't here... He won't be coming.'

'What do you mean?' Dan's question was automatic but as he was saying it his subconscious mind registered the potential meanings of what the Pastor had said. His legs weakened and he collapsed onto his bed. He managed to say, 'Why isn't he there?'

***

He rang home. Shirlene said few words and passed the phone to Ryan. The little boy's conversation was excited and mostly about what he'd done in school that day, followed by what his favourite cartoon character had been doing on TV that evening. Dan listened and didn't interrupt. He had let down everyone who relied on him. He knew, in a place deep inside himself that he didn't want to examine, he would let down Ryan and Lilly-Anne one day. It was inevitable. He choked back a sob and managed to say that Ryan was a good boy and that he loved him. Then he asked him to put Mommy back on the phone.

He convinced Shirlene to hold the phone next to Lilly-Anne and as she gurgled and giggled, he told her he loved her too.

'Is that enough?' Shirlene said, breaking the spell of his daughter.

'Yes. Thank you. That is enough.'

'Great. I guess I'll see you when you're home,' she said and ended the call.

Dan stared at the screen for a long time. Then he made his way into the bathroom and showered.

He stacked the uniform he'd worn on the exercise in the small laundry hamper and squared away the rest of his kit. Then he lay on top of his bunk and shut his eyes.

***

It was 4am on Saturday morning. It would be 10am in London. Dan lifted his phone. The number wasn't stored in it, but he had memorised it a long time ago and he had to hope it had never been changed. For all the times he had wished to do this and for all the times he had denied it, he knew once and for all that life was too short.

He also knew the very moment he texted a message that the die was cast. Shirlene checked his phone records every month and had done ever since they'd returned from the UK. Angry she may have been, but not stupid. Even a good old Cornhusker girl like her knew what an international dialling code looked like. Perhaps he could have bought a burner, but then she'd have seen the transaction on their bank account and anyway, the truth was, she had been right in that last call to her. He'd had, and it was, enough.

He took a moment to compose the message he had thought about sending for a long, long time.

'Luke. It's Dan. I can't do this anymore. Can I come to you?'

He pressed send.

***

My parents went back home late on Friday night and were back to sit next to my ICU bed the following day.

Finally, at the insistence of a nurse, who told them they needed to look after themselves, they went home to try to sleep on Saturday night.

At 10pm, still not anywhere near to sleeping, but sitting in their kitchen drinking tea and hugging each other when one or other of them started to cry again, a loud tone of a mobile phone sounded in the house.

My dad sprung to his feet and grabbed his, even though he knew it wasn't. As the tone played on he went into the hallway. The sound was upstairs. By the time he got to my room, the call had rung out.

He saw the message notifications on the screen. He hoped that I hadn't deviated from what the family had always done. Entering a four digit code, sure enough the phone opened. He smiled at the fact that his cyber-security expert of a son still used the family code that they'd always used. On reading the text messages, he stopped smiling and hurried downstairs. By the time he reached the kitchen there was a new notification. A voice message. Sitting next to his wife he pressed play.

It took them almost exactly an hour to decide what they should do.

He'd been like a son to them. They knew their son had loved him and he had reciprocated. They also knew the circumstances had been wrong. The timing, lousy.

'Nowhere near as bad as now,' my mum said.

My dad pressed the call button and the phone took a short time to connect.

The voice sounded like he was in the next room.

'Oh thank God, Luke.'

***

Dan had sent three more messages over the course of the next ten hours. Luke may have been many things, but forgetting to carry his phone or respond to messages wasn't one of them.

Finally, twelve hours after his first message, Dan, clinging to the hope that Luke had changed his number, pressed the call button. The phone rang out and went to messenger.

'Hi, this is Luke. Thank you for calling. Please leave me a message and I shall get back to you.'

The brief joy of hearing that voice was crushed by the fact that yes, it was his phone and that therefore, yes, he was ignoring Dan's texts. Perhaps a message might make a difference.

'Luke. It's Dan. I need you. Please call me.'

An hour later his phone began to vibrate. A UK number. Dan grabbed it up, 'Oh thank God, Luke.'

'No Dan, it's his father. I'm sorry, but I have some bad news.'

***

Staff Sergeant Chappell gave a semi-formal salute from behind the high counter. 'Good afternoon, Captain Stückl, how can I help you on this bright and beautiful Sunday?'

'Good afternoon Staff. Do you never take time off?'

'My turn for weekend duty, Sir. That's how it goes

sometimes. Even old hands like me have to do our turn. Show the youngsters we still can,' he said with a deep laugh.

Dan was instantly reminded of another old hand of a Staff Sergeant. The smile he returned to Chappell did not go beyond his lips.

The moment stretched. Dan felt a hot Afghan wind blow across him. He shivered.

'Sir?'

Back in the moment, he refocussed. 'Sorry... Eh, yeah, I wonder if I can take advantage of your fabulous facilities?'

'So you can be lucky again, eh, Sir?' The Staff Sergeant gave him a mischievous wink and tapped the side of his nose. 'I knew it was all about skill and practise, Sir. And yes, you are certainly more than welcome to avail yourself. It's a pleasure to see someone with such a talent. What's your preference?'

'Well, we did a lot of work on the M4s over the last few weeks, so maybe the M9 today?'

'Absolutely. Do you want to use the combat range or the indoor bays?'

'Indoor I think. Just to get my hand and eye back in.'

Chappell hustled away and returned in less than a minute.

Dan took four magazine clips and the offered M9 Beretta. The standard sidearm for the US Army. He'd carried one on every operational deployment of his Army career. He'd once stared at the wrong end of one as he sat on his cot in a darkened room in Afghanistan, but had resisted the urge he'd felt.

Signing for the weapon and the ammunition he walked through to the indoor firing range, lifting a set of ear protectors as he went.

It was a Sunday afternoon. Most soldiers on base would be out on personal time. The married ones would be in their houses having family time. The duty staff, like Chappell would be at their posts. No one, apart from Dan, was down here.

He walked to booth number twenty, for no other reason than it was at the end. He set the ear protectors on the counter top and loaded the Beretta with the first of the 15-round magazines and dropped the hammer. The gun sat neatly in his hand, the weight of it somehow comfortingly familiar.

He thought of Cody. Hanging from a makeshift rope in the hallway of his home. Found by his father an hour before they were due to leave for the Church of the Risen Son. He thought of Luke, dying in an English hospital. Was his way any less self-inflicted than Cody's? Yet at least Luke would be surrounded by those who loved him. Well…by almost all of those who loved him.

Dan turned the weapon, so that the muzzle pointed up at his face. A push of his thumb and the safety would disengage. A double pull on the trigger and that would be that. Those had been his self-same thoughts that time in Afghanistan. He'd not done it then.

This time was different.

27

Dr Wakefield lifted the clipboard charts from the foot of my bed and, as she had done each and every day she called by to see me said, 'Remarkable.'

I shuffled myself straighter in the bed and said, like I had every day she stopped in, 'I know.'

We shared a laugh while she asked me her usual questions, all of which I answered in the same way I had for the preceding two weeks.

'Now,' she said replacing the charts, 'I have a few student doctors in the hospital today. Would you mind if I were to bring them in? Rather a guinea pig in a cage type of thing, but given you are the first to receive the experimental treatment, I think it would be very useful for them. What say you?'

'I say yes, Doctor Wakefield. With pleasure.'

She parted with a hearty cheerio and I thought that the woman could ask me to chop off one of my legs and I'd say yes. I was, after all, even in the best case scenario, meant to have died last week. The fact that this specialist Gastroenterologist with a liking for liver, mine in particular, had embarked on a series of drug cocktails, that although very recently approved for use, had never been used on a patient in my condition was the only reason I was here.

Nor was her revolutionary suggestion expected to work. In fact, ten days after being admitted and with either ten or thirty days left to live, depending on which odds you were backing, the choice was put to me quite starkly.

'Luke, nothing we have tried is working.'

I knew that. My organs were failing. My skin, on every part of me, not just my arms, was a deep ugly shade of brown-yellow. I hadn't had a drink in ten days and I felt as sick as I had ever felt. I also was strangely at peace with the idea of dying having come face to face with it in Kyiv. This relatively slower and more painful way seemed altogether more sadistic.

'So I suggest,' she was continuing in her Yorkshire, edged with a bit of Tyneside, accent, 'that I start you on a mix of steroids in conjunction with a drug that's been pre-released but not fully signed off on yet. You okay with that?'

'Okay, if you think it will help. I'm meant to be dead soon anyway, so what harm can it do?' I'd managed in a weak voice that annoyed me more than my weak body.

'That's the thing,' she said. 'I do think it will help, however, there is no guarantee and you do need to be aware,' she paused and for the first time that I could recall, placed her hand on mine, 'very aware, Luke. If it doesn't work, it may have more detrimental effects.'

'How much more detrimental can it get?' I asked.

'Even if it works you might only have a four in ten chance of being alive this time next month. Of course, if it and you react badly, the truth is, it could kill you quicker.'

I raised my eyebrows. 'How much quicker?'

'Half the time.'

Without hesitation I said, 'Let's do it. Do you need me to sign something.'

She did. I did.

'One other thing, Luke.'

I nodded for her to go on. I was too weak to talk.

'Honestly, a lot of what happens now won't necessarily be down to any drugs or treatments. It will be down to how much you want to live.'

I coughed and swallowed hard. 'I've cheated him once, not so long ago. I don't fancy handing victory to him so soon after that.'

She squeezed my hand gently and said, 'Good to hear.'

Three days later, the irreversible conditions leading me to my death, reversed.

Now, thirty-five days later, I was almost back to being my usual shade of pinkish-white. My urine, no longer the colour of tea without milk, was now between clear and mildly yellow depending on how many little cups of water I was managing to drink a day and my weight had fallen by fourteen pounds. I felt terrific. I also had no clue, nor no care for the world of cyber, Mac, Jules or any of the rest of it as part of Dr Wakefield's treatment had been for me to be as stress free as possible. That meant no phones, no computers, no email, no work. The first few days had been like a secondary withdrawal. The booze and the buzz. Afterwards, both got easier. Now, I wondered if I would ever go back to the latter. I knew I would never be able to go back to the former. Also, critically, I didn't want to.

I'd expected crippling traumatic shock from my experiences in Kyiv, yet with the booze out of my system, it hadn't come in the way I thought it would. Sober, I looked back on that morning as a series of lessons. Don't refuse to do necessary actions based on anyone else's ego. Do rely on friends. Don't waste your life anymore. There were more, but most importantly, out of all of them was my sure and absolute knowledge that in my time of dire peril, it was my family who had come to mind.

My parents had been in every day, even those first four days when I'd been in an induced coma. My brother arrived on that fourth day, having flown in from Australia with, he said, the intention of staying until I was better. A week or two later, when I was on the mend, I realised he must have come initially with the intention of staying until I was dead. Either way I was quite touched. Others had come. Steve and Paul, with a sotto voce confirmation they had done and prepared all I needed. Emma, Mark and his wife, who had flown over from Cyprus just to come and see me. I was beyond humbled.

Rachael Kennedy and Ashley Young, Josh Long and Ritchie Adams, who was still so broad in his Scottish accent I mostly nodded when he asked me questions. Even Steph, the Office Manager from my time in MOD. I wasn't sure she'd ever been north of Watford before. A good few others sent cards. The one from Mac was, because I knew Mac's writing, signed and sent by Alexis. That was okay. Karma would find a way. With a helping hand.

Despite the cards and the visitors, I had given a promise to Dr Wakefield not to enquire about any form of work, past, present or future. Steve had volunteered his information, so I felt I hadn't broken my word.

Now though, if I was going to be a specimen for inspection, I felt that perhaps I was strong enough to face the outside world again. A week was apparently a long time in politics. Tomorrow would mark seven weeks since I'd been admitted to hospital. I was still thinking about that when a barrage of fresh faced kids, who looked like they might be just out of high school, came in wearing white coats. When they left I asked Dr Wakefield to remain. I might have known she and my parents were, of course, one step ahead.

***

The agreement was, I could go home. The stipulations were I would come back, almost every other day, for blood tests and physical evaluations. I agreed. First though, my parents would be in to see me and later I'd have a visitor coming from Twenty-Twenty. There was some information I needed to be told and Dr Wakefield wanted me to be in a safe place when I learnt it. I wasn't stressed. I was intrigued. If all was okay after those two and the weekend passed easily and without drama, I could go home on Monday.

The following morning, I sat with my parents in the day room for in-patients. It was early and the room was bright, light and empty save for us. My father took me through the fact that Dan had reached out to me. I asked him for the details. He told me all he knew. The text messages, the voice mail. He let me listen to it. He told me about the call he had made back and what he had told Dan at the time. He told me he'd tried on numerous occasions since to call back and update him on my improving condition, but there had been no answer.

Intriguingly, seven weeks before I would have entertained no further discussion. I'd have punched the call back button and given my all to talk to him, yet here and now, after Kyiv, after the seizure and after not drinking alcohol for more than a month, when I had heard Dan's voice on the phone I'd felt... not nothing, I'd never feel nothing. More it was a mild detachment. An interest in a friend who I'd lost touch with. Sitting here, with mum holding my hand, I knew my priorities in life had changed.

Dan hadn't featured in my last thoughts in that open square with a pistol pointing at me. It had been the same at the hospital. When I'd come round from the induced coma and saw my parents and brother sitting by my bed, they had been enough. I hadn't thought of Dan, hadn't imagined him there. Lastly I knew that for far too long my melancholy had stemmed from the drink and I drank because of my melancholy. Clear of both, I had a new perspective. There would be no more grieving for what I could not have.

'Are you okay, son?'

'Yes, Mum. I am.'

***

Two hours later, Pat Harris strode into see me. I was again humbled. Though with Pat here, I couldn't see how to avoid talking about work. As he stepped to one side, Dr Wakefield was behind him.

'You are released from your promise,' she said and walked away.

'You didn't have to come all the way across the Atlantic,' I said embarrassed at the kindness.

'I did,' he said and leant forward to give me hug. Something he'd never done before. 'I'm glad you're alive buddy.'

'Me too. So is it trite for me to cover my English embarrassment and ask, what brings you here?'

He gave a laugh and took a seat. 'Ailinka pulled out. Word is Mac did indeed ask for all of those things Emma warned you about.'

I shrugged in as Gallic a way as I could muster.

'A few of the others who had been sniffing around also went. Each approach of course came at a reduced offer.'

'No surprise,' I said. 'Do we have any value left?'

'We got a last ditch approach and I decided that the SVPs would handle it. We threatened Mac that we'd lock him in a janitor's cupboard if he opened his mouth. With him suitably warned, we kept him out of the final sale negotiations and without his grandstanding and stupidity, we sealed the deal at a much better price than he was on track to get us.'

I smiled, knowing Pat probably wasn't joking about the janitor's cupboard. 'So who and how much?'

'VecThreat.'

'Bloody hell, they were smaller than us when Mac started on his crusade.'

'Yeah. By the time the bids fell lower and lower and then the trade press started reports of all cyber being overvalued, we were lucky they muscled in.'

'All cyber?' I asked my interest piquing.

'Bad actors in a couple of companies. Paying third parties to manufacture threats,' Pat said, stone-faced.

'Bugger. Imagine that. Who got caught?'

'Couple of smaller firms out west, but it sent enough shockwaves through the trade to rattle confidence.'

'I'll bet. So are we in the process of selling? Do we have to redo all the due diligence? Do we still have our bad egg?'

'No, not quite and no.'

'Go on,' I said.

'The deal completed on Tuesday. Unless you'd been scouring the inside pages of *Computer Weekly*, you'd have missed it. Not the big Ailinka Software coup we'd hoped for. No fireworks and razzmatazz!'

'No smoke and mirrors either,' I thought to myself, but instead said, 'No, I guess not, but still, a sale's a sale. How come the due diligence completed so quickly?'

'I'd been setting us up for due diligence since I came on as SVP. All the preliminary work for Ailinka stood up for VecThreat, although I was still planning for about 60 days.'

'What happened?'

'They wanted us and their board were well aware their own value was getting knocked about too, so they accelerated everything. Threw people from their end into checking everything and as all our information was already there, they did it in 31 days. I was impressed.'

I nodded. It was quick for an acquisition, but not the fastest I'd heard about. 'And Jules?' I asked, hoping he had fallen under a Parisian metro train.

'Your lists matched.'

'Yeah, I figured. Julien Guérionne?' I asked.

'Yeah. Not a stone's throw from Jules Guérin.'

'And?'

'And I told Mac he was to show Jules the exit door or I'd blow the whistle.'

'He finally agreed?'

'He did, but if you hoped Jules would walk away broken…'

'No. I knew we'd have to buy his silence. How much?'

'To leave quietly, the week of the sales announcement, he'd get a package equal to what he was originally entitled to.'

'Fair enough. If it had gone any other way we'd all be broke.'

'True, but I attached some strings,' Pat said with a grin.

'Around his neck?'

'Ha! No, but his pay-out is staggered. Unlike ours. His will be paid in annual lump sums over seven years and if he so much as breathes a word about what went on, he defaults on the rest. I figured no one would care in seven years.'

'Well, that's better than I could have hoped for. Nice work, Pat,' I said and meant it. Jules could have destroyed every last vestige of value in the company. He had to be kept quiet and short of trying to kill him, like I know he had tried to do to me, buying his silence was the best way. 'So, you said our pay-out wouldn't be staggered,' I continued. 'Go on then. How much did we get?'

Pat stood, took a folded piece of paper from his back pocket and handed it to me. I had a vivid memory of him doing the same thing in my old office in Bateleur Bank. On that piece of paper had been a number which I initially mistook for his re-dundancy pay out and which had turned out to be mine. This time I paused. Holding the square of crème coloured paper I asked, 'Is this the amount we sold the company for, the amount you're getting or the amount I'm due?'

'The latter,' he said retaking his seat.

In the same way as I had lost all my eloquence when I had seen Lily in GCHQ, so when I opened the piece of paper I simply said, 'Well fuck me! That *is* a big number.'

'Quite,' Pat said and reached out to shake my hand.

After a lot more congratulatory handshakes and back slaps, gentle ones on his part, Pat rose to leave with promises to keep in touch and invites for me to come to his lake side house. I agreed and I knew, when I could, I would. This was not the smoke and mirrors or superficial friendship of Mac.

'Oh Pat,' I called and he turned in the doorway.

'I assume Mac's reaped his own payday?"

'Yeah. Relatively. He and us would have got a lot more had he managed to keep his mouth shut in the original negotiations.'

'True. When do you think all the people we know and like will have taken their full options as cash assets?'

'Eh...' Pat hesitated and frowned. 'Nine months tops. Why's that?'

'Just wondering. Cheers to us.'

'Cheers to us. Stay well, Luke.'

28

London – April 2011

I'd been out of hospital for six weeks when I got a cryptic call from Andy Gibson.

For that month and a half I'd stayed with my parents, been fussed over and fed almost continually by my mum, gone on walks with my dad, arranged to break the lease on my London apartment and contracted a removal company to clear all of my belongings into long-term storage. I'd also not had any alcohol. The seven weeks in the hospital had been one thing, the six on the outside certainly harder, but strangely nowhere near as hard as I imagined it would have, or could have, been.

Also not as painful as I'd imagined had my thoughts been of Dan. At my request, my dad tried a couple more times to ring the number we had. I didn't want to do it as I could imagine the conversation if Shirlene got to the phone first. Hearing my voice would have sent her into a complete fit, but I figured she'd be so confused by my dad's voice she'd hand the phone to Dan with little delay. Each time we tried and there was no answer, the twinge of regret I felt weakened. After three weeks, having tried at least once a week, when my dad asked if I wanted to try again, I said, 'No. I think we're done now. I need to move on and live.'

He had reached up and given my shoulder a squeeze. That had been enough.

With no booze and walking every day, even with my mum's fattening of the prodigal son, I had lost another twenty pounds in weight, so I was in a clothes shop in Newcastle when my phone rang.

'Luke, it's Andy. Want to come and work for a living?'

'Finally! I thought you'd never ask. Will I be double-oh eight?'

'Double oh heck would be closer.'

'Charming. I have a recruiter friend you could learn from. So if not a secret agent, what would you like from me?'

'Our mutual friend, Paula and I are thinking of exploring what might be on the horizon. New cyber problem sets from the Chinese Government and others.'

'Okay, and you'd like me to... what?'

'Bring that problem solving knack of yours. Let's see what we can scope out. If we make progress, then we'll put together a working group. Draw in some specialists. But for now, just the three of us, looking at Paula's specialist subject. It's well paid work. Travel and accommodation too. Interested?'

'Where?'

'The office we used the last time we worked together.'

'For how long at a time?'

'One or two days a week? A bit more frequently if required.'

I was certain I wouldn't drink again, but being isolated in a hotel for extended periods might not have been smart. One or two days a week would be manageable.

'Sure.'

***

The problem sets Andy, Lily and I had worked on had been fascinating and Lily had been every bit as brilliant as I always knew she would be.

The work was fun and the contractor money was very generous, but it was hardly like I needed it, although it was also one of the few ways I could continue to work in the cyber field. Part of the buyout terms was that anyone taking the cash immediately, like Pat and I had done, couldn't work in the commercial cyber intelligence industry for at least a year. Client confidences apparently. It suited me, yet I'd worried about losing touch in such a fast-paced industry. This strange workshopping between me, GCHQ and SIS was perfect. It was cyber, but definitely not industry. On my first day back in OWOB I'd asked Andy, 'So what's the plan?'

'I need you to conjure up potential cyber threats and how they could manifest themselves in the real world, then Lily will apply her expertise to see if those things could actually be done. I'll add what I know about our probable adversary and then, when we're ready, we can expand the group.'

'And by your knowledge of our adversary, I'm assuming you mean your Chinese knowledge and not your French?'

Andy flashed a grin, 'Of course.'

'Shame,' I said and walked off to make a tea for us all.

The six months since then had flown by and now I was back in town for the latest session, ready to turn my mind to whatever new threats Andy had on his radar.

Rising early, I strolled into a bright, cold April morning and, as I had been so often since leaving hospital, was struck by how much brighter and faster my thoughts and actions were without the heavy overcoat of booze.

The walk to OWOB from the InterContinental Hotel, Park Lane, took exactly thirty minutes on what I considered the scenic route, through Green Park and St James's Park, crossing the lake and making my way along Birdcage Walk. A quick, informal nod to 'Winston' on his plinth at the corner of Parliament Square Garden before turning up into Whitehall. Another more solemn nod to the Cenotaph and then into OWOB, except this morning, Andy Gibson was on the steps waiting for me.

'Have you forgotten, I have my own pass thanks to you,' I said waving the yellow card.

'Yeah,' he said, turning away and beckoning me to follow him back down Whitehall. 'I know, but I've had a request. Are you okay to come with me for a coffee?'

'Yeah. What's up?'

'I had a call late last night from a mutual acquaintance. He asked after you. Wondered if I was still in touch. Told him I could give him your number, but once he realised you were in town he asked for a face to face.'

'And who is this acquaintance?' I asked and as I did Dan's name popped into my head. I wondered if the US military had needed him to take a quick trip across the pond and he'd reached out to Andy. But then, why wouldn't he have just reached out to me? As I processed the thoughts, I was struck that his name no longer brought the peaks of joy or despair it once had. It had been nearly eight months since the Mental Asylum in Kyiv. I was living back at home, my working life was free of stress, my financial situation was, as an understatement, comfortable. My health was excellent and my dependencies, I realised, both alcohol and Daniel Stückl, were reduced to zero. If Andy said his name, I would be pleased, but I wouldn't charge down the street looking for him. A lifetime ago I would have. That's how I thought of me pre-Kyiv. A different lifetime.

'Steve Jäeger,' Andy said, interrupting my reverie.

'My, there's a blast from the past.' The surprise was accompanied by me registering I hadn't been fooling myself. The fact it wasn't Dan's name had not caused me a wave of angst or sadness. 'What does he want?'

'Probably better to hear it from him,' Andy answered as I passed the Cenotaph for the second time that morning. Once more I gave a small nod. From the corner of my eye I saw Andy do the same.

'Okay,' I said, intrigued, but not perturbed by his answer. In the time it took us to walk the short distance to the nearest Caffé Nero, diagonally across from Sir Winston Churchill's statue, I instead asked what he knew about the mysterious, one-eyed Steve.

'What do you want to know?'

'How'd he lose his eye?'

'Aww, that's no secret. Flying helicopters in Vietnam. He'll tell you if you ask him. He got the Air Force Cross for it. Not that he'll tell you that bit. Second only to their Medal of Honor.'

'And is he Langley?'

'Of course, what did you think?'

'I did think that, just hadn't found a good time to ask.'

'Ha, you crack me up sometimes, Luke. Yep, he was USAF during the war. Then Langley. Was a former head of section out in the far east, not quite sure where. Maybe Thailand? He got London in what was meant to be a cushy tour on the wind down. Then got really wound up about Chinese state sponsored cyber espionage and the US lack of annoyance about it.'

'And the UK's as I recall,' I said, thinking that a lot of me being where I was now, with a bank balance the like of which I never, for one second, thought I would have, was down to Steve Jäeger getting annoyed at the Chinese.

'Yep,' Andy said rounding the corner. We walked into Caffé Nero and were greeted with a wave from Steve, ensconced in the far rear corner of the café, within a small booth-type seat.

Having placed our orders at the counter, Andy and I went across and joined the man who I had last spoken to outside a ward in Saint Thomas' Hospital more than five years earlier. He was of course older, but as he half rose out of his seat to shake my hand, I was reminded, as I had been the first time I met him, of a silver wolf. A predator.

'I'd arranged with Andy to meet you in The Lord Moon, or next door in St Stephen's Tavern, but he tells me you've turned a leaf?' Steve said, retaking his seat.

'Something like that,' I answered with a smile, remembering how at our previous meetings he would drink non-stop cups of coffee whilst I matched him one for one with gins.

'Thought not dying was a better option,' I added, meaning it to sound glib and humorous, but Steve's half-frown, caught on his face for a moment. Obviously I'd misjudged it. I hadn't thought to ask Andy what he'd told him about me, but assumed he would have filled him in fully. It wasn't a secret. I thought it better to press on.

'So what do you need to see me face to face for, Steve? Another cyber revolution for me to launch?'

He smiled a tight lipped straight smile, that didn't reach even his good eye. Then he did the most bizarre thing I could ever have imagined this man do. Reaching forward he laid his hand on top of mine.

'I'm sorry, Luke, but I only found out myself a few days ago and I initially assumed you would have known. When I called Andy to see how you were, he said he didn't believe you did.'

'Know what?' I asked and somewhere in a deep recess of my mind I knew what was coming.

'It's Dan.'

With Steve's hand on mine and the gravitas in his voice, my heart lurched. 'What about him?' I asked, not needing his reply to know.

'He's dead, Luke. I'm so sorry.'

I breathed deeply and sat to my full height. My world did not implode. My vision did not tunnel. My heart, though as heavy as I could remember with sadness, did not break. Instead, I looked out past Steve and Andy to the Houses of Parliament and Big Ben. In my mind's eye I imagined looking through and beyond them to Vauxhall Bridge and the apartment Dan and I had shared. The place where we had fallen in love and the place I once thought my life had ended. But I had been wrong.

'How?'

'Suicide. Fort Hood, Texas. On a firing range. He turned his sidearm on himself. It would have been instant. He wouldn't have suffered,' Steve said, with a strange mix of sympathy and efficiency.

'I imagine if it was suicide all the suffering was done up front,' I said, trying to sort the cluttering jumble of thoughts and emotions. I took a deep breath, but I had to know.

'When?' I asked, dreading the response.

'August 15th last year.'

He had tried to call me a day or two before, depending on the time zones, and had been told by my dad that I was dying. Was this my fault? What had happened to make him try to call me, to abandon the family he so loved? Was me not being there the final thing to push him over the edge?

I voiced none of my thoughts. The barista called out Annie and Lock, which despite what I was processing, made me smile.

'I think that's us,' Andy said, getting up quickly to retrieve the drinks.

'What can you tell me, Steve?' I eventually asked.

Over the next half hour Steve told me what he had managed to piece together from official records and calling in a few friendly favours over the previous couple of days. I wasn't in shock and I wasn't numb to the pain, but I was wrapped up in images and memories, so I missed some of what he said but I caught words. Conversion therapy, Shirlene, Dan's father, the church. Afghanistan attached to the infantry for an extended tour of duty. Ambush, wounded, squad members killed. Daily firefights. New daughter. Then a final patrol in a valley, the name of which I missed completely. The man walking next to him killed by a sniper. More conversion therapy visits to a church in Nebraska. A warning order for an Iraq tour. Then another suicide.

I refocused, stopped Steve and asked him to go back.

'The young man was called Cody. He'd been abused by a Pastor at the church. Dan had tried to intervene and help but the second time he was in Texas on a training exercise so couldn't. Before he took himself down to Fort Hood's range, Dan documented it all in a detailed testimony, including assaulting the Pastor and warning him away from ever touching the boy again. In the testimony he alleged there would be numerous others and that at least a little proof could be had by the injury he had inflicted to the Pastor a few months earlier.'

'Injury?'

'Yeah, he'd broken the man's jaw. According to the medical reports whoever hit the pastor had nearly taken his head off his shoulders.'

I remembered Dan's physique. A full force punch from him would have been an event in itself. I realised Steve could have readily accessed the military report on Dan's suicide, but this was different. 'How did you get a civilian's medical records?' I asked.

'After Dan's testimony was found it was processed through Army legal. Eventually it was handed to civilian law enforcement. The case came to a head in Nebraska last week. Local news, not a big deal, but Dan's name was on the wire feed and a colleague of mine notified me. That's how I found out and when I started digging into what the hell had happened.'

'The case was settled? That's quick isn't it?'

'Yeah, a little. The fact a serving member of the military had made a deathbed allegation and a minor had committed suicide a few days earlier, meant there was momentum behind it, but it helped the local sheriff election returned a brand new incumbent aiming to make a name for himself. Dan had been correct. Fourteen other boys came forward. The Nebraska DA went all out because he has his own ambitions. Faced with the odds, the pastor pleaded guilty. Quick and simple. Fourteen counts with 15 year minimums to run sequentially. That's 210 years.'

'Seems Dan did some good work before he left?' I said and felt a lighter lift to my heart.

'He did indeed,' Steve said. I saw the nod from him and watched Andy rise to order more coffees.

'He also left a final page in his testimony, Luke, but being August of last year, the military police investigators detached it from the official records that were forwarded on to their civilian counterparts.'

'Why?'

'This is last August. *Don't Ask Don't Tell* was still in force. President Obama hadn't made the changes. The military were working on keeping the reputation of an officer intact. They

were wrong of course. There was nothing wrong with his reputation. At any time,' Steve said. Reaching into his inside pocket
he handed me a single sheet of paper. 'I'll go help Andy with
the order,' he said, slipping out of his seat.

I recognised the hand writing.

Dear Luke,

*I have been told you are dying with only weeks to live, so in
all likelihood, you will never read this. Throughout our time
together you made it clear that you don't believe in God or
an afterlife, and I have now come to completely share your
thoughts on the matter, so I shan't even get to tell you when
you catch me up in a few days' time. There are no clouds with
harp playing angels to serenade us as I lay down why I am
doing what I do.*

*So why am I writing this if not for us? That is easy. It is
for Shirlene and my father. It's for every member of the
military who ignored the conversion therapy camps, for every
person who said that you and I were broken or twisted or
depraved. For every religion and church pastor who thought
they were holier than their flock. It's so that none of them can
point to you or my love for you as having been what is
causing me to do what I am about to do.*

*You are not, nor could you ever be my final straw. Your
dying actually makes it easier on me. I could have run to you,
I could have shared a life, but I would have lost my children
and I think, in my heart of hearts, I would have reached the
point I am now, only later and in England, not in Texas. All it
would have meant is that you would have to clear up the
mess. You that would have to explain to others.*

The world is not fair and innocents get hurt every day. Good people who shouldn't die, do. I have tried to protect them all and I have failed. Your death is just the latest in a line and I am certain, if I stay as I am, then my son and daughter will be the next. So I leave for them. I leave for all those I failed and I offer what sacrifice I may have in me to protect my children.

Lastly, for those reading this. I am a serving member of the US Army and I fell in love with a man. Yet I could still pick up a gun and fight for my country. I want you to ask, so I can tell.

Luke, I hope you pass as quickly as I intend to.
Dan x

I swallowed hard and wiped a single tear from the corner of my eye. As Andy and Steve slowly returned I got up and inclined my head towards the door marked 'Toilets'. I got two small nods in return.

***

'Apart from this, how's he doing?' Steve asked quietly as he slid into his seat.

'Good. As he always was. Incisive, sees things others don't, or sees them quicker, even if they do eventually catch-up. Opens up possibilities.'

'You doing okay for technical support? I know he was never the most clued up on that side of things.'

'No, but we're okay now. We've made massive leaps since back in 2005 when you and I sat in here and set-up the initial email to Luke,' Andy said.

'That's only six years ago,' Steve said. 'A lot of water unde—, Jeez! Sorry man. I didn't mean for that phra—'

Andy waved a calming hand. 'It's okay. I know you didn't. And that's okay too. We did our best.'

Steve gave a slow sigh. 'I do like Luke and I'm delighted and committed to getting him back into cyber intelligence under your direction, for God alone knows we need all the assets we can get…'

'I sense a but,' Andy said.

'But if he had stayed in his Goddamn apartment that night, Lily would still be alive. She was the best inside track we'll ever have into the PLA units. I don't have many regrets, Andy, but that's one of them.'

'Yeah, but we win some, we lose some. It's okay. Maybe we'll get another shot one day.' Andy paused, contemplating how even the closest of colleagues and allies didn't get to share everything. Lily was strictly a UK asset. He took a sip of his coffee before continuing, 'Speaking of our PLA pals, I read what you sent through last week. How solid is that?'

'Confirmed. They're shifting focus. Understandable. They have so much engineering intellectual property now they could probably make their own fleet of Boeing aircraft,' Steve said with a shrug.

'Or Airbuses I guess,' Andy agreed, knowing that the complete set of plans for every new Airbus design going back a decade had been hoovered up by the PLA cyber units. He didn't know when the Chinese would start building their own indigenous airliners, but when they did, he figured they'd look a lot like an AirbusA320. 'But pharmaceutical?' He continued. 'That's a leap?'

'Big money in big pharma,' Steve said. 'Even more opportunities for disruption. If they could rip off a drug company's intellectual property imagine the amount of R&D and trial expenses they'd save.'

Andy shook his head and was about to take another drink but stopped short. 'Imagine if they used the knowledge of what a drug could do to come up with a counter threat.'

Steve nodded slowly. 'Yep. That's the sort of thing I'd like our Luke to apply himself to. See where his thought processes lead. Take a look at the pharmaceutical angle, what the Chinese government are stealing via cyber espionage and then maybe we can look at getting him back into the cyber intelligence game proper?'

Andy paused.

'What's up?' the American asked.

'The Conservatives have been in power for just on a year now. I'd hoped they'd be less inclined to climb into bed with the Chinese, but it isn't that way at all. If anything, they're more desperate to.'

'Yeah. I saw the latest reports about the so-called China Fund. And?'

'And I can't see Luke going back into official government circles. Not when the Prime Minister himself said it's not in the best interests of the country to deter Chinese investments.'

'Well, we can still direct him if he's in a commercial cyber setup.'

'Sure,' Andy agreed. 'In fact it'd probably be more effective.'

'Let's aim to do that then,' Steve Jäeger said and raised his coffee cup to toast Andy.

***

I stared into the bathroom mirror in a London café and waited to crumple, but I didn't.

Dan Stückl had been the great love of my life. Now, he was gone, yet since he had died, almost to the day, my spirit had been renewed. Perhaps this was how things had to be. Maybe balance had been restored. Or maybe it was just random chance and coincidence.

I, the committed atheist, hoped there was a reason to it and that karma and balance were the key. His death, whilst causing my heart to physically hurt and my mind to feel intense grief, might also have been the catalyst for me to live.

Perhaps.

Had I died in August, I'd never have known. Had I known prior to August, I'd never have survived. I owed it to myself, my new self, and to Dan, to keep moving forward. To be better. Looking back was good at times, for history was a great teacher, but I had to go forward with no regrets.

I looked again in the mirror and thought about Dan and the past and my future. I decided that I would reframe a thought.

Dan Stückl had been *a* great love of my life. But he would not be my last.

Epilogue

I arrived for the latest meeting of the Problem Set Working Group, as I had christened our efforts after deciding we needed the help of others to explore the potential cyber threats we faced.

I had at first thought to call it the China Working Group because everyone one who attended knew that China was the real problem, but Andy, used to moving in political circles, said that the Ministers wouldn't like that. I knew he was right. The government couldn't even admit to the threat, so we needed to have a more subtle name.

For the first and second workshops Andy had invited three of the most senior military officers in the country. Again I was struck by how quickly life had changed for me. Not many years earlier I had been a junior officer and these men would have been unlikely to spare me the time of day, unless I'd been asked to brief them. Now, they were listening to my opinion, not merely using me as an information source. We were also joined by two police Chief Constables, one from either side of the Scottish Border. I didn't miss that one of their regions hosted the largest nuclear facility in Europe, whilst the other had, until recently, its own nuclear power plant. The latter, decommissioned or otherwise, still had a reactor on site.

On the third visit we'd had the company of a number of country specialists from Vauxhall Cross and Defence Intelligence. On the fourth, three chairmen of British companies that were industrial or commercial icons and an entrepreneur whose reputation in Britain was approaching 'national treasure' level.

On that day I had taken the first opportunity I got to ask Andy, 'These guys have security clearances?'

He'd shrugged nonchalantly, 'Of course. These guys, just these four, have money and assets totalling over half a percent of the UKs GDP. Which,' he added quickly, seeing I hadn't fully appreciated the number, 'is a staggering amount. Also, the companies they run would practically stop the UK economy if they decided to shut up shop or couldn't operate. So yeah, they have clearances, because they get to talk to and be engaged by some of our more secretive branches of Government.'

Their insights and unique perspectives on the potential harm of cyber were a revelation to me. Lily and Andy had been equally surprised by some of their concerns.

Now, on my latest visit, beginning on the Monday which marked a full six months since I had walked out of hospital, I entered the room to find all the preceding attendees gathered together. It wasn't a surprise, Andy had pre-warned me in his own cryptic way when he'd called to arrange the meeting.

'All our old friends will be there this time.'

I did wonder if he would start wearing a red carnation and carrying a rolled copy of the Financial Times.

'Oh and Luke, this one is over three days.'

My pre-warning hadn't included the identities of the two new faces in the room. As the round table introductions were made, Felicity informed us that she was a senior Professor of Virology working with the Health Protection Agency, and her companion, Justine was the deputy chief finance officer for a major pharmaceutical company.

As in our previous days, Andy laid out his objective; to explore potential threats to the UK infrastructure that could come from direct or indirect cyber warfare attacks launched by China.

Lily, who was always called Paula in the sessions and never once had her background referred to, provided technical input, direction and correction. I provided historical context and future threat scenarios, the rest provided insights with their specialist knowledge. I enjoyed it. The exercises were stimulating and thought-provoking and it was certainly keeping my hand in with the cyber world as I was constantly having to keep myself updated on the current environment, but this day was different.

Three hours into the day, as Andy continued to facilitate the discussions and specifically as Justine wrapped up what she knew of the latest Chinese cyber espionage manoeuvrings within her pharmaceutical world, I was aware of entering my own bubble. The conversations progressed around me, but as I had discovered so many years before, when my mind freewheeled a problem, I had a peculiar ability to detach.

It wasn't something I'd known before joining the military, but as my intelligence career exposed me to new problems, I'd discovered I had a knack for seeing the whole from disparate pieces and recognising patterns. When I'd been asked about it, shortly after spotting a pattern to Iraqi insurgents targeting Baghdad Airport, I put it down to learning music at a young age and being slightly dyslexic. To see the notes or the words my mind conjured the separate parts, like a 3D puzzle. Then they coalesced into meaning. I couldn't explain how I did it, the action came naturally but I also knew that certain people had been impressed enough to brief others about me. When I'd slipped almost trance like into a contemplative state in front of that American, Steve Jäeger, in the Lord Moon of the Mall pub, he hadn't been perturbed. He'd known what I was capable of. As did Andy, hence why when I stopped thinking and stood up with a whiteboard marker in my hand, he brought the conversations to a temporary pause.

'Sir Geoffrey,' I said, addressing the entrepreneur and ignoring his preference to be called Geoff. I couldn't handle the informality. 'What would it take to ground all your aircraft?'

He pondered for a moment. 'All of them? Well that would need a common denominator. A single aircraft crash would temporarily halt the flights of that model, but we operate Boeings and Airbus, so I suppose, fuel would do it.'

'But when you were in here a few weeks ago, we identified that your fuel comes from four different sources. Or was it five?' I asked.

'Four usually and a back-up from the Tyneside refineries of North Sea crude if we ever needed it, but that would only ever be in a declared National Emergency,' he confirmed.

The senior army officer, Lieutenant General Stuart Barnt, head of Defence Logistics Support, and who, I was glad, had never said, 'Call me Stu', piped in. 'If a National Emergency was declared, my chaps would mount armed convoys to take the fuel to hospitals, government centres and transport hubs.'

'Exactly, thank you, both.'

I drew the outline of an aircraft and a series of lines to individual 'thought bubbles' for fuel sources and the various airline types, most of which I knew as it played to my quite geeky love of civilian airliners. I added a final line to a fifth fuel source but marked it with a double, heavy line to show it as protected.

'And Frankie,' I said, turning to the septuagenarian owner and still active executive of the largest privately held haulage company in the UK. 'To stop all your trucks?'

'Short of a general strike, that calls all the unions out, nothing really. Even then, most of my drivers aren't unionised any more. There'd be enough of them and they'd get protection,' he said looking over to the two Chief Constables who nodded their approval.

'And fuel?' I continued.

'Same as Geoff. We have agreements in place for National Emergencies. We'd keep a skeleton backbone of ground transportation and deliver whatever, whenever. Us and the Post Office as they still have by far the biggest fleet of trucks in the country.'

I knew that from our previous discussions a few months earlier, but I wanted it to be shared with the people who hadn't been in that session.

As I continued around the room, the board filled with outlines of trucks and boats, planes and trains, electrical power generation, high street shops for food and other essentials and finally military capabilities. Each one was linked to various sources of 'enablers' that allowed them to function. All of them, including I was personally glad to see, the military capabilities had multiple redundancies and options that would insulate them from complete disaster in a single cyber-attack.

'Almost done,' I said as I drew in a line between my outline version of a supermarket and a tractor in a field. 'All in all,

Paula, do you think they have the capability to launch the number of separate attacks to stop all of these?'

'Yes, but only if they stop all other operations. That is a very large effort and it would be an undeclared war. It is much too aggressive to tie in with their current objectives.'

Those objectives, that we referred to as the 'Chinese Jewel', were written on top of a separate whiteboard at the start of each day:

Disrupt without conventional warfare
Undermine 'Western' economies
Enhance China's influence in the world
Leverage 'projects' for favours

I turned to Justine. 'Can you repeat what you said about the cyber-attacks your industry got hit with two years ago?'

'Certainly,' she said. 'My company was the latest in at least six that we know of where the attack was against intellectual property surrounding drug development. In our case, we lost a decade's worth of research and development into a family of drugs developed for specific respiratory diseases. As happens many times in these cases, the breakthrough discovery had come about when our scientists were researching something completely different.' She looked across to Felicity the Professor for a confirmatory nod.

'True. I was part of the oversight on the final trials and I remember the initial research had been into asthma. Whilst in the very early stages the team had realised they'd stumbled into an effective vaccine for the H5N1 infection,' Felicity confirmed.

'Thanks,' I said. 'But specifically, Justine, before when you finished your overview, you mentioned something about 'well that variant, not much use for new ones'. What did you mean?'

'Oh, I see. Probably easier for Flick to take that,' she said, looking again at the Professor.

'Yes, that variant. The H5N1, or Avian Flu as it's usually called in the media is highly adaptable. The next time it occurs it would likely be mutated. The work Justine's company has done is a good basis and works against a strain, but if a new one rises then they'd still have to come up with a new vaccine. Stealing the IP on it seems a limited move.'

'I agree,' I said. 'But if they have stolen it and as we heard, five more, would that give whoever is getting this R&D a good start in developing their own vaccines?'

'Yes. Of course. It would give them about a fifty-year accelerated learning program,' Felicity said.

'In only two years,' Andy added.

'Where are your thoughts heading, Luke,' Frankie asked, reaching for a bottle of water.

'It was Justine's remark about a new variant. Sparked an idea in my head. I'm sure most of you would have seen those movies where a virus kills off humanity,' I paused and got a few nods around the table. 'I don't mean anything like that of course, but I wondered, for a very contagious virus that made people too sick or frightened to go out to work, what would the likely steps be to contain it?'

'The only example we really have is Spanish Flu,' Felicity said. 'Obviously we wouldn't accept the percentage of deaths they dealt with back then, but we have much better response times and vastly better scientific capabilities. However, in the early days of anything approaching that level of pandemic, then the standing recommendations haven't changed all that much.'

'And they are?' Kerry, the Chief Constable of Dumfries and Galloway Constabulary asked.

'Isolate the population. Ramp up hospital capacity. Develop a vaccine,' Felicity said it like a times table she had learnt by rote in primary school.

'How long does a vaccine take?' This time it was Tom, Kerry's southern counterpart and the Chief Constable of Cumbria Constabulary asking.

'Two, perhaps three years normally,' Felicity said.

There were actual gasps around the room. I had managed to stifle mine, but that timescale was a lot longer than I had imagined. However, it hadn't been what started me down this path. I needed to return to that. 'Frankie, you asked where I was going with this?' I got a slow nod from the older man. 'I started wondering if there was a contagious flu or the like, what the reaction would be and I pondered it might be everyone staying at home, almost medieval plague type of scenario, where no one leaves their own village. Felicity has confirmed it through her mention of isolation as the first step in any response. By that, I assume you meant no one goes anywhere?'

'Yes,' she confirmed. 'Isolate in regions, or towns and if that isn't enough, then potentially into your own house. There are contingency plans at international level with the CDC and the WHO.'

'And they'd be known by everyone?' Andy asked.

Felicity nodded.

I was still at the board. I drew a circle around everything already drawn on it and turned back to see all of the faces looking at me. 'If you made it so you isolated the whole population, would that ground your fleet, Sir Geoffrey?'

He looked from me to the board and back again. 'Yes. If there are no people to fly the aircraft and no passengers to fly, of course it would stop us.'

'And your trucks, Frankie?'

'Yes. No drivers allowed to travel outside of their own town kills off my industry pretty quickly.'

Asking the same of all sitting around the table, the unfolding scenario was a collapsed economy and the potential for unprecedented social upheaval. At the end of a spirited discussion, but quite depressing few minutes, it was Rear Admiral Anthony *'Call me Tony'* Stock who asked, 'I find this fascinating, but we are here to focus on cyber threats.'

Before I could offer my explanation, Lily, or as she was here, Paula, said, 'You are right Tony. The threat is simple. The theft via cyber I think has already been done,' she paused a moment. 'Felicity, with the material on drug and vaccine research that has already been stolen, could you engineer a new strain of disease?'

'Easily, but,' she said to cut off the reaction around the room, 'anyone with a half-decent science degree could do that already. Beijing have people far more competent and capable. However, this level of R&D would allow you to come up with a new strain so removed from what we know about, as to make a vaccine that much more difficult to manufacture. It could be three or more years to get one developed and cleared for use through our existing procedures.'

'During which time what would happen and perhaps, more importantly, why would anyone do such a thing?' Andy asked.

His question sparked a new debate which rolled on through and after lunch. By mid-afternoon the likely causes ranged from seeing if it could be done for future actual warfare, through to a diversion to distract from potential land grabs in the likes of the South China Sea, to being able to influence poorer nations by acting in a beneficial way in the midst of a global pandemic.

This last one prompted actions like distributing free medical equipment or sending huge numbers of doctors and nurses into badly hit areas.

Andy eventually brought the discussions to an end by testing each one against the 'Chinese Jewel'. Sadly, they all passed.

'Okay everyone,' he said. 'That's been a fascinating day. As they say on that real-crime TV programme, don't have nightmares. This is simply a thought exercise,' he said and I wondered how much he believed that. 'Nonetheless,' he continued, 'tomorrow I'd like us to look at how we can protect the IP of UK companies in each of your particular fields. That'll also include doctrine and policy for you guys,' he added, sweeping his arm towards the uniformed attendees.

BUSINESS NEWS
Dateline 26th July 2011

Canadian officials took Stuart MacLellan, founder and former CEO of Twenty-Twenty Security Incorporated into custody yesterday on charges of bribery, corruption, money laundering and espionage. The arrest comes nine months after the sale of his cyber start-up and only days after the former executive's wife filed for divorce and is believed to involve money traced to accounts in Macau and Romania.

A source in the Department of Justice who was not willing to be named, said that an anonymous tip had led to Canadian investigators tracing a money laundering path from Macau, into Romania and then to France. Department of Justice officials are believed to have liaised heavily with their French counterparts to secure the evidence needed for the charges to be laid.

Mr MacLellan has been remanded in custody as he was deemed a flight risk by presiding judge, Madam Justice McConnell.

Speaking outside the court, the Public Prosecutor Ms Lesley Desalles, said, 'Given the "injury assessment" provided by the Canadian Security Intelligence Service at the remand hearing, we believe the nature of the liaison between Mr MacLellan and a foreign entity has caused severe and irreparable damage to Canadian interests. This is why when he is convicted, as I am sure he will be, I intend to press for the maximum term life sentence."

The End

To Be Continued ?

Post Script

This book is based on events that happened over seven years and the events of the full *Luke Frankland Trilogy* stretched over some fifteen years in real life. However, for the purposes of drama and pace I have reduced that timeline within the books.

It is also worthwhile considering the changes that occurred during my career... Nearly 25 years ago, I had to tell the biggest lie of my life to get my first job; that I was not gay. I found that lie easy to adapt to as I lived in the world of intelligence where, in some way, we all lead a double life. However, for others it has not been so easy and some have suffered terribly as a result of not being allowed to be themselves. I am now proud to lead a team in my day job (writing these books has been done in my spare time) where over 20% of my team are gay. This is not through any form of positive discrimination. It is simply select-ing the best people for the job. It gives me immense pride that my team can come to work, be themselves and be respected for who they are. No one should be made to feel uncomfortable in the work place based on their sexuality. It is easier to embrace diversity and learn from those who are different from us than it is to hate or discriminate against them.

When I started in cyber security it was almost 100% dominated by men who collectively shared very similar backgrounds and views on life. Diversity of thought was binary to say the least and those men tended to recruit similar men in order to preserve the culture and stay in their comfort zone. Women hardly featured in the work place and the civilian security profession did very little to attract them. In my books I have tried to represent women fairly and with equality throughout and have placed them in some very significant positions that were not, and unfortunately in many professions and cultures are still not, filled by them in real life.

I am proud of the team I currently lead within the world of commercial cyber intelligence because a third are women and that proportion continues to increase, as it should. The world will be a much better and productive place when women are truly emancipated and have equality on a global scale. If your religion, society or culture, or all three, prevents you from respecting women and treating them with dignity and equality, it is your religion, society and culture you should be questioning and not the ability of women.

In my books the cyber threat has been the main focus, but I believe that religion on our planet literally poisons everything and is a huge threat to peace and harmony globally. I have only been able to make fleeting references to my disdain for religion in these novels, (such as some church's attempts at conversion therapy, the many cases where children have been abused by Catholic clergy and the systematic cover-ups engineered by various people in authority) but my opinion is that religion causes more pain, suffering, war and death than any other contributing factor in our world. Just be a good person and do good things – you do not need a bible or a religion to teach you that. Some of the most inhumane and unthinkable acts in our history have been committed in the name of, and justified by, religion. Humans have inbuilt humanity and compassion that has been around long before invented religions. Good people will be good, bad people will be bad, but to get a good person to do truly evil things, it takes religion.

Another recurring theme in Luke's story is of course his drinking. It is no surprise that alcohol in sufficient quantities is a killer. Since my university days and until my 38th year I enjoyed alcohol and it was an integral part of my way of life. I was never a binge drinker, nor was I often 'legless'. I was one of those consistent drinkers. Always just enough to keep that certain buzz and to ensure my blood to alcohol ratio never dipped below a certain point. However, without realising it I adapted my lifestyle to encompass a drink at every opportunity. I would never hold a business meeting over breakfast, for without alcohol, I thought it the dullest meal of the day and would often skip it.

In my private life on weekends or holidays, if breakfast was to be indulged in, it would always be with a strong and spicy Bloody Mary or the cracking open of a good Champagne. I even made other sparkling wine arrangements for those guests who wanted to dilute the good Champagne with orange juice.

My work life almost always allowed me to indulge in at least a glass or two of wine at lunch time that would see me through to happy hour, which over the years became earlier and earlier in the day. Friday nearly became a day long happy hour, even at work. Dinner was accompanied by wine and then the post dinner quaffing as conversations went deep into the night. Then, with the hair of the dog in the early hours, it would start all over again. I had tremendous fun and do not regret a drop. I enjoyed it. It eased me in my social circles, took the edge off any anxiety and helped a great deal when entertaining clients.

Most of my working life was also spent traveling long haul several times a month. I was lucky enough that my employers decided that warranted a civilised class of travel so I would arrive 'refreshed' at the other end; ready to work. That meant access to airport lounges and I would arrive several hours before the flight to enjoy the fine wines, vintage Champagnes and premium spirits oozing from the walls. This did not stop once on board the flight, nor in the club lounges of the hotels I stayed in. Life went from one drink to another, my lifestyle became accustomed to it and I was unaware of the damage it was doing until it was too late. Almost completely too late.

But one day it all caught up with me as I have tried to reflect through Luke. I had ploughed on regardless and lived with alcohol dependency for a long time before my body simply gave up. First the whites of my eyes yellowed, days later that spread to around my eyes and parts of my face. A week or so later my chest started to turn yellow and brown as did parts of the arms. I ignored it and thought it would go away. However, my parents took me directly to A&E as soon as they noticed. That move saved my life and the NHS, thinking at first they would only have to look after me in a humane way until my body finally gave up, managed to kick start my recovery and for that I will be for ever grateful. Several years later and I have not had a drop of alcohol since. I do miss it and would say I am a reluctant tee-totaller, but I have a much better enjoyment and appreciation of life post-drinking than I did when drinking. Would I change it if I could go back in time? Likely not, though I do believe that learning from the mistakes of your past is the best way to learn. My only regrets are the burden I placed on the NHS and the grief I caused my parents in those 'final days'. Both of those are lasting regrets, and both everlasting debts.

Another thing to be mindful of that I hope I've highlighted in these books, is that men suffer from domestic abuse, violence and psychological torture as well as women and children.

Always consider this and be on the lookout. Not everyone is fine or safe behind closed doors because they are the 'man of the house'. Dan was an example of this. Be aware of this and you may be surprised how many signs and signals you see.

It is not only the younger generation who are involved in cyber-crime and I tried to depict that in these books through Tom Solomon, an octogenarian. It is a good lesson in life not to fall for stereotypes. Traditional criminals in the real world have adapted well within the undefined borders of cyberspace, the lack of legal jurisdictions and the fact that it is lawless. Global governments are yet to conclusively work together to define cyber space to allow clear legal jurisdictions and therefore meaningful international prosecutions. As cyber-crime now accounts for more money than the global illegal drugs trade, it is no wonder traditional criminals have adapted their criminal mindsets and methodologies to the cyber world. Many are known to be guilty, but attribution for cyber-crimes that transcend borders make prosecutions by law enforcement often impossible.

I have also tried to relay that you do not need to be technical to succeed in the cyber world. I wanted to make the books accessible and understandable for all and blow up the misrepresentation that because cyber is about computers, it has to be complicated and technical. In my personal life I have a particular dislike for computers, technology and social media, being much happier tending my fruit trees. However, I have made a good career in intelligence and cyber security despite these misgivings and a lack of understanding as to how technology works, as reflected by Luke in my books, is no barrier to success. Technology is all well and good, but technology originates from and was designed by humans. To understand and overcome the majority of cyber threats and technology incidents you need to profoundly understand human behaviours. Technology does not work in isolation.

After 20 years of focusing on the threat from Chinese state sponsored cyber espionage from many angles and vantage points in my professional life in the public and private sectors, I assess that state sponsored cyber espionage from China is the largest long-term threat that we face. It is already well advanced with much of the groundwork done to reach the long-term objectives the Chinese Communist Party has for eventual superiority, by every measure, over 'the West'.

I hope one day we will be able to hold generations of world leaders to account for purposefully ignoring this threat and focusing policy with China on short term economic gain over long term national security, as it is not 'in the best interests' of their small-minded four-year election cycles. This narrow view from largely ignorant and unworldly career politicians precludes any government from simply doing the right thing and confronting China head on. In less than 10 years we will not have that option.

Lastly, as to the characters that have appeared within the trilogy; some, in concert with their actions, have been exaggerated and dramatized, others have had their excesses and flamboyancy toned down. Fact was stranger than fiction.

As for Luke and Lily, their adventures do continue, with twists you could never imagine, but sadly unless I find an agent and get offered a traditional publishing deal, this may well be the end of their adventures. If you do know any, please get in touch!

I hope you've enjoyed reading the trilogy.

Tim
France, 2021

Acknowledgements

Yet again, I owe a debt of gratitude to various people without whom this book would not have been possible.

Thank you to my editor, publisher and friend, Ian Andrew and his wife Jacki. Without their help, advice and mentoring I would never have been able to adapt my diaries and unpublishable biography into these cyber thrillers.

To my husband Peri, for giving me a tranquil and loving home life that allows me to work on these books when I am not busy with my day job, still working in the security intelligence and cyber threat intelligence fields.

Sadly, and because I am still within that world, I cannot name the real people who are the inspiration behind many of the characters. I've had such good fortune to share amazing experiences with them and I trust they will know and recognise themselves.

To those of you who have been assholes, I also thank you. Every book needs its villains and you provided the best material I could wish for. It is such a shame that so much of it had to be left out.

For giving up time they will never get back, a great thanks to my Beta readers, Howard, Lewis, Ian and Susan, who helped me to make tweaks here and there in the final stages of editing.

My deepest love and thanks go to Peri, Mum, Dad and Jamie for being such a loving family. I owe you so much.

Lastly, as with all my books, I would like to end by thanking the National Health Service, Dr Topping and the team at South Tyneside District Hospital. You saved my life and I have tried to reflect those events as appropriately as I can through what happened to Luke in these books.

Tim
France
2021

Publisher's Footnote:

In August 2013, the United Kingdom Government, under the leadership of Prime Minister David Cameron, announced that the Old War Office Building would be sold on the open market.

On 1 March 2016, 110 years after its opening, OWOB was sold for a figure in excess of £350 million, on a 250-year lease, to the Hinduja Group and OHL Developments for conversion to a luxury hotel.

About the Author

Tim Hind was born in Sunderland and joined the Royal Air Force as an Intelligence Officer after reading Law at university.

During his time in the Service he initially focused on the Middle East before specialising in cyber warfare. He later joined Barclays Bank in a Global Information Security role with stints in the Middle East and emerging markets. Subsequently he headed up the bank's global cyber intelligence capability.

He then moved to America to lead another cyber intelligence team in his position of Vice President within a start-up cyber intelligence company that was sold in 2016.

Tim now lives in the south of France and is a senior director in a privately held security intelligence company. He leads cyber intelligence teams located in Europe, the Middle East, Africa and the Asia/Pacific regions, who service clients globally in the public and private sectors. When not travelling the world for business or pleasure, he enjoys reading biographies, cooking, walking and skiing. He is also a qualified scuba instructor and, by his own admission, a commercial aviation geek. Despite all of these activities, he is at his happiest in the gardens of his home in the south of France with his husband, family, friends, two rescued dogs, an adopted cat and numerous fruit trees.

The Luke Frankland Novels

In The Best Interests (Book 1)

Luke Frankland, a junior intelligence officer home from the Iraq War, finds himself cast into a world of cyber espionage and state-level politics. Out of his depth and with no one in the Government heeding his warnings, he forms a makeshift team and tries to establish who is waging a new kind of war from behind a keyboard. The truth will leave him plunged into an arena he little expected and where the real cost is not measured in 1s and 0s but in human life.

In The Best Interests is the first in the Luke Frankland Trilogy of cyber thrillers. A series of novels based on the real life experiences of the author within the world of cyber warfare and espionage. They will take you on a chilling and personal journey that will leave you wondering where the fiction ends and the facts start.

The Luke Frankland Novels

Pick a Packet or Two (Book 2)

When a British bank, investing in emerging markets and hoping to help some of the world's poorest, starts haemorrhaging money, Luke Frankland is called in to find out who is to blame.

He soon finds himself in the middle of a multinational game of treachery, extortion and murder. His home life should be his refuge, but that is about to get equally complicated.

The Book Reality Experience
An Imprint of Leschenault Press